Praise for earlier volumes of Katha Prize Stories

Volume 8

... a fistful of gems to treasure and share with friends.

– *The Hindustan Times*

Over the past eight years, the *Katha Prize Stories* series have undoubtedly more than established the importance of regional fiction. Its publishers can justifiably take credit for creating a growing interest in regional literature.

– *The Hindu*

The wonder that is regional literature. – *India Today*

Volume 7

One of the most important publishing initiatives in recent years ...

– *The Telegraph*

The boom in the last few years in English translations of Indian fiction ... owes much to Katha's trailblazing effort. – *The Week*

Volume 6

The editors of Katha need to be complimented for showcasing the best of Indian short stories. – *The Hindu*

The stories here hold up mirrors to India that reflect the country as it is, not as we would like it to be. – *Business Standard*

Volume 5

Another truimph for Katha ... – *India Today*

... a rewarding experience for the reader ... the choice of stories has been made with admirable circumspection. – *Outlook*

A brilliant and stunning patchwork quilt, every piece standing out and holding its own. – *The Pioneer*

By buying this copy of Katha Prize Stories, Volume 9
you give Rs 25/- to help educate a child at the

Katha School of Entrepreneurship

Giving has never been so enjoyable, so affordable.
Come join our world, make it yours ... Turn the page!

My name is Asma. I am three. My preschool is getting me ready for formal education.

"I think many of our schools in the UK could learn from your work and teaching methodology."

– Kate Alexander, Care UK, London

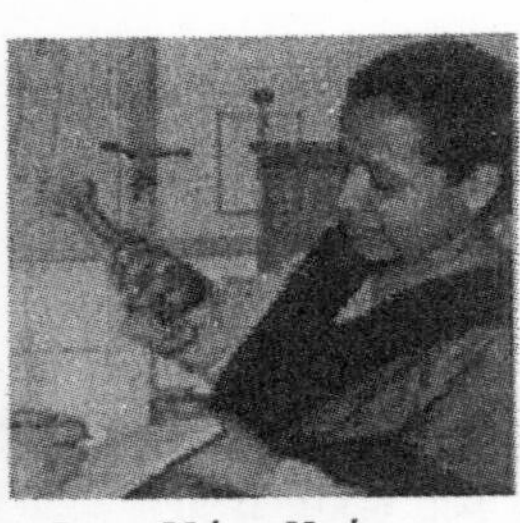

I am Usha. Katha prepared my sister and me for college. Katha is our family. It has stood by us. I shall stand by Katha when I am a successful entrepreneur!

Come join ... MY WORLD

... and the 1,200 happy kids of Katha. See life in a satisfyingly different way!

KID

Cs: Curiosity, Crea

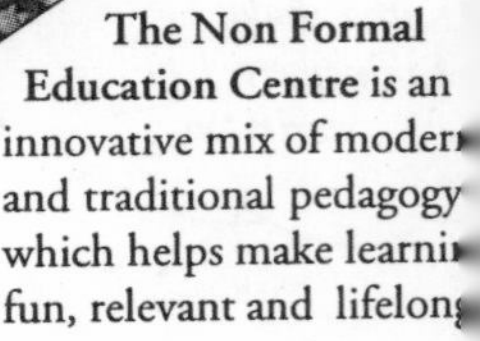

The Non Formal Education Centre is an innovative mix of modern and traditional pedagogy which helps make learning fun, relevant and lifelong

KATHA

A-3, Sarvodaya Enclave, New Delhi 110017 katha@vsnl.com

PRESIDENT: ABID HUSSAIN EXECUTIVE DIRECTOR: GEETA DHARMARAJAN

DIRECTOR, KATHA-KHAZANA: SARASWATHY SUBRAMANIAM

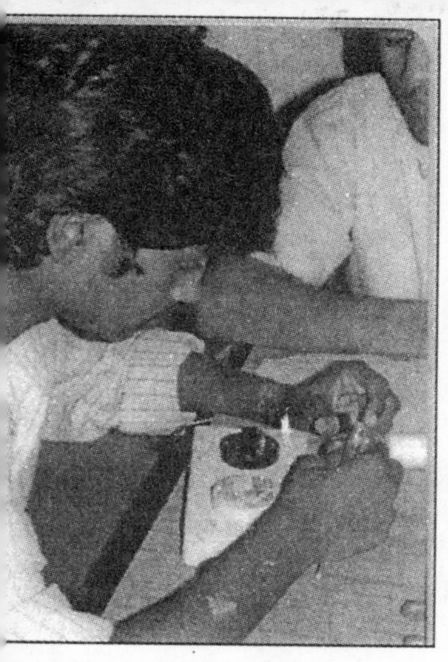

I am Anju. I am twenty two. I started coming to Katha soon after it opened. Today, I am the supervisor of the Katha Khazana Bakery, earning Rs 2400/month. Thanks to Katha I enrolled with the National Open School. I topped my class with 76% in the bakery course!

The Katha School of Entrepreneurship has children aged 10-16. It has a specially designed curriculum that combines scholastic and vocational education to help make our students self-reliant. Volunteer to teach in your spare time!

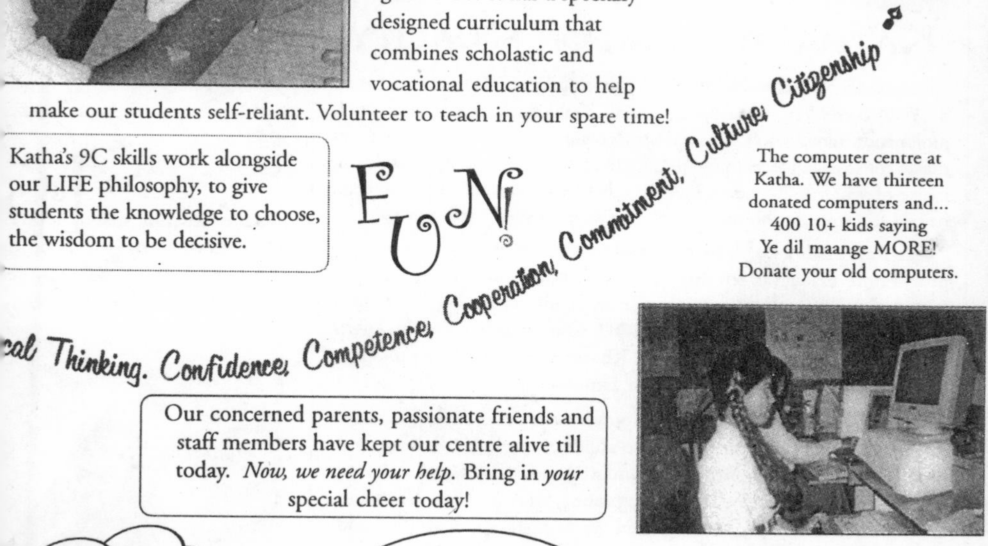

Katha's 9C skills work alongside our LIFE philosophy, to give students the knowledge to choose, the wisdom to be decisive.

The computer centre at Katha. We have thirteen donated computers and... 400 10+ kids saying Ye dil maange MORE! Donate your old computers.

Our concerned parents, passionate friends and staff members have kept our centre alive till today. *Now, we need your help*. Bring in *your* special cheer today!

My name's Pinkie. ...am 13. I used to work ...a house maid. Perveez didi brought me to Katha shala. I learn baking here. I write stories too.

I'm Chhoti. I am two. My mother sells ground spices. Katha takes care of me during the day. So my elder sister can go to school. I play here and Didi gives me yum...! food.

50 happy babies make **Our Creche** a happy place.

Volunteer today. The treasure is inside you!

We need you ... Call us at 6868193, 6521752 or 6994440 or Visit us at Katha-Khazana, Demonstration Block, Bhumiheen Camp, Kalkaji Extn., Govindpuri, New Delhi - 110019.

A large number of our teachers have been with us since 1990!

My name is Sh
I am 16 going o
17. I work as a
housemaid but w
it is 12.30, it's ti
to study! I study
KSE, the Katha School of Entrepreneurship.

Katha, a voluntary nonprofit organization, was registered on September 8, 1989. Over the last ten years, we have striven to reiterate that ...

KATHA STANDS FOR QUALITY

Kathashala was **started in 1990** with six children. Today, we have more than 1200 children, from 0 - 16 years. Katha has a **creche, preschool, junior and senior schools.** An exciting mix of formal and nonformal methods makes for sustainable learning for our children. More than 5500 children, many of whom have never been to school or are dropouts, have been helped to move into formal schools; we support them with **tutorials.**

The Katha School of Entrepreneurship is an exciting one-of-its-kind programme that gives scholastic, vocational and entrepreneurial skills to young people. It is an accredited study centre of the National Open School and is associated with IGNOU. Our latest batch of graduates earn up to Rs 2,500/month, today! **Khazana students learn to shape their own futures, and that of their families, too!**

Shakti-Khazana is our women's empowerment and income generation programme. It helps women earn, so children can learn. Belonging to families that earned about Rs 1000/month, today our women earn up to Rs 2,500/each! We believe getting money directly into their hands is one major reason why our children get to high school and beyond. Katha's learning centre is in Bhumiheen, Navjiwan and Jawahar Camps, a large slum cluster of about 1,00,000 people, in Govindpuri, New Delhi. It is supported by MCD Slum Wing, the Government of India, AUSAID, and donations from wellwishers.

Katha's REACH! Initiative strives to build a corpus for our work with working children and children from poor families.

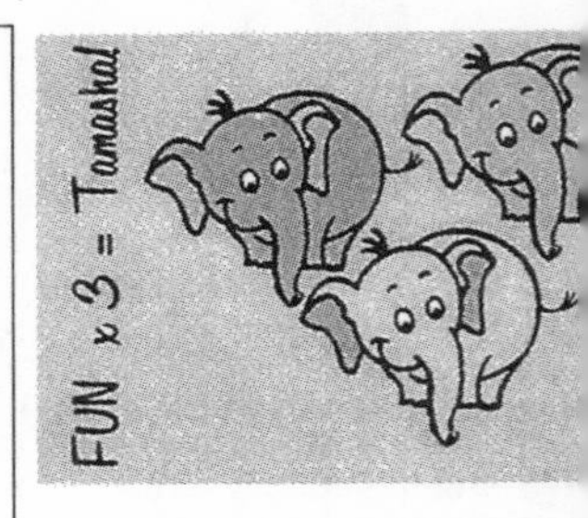

For the last nine years, **Shakti-Khazana** has provided income generation training for membe of the **Khazana Coop!**

Our women are teachers toda Others are experts in baking, catering, tailoring, and food processing. Our bakers have b trained by the Taj Mahal Hot chefs.

Order your cakes and cookies from us. Call us today!

Our students: Good sportsmanship and winning ways!

Phulwari is a loving home for our physically and mentally challenged children. They learn lifelong learning skills here.

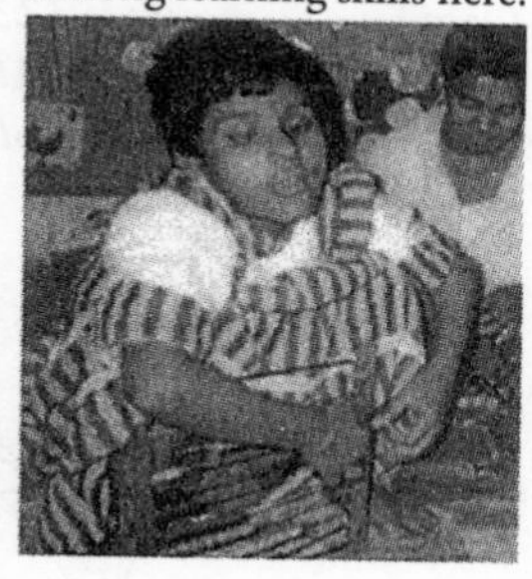

The Maa Mandal: 650 mothers meet regularly to discuss ideas like income generation, health, children's education, basic services. Two years ago, we started the **Bapu Mandal**, at the request of the community.

Jathas facilitate family well being, health and empowerment for the whole community.

"I know Katha is sincere and honest. That's why I have been with them for so long."

Raj Malik is a volunteer at Katha

Katha
Enhancing the pleasures of reading in the literacy to literature continuum!

Doctor, engineer, policewoman, nurse, mechanic, designer ... what will I be?

What happens when 1200 children, many of them working, 40 determined teachers and a whole community come together? Sheer magic!

You'll find this excitement in the air when you enter the low-cost, brick building that houses Katha-Khazana. Children running around, women entrepreneurs at work, people from the community taking a keen interest in the lives of their children.

The children and women of Govindpuri say they have come a long way in the ten years we have been together. Many of the children who come to us are still working to support their families, but see where they are! Doing their BAs and BComs from Aurobindo College, Gargi ... determined to be more confident, creative lifelong learners, to take control of their own futures. For example, Shazia is a teacher at YMCA, Haroon has graduated from Deshbandu and is now running his own shop ...

Once they had mere dreams of becoming doctors and engineers, computer specialists and catering managers ... Today, they know they can make those dreams come true. And they are doing everything they can to move out of the prison of poverty.

Participate in this excitement. Help shape dreams!

Supporting a child's education at KSE, annually, or through the REACH Initiative is simple. It costs just Rs 200/month/child! That is Rs 2400/year. You can –

- Send a cheque or DD, made out to Katha, to us at A3, Sarvodaya Enclave, New Delhi 110 017.

Giving has never been easier, or more affordable!

- Or ... better still, come volunteer. Your time, your experience, your ideas are important for us.

PRIZE STORIES VOLUME 9

The best short fiction published during 1998-99 in sixteen Indian languages, chosen by a panel of distinguished writers and scholars

Edited by
Geeta Dharmarajan
Nandita Aggarwal

Katha
New Delhi

Published by

A-3 Sarvodaya Enclave
Sri Aurobindo Marg, New Delhi 110017
Phone: 686 8193, 652 1752
Fax: 651 4373
E-mail: katha@vsnl.com
Internet address: http://www.katha.org

First published by Katha in January, 2000
Second printing, January, 2000

KATHA is a registered nonprofit society devoted to enhancing the pleasures of reading. KATHA VILASAM is its story research and resource centre.

In-house editors: Chandana Dutta, Chandra Ramakrishnan
Assistant editor: V Sri Ranjani
Cover design: Taposhi Ghoshal
Logo design: Crowquill
Production-in-charge: S Ganeshan
Typeset in 9 on 13pt Bookman at Katha and printed at
Param Offsetters, New Delhi

ISBN 81-85586-98-5 (paperback) ISBN 81-85586-99-3 (hardback)

CONTENTS

This book
has been made possible
by a grant from
The India Cements Limited

THE NOMINATING EDITORS

Asomiya

PANKAJ THAKUR

Bangla

DEBES RAY

English

PANKAJ MISHRA

Gujarati

KANTI PATEL

Hindi

ASAD ZAIDI

Kannada

RAMACHANDRA SHARMA

Maithili

UDAYA NARAYANA SINGH

Malayalam

K SATCHIDANANDAN

Manipuri

ROBIN S NGANGOM

Marathi

USHA TAMBE

Oriya

R P MISHRA

Punjabi

RANA NAYAR

Rajasthani

VIJAYADAN DETHA

Tamil

JAYAMOHAN

Telugu

AMARENDRA DASARI

Urdu

SADIQUE

KATHA AWARD WINNERS FOR 1999

THE WRITERS

Afsar Ahmed, Chandra Prakash Deval, Gopini Karunakar, Gracy, Imran Hussain, Jeelani Bano, Keisham Priyokumar, Meghana Pethe, Minakshi Sen, Mohammad Khadeer Babu, My Dear Jayu, Na D'Souza, Pratibha Ray, Prem Gorkhi, Roschen Sasikumar, Sarita Padki, Sutradhari, Vibha Rani, Yogendra Ahuja

THE TRANSLATORS

Aateka Khan, Aparna Satpathy, Bageshree S, Chandana Dutta, Hina Nandrajog, Kalyani Dutta, Mukta Rajadhyaksha, Nandana Dutta, Nandita Aggarwal, Neer Kanwal Mani, Pranava Manjari N, N Ramakrishnan, Rashmi Chaturvedi, Robin S Ngangom, Rukmini Sekar, Sumedha Parande, Tridip Suhrud, Vidyanand Jha

THE JOURNALS

Andhra Jyoti, Baromas, Binjaro, Dainik Pratidin, Huns, Jhankara, Kalachchuvadu, Karmaveera, Mathrubhumi, Miloon Saryajani, Nagmani, Pahal, Prantik, Sahitya, Sandhan, Tanazur

Stories like Love

Yellow roses, sudden happiness ... "The sea filled his mind with the same vigour with which Gangayi suffused it ... how she softened and blushed when she saw Narayana! He longed so desperately to see her always, talk to her, day and night." *Young love, forever love and the love between those who have seen the sorrow of sudden or everlasting chasms ...* "I know now, Subha's fat body conceals feelings as refined as the sweetest music ... She has proved that neither of us has grown old. Old age is merely a shell – remove it and within it brims rasa."

Each of the stories in *Katha Prize Stories, volume 9*, is complex, refreshingly creative and lend themselves to multiple readings. The stories came to us as some of the best written in 1998, '99. But while looking at them closely, we found love. Love, like stories, happens. Serendipitously. You find them in the most unlikely places. And ...

Love comes wearing many faces. Shy, sometimes self-adoring, often thoughtless ... "Finding her husband waiting patiently, after a reluctant while, Krishnaa took off her clothes. And, with a thin smile he said, Yudhishtiran can spend hours investigating the Vedas, the Upanishads and the Dharmasamhitas. But women bring him quick satisfaction."

It is love, too, when it is secret, and she will not reveal it, even when ... "All the three bhuvas hovered over her shouting and screaming, come out, come out into the open, you bitch. Whoever you are, face us ... Natha's wife was trembling, as Savaji picked up a chain and roared, Are you coming out or shall I rip your hide?" *And that other kind? Some do call it a kind of love when it is jealous, violent, cruel.*

Love after an arranged marriage can be romantic love or ... "On her wedding night she had drawn herself thousands of lines and checks, carefully measuring the gains and losses of every move, eager not to transgress the limits, All his worries should now become yours! Aapi had said. All his worries, last wishes, shattered hopes. He's my sustainer, my Khuda." *Yes, lovers wear many faces* – "One afternoon, asking Togor to pluck out the grey in his hair, he lightly touched her budding breasts. Togor was not frightened at all. In fact, a strange pleasure thrilled her virgin body." *Lust too is called love ...*

But then, luckily for us, there are other ways of showing love ... The worrying, eye-shining love of parents, the doting-on-your-child love ...

"Munia turned and Munia crawled, Munia grew, day by delightful day ... people saw her on Chhat Ghat, Munia at her mother's waist, Munia running, the tinkle of pajebs around her baby ankles, Munia twirling in a red dacron frock ..." *Or that wide-eyed, cuddle-me-close warmth between grandmother and grandchild.* "We all like Guddavva so much. And Guddavva, she loves us ... You got to keep an eye on Guddavva when she is telling a story for, in the middle of it she may suddenly prod the clouds with her stick and bring rain. Or she'll make the great big seas to rise in fury. Sometimes she can even magic the trees to burst into flowers!" *But then suddenly the children are all grown up and have reached a point when they love, yet cannot express it ...* "Did she look at me? Recognize me? Was there a smile on her lips? I don't know. But I felt light, as if a huge burden had been taken off my mind. I threw myself on the small bed next to Aai's and drowned myself in the sleep that I had been craving for."

And when our heart breaks at the death of a bird, a dog, is it not love? ... "Slowly, he lifted the bird in his hands. Its body already felt heavier though it was still warm. He was not sure what to do next. It occurred to him that he could bury it, but he doubted his mental strength to carry out the task." *Cowardice ... isn't that love, too? And pain.*

There's love of the theatre – looking for the eighteenth camel, purpose, passion and perfection. And love as theatre – anguish and drama and role-playing, playacting – "When will the curtains come down, Aaba?"

Longing for a homeland ... Nostalgia ... is it not love? "If I wanted to come to this town, it was only because I wished to die peacefully, secure in the knowledge that I would be buried in my native soil."

Isn't concern, anguish over the death of someone one does not even know, a kind of love? "... nine days before Sanju's suicide, a young boy took two days' leave from his hostel to return home, to E-3, downed thirty sleeping pills, and closed his eyes to the world forever. Even on that day, I did not say, What is the meaning of all this? These things must stop. Instead I thought meaninglessly – No meeting with a mermaid happened."

Love between friends is refreshing love, or between a guru and a sishya. And here you'll find universal love that brings universal responsibility, or suddenly shows the self as a marauding black buck.

Cynicism too is sometimes love! But finally, love is all that is simply human as in the trust between a Kuki and a Naga that starts this collection ... "Just three simple words but inside them raged all the fire in his heart."

It is love of another kind that made this book possible: I thank our writers, our translators and, most of all, our nominating editors. Sincere thanks to Sri K Srinivasan and India Cements for once again supporting the publication of this book. And to our friends who gave spontaneously, specially, Alka Nanda, Ananda Rao, Arvind Dixit, Bimbisar Irom, Bonita Baruah, C K Hota, Indira Chandrasekhar, Kranti Sambhav, Krishna Chawla, Maya Sharma, Mini Chandran, Prabhavati, T S Rama, Ritu Bhanot, Roomy Naqvi, Sadia Mehdi, Sangita and Arvind Passey, Savita Goswami, Shankaranarayanan, Sharada Murthi, Sharada Rao, Sumangala Bakre and Zakia Zaheer. Friends of Katha, thank you.

This book celebrates the magic of 9,19,99,1999. This ninth volume of nineteen prize stories is Katha's 99th book, offered at the end of 1999! 1999 was Katha's tenth year, made possible by my pleasure-to-be-with team at Katha, starting with Air Commodore Dutta, the editors, especially Nandita, Chandana, Chandra and Sri Ranjani, to Swapna, Sandeep, Suresh, Jose and Ganeshan. And those at Khazana, the Katha National Institute of Translation, in marketing, networking, administration, accounts – the rest of the best team anyone can wish for. Thank you!

This is one of the easiest prefaces I have ever written – but then love is like that isn't it? Easy as long as it isn't difficult. Each of these stories, in a way, is a thought-experiment, a heuristic device to capture emotions that play on faces and eyes and fingertips, but translate with great difficulty into words. Betrayal and fidelity, intuitions and perceptions, vindictiveness and melting love, worlds nestle within words, words within worlds and suddenly, there are more than nineteen ways of showing love in this volume that you hold in your hands. I offer this book to you with all the love I can muster.

Enjoy! The stories, the year 2000, the decade, century, mille...

19.9.1999 Geeta Dharmarajan

KEISHAM PRIYOKUMAR

ONE NIGHT

TRANSLATED AND NOMINATED
BY ROBIN S NGANGOM

First published in Manipuri as "Ahing Ama" in *Sahitya*,
November 1996, Imphal

What if his head was bashed in while he slept? Or a machete plunged into him unawares? Stephen woke with a start.

He opened eyes still heavy with sleep and stared uneasily at the bed opposite. Lingpao lay with his legs outstretched. He had not moved at all. Stephen breathed a little easier but then thought, He used to snore so loudly every night, now he lies there like he is not even breathing, is he still awake?

Stephen could not sleep after that. His eyes swept the objects in the small room dimly outlined by the faint light of an electric bulb that trickled in. Near the wall, the rice pot, the stove, a few bottles, a basket, the plates and bowls, lay undisturbed. Where was the machete that always leaned against the wall? He panicked and looked around.

Lingpao stirred. He turned in his sleep and rolled on to his side.

Stephen almost sat up, then decided not to. He remembered he had placed the machete under his bed. He craned his neck to check if it was still there. The machete lay untouched, a little further down, exactly where he had hidden it. Stephen exhaled. But he still could not bring himself to shut his eyes.

What time was it? He couldn't hear a single human voice and except for a couple of dogs barking in the distance there was a deathly silence. Was sleep not going to be possible tonight? He tried to quell the rising fear in his heart. He looked again at Lingpao who lay as motionlessly as before. Was he really asleep? Would I have to stay up till daybreak without getting a wink of sleep?

Stephen and Lingpao had been staying together in a tiny room at the far end of the horizontal office building for almost four years now. But never had Stephen's mind been in such torment.

"Would you still like to lodge together?" the official had asked, summoning the two of them earlier that day, and neither of them had replied. They had no idea how to respond. For a brief moment they had looked at each other, as if by accident, but their gaze held only for a mere second. Then, lowering their heads, they had both remained seated quietly, each waiting for the other to reply.

"Nothing will go wrong between the two of you, I know, but then who can predict human nature? If something does happen, then we'll all have to get involved," the official continued. "And then the chowkidar's job and the sweeper's will have to be performed jointly by one man. Or else, since we have no separate living quarters, one will have to live in a rented room. The two of you better decide by tomorrow."

This time too they had not replied and had walked silently out of the room. Having lived together all these years, having befriended each other, they were now separated by a great divide. All of a sudden, they could not look each other in the eye.

"A Kuki and a Naga living in the same room? If they murder each other at night, won't it be a slur on the name of this office?"

This was the thrust of the conversation in the next room. Stephen clearly heard what the head clerk, Kulubidhu, said and knew that Lingpao had heard it too. If someone had made such a remark earlier they would have laughed it off. Now he could not bring himself to join the others who talked and joked noisily. He wanted to run away – somewhere, anywhere. Lingpao, equally at a loss, stood rooted to the threshold.

Stephen wasn't sure whether he considered Lingpao an intruder on his land.

"Lingpao, don't you come from Pashong? Look, the paper says someone called Songkhulun Chongloi, his wife and three year old daughter, have been killed in a field near the Ihang river," the typist, Tombi, had said, holding out the newspaper.

Both Lingpao and Stephen had felt their blood run cold. Lingpao had almost snatched the newspaper from Tombi's hands and read it haltingly as if feeling his way through the news. His hands shook.

His eyes turned red. The paper slipped from his hands and he turned and left without a word.

Stephen knew that Songkhulun was Lingpao's brother. But Lingpao did not want to talk about the incident with anyone.

"Your killings, attacks, and burning down of each other's houses are not going to end just like that. Many more will die. Yesterday or, was it earlier, weren't some Tangkhuls killed in Monlom?" said Tombi to Stephen as he turned and walked away.

Stephen looked intently at Lingpao as he lay on the bed. Lingpao hardly moved. Was he asleep? But how could he sleep, having heard that his younger brother, his wife and child, were dead? Songkhulun had been barely thirty years old.

Lingpao had returned late at night, his eyes bloodshot, reeking of liquor, and had gone straight to bed. Stephen had thought Lingpao might already have left for Pashong. He wanted to say something, express his anguish, but seeing the state Lingpao was in, he hadn't had the courage to speak up.

Instead, he felt fear rising in his heart.

As the silence of the night deepened, Stephen lay back again and gazed at the ceiling, but his eyes glazed over the torn matting above. He was far away, with his mother, his wife Mary, and his three small children, in Sanakeithel village, on a broad flank of the mountain near Ihang river – the Kuki village of Pashong nestled on a mountain not very far away. In the small market of Sanakeithel, his mother sat through the afternoon, selling greens and herbs plucked from the forest. Pashong folk too came to this market to make their purchases. The level fields on the banks of the Ihang belonged to both villages and people from both villages caught fish in the river together, whenever they wished ...

But now? Stephen drew in a long breath. And Songkhulun? His face, chest, belly smeared with blood from cutting meat, the man who laughed easily, Butcher Songkhulun? Because Stephen was a friend of his elder brother's, Songkhulun would often gift him a chunk of meat before he returned to Pashong. Sometimes, like Lingpao, he would spend the night with Stephen's family and return the next day.

"Songkhulun, they're going to recruit men from the adjoining village for this dam they're building on Ihang river. Why don't you join us?" Stephen had asked him one day.

"Me? I've no education. And they'll ask me to live in Imphal. No no, let me continue living in my own village."

"You want to spend the rest of your days chopping meat, then?"

"I don't like cutting meat. I feel bad killing animals all the time. It's not good to sin. I'm doing this to stay alive. Who knows, I may die like an animal one day."

"Don't say that, Songkhulun. The Lord will protect us."

"True. He thinks only for the good of mankind."

It had been a black, moonless night. Ukhrul's mountain ranges, fields, rivers and the Sanakeithel village were all shrouded in the dark. The hymns emanating from the nearby church echoed loud and clear. Songkhulun joined in, singing hymns in his native tongue. After humming the songs gently for a while, his voice rose, clear, distinct, powerful and melodious ... Even now and so far away, when he went to church, Stephen remembered the songs Songkhulun sang at home.

A few teardrops fell from his eyes without warning. Stephen did not wipe them away.

How silent the night was. Stephen himself was not aware when the fear in his heart dissipated into the night. He heard the sound of Lingpao snoring, and wearily closed his eyes.

"How many hours to daybreak?" These were the first words Lingpao had spoken to him since last morning.

Stephen got up, and opening the window near his bed, looked out. It was dark all around. The plains of the Lemphel wetland, the trees and bamboos, were all submerged in the inky darkness. Not even a star in the sky. He closed the window.

"It'll still take quite a while. Can't you sleep?"

"How can I?"

Just three simple words but inside them raged all the fire in his heart.

"Won't you go to the village later today?"

"I don't know. How can I go without an armed escort?"

"Couldn't you get the escort yesterday?"

"No. Before the burial, I want to see Songkhulun, my sister-in-law, my niece."

Lingpao could not speak any more. He got up, picked up the broom from the corner and stepping outside, gently shut the door behind him. Stephen could hear the doors of adjoining rooms open. Closing his eyes, he tried one last time to sleep. But soon, he sat up with a start as if remembering something. He removed the machete from under his bed, and put it back where it belonged – against the wall where it was clearly visible. Then he went back to bed again and lay down hoping to get as much sleep as he could in what little was left of the night. He shut his eyes.

He knew exactly what his reply to the official was going to be.

ꝺ

AFSAR AHMED

... HEADMASTER, PRAWN, CHANACHUR

TRANSLATED BY CHANDANA DUTTA
NOMINATED BY DEBES RAY

First published in Bangla as "Arthaheen Katha Balar Nirbharata" in *Baromas*, September 1998, Calcutta

I am forced to weave together meaningless activity and thought, and have reached a point where there is no other way out. I must live with them. Without solutions. My body, its numerous parts, strike different meaningless poses, constantly. I lose myself in neverending meaninglessness, seeking refuge in it. And yet, my neighbours, my colleagues, my wife, my daughter – not one of them has found my behaviour or my gestures, strange or unreal. Perhaps, they have found an element of truth in all these.

Like now. The doorbell is ringing. I am inside our flat, standing at the front door. Yet, I don't open it. There is no reason for my not opening the door. But, to my wife and daughter waiting on the other side, I present a plausible explanation. I am in the bathroom, or in the bedroom napping, with the door shut, or at this very moment, am pulling on my shirt and trousers to come open the door. But the fact is, when I went on to the balcony of my second floor flat a few minutes ago, first a splash of red caught my eye, then the flower-laden krishnachura tree, and finally, through the gaps in the branches and leaves, my wife and daughter – my wife had gone to pick up our daughter from school. I came to stand at the door and yet I delay opening it. And to think that I hadn't even bolted the door after Pramita left. As soon as the door closed behind her, I'd come to the door, fiddled noisily with the bolt but left it as it was. I take solace from such meaningless gestures.

Even now, Pramita and Tinni stand outside, sweat drenched, firm in their conviction that I have latched the door and am inside the house. If they push a little, the door will open. But because they consider the untruth of my existence a living truth, these two creatures somehow continue to exist, to think I am in the bathroom, or napping with the bedroom door shut, or pulling on my shirt and trousers. I am getting sucked into the reality of the false.

I make a noise with my hand on the latch. And still the latch remains where it is – at the same distance from the upper edge of the door and the crack between the door and its frame. Then, a slight shove and Tinni hurls into the living space.

I am face to face with Pramita. She is holding a triple fold umbrella in her hand and wearing her sunglasses. Meaninglessly, I stretch my hand towards her and say, "Hello!" Accepting this gesture as true, Pramita retorts, "Don't be stupid," and with her sunburnt, red-radish face, stomps into the bedroom like a reckless, uncaring bull in the streets of an overcrowded market place. "Uff! Once again today they could not rescue the child from the manhole." Her face is stamped with terror.

I do not wish to acknowledge such talk. Walking a few steps behind her, I stop short. Then I return to the door. I know it is latched, and yet I pretend to latch it.

Pramita is standing at the bedroom door. She turns back to stare at me. "What? Had you left it open?"

I bite my tongue. Then give sound to meaningless words. "One night ..."

"Had you left the door open?"

"... rain ..."

Pramita thinks I'm reminiscing about a particular rain-filled night. My silence stops her from probing further. She saves her questioning for another time. But my "one night – rain" had not been intended to start a conversation nor was I keen to share memories or the description of an experience. I had just wanted to say something meaningless. Pramita goes into the bedroom, and I surrender myself to the sentences in my mind:

One night
rain
a lot of rain
the juice-filled fruits are dry
birds fly, their feet pointing downward, their spines ramrod
water crocodiles collect the colour blue at the root of the banyan tree as they yawn
the water-borne moss against the mountain face flaps its wings and chaffs its knees
Oh! my poor birds, don't go into the water, float away like the clouds

Snake-like evening
ink-filled night
naked breeze
all these in our rooms
pit caves, tar flies, children's lessons
meetings with a mermaid have not yet happened

I lean out a little from the balcony and feast my eyes on the red glow around the krishnachura tree. I enter my daughter's room with its neatly arranged rows of books and exit from the other door. A friend has come to ask Tinni out to play. She goes down to play, bathed in the same red glow of the krishnachura. There are a couple of concrete benches and swings down there. Or perhaps she's playing ball.

"Hanh! I think I remember your saying that one rain-filled night someone had fallen into the manhole. What a country, what a city, the height of being unsafe."

To fuel more false meaninglessness to Pramita's false notions about myself I repeat, "Yes. One rain-filled night" – and then I say, "No meeting with a mermaid happened."

I shake my head and sigh. *No meeting with a mermaid happened.*

"I am afraid of letting Tinni come back from school by herself."

"It is something to be afraid of."

Pramita's remarks cause more meaningless words to silently infuse into my thoughts. *Dak-peon, remark-book, headmaster, prawn, chanachur, swadeshiness, Indianness.*

"Are you never afraid?"

"Of course, I am." *Headmaster, prawn, chanachur.*

"Murders have gone up in the city, so have rapes."

... *headmaster, prawn, chanachur.*

"The budget session is approaching. Who knows what madness the ministers will indulge in this time."

... *headmaster, prawn, chanachur.*

Pramita goes to the balcony to pick up the clothes left out to dry. She wears a solemn face. The evening breeze is blowing, the door and window curtains flap and flare. Unknown to her, I pull faces and dance mockingly, brazenly, behind her back. I think about the result of my dancing and my gestures. If only there would be rain. No, there is no rain anywhere, there is no ocean anywhere, there are no trees anywhere, there is no earth anywhere, only this taunting dance as I kick my feet high in the air. There is no rain anywhere, there are no torrents anywhere at all.

The fragrance of fried hilsa. Shrieks and cries fill the kitchens – Where *are* the hilsas?

There is no rain anywhere.

Pramita descends into my rain-filled thoughts.

"You know, Rajat said the other day, there is a price for everything. Nothing happens anymore without a bribe."

I can't see any rain. But in my mind I see a spray of rain on Pramita's forehead, a few glistening drops waiting to roll off the strands of her hair.

"Wherever there is someone responsible for some work, they are waiting with their hoods raised to take a bribe."

"Where have all the hilsas gone?" I ask.

"You are absolutely correct. Otherwise, how can they buy hilsas worth more than two or three hundred rupees."

"Uff!" *There is no rain anywhere.*

These days Pramita has become quite impossible. Today, more than ever. She has been terrified since last night because some kid fell into a manhole. She had watched the people looking futilely for him. They had searched for him all of last night. So much time has passed today, it is evening, and yet there is no sign of him.

Pramita is feeling bitter, restless. Every once in a while, she shudders. Last week there were two dacoities in this colony. The week before, the police fished out a headless body of a youth from a canal. Sometime earlier, a young girl from the basti was abducted and gang-raped in the park nearby. And even before that, about a month and a half ago, the police came to this S-7 flat of ours, to this flat where Pramita, Tinni and I live, to look for a young boy whose limp body hung from a ceiling fan. Pramita had shuddered at what the police told her. On the telephone the police had heard S-7 instead of N-7. Just two blocks away. N-7. The parents are busy doctors. Sanju. What a decent, lively boy. Twenty one years old. One day just hangs himself from the ceiling fan. A social disease has stolen him from us, Pramita had said.

I have stayed in a state of drowning in the meaninglessness of my thoughts, in words like headmaster, prawn, chanachur. I have, of course, been extremely unhappy about this, and yet I have remained sunk in such chanachur-like words. *Wooden plate, knife and fork, bardariya, posta bazar,* I say, taking refuge in meaningless words, in absurd conjunctions, in mismatched half sentences. One and a half months ago, nine days before Sanju's suicide, a young boy took two days' leave from his hostel to return home, to E-3, downed thirty sleeping pills, and closed his eyes to the world forever. Even on that day, I did not say, What is the meaning of all this? These things must stop. Instead I thought meaninglessly – *No meeting with a mermaid happened.*

Then, last evening, the child fell into the manhole, and vanished without a trace. He has not been found till this evening. Pramita is extremely nervous and crabby. But what I'm trying to say is, isn't Pramita's coming into the kitchen after having dumped the clothes on the bed, the scurrying away of the cockroaches as they collide with her anchal, these cockroaches crawling on the kitchen wall, equally meaningless? At least it is not less meaningless than my pulling faces and kicking my feet high in the air.

The police had rung the bell to our flat. I'd opened the door and invited them inside. At a distance, Pramita stood huddled, holding Tinni behind her. When the police asked to see the corpse, I'd asked them into our bedroom, immediately swinging into an act of meaninglessness, to imbue this typical police endeavour to incriminate criminals, with reality. Pramita had set things in order, pointing out the mistake to the officer. All I had wanted to do was to use my meaninglessness to present the police with all the evidence of a suicide in my bedroom.

Later, I fell into a beguiling daydream of N-7 and S-7. To do this well, I prepared myself several times, to imagine my lifeless body hanging from the ceiling fan in my bedroom. Relishing the sense of falseness, I'd stammered in front of a policeman and had looked sufficiently scared for him to take a sharp look at me.

"What do you do?"

"I inflate balloons."

"What do you mean? What sort of work is that?"

"You know, blow things out of proportion in a newspaper office."

"What did you do before that?"

I understand that my age and the way I look has aroused his suspicion and he thinks I am hiding a dark political past. But what good would it do for the police to hunt for such a person?

"What period are you referring to? It is four years since I left the work of a schoolmaster. I taught for ten years," I say.

"No, no, before that, when you were younger, in your adolescence or early youth."

"Headmaster, prawn, chanachur ..." The words escape my lips and the police officer goes away laughing.

I am yet to understand what sense of reality these three words had given him for he had left hugely satisfied about something. This was a big surprise for me. To this day I have not been able to understand why these three meaningless words gave him such a sense of peace, why they seemed to liberate him. The police officer's abrupt departure appeared to me like that of an irritating lunatic who immediately leaves you when you ask him to stay. Maybe, the self-realization of his own youth dawned on him through those three words. *Headmaster, prawn, chanachur.*

That night I could not sleep for a long time. Kept looking up at the ceiling fan. The scene of the police officer, almost fleeing our house, perplexed me. What sort of self-satisfaction did he derive from my trio of headless, meaningless words? To me of course these three words were a form of protest against my incapacity to land a smart slap on the right cheek of the policeman. In fact, they conveyed the meaninglessness of protest.

Afterwards I gave two people the wrong number to my flat. N-7. When purchasing a phone from Chandni, I asked the shop to home-deliver it. The phone has now reached the home of the parents of the only son who had committed suicide. The parents are convinced that the boy had ordered for the phone before his death. Now my phone instrument rings beautifully in their house. It sounds like the cooing of a strange bird. I haven't breathed a word of this to Pramita. A phone purchased for my flat, coos like a bird at N-7 and showers consolations from relations and well-wishers, pours requiems for the dearly departed.

Standing in the dark balcony of my flat I hear the cooing of this bird. Whenever I wish to sleep restfully in my bed, it echoes strangely in my ears. During the day sometimes, I stand on the tarmac below N-block so that I can hear my bird trill every time a call comes through. The phone instrument which could have been mine, had I so much as reached out for it, is now in the room of a recently dead youth. His parents have embraced this falsity as being so deeply true that I don't stand any chance of introducing myself as the rightful owner now. I have no existence there.

The second person whom I gave the wrong address to was someone I bumped into after a long time, just like that, in the street. I ask him home. The same trick again. His name is Ananya, a friend from my heady political days. Nearly forty. No longer so young. Works on a lathe machine. A machine-mate, working on strictly specified and accurate dimensions. But he still retains the dreams in his eyes. He enters N-7 straight away. Bends down in pranam to the doctor and his wife, thinking them to be my parents. Introduces himself as a friend of their son. The parents burst into tears. Ananya stands face to face with the news of my suicide, shouldering the grieving wails of my parents.

When Ananya is walking below the krishnachura tree, returning from N-7, with reddened eyes and a saddened mind, I am sitting in the balcony with a newspaper in my hand. I have just woken up from a dawn to noon nap, after being on duty the previous night.

"Ananya!"

He looks up. "Arupda? You here?"

"Yes."

"But why are you here? You are supposed to be ..."

"Headmaster, prawn, chanachur."

"Arupda, you ... here?"

"Yes, I live here."

"But then ..."

"I am dead, right?"

"Arre Arupda, what a strange thing this is ..."

"Don't come upstairs. It is more fitting for you to return home in mourning."

"Yes, I should return home. In any case, I'm not able to understand this ..."

"Are you afraid?"

"Yes I'm afraid, but I do not understand what I'm afraid about."

"Perhaps it is some kind of miracle, hain Ananya? You should remain in the reality of N-7 to which you had gone."

"How are those two people at N-7 related to you, Arupda?"

"My parents."

"And the one who has committed suicide?"

"Their only son."

"Then ..."

"There is no then. Just go back home. I will now peruse eight newspapers perched on the commode. From these I will search for an advertisement for a post and will then quickly write out an application ..."

Scared, Ananya hurries away.

Later, while buying a cigarette on the road below, a jeep stops behind me. Looking back I find the police officer peering out of the jeep. "Headmaster, prawn, chanachur!" he guffaws and drives off.

Recently, a rape case, a murder, and two robberies in the area have left Pramita deeply agitated, worried about the lack of security. She raises questions about our democracy, the negligence of the administrative system. She talks about corruption, about social decadence, about the dangers of forming a new government. But, I alone cannot vote for millions of people. This helplessness leads me to depend on meaninglessness.

Today is a holiday for me. I am settling down for another bout of sleep after having slept through the entire day. All arrangements have been made for this. Pramita has fixed the mosquito net. The curtain flutters in the breeze. As on every night, Pramita is finishing her chores before turning in. The bird continues to coo at N-7, my cigarette continues to smoulder between my fingers.

"Can you hear it?" I ask Pramita in a hushed aside.

"Hear what?"

"The bird, the cooing of the bird, the bird of our house."

"Oh, that is not a bird, that is a phone ..."

"Is that not a bird? A bird's voice?"

Whenever Pramita is busy, she cuts the conversation short, putting off the talk for later.

The nightly television news bulletin has just announced that efforts to extricate the child from the manhole have not yet been successful. I do not like to think about the implications of such things.

I cling to my dependence on meaninglessness as I grind out my cigarette in the ashtray. As if I have escaped to an enchanted hill. Or to a lonely lake on whose cool waters bob many a road. The lotus leaves are all water-like below the waters.

The fire is more imaginative than the ants
when the clouds enter Patal, the legs grow increasingly itchy
a hundred pins are afloat on the closed door
red radish, bums, carpet
chicken pox, eye-grime
mixture, abortion, ashshaora trees, haritoki
a planked floor
temple of the Union, ankle bells, beef
stockings, cut-lips, mask, insurance, pickles, mankochu

One rain-filled night
manhole
the ringing of the phone as if the bird is alive
the meeting with the mermaid never took place
Patal spreads out in the hot sun

Pramita says, "The police are really terrible, aren't they?"

"When the clouds enter Patal, the legs grow increasingly itchy," I respond.

Pramita laughs.

"Why did you laugh?" I am amazed to find Pramita making sense of my meaningless words.

Pramita laughs again. "When the clouds enter Patal the legs grow increasingly itchy," she repeats nearly in splits. "But suppose that policeman returns and rings the bell on such a night?" she asks sobering up.

"Then he will go back laughing deliriously as if somebody has tickled him, when I utter a few of these words."

"But why should he come?"

"He will come. He will come to take down the bodies of the suicides from the ceiling fan. It satisfies him. He is suspicious of you only when you want to live, and then he immediately becomes serious. The extremists are becoming active. Otherwise, the police is fun-loving. Either they eat laughter or have the human brain for breakfast."

"I thought you had stopped talking like that."

"I had."

"Then why did you say that now?"

"It was a mistake. Ananya had come the other day and was standing below our balcony, under the red krishnachura tree. I asked him to turn around and then landed him a kick on his rear. He was terrified and fled."

"Terrified? Terrified of what?"

"A hundred pins are afloat on the closed door."

"What is that supposed to mean?"

"Nothing. That which does not have any meaning may have several meanings. *A hundred pins are afloat on the closed door*. Maybe you can derive your own meaning from this."

"Well, I am able to and then again am not."

"Can you hear the phone ringing in a bird's voice in Sanju's parent's flat?"

"Yes."

"That phone was supposed to ring in my flat. Instead, it is making consolatory noises to Sanju's parents. After that address became mine, Ananya visited that flat. He conveyed his pranams to my parents and expressed sorrow at my suicide. He became terribly afraid when he saw me alive in this flat. But he could never comprehend my desperation to remain alive. I had wanted to tell him that the ants are more imaginative than the fire. This would have helped him understand the fact of my existence. But instead he became afraid, not being able to understand the sheer helplessness of these unbearable times. Having asked him to turn his back to me, I had to give him a resounding kick. That completed the whole episode. But if Ananya had tried to come up directly to my flat, I would have welcomed him by saying that the ants are more imaginative than the fire. The point is, why should he go to a wrong address, just because somebody gave it to him? Are you feeling sleepy?"

"No, go on. I am scared."

"Scared?"

"Yes."

"If you separate me from my flesh blood and marrow, you are certain to feel terrified. Obviously you will feel scared if you see me dead. Just try to see me both alive as well as dead. Maybe you will get something from it."

"Rajat was saying that an elderly friend of his, Niharda, was terrified when he saw the breakdown of the way hospitals function."

... *red radish, buttocks, backside, carpet, chicken pox*

"Shikha's brother-in-law died because of a wrong operation."

... *ashshaora, haritoki, a planked floor*

"The son of your colleague could not be traced for the last five months."

... *ashshaora, haritoki, a planked floor*

"They are fed heavy doses of politics and religion, and people are also happily devouring this."

... *red radish, buttocks, carpet, chicken pox*

"Communalism is on the rise."

... *headmaster, prawn, chanachur*

"Sleeping?"

"No, one rainy night ..."

"Then?"

"The fire is more imaginative than the ants."

"That sounds good."

"When the clouds enter Patal, the legs grow increasingly itchy ."

"Are you saying something?"

"I am trying to say something without saying anything."

We fall asleep.

Next morning we are woken up by the police officer. Sitting on my only sofa he says, "I thoroughly enjoyed your words, sir, really, headmaster, prawn, chanachur." And he laughs as if someone had mercilessly tickled him.

I circle him twice. Then, bringing my face close to his I inhale the stink of his body – a stink which clings to the body, a stink which comes from the constant handling of putrefying corpses.

The police officer says, "This is the smell of genuine foreign scotch whisky, my dear man."

"Right."

"I want to inspect your bedroom."

Pramita stands at a distance, her eyes reflecting her terror, shielding Tinni behind her.

"Have you got orders to inspect my bedroom?"

"Orders? What orders? I just want to see your bedroom. You know what the times are like these days?"

"What do you want to see?"

"I just want a look," the police officer advances towards my bedroom. "Your bedroom walls have a very pleasant colour."

"The colour that you see is not really the colour of the wall."

The officer turns his head towards me. "Are you acting fresh with me? Do you know what I can do to you? How dare you joke, saying that the colour of the wall is not really the colour of the wall?"

"I am not joking at all. Maybe I can explain ... Do you see the krishnachura tree below? The colour of its blossoms are reflected on the wall giving it an altogether different shade."

"Arre! Really. You are right. It had me completely fooled. That tree must be felled tomorrow. Now tell me, what is the height of your ceiling from the floor?"

"It is not more than the usual height."

"So, what is your height?"

"You can see for yourself."

"No, I want to hear it from you."

"Five seven."

The police officer looks up at the ceiling fan, "Very beautiful."

"What?"

"Your wife and daughter."

"The flies from the oven alight on the cheeks and the flies from the cheeks are snapped up by the cat!"

"That sounds so lyrical."

"Really?"

"I mean, it is like a song. The flies from the oven alight on the cheeks and the flies from the cheeks are snapped up by the cat. If you sing it in tune, it will sound even nicer."

"One night, rain ..."

The officer is excited, "Yes, go ahead."

"One night rain, a lot of rain, the juice-filled fruits are dry, birds fly, their feet pointing downward, their spines ramrod ..."

"It sounds beautiful, tell me more."

"Water crocodiles collect the colour blue at the root of the banyan tree as they yawn; the water-borne moss against the mountain face flaps its wings and chaffs its knees ..."

"Really, this is very beautiful. Your meaningless words are beginning to intoxicate me."

"Why don't you take off your cap and scratch your bald head once? It will make you feel even better."

The officer takes off his cap, scratches his head, and sighs in pleasure. "Brilliant!"

"There is vulture shit on your head."

"Every now and then I have to go to the morgue. I have pet vultures close to the morgue. It must be their shit." He bursts into laughter. "Fact is not all corpses in the morgue can be disposed off properly. We also do not always hand over the corpses to the next of kin."

"How do you live with dried bird shit on your head?"

"Oh, my dear sir, we too are types of vulture."

"Are we?"

"Are you scared?"

"Why don't you take a cigarette? It makes you look a little human."

The police officer lights a cigarette, inhales deeply and blows out some smoke. "You have three ashtrays, don't you? One in this room, one in the bedroom and one in the bathroom."

"Headmaster, prawn, chanachur."

"You know, I have to keep tabs on you."

"Headmaster, prawn, chanachur."

"But you are more dangerous at home. Can you guess why?"

"Oh! my poor birds, don't go into the water, float away like the clouds ..."

"Look here, I am beginning to fall in love with your kind of talk, but I have to go take charge of the corpses soon. Something of that nature is about to happen."

"What is stopping you from fishing the child out of the manhole?"

"Oh, there's a problem in it. Unfortunately I cannot tell you everything about it. Suffice to say my dear friend, it is a conspiracy against the police. So long, I am leaving now. I will come again."

"Headmaster, prawn, chanachur."

The officer hoots wildly, beside himself with joy, at my rejoinder.

He walks out and I slam the door behind him forcefully, as if kicking him in the butt.

"Did he say he will come again," Pramita asks in a frightened voice.

"Certainly he will." I do not care to think about the stark implications of such conversations. Because I am helpless.

I open the door and step out.

"Where are you going?" Pramita thrusts her face out of the door.

"In the shade of the sun in the netherworld."

"Why are you going?"

"Because I am not able to do anything."

"When will you return?"

"I will be back soon. I will be back because I will not be able to do anything. And then I'll go again."

"What are you thinking of?"

"Some meaningless thing, like ..." I say, illustrating my point by lapsing into silence.

I go down the stairs. But, at the bottom, right in front of me, I find another flight of stairs. Climbing up the new staircase, I find myself back at the door of my bedroom. A funny way to return to base, I think, feeling my senses come alive.

ക

MEGHANA PETHE

THE EIGHTEENTH CAMEL

TRANSLATED BY SUMEDHA PARANDE AND THE EDITORS
NOMINATED BY USHA TAMBE

First published in Marathi as "Athrawa Unt" in *Huns*,
Diwali Special Issue 1998, Pune

A bunch of fresh roses arrived early that morning. Sanjeev received them and, as he went back into his study, squinted at the card. *For Sujata and Sanjeev, Many Happy Returns of the Day – Sherikars.* There were twelve pink-edged, yellow china roses in the bunch – some about to bloom, others still tightly closed. Sanjeev held them close and inhaled deeply. The water sprinkled on the roses wet his chest. Well, he thought, their twelfth wedding anniversary has begun auspiciously enough.

It occurred to him to put the roses in their bedroom near Sujata's feet so she would have a surprise when she awoke. He opened the door stealthily, crept in as quietly as he could. She must not be woken. She didn't like her sleep disturbed. The lady's mood was volatile and there was no telling what could ruin it. Once miffed, everything, including the bouquet, would be in vain and it would take a thousand pleas to return her to normal. He couldn't afford that. Not today. There was a party in the evening.

The moment he remembered the party the tension set in. There was so much still to be done. Sujata would help, but it was tacitly agreed that entertaining guests was his responsibility. She hated parties, and it was only after great persuasion that she agreed to it, in a sense obliging him with her presence, which was not to be scoffed at either. She would be the life of the party of course, radiant as a full moon, laughing, looking gorgeous, playing host so convincingly that no one would imagine she was less than supremely happy with the state of her marriage. But then, after twelve years of married life, especially when it is supposedly a successful one, anyone is capable of putting on an act. You didn't have to be Sujata Sane, Maharashtra's Ingrid Bergman, to do that.

The phone rang as he was placing the bouquet on the table. His slippers flapped noisily as he hastened out to answer it. Damn!

But Sujata had been awake the whole night watching a crow on the window ledge. It perched noiselessly, its beak buried deep in its neck, now hopping around, cocking its head in the cross-eyed way that birds have. Every once in a while it flapped its wings and then, arre!, it was off! As if its focus had been clearly identified.

That's what Aaba always said: Focus. Sometimes our actions help us attain focus, sometimes they distract us from it. It is for the actor to decide on the action when interpreting a scene so she achieves the right focus. Yesterday, Sujata had tried to explain Focus to Abhay. But she who could convey something so precisely through action had found herself helpless with mere words. Unlike Aaba. she thought wryly, Aaba and his Birbal – Zindabad!

Yesterday's rehearsal had been complete drudgery. The venue had changed at the last minute – a stuffy room, a forlorn, lethargic fan and Abhay smoking on despite her protests. He and Mhaskar had not bothered to learn their lines. There were a couple of hangers-on, as if Sherikar didn't know that she hated strangers at rehearsals. And, to top it all, the tea was cold, there was no coconut water and no news of the costumes. Savani had quit fifteen days before the first performance. Sherikar had managed to rope in a slip of a girl as replacement, someone that he, no doubt, had got cheap, or who hadn't demurred when he'd pushed her down on to the casting couch. It was enough to split one's head. A Dombari gypsy show would have been better organized.

But what could she do? For what was she without theatre? What did she live for? She remembered how it used to be before she started acting on stage. Luckily, there had been many plays in the past many years and each had added to her sense of self-worth. And now, however much it pained her, she had to concede that without theatre she would be like a straggly, plucked hen. It would be a different story if one didn't have the feathers but now she couldn't even think of life without the limelight. She was Sujata Sane after all, Maharashtra's Ingrid Bergman.

She had returned home, exhausted and restless (she never voiced her discontent at rehearsals. Sushma did and everyone commented on how foul-mouthed she was, so why get into that) and gone straight to the bathroom to weep out her frustrations.

When she came to bed, Sanjeev was reading by the light of the bed lamp. The music system played desultory music. She leaned abruptly over and switched it off. Sanjeev didn't react. He just closed his book and switched off the light. Minutes went by. Then she felt Sanjeev's hand on her bosom trying to draw her closer. She pushed it away, half-hoping he'd call her "Bali" and try again. Tomorrow is our twelfth anniversary, maybe he's waiting to wish me, she thought. She turned to him, but Sanjeev was already asleep, his mouth wide open. His attempt had been a mere ritual. The fire inside her remained unextinguished.

Overcome by a deep weariness but too tired to sleep, she lay awake marking the seconds by the cuckoo clock with its incessant pecking: tak, tak, tak ... remembering countless nights in those twelve years ... so many days ... so many years ...

In the morning she heard his chappals flap as he walked past. Why was he here? Normally he was in his study at this time, contemplating, writing, a schedule he never missed. Earlier, in their one-room apartment in Malad, with a lone bulb hanging from the ceiling, he did his writing in bed, his notebook resting on a pillow on his lap. Every once in a while she would feel his fingers stray off the pages, into her hair and she thrilled to their loving caress even in her sleep. She shivered as if she could actually feel his fingers in her hair. But now, he had his study and it had been five years since they'd moved into this house ... Actually his fingers had stopped ruffling her hair much before that. May be after I started acting on stage, she thought. *Habits can be lost in the same way that they're acquired. But their memories persist.*

Bored with lying around in bed Sujata got up and immediately saw the roses. They were really pretty. She picked up the note with a glimmer of hope, perhaps they were from Sanjeev, "For my Bali, for twelve years, yours, Sanjeev." But they were from the Sherikars.

She yawned. The bastard. Then she remembered the party.

Couldn't it just have been the two of us, Sanjeev? Who are these upstarts trying to celebrate our wedding anniversary? What do we owe them? What is their interest in our marriage?

Of course, knowing Sanjeev, he wouldn't look at it like that. He thinks a marriage is to be exhibited. Like a woman flaunting her priceless antique jewellery.

How different were our reasons for marrying each other. She had accepted Sanjeev, that amalgam of good and evil, and for what he was or what she had thought he was. But Sanjeev? Had he really married *her* or could he have made do with any healthy, beautiful girl from a good family with knowledge of the social graces? A girl who opened the door for him when he returned late in the night, who fed him and warmed his bed. Like a candle picked by a blind man he'd picked her and had married her for the most common of reasons – to make sure there was a woman who was his and his alone.

But she *had* married Sanjeev. And it had taken her a long time to understand the difference between them, or why he could remain calm and in control when she was going to pieces.

Then she remembered the party again, and felt like screaming – what's the big deal in being married for twelve years? Twelve years or twelve thousand – what the hell was the difference – the two, like two logs in serene waters – they could bloody well drift on till kingdom come. Break? What could break? Wasn't it too unimportant even for that? Both lived parallel lives. If she wanted, she could snap it in a moment, make a simple announcement that evening – Our marriage is over.

Will Sanjeev understand me at least then? Or will he carry on as always, a faint smile on his lips, politely serving drinks? She stretched lazily, imagining the party and her announcement like a scene from a play – the thought of the stunned reaction of the people, brought a smile to her face, what would the composition of the party be before and after the announcement.

A grand stage moment, she thought wryly.

Sanjeev peeped into the room when it was time for a second round of tea. Ah, she was smiling. He was reassured even as a strange thought rose inside him: She only smiled to herself these days, never at him or anyone else. Years ago, when his eyes opened to the shrill of the alarm clock, he would find her awake, holding his hand in hers and looking at him, a faint smile on her lips. But that was years ago, many years ago. Had he understood the evanescence of happiness he could have preserved the purity and innocence of her smile, freezing it forever in his heart. Alas! one was too callow then. He had never thought anything would change between them. And why it had was still a mystery to him. He hadn't changed. Perhaps that was the reason?

Sensing her good cheer he seized the opportunity and called out, "Bali ..."

Once this had been a surest way of winning her over. No matter how bitter the argument, when he called her "Bali," she would look at him with different eyes. Not really forgetting the quarrel, but like a child lost in a mela who pricks up her ears hopefully at the sound of her mother's voice, waiting to be reclaimed. "Bali" was the key to her heart. It was the nickname given to her by Nana whose beloved, only daughter she was.

Nana never approved of him. He was stunned when he found out his daughter was about to marry a vagabond. How he had tried to dissuade her from the relationship. She was the apple of her parent's eyes. And, how would Sanjeev possibly support her?

Sanjeev had avoided her completely for fifteen days. But one evening, there she was at his doorstep, clutching a small bag with a few belongings. He had come home at a godforsaken hour and found her sitting there – frozen, like a statue. He went in and switched on the light – a lone bulb with a few cobwebs hanging from it. His bedding, a stove, an earthen pot with a little water at the bottom, an unwashed kettle and a tomcat, that was all he had. The cat purred in welcome and slunk between her legs. Gulping down the musty water from the earthen pot, she said, "I have come."

They were both dirty and wet with sweat. Both desperately hungry.

Stuffy room, feeble light. And the tomcat weaving between their legs. He was dazed and confused. She was edgy and traumatized. They sat up the whole night, their hands entwined.

They had met at a college play. His first script. Her first play. She had come to him on the strength of that encounter, forsaking her huge house and her doting father. By morning, she was fatigued. She had no more tears left. Between dry sobs, she had said, "Don't ask me to leave." And immediately thereafter, "I miss Nana." It was then that he had called her "Bali" for the first time. "Bali, I am with you. I will never leave you." And she had looked at him, like, like a lamb at Jesus Christ.

Ever since then he had used the name almost like a magic word. "Bali ..." meant – All is well or Forget what has happened or Let's make love or I am wrong or I accept defeat or I was right but I have forgiven you ...

"Bali," he called now as in those days. And she smiled at him. Vacantly. Without love, without rancour, without forgiveness, without seeking forgiveness, simply abiding by convention. Ritual without religion.

He sensed all this. After all, he was a dramatist who captured and conveyed the finest nuances of human feeling through the crude medium of plays. How could he miss it? But why had things turned out like this? He did not ask this question even to himself, let alone her. It would have made sense to ask if there had been just one reason. But how can there be only one reason for staying together for twelve years? Ah, but there's the rub. The reason is always the same though the pretexts are many. There is only one reason ... Ever since Adam and Eve, every couple who has spent twelve years together, always knows the reason in their hearts even if they are unable to articulate it. But a playwright of Sanjeev Sane's calibre should be able to capture it in words. He tried ...

Only one reason – he had guessed wrong. Only one regret – he had lost the gamble. And Sanjeev Sane thought: I must use this line in my next play. Even in this situation, he was pleased with himself.

But suddenly he checked himself and said, almost coyly, "Bali, happy anniversary." He wanted to close his eyes and kiss her soft, shapely lips but could not even look her in the eye – he was actually scared of her deadpan face. But she solved the problem by taking his hand and shaking it. She signalled to him that she was going to brush her teeth.

He felt somewhat let down. But one had to accept it today, as he had the night before. There was a party in the evening. And it was imperative that the lady stays in good humour. Aaba, Abhay, Sherikar, Lalya, Sushma now with Mukul, and ... The phone rang. He got up, happy to have an excuse to get away.

A Rashid Khan CD played soulfully in the backdrop as Aaba sat meditating in padmasan. Lalya, Mhaskar and Sarang were playing teen patti. The china roses sat in a vase atop the delicate centre table. Sherikar sat on the sofa, channel surfing while Sunanda Sherikar – whom he only half-jokingly called his "Bad Conscience" – sat stiffly beside him sipping a Coke. On the mattress near the wall, Mukul hovered over Sushma and the confirmed bachelor of the theatre, Chetan, having wound up a long discourse on the science of palmistry, had just built it up to the point where he could finally grab her hand and read her palm.

Everyone was holding glasses. The liquids were all colours and everyone was high on whatever they were drinking. In the midst of them all, Sanjeev, ever the gracious host, moved around, refilling glasses, making sure everyone was having a good time. The party was in full swing.

Sujata felt like a spider hanging among them. She got up to go to the bathroom. The light in their bedroom was turned off. High up on the wall was the cuckoo clock that Aaba had presented to her after her first play, the only thing they had brought from their old house. The bird in it moved up and down every second, seeming to peck grains ... Sujata's companion for many years now, alerting and inspiring her ... tak, tak, tak. Sujata paused for a minute.

Was it already eight? Looks like Abhay won't come now, she thought. She switched on the light shrugging away her disappointment, to find Sharvari lying on the durrie on the floor. Sharvari got up quickly the moment she saw her, nearly upsetting the glass by her side. She gulped the tepid drink with its thin slice of melted ice and mournfully asked: "Has he come?"

Sujata shook her head with a smile at Abhay's would-be wife and entered the toilet. When she came out, Sharvari was still there, leaning on one hand, staring at an empty goblet. She looked as if she'd crush the glass any minute. What was it? Anger? Disappointment? Insult? Helpless attraction? The determination to put everything at stake or the need to sacrifice everything?

Sujata strode to the mirror. Sharvari's back was visible in the mirror and something stirred in the deep well of her memory. In Sharvari she spied the Sujata of those many years ago, the Sujata who had abandoned the security of her family and her home and had sat waiting on Sanjeev's doorstep. How that waiting had continued for years. Getting nowhere and hoping to keep her mind off his absence by engrossing herself in meaningless work, she had continued to wait for him till that evening at Malad station when she had woken up to reality.

The test that day had only confirmed what she had sensed all along. She was pregnant. She had waited though she wanted oh so desperately to share the news with Sanjeev for he was completely absorbed in his new play and she didn't want to add to his worries until she was absolutely certain. Also, he was always so tired when he returned, usually well past midnight.

The play was written but he was shuttling around for readings, preparing new drafts, absorbing new ideas. Something was finally working out somewhere, but that meant looking for finances, for heroines, having discussions with the director. Too often his mind clouded with worries about failure and success.

She understood. After all she had been in much the same state for the past two months. But that day the pregnancy test was clearly positive, and her first thought was, Sanjeev! She rang up everywhere before she found him. On the phone, all she said was, "Come early, there is a celebration, I will tell you when we meet. Let's eat out. I will wait for you." She hung up after deciding where they would meet at the station.

7:20. She had reached the station ten minutes early. The pre-decided bench was occupied, so she waited patiently.

7:35. She found a place and sat down immediately.

7:50. She sat as though glued to the bench. You never know. If she got up to have a drink, they might miss each other. She did not want to take that risk.

8:00. It was getting late! Mumbai does run by the clock, but sometimes there are miscalculations.

8:10. Should have got something to read ... Should I go and get it? A drink ... I have been thirsty since ...

8:30. No. Not for the temptation of a minute.

He should be coming ... Anytime now ...

8:40. How full these trains are! Where do people go all the time?

So many people? I don't want any of them. I, I want only one.

9:00. Everyone's returning home, only he hasn't come. Everyone but him.

9:15 ... Her throat is parched. She gets up to have a drink, but looks around even while gulping it down ...

9:30 ... She scans the station ... Is he standing somewhere else? Slowly she comes back to her place.

The station is getting deserted now and only a few paan-chewing drunks lurk about. Those greedy stares! Where is he caught up? Has there been a riot somewhere? An accident? No, no, no ...

Sanjeev please come. I am waiting for you without getting angry.

A pock-marked Gujarati lifts his dhoti to his knees and sits next to her, pretending to read the newspaper, adjusting his specs above his nose.

10 o'clock. The station is so quiet. She can hear the flapping of people's chappals as they walk about. What if Nana found out that

she'd been hanging about alone like this? He used to insist that she return home at the stroke of seven and would create a scene if she were even five minutes late. If he were to see her now?

The Gujarati refused to move. Why did I wear this peacock blue saree? Celebration ... I am here to celebrate the arrival of a newborn. She continues to sit as if she has forgotten her way home. She has stopped looking at people. She is scared. Should I go home? Has he sent a message home? Should I ring up again?

She tries to get up and the Gujarati stirs. She is actually scared inside but doesn't let it show. And then anger wells inside her. What sort of a man is Sanjeev? How could I have chosen him ... She sits with her eyes downcast.

Suddenly she turns alert. Immensely alert. Same walk, same height, same cut, she hurriedly walks in that direction. The Gujarati walks behind her slowly. No, it is not Sanjeev. She turns around and nearly collides with the Gujarati.

"Coming along?" he asks.

Since the morning, she has not had anything except a drink. She's churning inside. Doesn't Sanjeev realize that his good-looking wife can get into such a situation? Filled with rage, she hits the Gujarati hard on his cheek. Two, three people stop.

"What happened? What happened?"

She does not want a scene. She wanted a celebration. Even that she doesn't want now. She wants to go home, but home seems so far away. Sobbing she returns to her bench. One of the strangers mocks at the Gujarati – "What, man! Couldn't agree on the rate?"

"How would I know, I was only trying to check ..."

"What a woman! Why doll up and hang around here, so late?"

Ten more minutes. A police constable approaches, striking his baton. Should she ask if he can drop her home ...

"Bhai ..." She is about to call him when a train pulls into the station. And Sanjeev arrives. Smiling, a look of surprise on his face. "You still here?" Confident of his ability to appease her, like a hunter sure of the bird in the net he says, I thought, indeed expected, that you'd have gone back home.

She is silent, still, only her eyes flicker and "Come," he says sensing something. He has eaten a paan, something he always does after a binge, knowing she hates the smell of alcohol.

She gets up. She would have flung herself on the railway tracks. But that's not possible, not now, she is carrying a new being, an enchanting mirage in a desolate world.

Sanjeev keeps walking. He puts a conciliatory arm around her shoulder. She lets it rest there till they emerge from the station. "Well dear? What celebrations? Where should we go for dinner?"

"Home," she says calmly.

"Know something?" he prattles away. "I managed to land a big fish today. Suchitra Banner has accepted my play. You know they're very sticky customers. Such detailed discussions. I had a hard time convincing everyone, but they finally came around. Had to come down a bit but at least that banner values quality production. No compromises. And they do seem to want to bring experimental theatre to the mainstream. This is quite a big thing. Let's see. After everything was settled, they said, Let's sit down for a drink and I couldn't just walk away. Come, I'll treat you to an ice-cream."

"Home." She keeps walking.

Three hours ... three hours, I waited for this man. She glances at his face searching for a hint of remorse, but he walks, totally absorbed in himself, his face shining with the thought of impending acclaim, triumphant that his years of effort and hardship had finally borne fruit, a face that bespeaks smug self-absorption.

She had called him because she had something to tell him. She had come eagerly, to celebrate the arrival of a new being with him, a being in whom a bit of him resided too. But now she wonders, Who is this stranger – a man whose life is independent of mine, who has a goal where I have no place, a purpose that I don't share, a centre around which only his sense of identity can revolve.

Should she share her secret, the secret that lingers on her lips, flutters in her heart, that stirs her entire being? What will he say? Will he be delighted? Or will the impending responsibility only sour his happiness?

She watches as he impulsively hands a ten rupee note to an urchin, bending down to give him a friendly pat. And then he turns to smile at her – a glance that seems to her just like the note he handed to the urchin, the smile not unlike the friendly smack on the little kid's rump. The happiness is his, everything is his accomplishment, his dream, his success ... She is exhausted and hails a passing rickshaw.

He has forgotten that she had to tell him something, as conveniently as he has forgotten his offer of ice-cream. And through the night she stares at the bulb hanging from the ceiling. In the early hours she feels herself beginning to bleed. Something between them dies that night.

He left for Delhi the next day, to represent Mumbai in a conference on street theatre. Take care, he said, his mind already far away. Street theatre was his first love after all. And once he came back there was the production of *The Story Of Two Sisters*, his new play. His first venture. Maybe he would be able to coax Sushma Mudgal to act in it. And she, her first venture, only hers, washed away, Her Story ... but he would not understand that. This is the story of a shadow, an age-old plot. She finally understood the difference between him and herself. The bare white walls of the nursing home completely depressed her. Why is the moment of enlightenment always so enveloped in a shell of pain? What is the way out? Do I become the light? She knows she must but she doesn't know how.

Sharvari was moping again, this poor bride-in-waiting. Otherwise an intelligent girl in her final year of MBBS, she had fallen in love with Abhay. Her people were scouting around for a doctor husband for her, but she wanted no one but Abhay, the smart and handsome actor Abhay.

Sujata was filled with pity. She felt like shaking her up, "Wake up, Sharvari, wake up!" She wanted to tell her so many things. But what? You have to experience to understand. And experiences cannot be handed readymade to anyone. The one common point is the waiting. But even Sharvari will find ways, her own ways, and play her own games. Her victory or defeat ... I can only watch.

Feeling like a retired player, watching from the sidelines, biting his nails, frustrated, she applied a fresh coat of lipstick, straightened her hair and moved away from the mirror. She switched off the light and peeped out. She was tired, tired of the forced smile, tired of performing her duties as a hostess. She wanted to sit in a corner alone. She saw Aaba lighting his cigarette. He had seen her, too.

Suddenly she remembered what Aaba had told her on the first day of their rehearsal. "Whenever you are on stage, even down stage, in the wings, half in and half out like a chorus girl, you must act as though at least one person in the audience is looking at you. Like a bridesmaid holding the lamp, you must bear yourself, till the curtains fall ..."

And, as if under his direction, she assumed happiness and cheer, and stepped back into the party.

Chetan was finally gazing into Sushma's palm. "Three."

"Arre, three! Three what?" shrieked Sushma.

"There are three men in your life," Chetan said, looking pointedly at Mukul.

"Oh, men," said Sushma with an exaggerated sigh, "God bless you. For a minute I thought, children. You had me scared!"

"Children? She must have aborted five by now," murmured Mrs Sherikar, unaware that Sujata was right behind her. Sujata saw Sherikar was still channel surfing, perhaps thinking of the nights spent with Sushma, two years ago. She was so wild then ...

"I am the third!" Mukul said nuzzling Sushma's shoulders.

"Oh come off it. What do you think? You Napolean me Josephine? Spouting dialogues like, I know that I am not the first man in your life, but I hope I'm the last. Idiot! That happens only in plays ..."

Mukul only seemed more pleased than ever as he twirled a tendril of hair across her forehead. It was like watching the primitive courtship ritual of some avian species. Was Mukul really infatuated with her or was he looking for a one night stand? And Sushma, what did she really think of his advances?

Chetan placed her hand on his lap and moved his fingers over the palm as if smoothing a crumpled sheet of paper. "Oh no! It can't be!"

"Now what?" Sushma was obviously enjoying killing two birds with one stone – leading Chetan on and driving Mukul insane with jealousy at the same time. Had it been possible Sushma would have hunted men in droves.

"Just look at this! There is a cross on the lower side of the index finger. You are destined to have a happy marriage. Maybe ..." Chetan smiled mischievously, "If you were to marry me ..."

Mukul lunged for his throat.

"Hey, I am not dead either," Lalya said.

"Happy Marriage? Very funny! Is that possible when women have only men to choose from?" Sushma laughed raucously.

"Why not? We have gathered here to celebrate twelve years of one such marriage," said Lele.

"Oh yes, of course ..."

"And Sanjeev will vouch for it."

"Oh yes, of course! Sanjeev the loyal husband. So Sanju, do you feel your loyalty has paid off?" The sarcasm was lacerating.

Sujata felt suffocated. Would Sushma ever forgive her? Would her jealousy ever let up?

Sushma had always felt that Sanjeev was her jackpot. Not only had Sanjeev married Sujata, he had no qualms about letting her act either. And after she had made it big, Sanjeev had never held her success against her, never made her choose between marriage and the stage, nor chased other women. Sushma thinks it has been a cakewalk for me. And not because I deserve it but because Sanjeev is not like other men. He is loyal. Oh ... Sanjeev and his loyalty! I have heard about this, many times, from many.

Loyalty ... What is loyalty? Is he loyal only because he has slept only with me? Does he force himself to sleep with me whether or not he likes it? Whether or not I am able to satisfy him? Or is he just a coward, too scared of going to another woman? Perhaps he's plain lazy, being content with what he has. Perhaps he just follows the golden rule that a bird in hand is better than two in a bush. Then again, perhaps he has no interest in anyone. Neither women nor men. He lives for himself! Is this loyalty? Does he have many temptations to contend with? Does he have the courage to pay for them? Or the willingness to invest in his emotions? The necessity, the capacity or the sheer energy? I care a fuck for his loyalty! Sushma, you don't have to be jealous of me. Once he gives me what I want I don't care if the left-overs go to another. But there is not much to him beyond himself. I'm not flattered by his loyalty. This is loyalty by default. Don't feel jealous of me, Sushma.

Sujata, lost in her thoughts, came suddenly back to earth and rearranged her lips into a smile. Lalya was cracking a joke – "There is this rich woman with lots of dough and ... luscious!"

"Go on," said Mukul.

Sushma laughed loudly. "After believing herself to be just a female body and always available ... what will she do after a few years?"

"Anyway, she says, I'll marry the man who satisfies me completely, and become his slave. I will even sign over all my property to him. All sorts of men are tempted to try their luck. Athletes, weight lifters, Sumo stars ... But she desires no one. They are with her only an hour or two before they get a boot in the rear. Our man Birbal is walking past. He thinks – Let me try my luck ..."

"Did you hear that Aaba? Birbal!" shouts Sushma.

Aaba smiles but keeps nodding his head to the music.

"Everyone tells him, Forget it, no one has succeeded. Not even Mukul. What chance do you think you have? But he is adamant. He enters. Everyone feels sorry for him and waits with bated breath. Within fifteen minutes Birbal walks straight out, with our lady behind him, her head downcast, and an announcement is made – Birbal is my husband and I am his slave. Everyone is surprised. They surround Birbal. What yaar! How did you accomplish it? What miracles did you perform? And Birbal says – Sometimes you have to use your head."

Everyone laughed as Sushma grabbed Mukul by his hair and said, "Get it? Use your head sometimes. Your head!"

Sunandavahini was the only person who didn't get the joke. Not a muscle twitched on her face. She went everywhere with Sherikar like the bunch of keys at her waist which tagged along with her. To Sherikar she was like a stepney, only remembered and required in emergencies. Sherikar gave her the house keys, she gave him children.

This is marriage too, like a free watchman service. Sujata laughed to herself as she went across to empty Aaba's ashtray.

The party seemed to have quietened down. Everyone was drinking silently. Sanjeev was going around refilling glasses, handing out plates. And then the bell rang.

Sujata ushered Abhay in saying, "Your lordship is late," creasing her face into yet another smile. Sanjeev said, "Better late than never!" gave him a brief embrace, asked, "What would you like? The usual, right? Vodka coming up in a moment."

Abhay held Sujata's hands, kissed her cheek and wished her. He held out a huge bouquet. Sharvari, who had reached his side by then, took the bouquet in her sweaty hands, sniffed it and deposited it on the centre table. She now waited tremulously for Abhay to notice her. What a beautiful smile he had! And when he looked at you from underneath his heavy lids ... what deeper happiness could one want? And what more poignant definition of pain?

"I thought you had decided to drop out," Sujata was saying to Abhay, her face bathed in the light of Abhay's smile.

Sharvari eyed Sujata enviously – She has such an imperturbable face. And her movements, so deliberate and measured, are never disturbed by any agitation. Such self-confidence and purposefulness. Abhay keeps talking about her poise while I am always fumbling ... How effortlessly and expertly she tackles Abhay's marvellous smile! Then Sharvari checked herself: What am I jealous of? The over-generous attention Abhay is lavishing on Sujata, the way he ignores me or am I envious of Sujata's dispassionate heart?

Sujata looked at Sharvari, a look of pity and compassion in her eyes. This woman, she thought, is perpetually waiting for a chance to patronize and something in the way she looks at him fills me with anger.

"Now sit with Sharvari for a bit. She has been waiting for you for ages." Sujata turned Abhay over to Sharvari and walked away.

Sujata went straight to her bedroom and looked around for the perfume she had bought for Abhay and Sharvari. Why was Sharvari looking at me like that, what did she think? That Abhay is in love with me? The neurotic woman! Yet, the thought brought a certain sadness. Doesn't she realize that he is only interested in my name, my standing in the world of theatre and my popularity, that if he works with me, I will recommend him to others. He is attracted by my success and fame and I by his youth. Don't worry baby, this isn't love ...

She suddenly felt disgusted with the party and longed to be alone. Let the party go to hell. Who do I care about here but Aaba. And he does not speak to anybody. Even during the rehearsals, he is like this, yet the play grows to perfection – tight and solid.

The cuckoo chirped. Ten o'clock.

When is curtain-fall, Aaba? How long do I have to maintain this mien? This appearance?

Aaba always said, year in and year out, even when she was confused, hopeless and defeated: Maintain the façade. An actor must maintain the façade at all times. Even when gripped by desperation. Even when sick to death. Like Karna who sat in unmoving concentration, even as ants nibbled at and gouged out a piece of his thigh!

Tak, tak, tak. The cuckoo in the clock pecked rhythmically. Sujata went to the window. She could see the turning at the end of the road. Aaba's house stood just beyond. She remembered her evening there. And the events that had led up to it, as if inexorably luring her to her destiny.

Sushma Mudgal had been roped in to act in Sanjeev's play *The Story Of Two Sisters*. He was thrilled. Sushma had more name than acting abilities. It was the Sushma Mudgal tag that drew people to the booking office.

After his return from Delhi, Sanjeev was completely engrossed in the play. Sushma was the heroine and Aaba the director. Sanjeev was relatively inexperienced and therefore had to be present for every rehearsal, constantly getting instructions from Aaba – change this dialogue, change this into direct speech, rearrange that scene, put intercuts here, the play will be fast paced ... There were umpteen changes that had to be made as the play acquired life on stage – a playwright can learn quite a lot during the rehearsals. Besides, Sanjeev had to do the PR, look after advertisement layouts, performance dates, a zillion other things.

He returned home dog tired. Even when he returned home, he was never really there. The play possessed him completely. At times he would smile to himself remembering something, or mutter things to himself and gesticulate in the air.

He had no time to mourn the loss of the baby. He was completely oblivious of what Sujata was going through. He had no time to give her. In that respect, the tomcat was luckier, at least, rolling at its master's feet, it managed a cuddle or two. Sometimes it would even get a morsel from his plate. Or a kick.

Sujata was sinking into a depression and had a hard time getting past the day. In the morning she would busy herself in work, the evenings were given over to waiting and the day's tiredness would bring sleep on swiftly at night. Morning, evenings and nights – these were relatively easy times of the day.

But noon was different. It paused, like a semi colon, holding up the flow of speech. Time hung heavy on her hands. And with its stark savage light, noon brought home the meaninglessness of life. It compelled questions about the purpose of existence and her total helplessness. To get through these afternoons she rolled papads, exercised, plucked her eyebrows, played with the neighbour's kids, read, heard Vividh Bharati, masturbated ...

But she still could not escape the big questions. Why am I here? Why are the others here? How will the noon ever pass? She often wanted to just get up and leave. But go where? To Nana? And accept defeat? No way.

Sometimes she wanted to die. To wipe out her existence. But she did not have the strength for it.

On one such afternoon, driven to despair by her loneliness, acting against Sanjeev's warning that Sushma didn't like unnecessary people hanging around while she rehearsed, she went there. By the time she reached the hall, she had lost courage and stood frozen at the door.

A scene was in progress. Sushma's monologue. Each word was enunciated distinctly and precisely and though rehearsed, each gesture seemed natural. Her voice was melodious, her face pretty. Each prop was dexterously handled and the pauses for music didn't jar. It was thoroughly professional. The scene over, Sushma flopped down where she stood. A couple of people applauded. Sanjeev, who had been gazing at her intently while the scene was on was startled when she yelled, Sanjya! Cigarettes!

He literally ran to her, bent forward, offered her a cigarette, but she simply pulled the cigarette off his mouth and inhaled deeply. She stretched one leg and massaged it and her pallu slipped when she whispered something in his ears and thumped his chest, laughing raucously. Sanjeev, somewhat abashed and embarrassed, nodded his head and knelt by her side.

Sujata watched all this. Only an old memory stirred in her and she thought, Is this scene going to be done this way? What a pity.

She remembered the morning after the night Sanjeev had written this scene, sitting on the bed under the lone bulb in the Malad flat. She had fallen asleep watching him work, her heart soft with love. In her dreams that night, she had seen her struggling lover attain success and fame. Her Sanju was famous. And she had woken early in the morning to Sanjeev's gentle fingers smoothing her hair. He stubbed out his cigarette, smiled a soft smile and, resting his head on her breasts had said, "Bali! I have finally done it. I'm free. I was stuck at this point for so long but today I've managed to write the scene to my satisfaction ... want to hear it?"

And she had listened, bright-eyed, as he read the scene. This same monologue, but read by Sanjeev. She had hugged him tight as the tears coursed down her cheeks. He had done it, her Sanju had done it! And later, in the terrible days and months and years of waiting that followed, she had said the monologue to herself a hundred times, uttering it on sad empty days in front of the mirror, laughing derisively at her own sterile efforts.

The play was nearly ready. She often wondered if Sanjeev remembered that she too had been a stage artist once. Did he remember that she had acted in his first one act play and that he had loved it? Should she ask him? No. He should. That would be a pleasure.

Of course no such thing happened. Sushma Mudgal agreed to play the lead role. He was so happy that day, he had forced Sujata to sip a little beer from his glass. He had even given a bit of it to the tomcat.

And now, she remembered her own rendition of the monologue with crystal clarity. There is something wrong in the way Sushma did it. The sentences are not meant to be delivered so clearly and precisely, oozing confidence. They must sound doubtful, unsure, the words modulated, the pitch lowered. And shouldn't every word be spoken with pain, like a light blue sky painted on a huge canvas with a small bird flying high above – the words were the bird, the light blue sky, the sadness. I can feel all this, Sujata told herself.

But who will tell Sushma? Anything she does is approved by everyone as they can't appreciate how different the scene was meant to be ... But Sanjeev ... Even you? She wanted to run into the hall and ask him but kept standing, like an unexpected guest on a doorstep. Who was she to ask these questions?

"Tell us, lady, when you are through with your puffing. We have to rehearse the trash that you dished out, again. And you others, take ten minutes."

Sujata looked around eagerly. Who was this that shared her

views. A man was walking up the aisle – Aaba Chaubal! No doubt! There was a stunned silence in the hall. Then everyone stood up. "Get me a Coke!" yelled Sushma.

It was Sawant, sent to get some stuff to eat, who saw Sujata. "Vahini, you? Why are you standing here? Come inside." And before she could tell him not to, he had called Sanjeev.

She went inside. Sanjeev was surprised first, then disapproving, somewhat taken aback ... She stood there uncomfortably. Sushma continued to sit there with her legs sprawled out, staring at her, saying, "At least introduce her yaar," to Sanjeev.

"Oh yes, yes," Sanjeev said grabbing hold of Sujata and taking her to Sushma. "Meet Sushma Mudgal who needs no introduction." Then placing his arm around Sujata he said, "This is my wife."

"Very sweet." Sushma shook hands with her.

"Come let me introduce you to Aaba."

Sujata protested and an irritated Sanjeev said, "Come, come." But Sushma hadn't let go of her hand.

How do I get her to release it, Sujata wondered.

"Go, go, that monster will not eat you up. He likes simple, innocent ladies," said Sushma, giving Sujata a little push and directing a poisonous glare at Aaba.

Aaba sat in a corner looking out of the window, calmly puffing a cigarette. He had a Walkman on his lap and headphones on his ears, and his fingers kept time on the window bars.

Sanjeev touched his arm and said, "Aaba ..."

He looked up and slowly removed the headphones. Then he took off his glasses and looked at Sujata quizzically.

"My wife ..."

Aaba greeted her without smiling. "Doesn't she have a name? "

"Oh yes, yes! Sujata," laughed Sanjeev.

He should feel ashamed, thought Sujata, and then, But is it his fault? I am just his wife anyway.

"What does she do?" Aaba asked him, looking at her.

Sujata looked out of the window.What more was there to say,

after all? I do everything that his wife is supposed to do.

"Where did you meet her?" teased Aaba with a straight face.

"We met in college," said Sanjeev.

Isn't he going to say, I had acted in his first play and my work was acclaimed, she wondered. Of course he won't mention it.

"Is she interested in plays?"

Oh, she too has struggled with me for my plays. I read the draft of the play – of which now you speak highly to her – and she invariably adds something invaluable to it. She recognizes the playwright in me – she left her home and came to stay with me when I barely had a place of my own. She has never complained about anything. She has always stood by me. She's given me courage. I was away when we lost our first baby and she managed alone. Even now she manages single-handedly. She is not interested in all and any plays, but in *my* plays.

Will he ever say all this to anyone! No. Never.

"What do you say, Sujata, are you interested?" Sanjeev teased, as if asking a five year old, Sweetie, do you know the three times table by heart? Let Kaka hear. Such condescension.

"A little," she said somehow. But in her mind, she said, Can I do the monologue Sushma just did. Not for the world ... but for you?

"That's good! It is tragic for artists when people at home don't appreciate their work. Of course I have no such experience. I have only the four walls of my house, and they understand my plays. I say this because I see it happening all around," Aaba said, inviting her to see how the play shaped up.

Sujata sat till the end of the rehearsal absorbing everything, storing it in her eyes, ears and consciousness. Then Sanjeev said, "You go on home. I will come right along. There are a few things ..."

At home, the tomcat, mad with hunger charged at her. She gave him eggs from the cupboard and said "Ai you, are you interested in plays? Otherwise, it will be tragic for the master. Lucky you! What a blissful life you lead – you can spend your day licking your body clean, chasing cats in the lane, gobbling stray rats, rolling at your master's feet. Try doing the monologue. Do you know how to deliver it? Listen!" And she recited it from memory. She finished and looked around. The cat had polished off the eggs and disappeared.

Sujata had stared into the mirror and broken into deep sobs.

The next afternoon she returned to the rehearsal. A different person. Yesterday's rehearsal had awoken something in her that had lain dormant. Overcoming her fears of rebuttal and inhibitions she went to the rehearsal. And she kept going. She had no hopes of being in the play and therefore no desire to be in it either. But she loved watching the words come to life and being given shape. She wanted to witness that journey. She kept going. Once, twice, and again, and again. And, after the first day, no one seemed to take notice of her. Or so she felt.

Aaba sat in a corner with the headphones on his ears. Sometimes he would doze off. But no one had the guts to slack off. If anyone delivered a flat dialogue or muffed his lines or played to the gallery, he only had to remove his headphones or change his posture to make the errant individual squirm with shame. He would snap his fingers and the scene would start again. But sometimes, when he was in a good mood, he brought along something to eat – pakoras or bhel. He would walk across to Sujata to give her her share and then return to the group, saying, "No scene is a fragment. It has its own climax." Or, "No line or gesture should be purposeless. If it is so, however exquisitely smart it is, one should ruthlessly drop it!" Or, "Though the actor should be constantly aware as to what is to follow next, the audience should never get the slightest clue ..."

There were endless series of such insights. Aaba would tell tales of Birbal. Birbal this and Birbal that, when Birbal laughed till his cheeks nearly split. Birbal didn't approve of this, Birbal was upset by that. Birbal stories illustrated points, conveyed insights, ways to act, criticisms. Birbal was his favourite character, was Aaba's weapon, his shield, and his veil.

Sujata would sit in a corner and listen to him intently, aware that it was not meant for her, knowing that even if she understood Aaba, it was of no use. She envied Sushma. Not because she seemed to be the focus of Sanjeev's attention but because she was in a position to learn from Aaba. But, she also pitied her. Because Aaba's Birbal was entirely wasted on her. Like water on a lotus leaf. She had no clue how priceless his insights were.To her, he was simply a man, someone she could arouse, flirt with, end up in bed with ...

The look on her face when Aaba spoke was either vacuous or insincere, Sujata thought. Here he is telling her something and she doesn't even have the grace to listen. She's hardly in the play. The only thing she has to offer is the hauteur of an attractive woman. She is just a body. What would I not give to be in Sushma's place!

She thought: Is the world always like this – Where it is desired, it is never given. And where it is given in abundance, it remains unsung and unwanted? The whole damn game is so unfair, so unjust.

Looking at Aaba, she would remember all the tales she had heard about him. Mostly about his womanizing. But if a woman were to present herself as a woman and nothing more, she would be used as such – why Aaba, anyone would use her that way. But she would ask, And I? Who am I? I am not even a woman. I am like the tomcat in Sanjeev's house. Only a pet!

When the rehearsals were over, she would leave without saying goodbye to anyone. No one noticed her absence, just her presence.

Several days went by like this. One day when Sanjeev came home around midnight he said, "Bali, why have you started coming for the rehearsals? Is it to keep an eye on me? You don't have to worry about Sushma. She's like that with everyone. But she *is* the heroine. One has to indulge her moods ..."

Did he really think that this was why she went there? Would he ever understand that suspended hour of bright noon? She was about to say something sarcastic but checked herself, realizing that no answer was expected. He had put the tomcat on his lap and was saying, "Hi hero? Are you angry? We will take care of your moods also. Oh! Oh! ..." Then he said, "Let me have my dinner. I want to hit the sack. The rehearsals start early tomorrow."

From the next day, Sujata stopped going to the rehearsals.

Then god knows what went wrong but Sushma dropped out of the play barely ten days before the opening day. Someone said Aaba didn't like her and that they were at loggerheads everyday and Sushma was fed up with this daily friction. Some said she was not satisfied by the offer made by Suchitra Banner. Others said she had personal problems – her husband was insisting that she choose between marriage and the theatre. All sorts of rumours were doing the rounds.

Sanjeev returned home so sozzled that night that Sawant had to escort him home. The tomcat tried to slink between his feet but all that he got for his efforts was a violent kick. And when Sujata tried to reason with him, he turned viciously on her. "What the hell! The house is mine and the tomcat is mine. Understand?"

"What's the matter Sanjeev? What happened? You are drunk ..."

"So what? Your father hasn't paid for the drinks. I drank with my money. You sit around the house all day, like some dumb bimbo and when I come home you start to nag. Okay so I am drunk ... What will you do? Leave me? Go get out!"

"Sanju ..." She felt a lump in her throat.

"And listen, spare me the tearful Meena Kumari routine. Do you have any idea what I face in the outside world? How can you? All you do is hop around from kitchen to bath and bath to bed!"

"Sanjeev ..."

"What else? Don't eat my head, let me sleep!"

"San ... "

"Now what? Bloody hell, warming the whole day, to extort your quota of highs at night, the bloody stud that I am. What else am I good for anyway. Come let me finish that job, make you happy ..."

Is this Sanjeev? My Sanjeev? He was never like this! How he speaks! At this unearthly hour. I can't even go away anywhere.

She reached the door. How much more indignity could she suffer, she wondered, feeling completetly unwanted. Just as she was opening the latch, he said, "Don't go, Bali. For my sake Bali, please!"

For my sake? she thought, but what have you done for *my* sake? Still she turned back.

She learnt only the next day that Sushma had quit the play.

Sawant had come home, bearing a summons from Aaba.

"Me?" she asked.

"Yes."

"Are you sure?"

"Yes."

Silence.

"Do you know Sushma has quit?"

"What?"

"Didn't Sahab tell you?"

She smiled.

"When does he want me?"

"Anytime. He will be at home, he said."

"But ..."

"You have been asked to come. Here is the address."

She finished her housework hurriedly and left a note for Sanjeev before leaving. She felt her heart thumping wildly all the way: At the station, in the train, and then as she searched for the house.

She rang the bell hesitantly. Aaba opened the door and invited her in. Then he sat down on a settee as she stood there wiping the sweat off her brow.

"Sit."

She sat down quickly.

"You must have heard that the lady has quit the play. And that you are going to replace her."

She felt as though a roof had crashed down on her. Me?

"Will you do it?"

What could she say?

"I am asking you, not the walls. Yes or no?"

"Yes," she said, feeling like a small child sticking her neck out of a collapsing building.

"Good. I am fed up with stars. I can create my own, you for example ..."

She wanted no flattery. "What makes you think I can act?"

"As they say, Ask and ye shall get, Seek and ye shall find. Well, that is true. Ask properly, seek properly. Ask for what you deserve and look for the important things. You will get what you seek. You came to the rehearsal that day. Why? What were you looking for?"

"I ..."

"No. There is no apparent reason. You were brought there by Destiny. I don't believe in it, like a fatalist does! But there's always a cause. Whenever you see effect, there is a cause underneath! Sometimes the cause is known, for example our actions. But when the ever present cause is not identifiable, I call it Destiny."

"But how do you know that I can manage it?"

"I don't. But I'll do my best. What are *you* willing to stake?"

She was totally confused. Where was this leading to? She felt faint. Aaba is a great director but his reputation with women ... Then she suddenly remembered the last night. The Monologue. Those empty noons. Leaving her father's house. It all seemed, purposeless, her life ... without any direction, lonely, wounded ...

"Everything ..." she heard herself say.

"Everything?"

"Yes, everything"

"And everyone?"

Sanjeev? Sanjeev ... Sanjeev. Where is he for me?

"Yes," she said as though intoxicated.

"Including your self-image?"

Self-image? What is my self-image? Sanjeev's wife? Nana's daughter? Bali? A trifle?

"Yes."

"Good! Let's celebrate. We will have a drink."

"I don't drink."

"No, say Didn't. Don't turn back. You were ready to sacrifice everything, that includes habits too!"

"I ..."

"Just have it. That's all."

He went to the sideboard. From the small bar he selected a bottle and, arranging the glasses he said,"We should not be a slave to habit. Drinking is bad but so is rigid abstemiousness." He placed a glass in front of her. "Come on ... have it! One peg is not going to kill you ..."

She was already feeling dizzy. She picked up the glass and took a sip.

"Good. It's okay if you don't drink the rest. Its okay too if you do." For the first time Aaba laughed. "Now stand in front of me."

She was scared.

"Here, here ... closer ..."

"Listen, I am only asking you to stand in front of me, not sleep with me. Of course according to our arrangement you should even do that. But for now all I want is that you stand in front of me."

So she stood there, her eyes turned to the window. A little scared. And he inspected her, from head to toe, intently.

The minutes stretched like hours.

"You can sit down now."

She sat down immediately.

"This was your first lesson. You are to be an actor. An actor must not mind anyone staring at her, okay? Sawant told me that you have acted in a play. The other day when I saw you, I said to myself, this one has some pain inside her. It's there, isn't it?"

She nodded her head vigorously. Yes, Yes, she wanted to scream. Liberate me. Free me from myself.

"Your life can be beautiful. But there should be a purpose. An aim, which concerns no one but yourself. That's the tragedy with you women. You bind yourself to other lives. Yes! Bind yourself. It's false to say that you get bound. You do it to yourselves. Then you get knocked around helplessly. Like those little children in the Gulf countries who are tied to the legs of racing camels to make the camels run faster. That's what happens to you. And it is the same with apparently successful ladies. Now that girl, that whore Sushma, her husband left her, that was all, and she just went to pieces. If your husband is going around with another women why should you feel so humiliated? It is beyond me. But now that stupid bitch is after every male. She wants especially to sleep with married men, to wrap them around her fingers so she can drop them. But let that be. That's her choice. I have something to tell you. Do you think you will be able to take it?"

She was startled. Now what? But she nodded.

"She even blackmailed Sanjeev, poor guy. I will act in your plays, sleep with me. That idiot nearly got trapped. But he refused and she left the play. This is not a guess. Yesterday he came and sat here. Drank plenty. And I asked him point blank ... After all, I've also been through the ordeal once! And he told me all."

In a flash, Sujata understood last night's episode. His incoherent raving, his frustration. But he had not made the sacrifice without regret. He had done so reluctantly, agonizing over the conflict. And he had avenged himself by insulting her. If loyalty was so important to him, why was he so aggrieved? He had the guts to insult me, only because my life has no purpose. I live through him. For him.

She found Aaba smiling at her. She looked at him with gratitude.

He said, "Your life will work, if it has a purpose ...

"Let me tell you a Birbal story. There was once a moneylender. He had seventeen camels. On his death bed he distributed them among his three sons. One third for the first son, of the remaining, half for the second son and the remaining five for the third. The children were confused. How should they distribute these seventeen camels without cutting one in half? They went to Birbal. Birbal came, bringing along his camel. The children said, No! We don't want your camel. Distribute these seventeen camels. Birbal said, Just wait for three minutes. He made his camel stand with the seventeen camels in a row. Now there were eighteen camels. One third to the first son. He got six. Twelve remained. Half to the second. The second got six camels. And five to the third son. Distribution done, Birbal walked away with the eighteenth camel.

"So what's the moral of the story? The purpose one gives to oneself is like the eighteenth camel. If it exists, life's puzzle can be solved. Understand? In other words, Ms Sujata Sane, please get the eighteenth camel in your life."

She smiled. After many days, a carefree smile.

"But remember, everything comes with a price tag. You have to pay the price. Maybe it is giving up old habits, dealing with defeat, with being a laughing stock, with loneliness. Once you choose the eighteenth camel there is no turning back. Now on to business ... When should we read the play?"

"The play?"

"I have to see how much work I must do on you."

"I know one monologue in it ..." And then she had enacted the monologue – as she had understood it – completely oblivious of Aaba's presence. When she finally emerged, she found Aaba mime-clapping his hands.

"Good, I like it. But remember this is just one part. Sometimes, the parts that seem the hardest are the easiest to do. And the apparently easy ones turn out tough. It's hard work. Are you ready?"

"Yes." She was getting used to saying Yes to Aaba.

"Are you ready for failure, for flops?"

"Yes."

"And hits."

"Yes."

Then he suddenly went near her and touched her hair. He said, "I want to kiss you ..."

His notorious reputation, Sanjeev, the Bali trap, those empty days spent alone with the tomcat ... everything swam before her eyes. And for a moment she couldn't decide. Right, wrong, yes, no, an abyss of alternatives loomed before her. "Kiss me ..." she said and waited with eyes closed, as if standing under a hanging sword.

But nothing happened. Aaba removed his hands from her shoulders and pressed them to her ears. He wiped the sweat from her brow and stared at her. "This innocence, this confusion, promise me you'll never lose it," he said as he walked away.

She had thought he would ask, Are you offering yourself as charity or as a price? Is this pity you feel or are you burning your bridges! But he only sat there facing the wall. He had put on his headphones and his fingers were keeping beat.

Sujata was overcome with sadness. She went up to him, kneeled and, removing his headphones, put them on. There was the hiss of a blank tape. She looked at Aaba, aghast and stood up removing the headphones hastily. Without thinking, she drew Aaba's head to her bosom and stroked and caressed it. After a while she held him away and, dabbing his wet cheeks with her pallav, said, "We'll meet at the rehearsal tomorrow."

"I only hope Sanjeev doesn't mind," said Aaba worriedly.

"No, No, he won't come between us," she assured him. He won't stand in the way. Never does. Nor does he walk with me. He does things only for himself. But now I have the eighteenth camel!

Before leaving she looked at Aaba and said, "A million thanks."

"What for?" Aaba said without turning his eyes from the wall.

"For the eighteenth camel."

Aaba only nodded his head, and the burden of emptiness, which he had appeared to cast aside a while ago, descended on him again. He set aside the headphones, smiling to himself.

He got up and watched from the balcony as Sujata left.

The rest is history. The play was a super hit ... and a star was born. After the first performance, Aaba had come inside and given Sujata a packet. It was a clock. With a cuckoo pecking grains, chirping the hour. On it was written: "To Sujata, for all times, Aaba."

She didn't even realize when Abhay entered her room asking, "Sujata, bored? Come let's do the lines. I have a new idea for the scene."

Sujata turned around.

Abhay? What is he doing here? Damned tomcat.

At just that moment, Sanjeev knocked at the door. "Bali ..." and looking at Abhay shyly said,"I mean, Sujata, will you come outside? Malkani is here ..."

Malkani was Sanjeev's new producer. He insisted that Sujata work for them. He'd rung yesterday.

"Mmm," Sujata mused. She had hardly read the play. In case she liked the role ... Sujata looked at Sanjeev. By calling her "Bali"

Sanjeev had discreetly told Abhay that she and he shared a special relationship, and the thought brought a smile to her lips. Sanjeev was not suddenly insecure, was he?

Abhay followed them out of the room. Sharvari was leaving and he said, "Oh, so you're leaving? Lalya will drop you. I think, I'll stay on for a while. There are a few things ..."

And he followed behind Sujata and Sanjeev to where the Malkanis were. Sanjeev said, "Mr and Mrs Malkani," and resting his hand familiarly on Sujata's shoulder said, "And this is ..."

"Come on yaar, who doesn't know her? The one and only SUJATA SANE," said Mr Malkani cutting him short. "Sujata, this is my wife."

"Surely she has a name?" asked Sujata, looking at Aaba but he was looking out of the window, keeping tap to some inside music.

"Oh yes, of course ... she has ... Vasanti, Vasanti is an ardent fan of yours ..."

Sujata gave her a broad smile. Then suddenly, embarrassingly, tears welled in her eyes and she quickly averted them, saying, "Abhay, you can leave with Sharvari now. We will discuss other things at the rehearsals tomorrow." And then, turning to Sushma, she said, "Care for a game of cards?"

Sushma was trying to get Malkani to notice her and now she left, saying "Hi, Harish!" giving him a peck on the cheek. And at the card table, she chattered on as she shuffled the cards. "Unlucky in cards, lucky in love, yes Aaba? Sujata, see, I'll win all the games."

"Who knows?" Sujata smiled silently as she pulled out the trump.

The party was over. All that begins ends anyway ... Everyone dispersed, leaving Sujata tired and relieved. She was exhausted. Like if she was in a make-up room after a performance and the make-up is being cleansed off.

In the morning, she had thought, No play today, no rehearsal, no script reading, how will the day pass? But it had and now she thought, How can I say there was no play? Didn't I rehearse for the evening show this morning when we visited Aai and Nana?

She had a long bath, like she always did on returning from an evening on stage, and entered the bedroom.

Sanjeev was at the window. She went and stood beside him. He was startled and looked at her suspiciously.

"What are you looking at?" she asked.

"At the road. This road turns and that's where Aaba lives."

"So? We've been there hundreds of times."

"Yes! But today, I'm thinking of a particular visit."

"What visit?"

"Aaba had first asked you to act in my *The Story Of Two Sisters*. You went alone leaving a note for me."

"Yes."

"That evening you returned late."

"And you came back nearly the next day."

"You never asked me where I went."

"Well! By then, we had long ceased asking each other anything."

"Can you see that red blob of the signal? There is a tamarind tree ten feet away from it. I stood there that day, anxiously waiting for you. It was nearly night when you came out. You turned to look back. Aaba stood in his balcony. He waved at you. And you got into a rickshaw at the corner of the street and ..."

"And came home to our Malad house."

"I was watching you all the way from Aaba's house to the end of the street. Your walk was different. There was a spring in your step. You seemed happy with yourself, totally absorbed. Your steps were firm, confident. As I watched, my heart missed a beat. I don't know why, but I suddenly felt ... "

"Why didn't you call out? We could have gone home together."

"... I suddenly felt you were not mine. I had lost my Bali. She had gone far away. I don't know why I felt this. Maybe Aaba's reputation with women ... Maybe because Aaba had come to the balcony to see you off and I know he never does that ... Certain things can't be proved by logic. Maybe the premise is wrong, but the conclusion is right! It is always right! One hopes against hope.

But something happened that evening. The whole night I wandered aimlessly, brooding over what it might be."

"Do you want to know what really happened?"

"No," he shrieked. He stepped back, still looking at her, like the crow on the windowsill that morning. Not shifting his focus. "I am scared of what you will tell me. Don't shatter my illusions, Bali."

"You are a bit drunk today, Sanjeev. Come let's sleep. Nothing happened there except for Aaba telling me a Birbal story."

He knew she was lying to him. But he was immensely grateful to her for her lies. Before she could say anything further he came closer to her and holding her face in his hands savagely pressed his lips on hers. Then he released her and lay back on the bed.

"Bali, my Bali, thanks for the lie," he said, his eyes fixed on the ceiling. "I need your wonderful lie. Don't leave me, Bali. Don't leave me."

He was stammering now, his body rocking, silent tears streaming down from the corners of his eyes. She turned his head towards her and, straightening his arm, lay her head on it, her perfume mixing with the smell of his sweat. His body smelt so familiar. She was aroused. Those nipples on his chest, like rosebuds, she moved her fingers over them. She felt him responding. She wetted those flowers with her tongue.

These were old known territories. Now both were treading familiar paths easily. The game had ended on equal terms.

It was much later that Sujata opened her eyes and saw Sanjeev's arm lie lightly around her waist. She got up, gently pushing his arm away. The light was on. She switched it off and caught sight of Sanjeev's face in the thin shaft of garden light that entered the room. He was sleeping like a baby, with his mouth open.

Her fingers touched the strands of hair that lay across his forehead. She pushed them back and looked at his broad forehead. He seemed to smile in his sleep. For a moment she longed to feel as she had that evening twelve years ago when she had sat at his doorstep waiting for him and ...

Chirr, chirr, the cuckoo in the clock chirped. It was three am.

She took her hand away from Sanjeev's hair and went to stand at the window. Outside, the gulmohar rustled in the wind. Beyond it lay the road, nearly deserted, like a lifeless strip bathed in pale light. The amber light of the signal flashed on and off. As you turn at the end of the road, you ...

"When will the curtain fall, Aaba?" Sujata asked. "When?" Wearily, she closed the window and went to sit once again on the bed.

The gulmohar rustled, and did a strange shadow dance on the window pane.

JEELANI BANO

CIGARETTE IN AN ASHTRAY

TRANSLATED BY AATEKA KHAN AND THE EDITORS
NOMINATED BY SADIQUE

First published in Urdu as "Ashtray Mein Sulagta Hua Cigarette" in *Tanazur*, July 1998, Hyderabad

Think of him as your God on earth."

Really, it was these words of Aapi's that began all the trouble. Naved became something otherworldly, a fantastic illusion, for Shama, as distant as the prophets and the stars. As if the small knotted thread that secured him to the ground had slipped and he'd slowly escaped into the skies, transforming himself into some huge power that scattered its brilliance in all directions. Aapi's golden principles, her efficacious home remedies, her grim warnings, had left Shama totally confused, vulnerable like a lamp to gusts of wind, flaring, flickering, glowing, snuffing out, with each suggestion.

On her wedding night she had drawn herself thousands of lines and checks, carefully measuring the gains and losses of every move, eager not to transgress the limits Aapi had cautioned her about, when to walk, when to stand still. The penalty for turning around to take one look, she had been warned, was to be turned to stone.

But nothing had happened the way Aapi had said it would. None of the beautiful fantasies and dreams, no romantic songs, nothing remotely like the innocent schoolgirlish whisperings of her friends that she had lived on and dreamed about these past seventeen years. The first thing he did when he came up to her was to light a cigarette. The cigarette-end flickered like the embers of a fire blown on from afar to stoke it. He drew in the smoke and held it, savouring its taste, the lit cigarette held lightly between his fingers, his eyes on the now flaring, now subsiding spark. She thought he was chimerical ... godlike ... like the paigambers.

He lay down next to her but when their hands touched there was nothing, no spark, no glow. She felt confused and tired. The buoyancy in her heart stilled. "*When your man laughs, light up or he will suspect you,*" her sister had said. The pitch dark of the night grew denser and she was almost swept away by a wave of fear – "When he laughed, why didn't I ..." All through the night she quaked with fear and her eyes burned – Oh to face the wrath and fury of the gods and their chastisement! And to think that she had once imagined being welcomed in through the gates of heaven.

Naved's fleshy hands groped around on the bed, sometimes

touching the pillow, sometimes her. Maybe he was searching for his first wife. Shama submitted to the restless impatience of his touch and tried to remember what it was Aapi had said she was supposed to feel now – happy or sad?

"This house is full of her belongings," said Naved alluding to his first wife. "It's just short of one thing ... a Maruti car. Her father was a great miser, you see." Naved saw himself at the wheel of a shiny new Maruti. And Shama, looking scared and subdued, her lips parting in fear, thought, If only she had not died, if only she had not died ...

"All his worries should now become yours," Aapi had said.

All his worries, last wishes, shattered hopes, are mine. He's my sustainer ... my Khuda ... If Khanam was unable to get him a car, then it is now my responsibility to get him one. It is my duty to fulfill all his unrealized desires.

Mornings, she looked around the house expecting to feel her saukan's presence everywhere. Instead she found ashtrays. There was ash on the bed, on the pillows, on the flowers, on the books ...

How many cigarettes turn to ash here, she would think while cleaning up the house.

"Don't object to anything he says. Don't make him rage."

Aapi had been married for five years. So she claimed to be an expert on men – how to take them apart and reassemble them with all the nuts and bolts in place. She wanted to bestow the extract of her experience on her younger sister. She felt that her sister was too naive and too emotional. "She is so trusting, Amma ... she is too young," Aapi had worried, looking at her with eyes full of such compassion that Shama immediately squared her shoulders and tried to look more assertive. What did she know of how lofty she felt from within? She was above them all, protected in the golden mesh of her dreams. She was a colourful anaar, waiting for marriage-the-sparkler to ignite all that lay suppressed within her, waiting to shoot up, gloriously, brilliantly, in one effulgent burst of light.

"Remember one thing, Shama ... never let him take your love for granted, otherwise he will turn away and doze off," Aapi had said, but here her husband slept soundly without even caring to extract any vows of love. How strange this man was, a unique prototype, a deviant who even discredited Aapi's theories.

"Our dulha bhai, scientist that he is, is obstinate, extremely suspicious, cynical by nature. And yes, remember Shammo, a man never does anything wrong. But you make one mistake and ..."

"Uffo Aapi ..." she had said holding her head in her hands. "Am I alone supposed to do his bidding? After all he will also do something, won't he?"

"Heh ... he ... he ..." Aapi began to laugh, and as she laughed tears welled in her eyes.

"Yes, and why not?" Shama asked indignantly. "Some dear wordly-wise Aapajan of his own must be sharing her insights with him right this minute. No doubt teaching him the art of ripping apart and mending the different aspects of a women's nature."

"You are totally mad ..." Aapi was getting really worried now. She thought, arre, foolish girl, are we ever concerned about the goat we sacrifice to atone for our sins? Though Aapi did not share this thought with her, the way she avoided looking at her and the bitterness lurking on her trembling lips made Shama uneasy.

"You are so naive, Shammo." Aapi's tone changed as she tried a different tack. "He's an unfortunate man, he has been heartbroken. The first wife burned to death. Such men are very sensitive. That's why he flares up every now and then."

When Shama was still unmarried, she had had an identity of her own. She had had her dreams. She had had her Khuda, her god. But now she was like a lump of sugar dissolved in water. She had neither a mind of her own, nor an existence. She was in accord with everything he said. She thought and did everything for him. After her marriage she had acquired a sixth sense. She could intuit Naved's thoughts. It was as if his thoughts declared themselves to her, commanding her to move, stop, laugh.

"Know ... When to ... when not to ..." Aapi used to say.

Aapi ... Aapi ... exasperated she would rip herself apart and then sit down with a needle and thread to alter herself to the new requirements. When he lay next to her, she would be at a loss. Now what do I do? There always seemed to be a lit cigarette in his hand slowly smouldering to ash. Naved would glance at it, but only to see how much was left to burn.

One day, weary of this game, Shama hid the cigarettes. Naved turned desperate. He searched the whole house. Shama, seeing him so distraught, laughed as she saw him run towards the door. "Where are you off to?"

"To get more ..."

Shama began to shiver and sank down on the sofa.

"You don't know how to play games, Shama."

And she nodded in defeat.

When Naved came home that evening, he was in a great mood. Her sixth sense spotted this. Today he is blooming like a lotus. He must have got some news about his promotion. His face looked different.

"When did you start smoking these?" Shama asked, picking up a cigarette pack lying on the table. It was of a different brand.

Naved was startled. As if he had been caught red-handed. He began to stammer. He snatched the pack from Shama's hands and fingering it lovingly, said, "Rano got it from America. She is an old friend. I'll smoke these when I want a change sometimes."

Shama looked uneasy.

The cigarette between his fingers turned to ash. "Rano has also got you a yellow saree. She likes the colour yellow a lot. She will bring it home tomorrow."

And suddenly Shama noticed that everything was yellow hued. The house was aglow with the luminous brightness of yellow flowers. The entire house was yellow.

This is a good thing. Now I will also wear a saree of his choice, for Aapi says when he is happy, you also should brighten up. But the smoke from the cigarette went into her eyes and undid the spell, and she rubbed her stinging eyes with the heel of her hand.

If you stand too far the smoke gets to you and if you stand too close the fire consumes you, sets you ablaze.

No one knew what happened to her that day. She ignited on her own and, once aflame, continued slowly to smoulder ... One night, haltingly, he began to tell Shama the circumstances of his first wife's death. She had been very happy that day and had been busy in the kitchen rustling up all kinds of things when ...

The cigarette in Naved's hands had begun to quiver as he spoke. As if, before telling Shama all this, he had run around aimlessly, for miles. Shama sat silently, her head lowered, watching the burning cigarette in Naved's hands. Would it ever happen that the cigarette burns itself out and Naved does not remember to light another? Naved was so engrossed in his talk that he forgot to bring the cigarette to his lips and it was slowly turning to ash. Why doesn't Naved ever hold it to his lips? These cigarette smokers are so careless, they light a cigarette and then forget all about it.

"Hmm ... so what?" Naved asked when Shama pointed this out to him. His face was creased as if he was lost in some unpleasant memory. He had forgotten her very existence. Then the dying cigarette stung him and he started, threw it into the ashtray without putting it out, and immediately started groping for another. Finally his eyes rested on Shama who sat dejected, feeling herself turn to ash with the smoke of the cigarette.

"Come on, forget it ... Why are you depressed?" he said pulling her towards him with his free hand.

"Laugh ... laugh, my dear," says Aapi ...

In the evening he came home with Rani. Enveloped in a bright yellow haze, a cigarette lay smouldering in an ashtray in the dressing room. "Oh that! ... I think I forgot to stub it out," Naved said, sheepishly.

NA D'SOUZA

THE BOAT

TRANSLATED BY BAGESHREE S
NOMINATED BY RAMACHANDRA SHARMA

First published in Kannada as "Doni" in *Karmaveera*,
October 1998, Bangalore

He continued sharpening each tooth of the saw and, though he was not interested, the conversation between his parents kept falling on his ears. Manavachari was telling his wife about the new job. Father and son had been working at Hegde's house and were now working in Mohammed Byari's house. Next, they might work in Munavel Fernandes' house. And then? There was no escape from the axe, the carpenter's plane, and the measuring tape, the adz, the chisel and the saw. Or from the sameness of what they did, thought Narayanachari. They perpetually made door frames, cut wooden boards for the ceiling, polished them, and then on the day of the housewarming ceremony, the owner gave them a new dhoti each, coconuts, betel nuts and betel leaves on a platter and joined his palms in thanks. Manavachari and Narayana returned home. How many times had they done this over the years? But still, Appayya must be feeling happy that a new assignment had come their way even before the present one was done.

"Whose work?" Amma was calling out from where she was washing vessels under the coconut tree.

"Work on a boat. At Thimma Sahukara's house in Honnavara," Appayya replied as loudly, as he poured water on his feet from the pot under the tree, and scrubbed them clean. He gargled noisily, spat the water towards the base of the coconut tree, and wiped his face with the towel on his shoulder.

"Boat?" Narayana asked.

"Yes, Sahukara wants a boat by Nugulu Hunnime. We will have to stay there for two or three months. Sahukara says, if our work is good, he will give us as much money as we ask for."

Narayana listened with growing interest. It was sure to be a new experience and, after such mundane jobs such as fixing hinges on doors and filling crevices in the wood with wax, exciting. Appayya had said "we" and that made him happy because it meant he would get to go along.

He got back to sharpening his saw with redoubled vigour.

"How hot it is! It would be good if it rains," his father grumbled, sitting on the jagli, fanning himself with the towel on his shoulder, as he continued to talk about the new job. Narayana set aside his saw, sprinkled some white stone power on a long wooden plank and started sharpening his chisel on it.

Thimma Sahukara's house was the biggest in Honnavara's fishing colony. He was an experienced fishmonger. He had three boats, a big rampane net and about seven or eight fishermen working under him. He also had extra nets at home which he would rent to other fishermen in return for a certain quantity of fish. Thimma Sahukara's son owned a tempo in which he took the fresh fish all the way up to Sagara town.

Outside Thimma Sahukara's house was a mango tree. Thimma Sahukara stood often, looking at it. Large and ancient – god knows when the sea had washed the seed ashore – it had been a sapling when he was a little boy. It was now so huge that two or three people together could not stretch their arms across its trunk. Thimma Sahukara was thinking of extending the house, and it was this tree that came in the way of his plans. Also, whenever he looked at the tree he couldn't but think of the excellent boat it could make – not that he didn't have enough boats, yet ... To make a new boat, one would have to scour the land for a good mango or dhoopa tree or buy planks of wood. But here was a tree right at his doorstep! A new boat, an extended house and both at next to no cost. What if ... Thimma Sahukara was delighted with himself.

"What do you say, bhava?" he asked his brother-in-law, Parusha. "How about getting a boat made from this tree?"

Parusha sized the tree with his eyes. "Yes, we should get a boat plus enough wooden planks to build an extension to the house."

So Thimma Sahukara had the tree felled. He put aside the thick

---

Many names in the story indicate the caste and occupation of the person. The suffix Achari, attached to the names of Manava and sometimes Narayana indicates that they are professional carpenters. Bhatta indicates that the person is a Brahmin priest. **Sahukara**: Rich man. It also becomes a term of respect, when he is referred to as 'sahukarre' in the course of a conversation. Achari also becomes "Acharre," "re" being an honorific. **Rampane** and **Goru** are two different kinds of nets. Rampane is a bigger net, handled by more than one fisherman. A Goru net can be handled by one person.

base of the tree, and used the rest to build his house. Now he had to make the boat before the wood dried up, and Thimma Sahukara needed a good carpenter. That was when someone mentioned Manavachari of Hosadi village. "He'll be the right person. When he starts a job he finishes it. He does not just pocket the advance and then disappear like the others."

The very next day Thimma Sahukara was at Honnavara port. He caught hold of Manavachari on his way to work and said, "You have to do this for me ... Stay in my place, take four months, if it is not possible in three. I will fill your palms with money."

"I have a job at Mohammed Byari's house, Sahukarre. We'll see once that's over."

"All right, Acharre," said Thimma Sahukara, "As long as I can have the boat by Nugulu Hunnime."

"I ... I'll come and see you tomorrow and then maybe ..."

"Yes come and take a look. The tree is just right for a boat, there isn't a single knot or crack in it!"

"To travel all the way from my village everyday will be difficult, Sahukarre. It's not just me, you see there will be three or four people."

"Didn't I just say I will make arrangements for your stay and your food? If you don't want to eat in our house, you can do your own cooking. I will give you rice, salt and tamarind. You'll have no problems. I want only you to build my boat."

Sahukara urged Manavachari to go with him to the Nithyananda cafe nearby for avalakki and coffee, which Manavachari politely declined. But Thimma Sahukara was not ready to let go. He kept persuading him till Manavachari more or less agreed.

Father and son disembarked from the tempo at the Durga Devi temple in the fishing colony and walked along the bank of Bandehalla tank where the fishermen's children were playing in the water. They pointed out Thimma Sahukara's house. It was a big, freshly painted house with five or six nets lying in front of it. Piles of fish were being dried some distance away. There were a couple of dogs. And there was the tree, lying on its side.

"Come, come!" Thimma Sahukara called out in a welcoming voice as he stepped out of his house, wiping his hands on one of the ends of his short lungi.

Manavachari and Narayana stopped to examine the tree. The wood was straight, there were no knots, no worms. It was not charred by fire, nor did it have cracks. If one fourth of the log was lopped off, the rest could be scooped out to make a boat. The wood was mature but their implements were sharp and they were confident that they would be able to do the job without much difficulty.

Manavachari went into Thimma Sahukara's house. But Narayana stood at the door and gazed entranced at the distant sea. Of course he had seen the sea before but this one was breathtaking with its jaunty fishing boats, the little silver waves that lapped the shore. Women with baskets gathered around the anchored boats while others, their baskets already full, were walking away, their hips swaying under the weight of their headloads. Hungry crows flapped around, hoping to pick something out of their baskets.

"Come in," said Thimma Sahukara again and then went straight to the point. "What do you think of the wood?"

"It's fine wood. But it may be fifteen or twenty days before we can start here. I must finish Byari Sahukara's work first."

Thimma Sahukara got up, pleased. He quickly took two betel leaves and some betel nuts from the tray and, looking in the direction of the inner door, called out, "Appi?"

A young girl put her head out of the door. "Yes Appayya?"

"Bring me a one rupee coin."

The next minute the girl stepped in with a coin in her hand. Narayana watched her quietly. Taking the coin from her, Sahukara held out the betel nut, leaves and the coin, saying, "Acharre, do this work for me."

Achari cupped his hands and respectfully accepted the offering. He said, "Yes, I will."

Both of them sat then, discussing the details. Manavachari

wanted a boatshed built around the log. "We'll need a roof of coconut palm fronds and some fronds on the sides too. With little protection from the sun and the rain, we can live there too."

When finally Manavachari and Narayana left the fishing colony, the sun was right over their heads. Thimma Sahukara's daughter, Gangayi, was walking towards the sea with a mori fish in her hand. Narayana watched her, pretending to watch the sea.

Manavachari had brought three boys along with him from his village, Narayana being one of them. They broke a coconut at the Haigali Durga temple, smeared the sacred bhadara ash from the temple on the mango tree, and got down to work. Work progressed at a slow pace. First they had to chisel the log into the shape of an egg, mark it with limestone, chip off the outer edges and scoop out the inner portion. The boys made wooden strips for the inside of the boat, planks for laying across the boat, the rudder board and other small things from the remaining pieces of wood. Manvachari would oversee everything himself, smoking beedi after beedi, picking up the axe or chisel every now and then. He watched the boys hawk-eyed, told them how and how not to do things. Any task he took up was swiftly done.

The rough log of wood slowly began to look like a boat.

Narayana was in charge of the cooking. Gangayi was given the responsibility of giving him rice, pepper, tamarind, salt and anything else that he required each day. But for the fish, Narayana had to wait for the fishing boats, which went into the sea at sunrise, and returned one after the other by about ten in the morning – any boat with one big oar standing erect in the middle, a piece of cloth fluttering from it, signalled Fish! Even while riding the waves back home, the fishermen sorted out the catch, bunched them together and decided on the price. Some boatsmen reserved their fish for regular customers, but there were others who sold to all.

Narayana did not manage to buy any fish for the first two days. But soon things were made easy for him. A portion of fish from

Thimma Sahukara's boat was reserved for Gangayi and now, another was set aside for Narayana.

Narayana did not know what to say when Gangayi held out two bundles of fish the first time, saying, "Here, Appayya said ..." She even offered to grind the pepper for him. Narayana felt thankful.

Gangayi soon was cleaning the fish for him, too. He watched with open admiration as she scraped the skin, expertly slit open the fish's belly with her sickle, removed the innards, sliced each into two or three pieces, threw away the tail, and then held out the edible parts to Narayana. While he boiled the rice, she ground the pepper for him. Making the fish curry in another pot was not difficult after that. Narayana managed to get back to work early enough.

Two things enthralled Narayana – the sea and Gangayi. He watched the tide recede all day and grow more and more forceful as evening fell. He would stand on the shore in the morning and marvel at the handi fish gambolling in the water, the waves rushing to the shore, the water dogs and turtles venturing on to the sands, then quickly scuttling back to disappear into the waves, the moment they got wind of a human presence. Hundreds of boats stood along the coast, different kinds and makes – maragi, pathi, halage – heaped with fish of all hues and sizes.

Narayana was learning to recognize different kinds of nets and as many kinds of fish. He watched the boats skip over the turbulent waves as they touched shore, now pushed back by the waves, now oared forward by the determined men. He watched with envy as the fishermen stood in their boats, in the middle of the ocean, flinging their spreading nets, effortlessly pulling in the crowding fish. What adventure, he thought, how much variety this life had! Weren't the fishermen who played with the tumultuous, unpredictable ocean and gathered fish from it mightier than the ocean itself?

The sea filled his mind with the same vigour with which Gangayi suffused it. Gangayi in her adda saree and the tight blouse of the coastal people. Gangayi of the sturdy thighs, strong neck and swelling breasts. Gangayi with the walk that accentuated the curves of her waist. How her teeth sparkled in her brownish face, like lustrous waves in the light of the moon. Yes, she had the sharp rough speech of a fisherwoman, but how she softened and blushed when she saw Narayana! He longed so desperately to see her always, talk to her, day and night.

The log of mango was still being coaxed into the shape of a boat. One day, Narayana was waiting for the boats to return while Gangayi also waited a little way off, leaning on a gali tree. There was a time when she ran from home just as the boats neared the shore, but lately she had started arriving well ahead of time. Now, she stood watching two boats come in, dragging a rampane net in its wake. It was a huge catch and the fish could be seen tossing and jumping in it. Seagulls followed the net, swooping into the water every now and then.

"Gangayi ..." Narayana called out hesitantly.

"Hmm?"

"Have you ever gone out to sea?"

"Mm."

"To catch fish?"

"Chee! Ever heard of women catching fish? We sell them. Catching fish is a man's job. Women can't spread the net."

"Why did you go to sea then?"

"Just like that."

"I want to, too."

"Go then, I'll tell the boatsman," she said.

And then, Thimma Sahukara's boat came in and shouting "It's come!" Gangayi quickly hitched up her short saree, and walked into the water. Narayana followed her.

And so one day, Narayana set out to sea. He had got his father's permission and the Sahukara had also given his.

The boat pushed out before daybreak, carrying a scared Narayana who watched the land recede with fearful eyes. He was surrounded by nothing but water. Blue sky above, dark waters below.

"Are you scared or what?" the fishermen laughed. "There's nothing to be scared of. Isn't the ocean our god?" they reassured him. "Here, start rowing," they said, passing him an oar.

Narayana watched the jumping fish, the other boats that passed by, the nets as they went in and came out of the sea, wriggling with fish that the men picked and strung together. Slowly, a reverence for the depth, expanse and volume of the ocean grew within him. He played with the nets, watched the fish do their last jump-dance in the boat, and didn't even know when the boat headed back towards the shore.

"How was the sea?" Gangayi asked later as she cleaned the fish.

"Oh!" he said, unable to find any more words.

Time went by. Gangayi and Narayana were meeting more often, finding many things to talk about. Narayana made friends with the fishermen, went to sea regularly, lending a hand to row, to turn the rudder and even to man a sailboat, directing the sail against the wind. And he, who didn't even know how to walk deep into the waters, now swam like a fish, jumping into the sea with the others each evening.

He knew his life had changed. Never before had he felt so charged. Gone was the Narayana who would eat his morning gruel and then spend the day with chisel in hand, in someone's frontyard. The only things he could look forward to had been the cup of tea and avalakki in the corner teashack, the occasional walk down the market-street to hear the latest news about Bhatkal and Honnavara town. And now, how things had changed for him! Even cooking here was different. And then there was Gangayi, throwing covet glances at him as she came out on to the front yard to now dry the clothes, now the fish, appearing all of a sudden at the door of the boatshed to talk to him. The boatshed was just a little way from the sea, and he had to walk only a few steps to the east and stretch his neck to see the blue waves and the amazing activity it generated.

Thimma Sahukara was rarely at home. His fishermen would take his boats to sea on their own and then divide up the fish they brought back – giving him something per net or boat. Sahukara spent all his time at the port, while his son left early each day for Sagara, his tempo loaded with fish and ice, and returned late.

Thimma Sahukara's wife, Beliamma, was soft-spoken. She used to sell fish before her marriage, but now, managing the house was her work. Gangayi brought fish home, cleaned them, marinated the extra ones and dried them out, went to Mammu Kaka's shop at the other end of the colony to get the provisions, picking a quarrel with him now and then. This was Gangayi's work.

She would be at the shore when the boats arrived to find out how many fish had been caught, how many sold and how much money collected. The fisherwomen took the fish on credit and Gangayi kept the accounts. If anybody was late in bringing the money, she would frown and say, "Sharavathi, you owe me ten rupees. No fish for you tomorrow if you don't give it by evening." "Gangi, you must have got a good price for the sorlu fish yesterday. Why haven't you brought money?" "Kamali, no more fish for you ... You have too many dues!"

Because Gangayi was strict, money always came to the doorstep. She was the one who disbursed the wages to the fishermen. Gangayi had dropped out of school after the Fourth Class, but she had picked up things on her own. Thimma Sahukara was always calling her when there was something to read or write. "Appi, come here fast," was heard often in the house. Narayana admired Gangayi's sharpness. He would watch her calculate wages and briskly write down things, nodding his head in appreciation.

One evening when the sun had inched towards the edge of the sea, becoming a ball of burning coal before it plunged into the water, Gangayi peeped into the boatshed. There was no one there. Manavachari and his workers must have gone to Durga Keri, she thought. But where was Narayana?

Gangayi crossed the front yard, and walked towards the sea. It had risen the previous night, leaving a mark on the shore and now was rising again, the waves making determined efforts to outsmart each other. Gangayi searched for Narayana all over the shore. Far away, a ship was starting towards Mumbai. One or two boats were coming in. Closer, a small pathi boat was being tossed on the waves, visible now and again. She looked closely and noticed that the man in the boat was waving towards the shore, and inadvertently blurted out, "O, Haigali Devi! Isn't that him?"

Her heart leaped to her mouth. One needed courage and experience to go to sea in pathi, maragi and other such small boats. Why was he so reckless? Fortunately the pathi boat began to draw closer. And Narayana reached the shore, dragging the pathi with one hand. He dropped the boat and held out something to her.

"What is it?"

"Fish."

"Oh? Have you given up carpentry or what?"

"So what? That work is no fun."

"Whose boat is that?"

"Damu's. I took it with his permission. Now I can row a pathi, a maragi and everything else."

Gangayi glanced proudly at him in the gathering dusk. He was wearing just a pair of short pants. Water dripped from his broad chest.

"Don't joke with the sea, hanh," Gangayi warned.

"It's no joke. If Appa says Yes, I will drop my carpenter's job straight off and become a fisherman," he laughed, drying himself with the dhoti he had left behind on shore.

Gangayi stood there a little longer, talking to him. The lights of a vehicle fell on the shore and then moved towards their house.

"Looks like Annayya has come," said Gangayi hastily getting up.

Her brother, who usually left the tempo at the port, had come straight home. He was standing on the jagli of the house, waiting for her when she got back. "Gangayi," he yelled, as she crossed the threshold. "Whom were you chatting with out there?"

"Boat Narayana ... Why?"

"You ask me why? Who's he? Is he of our caste? Our sect? He is the kind that carries a chisel and an axe around, chipping wood. What do you have to say to him? This is the first and the last time you will talk to him. Do you understand?" His nostrils flared with anger. Gangayi did not want an argument with him. But he turned to his mother and said, "You and Appayya have spoilt her. Keep an eye on her at least now."

Gangayi was pained by her brother's behaviour. But she did not tell Narayana about this. She just became a little more circumspect. She did not want him to pounce on Narayana.

Clouds gathered in the empty sky. The white clouds turned dark and ominous, and bolts of lightning scissored through them. Thunder growled in the skies. The waves heaved as if the sea was intoxicated. Boats pulled into shore and were quickly turned upside down, the nets and oars were rushed into homes. The storm was approaching!

Thimma Sahukara covered the boatshed with lots of coconut fronds, and Manavachari went home to his village for fifteen days, to make arrangements there for the rainy season. By the time he returned, having stored enough rice and pulses back home to last the entire season, it had begun to rain in right earnest. The trees shook dishevelled heads. The government had put up red flags to warn fishermen. The rain lashed so heavily that visibility was down to four feet. Waves, tall as human beings, hit the land. Most fishermen were at home, but some still stood at the edge of the wind-whipped sea, trying to catch fish with goru nets. The women were dipping into their savings. Sun-dried fish were in great demand. And every night Narayana lay awake worrying, What if the boatshed was blown away.

The boat had slowly acquired shape. Only the surface remained to be smoothened and the wooden strips to be fitted. There were still many days to go before the planks would be placed across the flanks and the rudder fixed. The boat would then be seasoned with fish oil and the pungent sap of the matti tree.

The fishermen crowded around it, saying the boat was coming along well. Most importantly, Thimma Sahukara was happy. "Haa, the boat is looking good, Acharre. Nugulu Hunnime is almost here. We should be able to offer coconut and gold thread to the sea on that auspicious day and send this boat to sea with the other boats the day after, shouldn't we?"

Achari counted the full moon and new moon days and said, "Leave it to me."

All activities outside the boatshed had come to a standstill but inside, work moved as usual. Narayana sat in front of the warm hearth and placed dried bangdi fish between the glowing coals, and covered them with more coal and ash. When they smelt done he flipped them. The smell of burnt fish was everywhere. He quickly pulled the fish out of the hearth, covered them with a bronze plate and weighed it down with a piece of wood – to prevent the wretched cats from stealing it.

"Has the sea caught fire or what?" Gangayi asked, walking in.

"Fresh fish is not available, and dried fish sticks in the throat. What is a man to do?" he laughed.

Gangayi had washed her hair and now it spread enticingly over her shoulders. Her face, scrubbed with soapnut, glowed pink.

"Have you finished cooking, Gangayi?" Narayana asked chattily.

Gangayi was doing the cooking at home those days as her mother was down with an infection caused by a fishbone prick.

"Yes. I too had only dried mori fish to fry. Kariya has taken a goru net to the sea and hasn't come back yet." She paused before she asked hesitantly, "Is what Appayya said, true?"

"What?"

"That the work on the boat is nearly over?"

"Yes. It's as good as done. In another month, the boat will be bouncing out in the ocean and we'll be back home."

He laughed. But she didn't. She stood there looking sullen, her head bent.

"Gangayi, what's the matter?" he asked.

Gangayi merely bit her lower lip, her face darkening.

It didn't take Narayana long to understood why. Though he had joked about being home soon, he had felt a stab of pain when he said it. Was Gangayi upset about it too?

Gangayi lifted her face and he saw her eyes were awash with tears. "Anna has brought an alliance," she said slowly.

"An alliance?"

"Yes," she nodded and told him the details.

The boy was in Sagara. His name, Sankayya. He belonged to their community. His family had moved to Sagara a long time ago. He was an attender in a bank. A good boy with a good job. The boy was to come and see her soon. The wedding would be after the rainy season. Gangayi would settle down in Sagara. Thimma Sahukara and his wife had agreed. Their relatives had to be informed. A wedding at a sahukara's house has to be performed in style.

Gangayi told him all that she had heard at home. She blew her nose and wiped her tears.

Narayana felt as if he had been knocked down by a tidal wave. Gangayi was to go away to distant Sagara. The news shattered him. For some reason, he wished such a thing would never happen. He did not want Gangayi to ever leave him. And then it dawned on him that she too nurtured the same wish.

He thought Gangayi wanted to tell him something more. When she wiped her tears and regained her composure, Narayana nodded at her, encouraging her to go on.

Gangayi stayed on because there was one thing she absolutely had to let him know. "Anna is suspicious," she said, not knowing how else to begin.

"Suspicious? Why? Who's he suspicious of?"

"Of us."

Gangayi told him what had happened that evening, when her brother had brought the tempo home. Her brother had promptly told his father and a day or two later Thimma Sahukara had called his daughter.

"Is it true?" he had asked her directly. "That boy has come here to work. They will leave this camp in another month. Let them be where they ought to be," he had told her patiently. "This is a question of the family's prestige. One small hole is enough to sink a boat. I won't keep quiet if I hear any more of this!"

And ever since then, her parents had kept a stern eye on her. But she had been coming to the boatshed secretly.

"Have you been disobeying Sahukara's words to come to me, Gangayi?" Narayana asked now, pride and concern sliding against each other.

"Do I have a choice?" Gangayi asked stoutly.

As he listened to Gangayi, Narayana began to understand the reason behind Sahukara's changed attitude. Sahukara, who used to speak nicely to him earlier, had lately begun to give him dirty looks. "Acharre, work on the boat is over, isn't it? Why don't you send back one or two of these people?" he had said once or twice, looking pointedly at Narayana, but had been silenced when his father replied, "I can't send them away like that. These people work wherever I work." And Narayana had occasionally noticed Sahukara's servants lingering near him. These things had not seemed significant earlier but now they fell into place.

"So, it's come to this," he murmured.

"Yes."

"What will you do now, Gangayi?"

"I will go to Parusha Mama's house," she said. Parusha Mama was her mother's brother and very fond of Gangayi.

"If the nagging worsens here I will go away there."

"But where will *I* go? Your father and brother will not leave me alone," Narayana said, laughing even at that tense moment.

"You could come there too, I will tell mama everything!" she said, breaking into a smile, too.

"Let's do that," said Narayana happily. "Let's go away together to Murudeshwara. The new boat is ready anyway."

Gangayi's face grew instantly serious. She felt bashful. She stood there a minute longer, considering Narayana thoughtfully and then pushing aside the fronds at the back of the shed, she disappeared into the night. Narayana put out the fire and came out of the shed.

"Can we have our kanji now?" asked Manavachari, smiling at his grim-looking son.

The rain let up a little but soon the clouds gathered and it started raining all over again even before people could walk out to the frontyard and say, "Oh, it's cleared." Fishing in the sea had stopped but some people continued to fish in the river. But in the boatshed, work never flagged. They had finished making the thick crescent shaped wooden strips and Manavachari had bought some long brass nails to fix them with. The work of polishing the interior and exterior of the boat was to get over in a day or two.

Only Narayana's heart felt heavy, like the mire-laden waves of a sea in storm. Gangayi and he had really grown fond of each other without thought of what was to follow. Their friendship, which gave them a peculiar happiness, had deepened. Narayana always waited to catch a glimpse of Gangayi, and she always found some excuse to come to the boatshed. Not that they had ever spoken of their love or attraction for each other. They had not thought of their future together even after Gangayi's brother had kicked up a row. But now, after her brother talked of the Sagara alliance, Gangayi had begun to think seriously about Narayana ..

In two months, Narayana had come to love Gangayi as much as he loved the sea. That he would have to leave both in a month's time worried him. He knew that unless he intervened, Gangayi would be somebody else's. Narayana lay awake at nights, listening to the waves strike the shore, the waters seeping into the sand with a slow whoosh.

The people from Sagara came to Thimma Sahukara's house two days after the rain let up and the sun began to shine. Gangayi's brother brought them home himself. Gangayi went through the whole ritual of adorning herself in a silk saree and her mother's jewellery with abbalige flowers in her hair, and sitting demurely in front of the boy and his parents.

The boy approved of her. The boy's father said, "Girl, you are lucky. You won't have to sell or dry fish any more. My son can't stand fish. You'll live happily and respectably like an officer's wife."

Gangayi got up and went inside as he spoke.

They fixed the date of the wedding before they went back to Sagara. "You are a girl of good fortune," said Gangi, Sharavathi, Manji and Chinni of the fishing colony. "You are going to a town. Learn some niceties," they teased.

The boy and his father visited the boatshed while Narayana was working there. They walked around examining the boat, wondering if wooden boats were any good any more. "You get fibre boats these days," they said. "You don't even need oars. There are machines now."

Narayana looked at the boy as he walked away from the boatshed. He looked good in his trousers, shirt, dark glasses and shoes even as he struggled to walk on the sand.

That evening Narayana sat alone in the boatshed. The rest of the men had gone to Durga Keri. They maintained that unless they went there for a couple of swigs of arrack every evening, the ache in their bodies never eased. They had gone after a long time, since the continuous rain had made it impossible for them to stir out of the house. As always the roar of the sea filled the boatshed.

Narayana turned around when he heard the palm fronds move. He could see Gangayi in the faint light of the lamp. Narayana got up and walked towards her.

"When are you going to Sagara?"

"It's all a joke to you, isn't it?"

Narayana sat on the edge of the boat.

"Did you like the boy?"

"Who ever looked at him?"

"Gangayi, tell me the truth. Do you like this alliance?"

"Do you? Tell me," she responded.

"Shall I tell you the truth?"

"Tell me."

"I don't like it. You shouldn't become somebody else's wife."

He couldn't see her face but could sense how distraught she was from the way her voice shook. "Then tell me what I should do?"

"You ... You ..." Narayana walked four steps forward, pulled her to him for the first time and wrapped his strong arms around her. "You are meant to be mine," he whispered, cupping her face in his palms. Then he let his hands stroke every inch of her body as he kissed her, confirming in action what he had just uttered in words.

Hearing Thimma Sahukara in the distance, Gangayi pulled herself away and sneaked back into her house.

Narayana stood there, his fingers tightening around the prow of the boat.

As Nugulu Hunnime approached, the boats on the shore were readied and set upright again. Most of the boats got a coat of choguru polish, some had been smeared with fish oil. Minor repair works were carried out, new oars, sails and nets were brought out.

As promised, Manavachari had finished building the new boat. It had been brought to shore on rolling logs of wood. Some of Sahukara's fishermen even pushed the boat into the water and went some distance into the sea. Narayana went with them, turning with the boat when the boatsmen turned it, moving in tandem with the boat when they rowed harder, Gangayi stood on the shore gazing at Narayana in admiration.

The entire length of the shore had been decorated with plantain trees and mango leaf festoons. The people of the valaga band from Durga Keri were playing music, sitting under the gali tree. Chandra Bhatta of Balehalla village came with his pooje paraphernalia. People brought the special food they had made at home, in little boat-like vessels made of hard palm fronds.

Some five to six boats were to carry the offerings to the Sea King. One boat was readied for Chandra Bhatta too, since all the rituals could be carried out at sea only by the Brahmin priest. Some men tucked their dhotis high and waded through the waves to get into the boats. Sahukara went in Chandra Bhatta's boat.

Sahukara had arranged for a special pooje at the Haigali temple, too and Manavachari handed over the boat to its rightful owner. Thimma Sahukara had been paying Manavachari every week, even so, he presented each of his men with a new panche, a length of cloth for a shirt and five hundred rupees. He gave Manavachari a gold ring.

"Sahukarre, may this boat bring you good fortune," Manavachari said, as he handed the oar to him.

Narayana came back with prasada in hand. He walked up to Gangayi, who was leaning on the new boat, gave her the prasada, and said, "This boat goes into the waters tomorrow, remember?"

She nodded.

The next day, the shore was full of people even before daybreak. People pushing boats into the sea, loading nets and oars, competing with one another to get in first, eager to take on the waves again. There were those who had come to send off the fishermen – old men and women, their children, their dogs. Pandemonium reigned. Three of Thimma Sahukara's boats were swaying on the waves. But his new boat?

Thimma Sahukara walked the entire length of the shore, Krishna, Ranga and Irodi, who were to row the new boat, following him, their nets on their shoulders. They walked from one end of the shore to the other. They were still searching when Thimma Sahukara's wife came limping to the shore shouting, "The girl's

---

Nugulu Hunnime is a big festival for fishermen of Karnataka. Coming as it does at the end of the rainy season, on this day a variety of foods are prepared at home and offered to the sea. Earlier, there was a custom of tying golden threads to a coconut and offering this to the Sea King. This practice is rare now. Instead, they offer the holy yajnopavitha thread to the sea. Work commences the next day.

not at home ..." Manavachari, who arrived just then, changed his mind even as he opened his mouth to say that Narayana was missing too.

The eastern sky grew red. Hundreds of boats moved eastwards. But one boat had entered the night sea when the world was asleep.

SARITA PADKI

THE WEB

TRANSLATED BY MUKTA RAJADHYAKSHA
NOMINATED BY USHA TAMBE

First published in Marathi as "Jaala" in *Miloon Saryajani*,
October 1998, Pune

Bandu-Gundu's school bus arrived and took them away. Leena, too, had left. She should be reaching her office by now. The stress of waking early in the morning, getting the children ready, making lunch, and the thought of having to drive forty kilometres after that, was always evident in her face.

I cleared the cups and dishes and then poured some coffee into a mug, one last cup before leaving for work, when suddenly the telephone rang. I wondered who it could be so early in the morning and said an abrupt "Hello."

"Hello?" came the reply after a long pause, and then the voice shook and broke.

It was Mavshi. I was so overcome that I didn't even realize when my hand started trembling.

"Laloo, Tai's condition is very critical. Your aai, your mhatari ... we've taken her to the hospital. She's in the ICU. The doctors aren't telling us much!"

"Mavshi, what has happened to her?" I asked, trying to keep my voice as calm as possible.

"She went to the door to buy vegetables and collapsed right there. The neighbours informed me. I rushed immediately and ..." Now Mavshi broke down, crying loudly.

"Mavshi, be calm, Mavshi ... "

"Come at once, Laloo. Or you'll not see her again." Mavshi spoke like one exhausted and then hung up.

I stood with the receiver in my hand. Now my whole body trembled. "Aai, you can't do this to me. You can't die on me ..." Tears welled in my eyes and spilled over.

To tell the truth, those of us who migrate to the USA snap all our ties with India before we come here. Or, at least, that is what we are constantly trying to do. Even on the flight out to America, Leena had said, "Look, now don't keep harping on about India-kindia, Aai-Aai, Gaja-Shrikya. All that is behind us. That part of us has broken off like a piece of groundnut chikki and, like a chikoo seed, we have slid out of there as cleanly as from the fruit. There's no need to attach any pulp to ourselves. It is only when we realize this that we can be happy in America. Now all we can afford to do is make a weekly or fortnightly call, pay a fifteen or twenty day visit every two or three years, and send them a cheque for festivals – an amount that'll probably be small for us but large for them, no?"

"Yes, yes," I had said, squeezing her arm and pulling her towards me. The thought that all her shackles were well and truly off, that we were now alone and belonged only to each other, enabled her to respond openly, snuggling into my arms with a soft sigh of satisfaction.

Now, suddenly realizing that I was going to be late for work, I raised the mug of coffee to my lips. I cleared everything rapidly, locked the house, drove at top speed and just about made it to my table from sheer habit.

The first two hours at work were gruelling. Discussions with the boss, answering the doubts and queries of clients, attending to sudden jobs that cropped up – I had no idea how time flew. And then Dhingra came by and sat down on the chair opposite mine. He's our client. A friend of the boss, and by virtue of being an Indian, a friend of mine too. Dhingra lowered his lanky frame into the chair and ran his eyes over my face. "Why are you looking like this, bhai," he asked, "What, bad news?"

I broke down, more from the concern in his voice than his question, and started sobbing. After a while I told him, "Dhingra, my mother's ill, in India. She's in the ICU."

"Don't be anxious, yaar. Your mother will get well. She'll be all right. But you should go there at once. Do you want me to talk to your boss?"

"No, no, don't. I haven't decided anything yet."

"What is there to decide? You have to go and that too immediately. If there's any problem, let me know," Dhingra said and left, leaving me wondering if he had heard me mutter, "Thanks."

I was trying desperately to concentrate on my work when the telephone rang.

"Hey Lalya, what are you crying in the office for?" Pakya, of course. Dhingra must have called him.

"Aai. She's in a critical state," I told him.

"So are you supposed to cry or leave straight away? And listen, nothing's going to happen to your mother. Absolutely nothing! She probably just wants to see you. You go there and come back. We'll look after Leena and Bandu-Gundu. But go fast."

As he hung up, the telephone rang again. I put my ear to the receiver. I was beginning to dread the telephone.

"So, Laloo Prasad Yadav, seems your mother's ill?" This was Madhya.

"Yes, Madhya. She's in the ICU. I'm ..."

"Why worry, yaar? These people don't die that quickly. Just look at my father. He's been bedridden for eight years now. He's stuck there and has my mother stuck with him too. I really wanted to bring her here. She's never had any rest at all. But you don't worry, Lalya. Nothing will happen to your mother. She'll survive. You'll see," he said and put the phone down.

My desire to bring Aai to America surfaced once more. But was it too late now? Would I ever be able to bring her? Would I?

The telephone trilled again.

"Laloo, Leena here," said a stern voice. "Laloo, news of home reaches me through outsiders. Is this how things stand between you and me now?"

"No, Leena. When the call came, you had already left for work. And I've been wondering what to do."

"About what? Going there?"

"I have to go Leena. Mavshi sounded really scared on the phone. But then what about things here? You, Bandu-Gundu ... Leaving you all alone here ... in this country ..."

"Laloo, I told you on our very first day here that we had come for good. We can't afford to involve ourselves with India and the people there. Have I been to my mother's in the last three years?"

"But one does *get* involved, Leena, I *am* involved, at least I am right now. This time I feel I should go."

"It's your decision. There's no harm in going if it's going to be of some use. We'll manage somehow. But call them up once before you leave. See if a visit is really warranted. Okay, bye. We'll talk when you get home."

So I left. And reached Bombay. I stopped the rickshaw at the hospital gate, picked up my luggage and was soon standing in front of the receptionist: "I'm Deshpande. My mother's here."

"Yes," he replied. His "Yes" reassured me in a deep, unknown way. I left my luggage with him and, after fulfilling all the nurse's conditions, found myself in Aai's room. I stood at the door. Aai's frail body lay on the cot with all sorts of tubes attached to it. She was like a tiny fly caught in a spider's web. And she wasn't even struggling. But she was alive and that was enough.

Did she look at me? Recognize me? Was there a smile on her lips? I don't know. But I felt light, as if a huge burden had been taken off my mind. I threw myself on the small bed next to Aai's, wrapped Mavshi's saree around me and drowned myself in the sleep that I had been craving for.

I woke up from a sleep as deep as the ocean to the soft caress of fingers stroking my forehead and hair. With eyes still closed I reached out and held the hand in mine and felt as if my heart would burst with joy. Having this hand for company meant that I had the strength to face any danger.

Aai was smiling. "Miyan, miyan," she whispered softly, not very clearly, a smile hovering all the time on her lips. There was no tube in her mouth now. Did that mean she had improved? A consequence of having her son, the light of her life, beside her?

"Were you flightened of the miyan?" Aai was asking me, teasingly, using my lisping, baby voice.

"Miyan?"

"You've forgotten? That's what you called an aeroplane as a child."

Me? Frightened of aeroplanes? I used to love aeroplanes as a child. When I heard the sound of one I would spread my arms, jump up and down and pretend to be flying in the air, making aeroplane noises all the time. This flying would go on and on, every time, till the aeroplane was completely out of sight. Suli, my next door neighbour, always said, "I know you will go to Am-berica when you grow up!" And Aai was saying that *I* was frightened of planes. How can our memories of things be so different? In that case, which is the true version?

While I was talking to Aai, the doctor arrived. "Hmm, Deshpandebai, no chatting allowed just because your son's here from America!"

"But," Aai started to say ... The nurse pressed her palm lightly on Aai's lips and Aai removed it with a laugh. In that single moment the load on my mind lightened and I said, "Aai, I'll just grab a coffee and come back!"

"And a masala dosa," said Aai with a wink.

"Deadly combination!" I said instantly, using an old favourite phrase from my adolescence, and the past that we both shared came alive. I had so taken to the combination of coffee and masala dosa that I called it a "deadly combination," a phrase used by my English teacher in class. When Aai saw how much I loved having the two things together, she started making them at home. She would put both dishes before me and ask, "How is it? Deadly?" And I would nod and attack them. After that whenever I was in the mood for a dosa and a coffee, I'd say, "Aai, let's make deadly." "Deadly or idli?" she'd giggle and, "Idli?" I'd say everytime, "No, no, deadly, deadly!"

I stepped out smiling. The fierce light hit my eyes like if I had emerged from a tunnel, the roar of the traffic and the clamour of the crowds almost deafened me. The odour of petrol and diesel assailed my nostrils.

I stood frozen for a second and then reminded myself, Hey, this is your country and these are your people! I made a bold attempt to walk ... and found that I could. I reached the gate of the hospital and found Mama there. Both of us just stood looking at each other for a while. How bent he looked, how grey! He hugged me with deep affection. Then he caught my hand tightly in his and said, "It's good you came. We were so frightened by Tai's state. We brought her to the hospital with the neighbour's help but we really thought we wouldn't be able to manage. Who would come here every day, stay here at night, do everything? It's good you're here!"

"Come, Mama, let's go and have a cup of coffee. Aai is a little better now."

We went to a restaurant and I ordered dosas for both of us. While Mama was eating he looked up at me and said, "Look, Laloo, I know that you hold some grudge against your mother, that there is some prejudice somewhere. You may have a reason. But now I'm asking you with folded hands to please cleanse your mind of it. Forget it. Look after her now. Even if she gets well now, I don't think she will ... for long ..."

Even as he spoke, Mama started sobbing loudly. The restaurant was near the hospital and drew most of its clientele from there, so there were only a few sympathetic glances when Mama broke down, but I was quite agitated. What on earth was going on in the minds of these people? What grudge was I harbouring towards Aai? Why did they feel like this? And did Aai feel the same way too? Is that why she had never asked me to return nor insisted on visiting America? What a strange madness this was! Such a huge misunderstanding between people who were so close!

"No, no Mama, I feel absolutely nothing of the kind. I bear no grudges against Aai, never have. How can I, she's such a wonderful mother ..."

Now, I too could not speak. Somehow I finished my dosa and coffee. When I felt my voice return, I told Mama, "I will not burden you with Aai's responsibility. Either I'll stay here or I'll take her back with me. But you don't have to worry about her any more."

"Deadly combination, uncle and nephew together!" exclaimed Aai when she saw us together.

"Look how this myna is twittering now. Who'd believe she couldn't speak a word the day before yesterday!" Mama said and both of us giggled. Immediately, someone hissed "Shhh" and we shut up.

"You go home and rest. I'll sit with Aai while I am here. Don't worry," I said to Mama, and watched him walk away, pleased and relaxed.

And then I literally shifted into the hospital. Fortunately, one close relative was permitted to stay around all the time. I ate wherever I could, bathed, slept, bought medicines. I fed Aai her first cup of tea and her first biscuit.

I also arranged to receive all my calls at the hospital phone number. I made sure that those who called would do so at a fixed time and waited for the calls near the telephone at the time we had agreed on. Leena called often to inquire after "Tarabai's" health. Once Bandu-Gundu, sounding very proper and grown-up, also spoke to their Dad. And once Leena's mother called.

"This is Leena's Aai here. How is Tarabai?"

"She's a little better now."

"Naturally, she has to get well now that her son has come. When are you coming to meet us?"

"I'm afraid it won't be possible this time. In fact, I've decided not to move out from the hospital. I'm needed here."

"See how much you're doing for your mother! Just teach our Leena to do the same. Ask her if it's enough to call once a month. Shouldn't she come to meet us? Or is it that once one goes to America, one's parents can perish?"

"No, no, it's not like that. She misses you a lot. But what with the housework, her job and the kids, she has no time."

"Great. Side with your wife! All right, the two of us will come and meet you," she said and hung up.

The threads of the spider's web around Aai started snapping slowly. The tubes were removed one by one. And after fifteen days, the doctor actually discharged her. I was taking Aai home like a triumphant warrior holding aloft his prize.

"Thank you, Doctor, you've done so much for my mother. Now I'm going back. Tell me, when will you permit her to come to America?" I asked before we left the hospital.

"You can take her after four or five months. She's progressing quite well. You'll just have to be careful for some time," the doctor told me.

When we came home and I unlocked the door, I understood why I hadn't come home all these days. I hadn't been ready to enter Aai's house without her.

Aai went inside and sat down on a chair. Aai, Mama, Mavshi, Krishnabai, me ... the house seemed so full of people.

I stayed for a couple of days more and then left for the US leaving Aai in the care of Mama and Mavshi, and especially of Krishnabai. Since I left promising to come back for Aai in four months' time, everyone, including Aai, bade me goodbye with a smile.

I reached home. Met Gundu-Bandu and Leena. I gave Leena the saree that Aai had sent for her. Then I went back to work. Answered Dhingra's queries with a smile. Called up my friends and gave them news of India. In short, I settled down again to my life in the States.

One day I was sitting with Bandu-Gundu watching television, when the telephone rang.

"Laloo, my boy, your Aai passed away yesterday." It was Mama on the phone. "There was no point in asking you to come again. The neighbours were most helpful and we managed to do everything that was necessary. I wanted to call you myself. Now everything is over and I'm free, and I thought I'd let you know. You did everything you could for her. So don't feel bad. You fed her water. She was happy when she died. Now come here when it's convenient for you and decide what to do about the house, the furniture and other things ..."

Mama hung up. I was bewildered but not shocked. I was shocked but I didn't collapse. But something must have registered on my face. Leena asked, "Who was it?"

"Mama. Aai passed away yesterday."

"What? Tarabai? Dead?"

I nodded.

And all of a sudden, Leena was crying. Huge racking sobs, loud and inconsolable. After a long, long while, she quietened down in my arms whimpering, "Laloo, I want to go down to India, I want to. To my Aai. I haven't met her for ages. I have to go ..." Her voice broke. I patted her back trying to console her. Or, perhaps, I was only trying to console myself.

GRACY

PANCHALI

TRANSLATED BY RUKMINI SEKAR
NOMINATED BY K SATCHIDANANDAN

First published in Malayalam as "Panchali" in *Mathrubhumi*,
September 1998, Kozhikode

It was a nazhi uri of milk that the mother-in-law handed to the bride on her wedding night. Sensing her embarrassment, ammayiamma said with a slight smile, "Phalgu's orders."

When Krishnaa walked into the bedroom, he was leaning back on the bed, smoking a cigarette. The foul smelling air that hung heavily in the room was enough proof of his having burned many a cigarette to ash.

He turned around when he heard her place the small metal measure of milk on the table. But his face was not his alone. Four, five people seemed to be crowded into that face!

Krishnaa gasped, her heart missing a beat.

With a smile that was hardly his alone, Phalgunan rose and held Krishnaa close to him. In a voice that she could scarce recognize, he said, "I was just remembering Krishnaa, what a rasika you were. You called the five of us Pandavas, loving each one of us equally, without a difference!"

She knew then that a calamity stood waiting, with huge gaping jaws, to swallow her whole life. She cursed the moment when those five young men had come to live next door to her. She was a ripe, full bloomed fifteen year old then. She had delighted in the fact that all five of them had a place in her heart. It was as natural as the blossoming of five flowers in one single bunch. She replied to the letters each of them sent her. She waited where each had asked her to wait. She even congratulated herself, for not once did any of them doubt her.

But now – almost as if he had tracked her thoughts and taken a short cut – Phalgunan said, "I studied with a vengeance. I participated in competitive examinations with great determination. Got myself the best possible job. And then presented myself proudly

---

Phalgunan: Another name for Arjunan. Named thus since he was born in the Uttaraaphalguni constellation. **Krishnaa**: Draupadi, the daughter of Draupada, the King of Panchala, was also known as Krishnaa, as she was dark-skinned. She is also called Panchali because she was from Panchala. Arjunan, one of the five Pandava brothers won her hand in marriage but when he and his brothers brought her home, their mother, Kunti, not knowing what her sons had brought home as alms that day, asked them to share it equally amongst themselves. Hence Draupadi became the wife of all the five brothers – Yudhishtiran, Bhiman, Arjunan, Nakulan and Sahadevan.

before your father. And he gave you to me. But I shouldn't forget my friends, should I? So from today, I shall share you with them, divide you into five."

Krishnaa didn't quite know what Phalgunan was getting at. And she felt nervous. She had not seen the other four in a long time. None of them had come for her wedding either. All of a sudden, a terrible fear gripped her. She listened keenly to the darkness outside. Could they be crouching there, waiting for their turn?

Phalgunan laughed. The sharpness of that laughter pierced her and she cringed. Picking up the milk, Phalgunan said, "Here's to our married life!" He took a sip of the milk and passed the vessel on to Krishnaa, saying, "Dear wife of Yudhishtiran, drink. Just one sip. Remember, the other four are waiting."

Krishnaa did not have the faintest idea of the denouement of this play. Despondent, she took a sip. He then took one sip each for Bhiman, Arjunan, Nakulan and Sahadevan. Each time, she had to become that person's "dear wife."

Yet she was relieved. They were, after all, nowhere near.

When the vessel was empty, Phalgunan continued with a rather sly smile, "Though it was Phalgunan who won Krishnaa, it was Yudhishtiran who first slept with her."

He took her by the hand and led her to the bed. "You know, don't you, that Dharmaputran is an honourable man, particularly in the matter of women. So, your ladyship, you may undress yourself."

Perhaps, she thought, perhaps after all, this game might not be as dangerous as she had feared. Yet she hesitated. Her vision of what her first night would be was not very different from that of other girls. Finding her husband waiting patiently, after a reluctant while, Krishnaa took off her clothes.

With a thin smile he continued, "Yudhishtiran can spend hours investigating the Vedas, the Upanishads and the Dharmasamhitas. But women bring him quick satisfaction."

With a perfunctory caress of her body, he entered her. And climaxed just as quickly. Krishnaa stared with growing dissatisfaction at her sleeping husband, who had turned away from her. She realized then that her heart was, indeed, cut into five.

She watched fearfully, as he transformed into Bhiman, his breath heaving and swelling heavily in his sleep. And the next night, Krishnaa tossed, turned and swirled like the Kalyanasaugandhikam Pond into which Bhiman had once descended. Her wounded lips, her neck drooping like a lotus stem, her bruised breasts, the broken rim of her navel, and her crushed waist – all dragged her into a fathomless abyss of emptiness. When at some point she opened her eyes, her husband's loud burst of laughter brought her ashore.

"Sabaash Krishnaa! You not only possess the mental strength, but also the physical ability to take on the five of us!"

It was then that she began to understand that matters were moving beyond her wildest imagination. With that realization, her divided heart, much to her own consternation, began to unite and solidify like a rock.

Arjunan walked in on the third night with a tune on his lips. His love-laden eyes caressed Krishnaa for a long moment. Then he undressed her without mishandling even her clothes. He placed her on his lap like a veena. "Oh, Krishnaa, how much I yearned for you, from the moment I set eyes on you!" he exclaimed affectionately. Erotic ragas multiplied on his fingers.

But Krishnaa did not melt.

On the fourth day, Krishnaa decided that she would visit her home and not return. But her hopes were wiped out completely.

"Oh no, we are not going anywhere, not before Nakulan and Sahadevan have each had their turn!" he said.

It was Nakulan's night. "Of all the five, Nakulan is the most handsome. But if he loves anything at all, it is his own body. He is not in the least attracted to a woman's body."

He then satisfied himself, ignoring the fullness of her body. After which he went to the bathroom, washed himself with a fragrant soap, and returned, looking more handsome than ever, to enter the world of sleep.

On the fifth night he became compassionate. "Oh Krishnaa!

Sahadevan is really very shy in man-woman matters. He will not even touch you. But are you not his woman, too? Therefore, the responsibility of arousing his manhood rests with you."

With intense self-contempt, she forced her fingers to travel. Sahadevan's shyness soon faded. He began to expand. And Krishnaa ground her teeth, gnashing them together, unable to bear his aggressive assault. She was quite sure then, that this game would continue forever, turn by turn.

The vacation was over. Her husband was leaving for office. As he was getting ready, Krishnaa's hate-filled eyes stabbed the back of his neck like a mutinous sword. Startled, he jerked around, rubbing his neck.

"Krishnaa, be ready, I'll take you to your house this evening."

He revved up the car and went past the gate.

For a long time, she stood there, numb. Then she bathed and dressed.

When Phalgunan returned that evening, he found the bedroom door shut. The door swung wide open even as he knocked. Krishnaa stood there, her hair dishevelled and her face soaked in sweat. The big kumkumam pottu on her forehead had spread, glowing like a funeral pyre. Almost singed, he peeped inside with trepidation. His eyes were blinded by the luminous pitambaram-yellow light that flooded the room.

Trembling, he asked, "Krishnaa, who is inside?"

Krishnaa burst out laughing. "It's true that Panchali had five husbands. But in her time of need not one of them supported her. Someone else was required for that. If you don't know who that is, I suggest you go read the puranas first."

Pitambaram: The yellow robe of Lord Krishna

ൾ

SUTRADHARI

THE LONE FEATHER

TRANSLATED BY N RAMAKRISHNAN
NOMINATED BY JAYAMOHAN

First published in Tamil as "Ottrai Siraku" in *Kalachchuvadu*,
January 1998, Nagercoil

Only when he was almost back at the shaded spot where he had parked his vehicle did he see the bird perched on the silk cotton tree. Its long, bright yellow beak caught his eye first. Then its downy neck, stippled nightblue and ash, then the pale blue and red feathers of its body that shone golden in the slant of the sun. The deep green of the long ilavum panchu leaves set off the colours of the bird wonderfully. It was almost as if the bird had been waiting to share in his depressed state of mind.

He began to observe it more keenly. The bird's darting eyes showed panic. He knew there was something wrong with the bird from the awkward way it hopped along the tree branch, as though it was about to lose its hold and, even as he watched, it careened down in a spiral of fluttering wings. His hands stretched out on their own to catch the bird but he missed and it landed on the cushioned seat of the scooter, its body twitching spasmodically. He immediately picked up the bird. Its warmth sent a frisson through him. Holding the softness of its feathers and the richness of its plumage – like holding a dream – was disconcerting. He saw its long beak open and close rapidly, its eyes roll back. Gently, he parted the bird's feathers for any telltale sign of injury. There was a reddish bruise on its underbelly. The moment his finger touched the wound, the bird's body convulsed violently.

The movement made him hesitate. A drop of water might give it some comfort, he thought. Placing the bird on the seat of the scooter, he dripped water drop by drop into its mouth from a bottle that he was carrying. As the water coursed down its throat, a semblance of calm appeared in the bird's eyes. He fed it a few more drops and cradled the bird in his hands once again. Its convulsions had not stopped. He felt helpless. Almost as if the bird could no longer bear his anguish, it leapt from his hands. It floundered on the ground, squawking in agony, its brilliant feathers growing dim with dust. Then its body convulsed one last time. Its glistening eyes grew still, as they gazed at the sky.

He stood there, numb from having seen death at such close quarters. The bird's shrieks still hung in the air. He felt his legs give way. He could hear the pounding of his heart and feel the dead bird's gaze boring through him. Sorrow choked his breast. The colours he had marvelled at, only a moment ago, now filled him with fear. Slowly, he lifted the bird in his hands.

Its body already felt heavier though it was still warm.

He was not sure what to do next. It occurred to him that he could bury it, but he doubted his mental strength to carry out the task. Undecided, he started walking towards a nearby well and placed the bird in the shade beneath its rim. He stroked the bird one last time, softly, took a hurried step back and, turning abruptly, walked quickly away.

The bird's calls seemed to follow him. Though he did his best to drive on unconcerned, the calls seemed to pursue him. It was only when he reached the gates of the hospital that he calmed down.

How long does one have to wait here? And that too after you promised to be here early ..." Irritation and accusation mingled in her voice.

He did not offer any reply. The eyes of the bird as they stared at the sky, still tormented him, its warmth still burnt his palms.

The sun was beginning to set. The brightness of its rays struck him as somewhat incongruous. He wished it would grow dark soon.

He was in the same frame of mind as they left the hospital. He drove on, unheedful of her questions as she sat behind him. It was as if the bird had snatched all words from within him. Still indignant at his silence during their visit to the doctor, she mumbled about his continued lack of response.

At the turning near the fruit godown, a little way off the road, he saw a crowd and, almost involuntarily, stopped the scooter. The place broke into his languor, and pulled him towards itself.

Telling her to stay near the vehicle, he approached the crowd. Shouldering his way through, he peered in. At first glance he only saw the overflowing garbage bin. He pushed aside one or two more people, and moved further in. Now he could see the white bundle, which was the focus of the crowd's attention. The thing wrapped in the white veshti moved, the cloth parted to reveal two tiny legs. The dampness of the cloth, and the blood that stained it, indicated that the child had been born not very long ago. Its eyes, mere slits in its face, had not yet opened. Someone shooed the flies that sat on the infant's forehead. The flies buzzed, flew about, and then came back. Using the thalappu of her saree, a young woman fanned the flies away again. The child's face puckered each time the flies landed on its face. The colour of the newborn baby as it lay there, was in sharp contrast to the garbage bin.

"Wonder what woman was heartless enough to do this ... Didn't even let the baby suck at her breast before throwing it away ..." The old woman's face was distressed.

"She would have cared for it if she had slept with someone in the proper order of things ... What can you say about the rascals who service their urges whenever they like?"

"At least if it had been dumped at an orphanage or an arasanga-thottil, it might have been all right. But like this, dumped with garbage ..."

The words flew thick and fast, but no one made any move to pick up the baby. The infant moved feebly every now and then as if to prove that it was still alive though too exhausted to cry.

He couldn't bear the sight any longer. Driven by an unseen force, he approached the baby. Bending down, he stretched out his hands to lift it up.

"Why should you get unnecessarily involved, sir ..."

The voice yanked him out of the crowd and walked him slowly back to his vehicle. He was unable to assert himself.

"What is it? Something about a baby. They were saying ..."

Ignoring her, he started the scooter and though she asked him all the way what it was he had seen, he did not reply.

Veshti: Otherwise known as dhoti. The soft cloth is often used as a swaddling for infants due to its softness and lightness. **Thalappu**: The Tamil word for pallu/pallav. **Arasanga-thottil:** Literally, the Government cradle. As a measure for preventing infanticide, the Government of Tamil Nadu provides cradles at public gathering points, churches or temples where unwanted babies are left, for adoption.

When the door opened, it was she who answered the anxious queries of those who were waiting for them. The questions were almost accusatory in their tone, and she answered in a weak voice, full of hesitation and fear, "The scan report will only be available tomorrow morning. The doctor said he would look at it and ..."

He lay in silence. A monstrous weight bore down on his chest. He squirmed, unable to escape its relentless thrust, and struggled to suppress the sobs that escaped him. She slept soundly. The wounds caused by all those unanswered questions must have been anaesthetized by the strain of the hospital trip. If she had felt even a bit of that pain, she would not be sleeping like this.

Behind his closed eyelids, the child stirred. Its feeble wailing grew louder and louder. He clapped his hands over his ears but could not shut it out. He struggled to escape the web spun by its tiny fingers from the blood and slime that covered its body. Caught in the web, he could move neither hand nor foot. He squirmed like a trapped insect and saw the grinning visage of a spider in the baby's face. Unable to bear its mocking laughter, he shook himself and opened his eyes. The thought that someone might have taken the child home brought him some comfort. After all, hadn't there been many people there? Without a doubt, someone would have picked up the baby and taken care of it. There were some women among them ... Surely they would not have left that tiny creature in the filth. Yes, it must be sleeping peacefully somewhere, warm and fed, with someone gently rocking its cradle at this very moment ... This brought him a measure of comfort.

But the thought lasted only an instant. His mind reverted immediately to its earlier train of thought. What if everyone had just gone about their own business – like him? What if everyone had the same why-should-we-get-involved attitude? Why am I not the one rocking the cradle? What kind of an act was it to turn away without even informing the concerned authorities about the baby? Wave upon wave of questions crashed against his mind.

He sat up. There was a knock at the door. A light sound, one that did not disturb the stillness of the night. He extricated himself from this web of thought and walked to the front room. Noiselessly, he opened the door. A cold wind blew past him into the room.

There was no one at the door.

An uninterrupted darkness ... bubbles of light flashed, here and there.

Disinclined to go back inside, he sat on the steps. The vepamaram swayed gently and each time it swayed, his feet would vanish into the tree's shadow. The dampness he felt in his feet slowly worked its way up through his body. He closed his eyes and waited for it to ascend to the tip of his head. In that instant, when the chill sprang from the top of his spine to his head, he heard the voice again. A voice unimpeded by words or meaning. The wordless cry of a child.

Senses heightened, he stood up. The voice was definitely coming from the tree. He stared intently at it. The dense darkness around the tree slowly receded and a radiance emanated from it. He saw the bird in that light. It sat on a low branch, preening its feathers. Even amidst the mottled patches of light and dark, its glorious colours shone brightly. It was as if someone were strumming the notes of the bird's song from within its glittering blue and red feathers. Suddenly, it rose with a flutter of its wings, and flew down to sit at his feet.

Stooping to pick it up in his hands, he suddenly drew back in disbelief. Swaddled in the blue feathers, the baby crawled at his feet. Its arms were lined with the brilliant plumage of the dead bird. The joy of flight shone radiantly on the infant's face, its happiness reflected in its glowing eyes. The baby smiled and held out its arms to him invitingly. It was an invitation he could not refuse. He moved closer and stretched out his hands, and the baby leapt into his arms like an effulgent ball. He sat on the steps cradling the infant in his arms. The soft warmth of the baby's body filled him with exhilaration. Its touch sent a thrill through him. The calmness in the baby's face pervaded his being. The feathers brushed against his belly. In his joy he bent over to kiss the child.

In that second the baby whipped out of his arms and brushing past his downturned face, floated away, laughing. Swallowing the kiss, he stood there disappointed. Clapping its hands, the baby wheeled above him. Coming within an arm's reach of him, it would dodge his outstretched hand and fly away again. Each time it escaped him, his desire to hold the child in his arms increased, its laughter spurring him on. Grasping the feathers that trailed from its wings, he pulled at them with all his might. As he pulled, the feathers coiled around his feet like a coir rope and the child soared ever higher. Flying with the wind, it moved away on the waves it had created.

His efforts wore him out and he slumped on to his back. Seeing him that way, the baby flew lower. The sparkle in its eyes comforted him. It came down and sat playfully on his heaving chest. But as soon as it had seated itself, a bolt of lightning struck the infant. As it began to wail, it was whipped up by a whirlwind reeking of garbage, of rotting polythene bags and putrefying plantain leaves which carried it away into the darkness. The arms of the wind ripped the feathers off the baby. Its voice cracked with pain. Torn feathers floated silently in the sky.

He watched, his head raised off the ground. Drops of blood spattered his face. At the outer limit of his vision, at a great great distance, he saw the arms of the whirlwind vanish with the baby. And the only evidence of the carnage, a lone feather, fluttering down slowly and settling on his chest.

In the morning, the lone feather continued to flutter inside him but it seemed to be weighed down by the unbearable burden of the previous night.

As he approached the garbage bin, he saw a crowd gathered there again. A dreadful stench pervaded the area, frightening him. His legs shook as he steeled himself to peer in. The bundle of cloth was still there. The white cloth had turned a disgusting shade.

Ants crawled over the infant's body. The stench was emanating from the putrefying corpse. There was a pit where the left eye had been. A black insect emerged from a nostril. The sight made his gorge rise, gagging him. He felt faint. Holding his head in his hands, he stumbled away and spat out the vomit that had pooled in his mouth. The fear that had tormented him had reached its peak. All his escape routes in blind alleys, and trapped in the centre of a road that lead nowhere, he felt he had nowhere to go.

Unable to cope with his inner turmoil, he immersed himself in work. Staring at the green digits on his monitor he tried to find refuge in the world of numbers. It was only when the phone rang, that his attention shifted from the square screen in front of him.

"Have you collected the scan report?" It was her voice on the telephone.

Her question brought the corpse he had buried deep into the ground, out in the open. The smell of its putrefaction enveloped him.

"Not yet," he replied.

"At least go and get it now – and show it to the doctor to find out what he thinks," she said. There was hope in her voice; at least they would know for sure.

"All right," he said, and put the receiver back on the hook.

What terrified him was the thought of the other report, the one about the child's death.

IMRAN HUSSAIN

BUTTERFLY

TRANSLATED BY NANDANA DUTTA
NOMINATED BY PANKAJ THAKUR

First published in Asomiya as "Pokhila" in *Prantik*,
October 1998, Guwahati

Togor paused to rest only when she reached the bank of the narrow stream. Her village was just across the little bamboo bridge and her house midway through the village. A short distance, but her body refused to take another step. She had been running along the forest path for almost an hour. Now she sat panting on a rock, her chest heaving with huge, gasping breaths.

Nine months ago, Togor's elder brother, the mainstay of the family, had died suddenly after a night of vomiting blood. After his death her old father too started to waste away. Of course the villagers tried to help with what they could, but the family that had always had two square meals a day now often had only empty plates to lick. That may have been the reason why little Togor, who was so lost in her own small cozy world, playing with the baby goats, was taken by her mother to the mondol's house and left to work there.

Togor had been thin as a bamboo reed then – all skin and bone. However, before the year was over, her body had begun to fill out. Her limbs grew rounded, her hips and her breasts began to show. As she worked around the house, her curvaceous body was even more apparent and the mondoloni, herself plain and sickly, became increasingly harsh in her manner to her. In contrast, the mondol's manner acquired a certain greasy smoothness.

One afternoon, asking Togor to pluck out the grey in his hair, he lightly touched her budding breasts. Togor was not frightened at all. In fact, a strange pleasure thrilled her virgin body. From that day on, the usually energetic and busy mondol began to complain of aches and pains, and ignoring his work, started to spend more and more time at home. He began to feel thirsty more often and suffered from headaches, and Togor was always having to set her work aside and attend to him. Their stolen moments together were filled with soft touches, tingling excitement and tantalizing desire.

But on that day Togor had a completely different experience – an experience that brought terrible bitterness in its wake. That afternoon the mondoloni, with her whining little son clinging to her like glue, went to attend a juron at the wedding next door, leaving Togor to wash the utensils. His wife was barely out of the gate when the mondol complained of thirst. As Togor entered his room with the glass of water, he lunged at her and pushed her down on the bed. She searched his face, uncomprehendingly. His nostrils were flared, his small beady eyes had dilated and the few long strands of hair that he carefully combed across his bald-pate, fell in long strands about his flushed face. His loss of control and the strange way he was behaving frightened her. She wanted to scream. But before she could, the mondol's thick, fleshy lips came down on her own half-open mouth and his foul breath made it difficult for her to breathe. Crushed under his corpulence, moaning, she began to scratch his face in an attempt to free herself from his unwelcome embrace, but after a while she stopped struggling. A little longer, and the ultimate misfortune might have befallen her. But suddenly, at the sound of a sharp voice, the mondol released her. From the bed, Togor saw, standing in the doorway, the mondoloni herself.

Her blazing eyes burned holes into her husband and her body shook in anger. The mondol was rendered completely witless by his wife's unexpected return. He rose from the bed sheepishly and moved towards the door. His furious wife pounced on him and began raining blows on his chest. Togor watched in fascination as the mondol cowered under the fusillade of blows and curses – a roaring tiger transformed into a cringing cat! She had seen husbands beat their wives but this was the first time she was seeing the converse. Gradually the mondolini's blows ceased. Her eyes flaming in her dark face, her hair undone, the sendoor on her forehead like a streak of blood, the thin, plain woman stood like an image of the goddess Kali.

Seeing her mistress in this terrible avatar of Ronochandi, Togor was petrified. As she trembled in a corner, the mondoloni turned on her, rushing at her like a wild wind, grabbing her by her hair and dragging her outside. She picked up a piece of wood and started beating her with it. "You bitch! You, who can only eat people's leftovers! You haven't reached puberty yet, and you are already trying to destroy my marriage! My curses on you! You'll be barren as soon as you flower! Get out of my house! Get out! You sly, wicked creature!" And she shoved Togor violently out into the street.

Confused and bewildered, Togor started to run. Everything had happened so fast that she quite forgot to cry. But, as she ran from the house where she had spent so many days, a deep feeling of anguish and hurt overwhelmed her. Perhaps at this point she would have given in to all her pent-up tears had they not been arrested by the sound of a loud wail from the house. Strange and pathetic, those heart-wrenching, broken cries of the mondoloni!

As Togor sat on the rock, going over the events of the day, a rough voice broke into her thoughts: "Who are you, girl? Aren't you Golapi's daughter?" She turned and saw old Basanti, the midwife, leaning on a stick and eyeing her accusingly.

"Yes Aai! I am ..."

"Your brother's wife is in labour – the water bag has broken – and here you are idling! Get up and come with me at once!" The old lady spat out a stream of betel juice and trundled off.

Stirred by her sharp words, Togor got up and followed old Basanti across the stream and into the village. Swiftly walking past seven or eight houses, she came to her own and saw a group of women gathered in the tiny courtyard. They all looked worried. Her bou's labour pains had begun and they all heaved with relief when they saw Basanti. The old woman barked out instructions – "Bring this! Bring that!" – and entered the labour room. The women rushed into action, running in with vessels of hot water, the thin skin of the bamboo, cloth, thread, and other things. Togor's Moini Pehi, her father's sister, had somehow heard the news and rushed from the neighbouring village, where she had moved to when she was married nine years ago. She had not lost any of her affection for her own people. Whenever she heard of any trouble she came promptly. She loved Togor dearly. But today, even she had no time for Togor.

The air was heavy with the pain of labour. Not knowing what to do, Togor sidled along the kitchen wall to the tiny cage-like room adjoining it, where her father lay asleep, his mouth hanging open, oblivious to the commotion around. His naked chest, with the ribs jutting out, heaved as he wheezed. Though he stirred briefly at the sound of Togor's footsteps, it was merely to stretch his legs. He lay there like a felled bamboo, almost lifeless. The sight was more than Togor could bear and she softly backed out and sat down on a broken pira.

Lost like her in the bustle of the house were her two little nieces, who, spotting her, delightedly welcomed her back with cries of "Pehi! Togor Pehi!" and climbed onto her lap. The two baby goats she had left behind came up to her and started licking her hand.

She was with the children and the goats when she heard the cry of the newborn child. This was followed by sounds of thumping on the wall, and within minutes Togor's mother emerged with a stormy look on her face. Picking up the thorny branch of the bogori tree, which had been used to block the doorway, she flung it aside in rage.

A crowd of women gathered around her like flies buzzing over a ripe mango. "Another girl, Golapi? Hori! Hori! How's the mother? Is she okay ... is there something?"

The questions tumbled around her.

Golapi sank to the ground like a severed plantain stem. With a derisive curl of her lips she said, "O come! What can happen to that cursed female? She screams and wails for nothing."

Surprisingly, all the women joined her, frowning, brooding, pretending to sympathize. The courtyard filled with the buzz of their voices but just as quickly quietened down. Soon everyone began to leave for their homes. Moini Pehi, promising to come again for a longer visit, departed as quickly as she had come.

Old Basanti remained sitting beside Golapi.

"My dear, you should not feel so sad. Girls are God's gifts. Women are as necessary as men on this earth – or else how would anything take birth and grow? You are a woman. Think of Malasi, your poor daughter-in-law, widowed so early with this child still in her womb. You are the only one who can console her, give her strength. How can you be so weak now?"

Basanti left but Golapi continued to sit, her head in her hands, staring vacantly ahead.

The house was eerily silent now, only the infant's feeble cries wafted out now and then. Togor was secretly angered by her mother's dissatisfaction. She failed to understand why the birth of a girl-child should bring such sorrow. "I'll go and see the baby," she told herself and, with the curiosity of a young girl, walked into the room where her sister-in-law lay.

She found Malasi lying straight and flat on the low bed. Sleeping quietly beside her, swaddled in clothes that only revealed its face, was the fatherless child. Malasi's eyes were fixed on the baby, her eyes unnaturally bright in her pale face. Looking around, Togor noticed that beneath the picture of the baby Lord Krishna, lay a few pieces of firewood and a cane basket full of fish. There were stains on the floor from the fish her sister-in-law must have been cleaning when the pains came. A few pieces of cloth lay scattered about. Togor became conscious of an unfamiliar smell pervading the room. Was it the damp wood or the smell of sweat, blood and dettol? She felt a wave of nausea sweep over her and rushed out to the yard.

Golapi was still there. The wind of the sot month had blown sand over her face and hair. Togor approached her mother and sank onto the ground beside her but Golapi was so absorbed in her thoughts that she just looked at her unseeingly.

The sun was beginning to set. Perhaps that was why the wind was so cold. Togor's heart felt weighed down in this atmosphere pregnant with unuttered sounds, like the stillness following a clash of brass cymbals.

It was only after a long while that Golapi became conscious of Togor's presence.

"When did *you* get here?"

"Some time ago, Aai."

"You were here only the other day. If you come so often, how will I feed you?" Golapi asked in a shrill voice.

"No ... I mean ... it was ..." Togor hesitated, wondering how to tell her mother all that had transpired that day.

"Has the mondol paid you? ... Why don't you answer?" Golapi asked impatiently.

Togor kept a guilty silence. Infuriated, Golapi glared at her daughter, and then turning her back on her, once again became absorbed in her own thoughts. Again that uncomfortable quiet.

Togor sat shamefacedly, biting her nails, furtively glancing at her mother who sat in a posture of supplication, her unblinking gaze turned up to the sky. Many minutes went by. Then, Golapi's lips trembled. Seeing her face soften, Togor felt emboldened to say: "Aai, I don't want to go back to the mondol's house."

"Why?" her mother asked, not too gently, her face beginning to harden again.

Togor answered limply, "Because ... oh ... just like that."

"Just like that?" Golapi suddenly scrambled up and slapped Togor hard on both cheeks. "Listen to her! Just like that she says! The witches incite you! You don't know when you are well-off. Who's going to feed you here? What's the matter? Why don't you answer?"

Togor stood up meekly and began to bite her nails again.

"What's the matter? Why don't you answer me? If you don't agree to go back, I won't give you any food today."

The whole day had been too much for her. She was already deeply distraught and the sorrow, anger and bitterness she had felt all day flared up at her mother's harsh treatment: "I won't go back! Even if you cut me up, I won't work in the mondol's house ever again. I won't go ... I won't!" she screamed recklessly.

"What did you say, you cursed girl? You dare answer me back!" Golapi rushed at her angrily and started slapping her again.

Togor just stood there quietly. And then all of a sudden she ran to the raised bamboo platform in the courtyard, the saang, and laid herself down. Her face smarted from the slaps of Golapi's work-hardened palms, her back was sore from the mondoloni's beating.

She felt hurt, exploited, betrayed. But not a single sob escaped her. A whole sea of tears dried up within her as she lay silently on the saang.

Different sounds echoed around her – the faint cry of the newborn, Golapi's shrill tirade, the clatter of utensils being washed, the spluttering of oil as something was put into the frying pan, the sounds of laughter in the kitchen, again the washing of pots and pans, and the clamour of barking dogs. In the midst of all this, she was terribly alone.

And then the sounds died down. Her nieces Mala and Ila, came out and curled up beside her. Their breaths had the fragrance of fresh mint. Togor felt the rumble of hunger. But her bruised ego prevented her from going to the kitchen. She waited expectantly for her mother's call, but only heard the sound of the kitchen door being locked for the night, followed a while later by the sound of her mother snoring in the next room. That was when she realized that she would have to go hungry and thirsty to bed that night.

The new moon was in the sky. She turned her head and looked at it and at the small puffs of clouds sailing by. As she gazed up in the silence of the night, her heart grew heavy with deep, primeval grief. She was cursed. The long pent-up tears broke free and began to course down her cheeks. Her vision blurred and the silent tears gave way to violent sobs that racked her entire body.

All night long the crickets called from the creeper outside the window.

And Togor continued to lie on the saang.

In fact, it was when the waves of her salty tears started sweeping over her, that she embarked upon her strange journey. Unknowingly, she had just stepped into another world. But was initiation into this world always so violent? Maybe that was the reason why she was so silent, almost fearful. Then, as she stared out at the moon, into the night, her eyes swimming with tears, she was again an innocent young girl.

The house came to life as if stirred by an earthquake. Golapi, coming out to the bathroom, noticed Togor sitting there, holding herself awkwardly. "Have you been bitten by a snake?" was her first query. But it did not take the mother long to realize that her daughter was having her first period.

But have I really grown up? Is this what it means to have warm blood flow? Togor wondered. And this thought weighed down on her as she listened to the talk around her. Why was she not allowed to leave this miniscule room for seven days? Why could she not comb the tangles out of her hair, or oil it? Why could she not look at herself in the mirror, not serve tamul to her mamas and khuras, not even be allowed to nurse her old, sick father? Did growing up and becoming a woman mean that even the touch of her shadow was impure?

Since early morning, the women of the village had been pouring in. One brought some milk, another a mix of pulses, still another a bunch of bananas and some sticks of sugarcane – and they all came with a hundred little do's and dont's for her. Moini Pehi heard the news and came to spend a couple of days. She had given Togor a pair of silver earrings along with some invaluable advice: Now that you've reached puberty you should not wander off by yourself all over the village, nor should you play with the boys.

But all that Togor could think of was that her stomach was on fire. Yesterday she had had no time to eat lunch at the mondol's house. And then she had silently borne the violent blows from the mondoloni and her mother's slaps. At night her furious mother had not even called her for supper. And today, apparently, she was meant to fast.

She felt she could eat even the unripe bananas and the rice grains kept in the ceremonial vessel, the dunori. But nobody paid her any heed. Her mother just came in to announce that she would be able to break her fast in the evening with some fruit. Helpless, she spent the day tossing and turning on the straw bed that had been prepared for her on the floor of that pigeon cote of a room.

It was only in the evening, after the blowing of the conch, and the trills of the unruli that she felt a sense of relief. She quickly gobbled up the pieces of apples and sugarcane along with the sprouts offered to her and demanded to be given more. In a short while, she ate up all the food that had been brought by the women in the morning. Everyone just stared, amazed and amused by her appetite.

The next day, she again feasted on a great variety of fruits. The apples and grapes in the dish surprised and pleased her. She had never tasted grapes before this, even though she had seen them at the mondol's house. She could not understand how her mother had procured them. She could not understand her mother at all. But as she ate the grapes one by one, lying on her straw bed, tasting the joys and sorrows of womanhood, all her resentment and anger faded.

But in her new state, her body experienced strange sensations. She tossed about restlessly, her back ached, and shooting pains coursed through her lower belly. The increasing wetness sometimes alarmed her. Sometimes she felt angry at the group of giggling little girls peering at her. At other times she looked at the silver earrings with which Moini Pehi had conferred the social status of a woman on her and blushed under the gaze of the young wives who sat close by, chatting animatedly and glancing at her every now and then from the corner of their eyes. A fascinating and inexplicable joy pervaded her being.

Mala and Ila, her nieces, continued to sleep on the saang, which Togor had earlier occupied. During the day, refusing to stay inside, they played hide and seek around the house.

Though now Togor had got used to being by herself, she felt incredibly restless on the day the women of the house prepared aakhoi, a delicacy that was made specially for this occasion. The strong wind blowing in through the cracks unsettled her still further, made her feel even more lonely, like a dried leaf falling from the tree to the ground. The wind died away towards the evening, but the sky remained overcast and gloomy, adding to her depression.

In the evening, after Togor had broken her fast, the women of the neighbourhood gathered outside her little room to help with the aakhoi. Their chatter matched the crackle of the roasting rice grains. But Togor watching them, continued to feel low, remembering the unpleasant experiences in the mondol's house and wondering at the sadness of a girl's lot. Her mother's harsh words following the birth of another girl-child to her sister-in-law, still rang in her ears. These thoughts kept her awake late into the night, long after Mala and Ila had fallen asleep.

She was about to go to bed when she heard whispers outside. The days of inactivity had whetted her curiosity and she approached the wall with the stealth of a cat. The words were softly spoken but they were audible to her and she recognized the voices. Moini Pehi and her mother.

"She's not a child any more. What can you do if she refuses to understand? Can you explain anything through a beating, Bou? When you get angry ..."

"Yes, I agree. The other day, I beat her so hard ... she's so stubborn. I felt very bad about it later."

"It happened that night, didn't it?"

"Yes, that's the night she got her period. She was very frightened, hid herself away. I found her like that ... Imagine!"

"Of course she would be frightened. Weren't we afraid? I'll never forget that first fear."

"And me! I was so scared that I didn't tell anyone. I kept away from people, walked around by myself. In the end, I went to Minoti Bou. You remember Minoti Bou of Phulguri? But my stars were lucky. This girl is going to make us all suffer."

"What does the astrologer say? Is it something bad?"

"Bad? It couldn't be worse. She'll never have a husband. Moreover it happened on a Shanibaar, in the middle of the night. It's bad luck all round."

"Yes, they say that if a girl gets her first period on a Saturday she is going to be barren. The time is inauspicious. You'll have to give daan-dakhina ... My husband's niece too had this curse on her, you know."

"Don't speak about daan-dakhina, Moini. The astrologer has already demanded a goat along with the usual gift of clothes. And if that isn't enough I'll have to hold a hori-kirtan for the purification rites. The mondol used to give forty rupees every month – now even that will stop. I don't know what has happened. I have no money left. We've had no food since yesterday – there's not a grain of rice even for my little granddaughters."

"This is too much, Bou. Why have you been buying apples and grapes?"

"You know Moini, that day after I beat her I felt so bad. She's already reached puberty. How much longer will she be with me? I broke into my savings in the clay pot."

"Bou, why don't you send her with me? She can work with our society, weave cloth, and help me sell it. You'll get about sixty rupees every month, and that's likely to increase later."

"What can I say Moini? I don't mind. But you know how stubborn Togor is. And as if that's not enough, my daughter-in-law refuses to eat plantain curry – she wants only fresh fish ... And she makes such a fuss. When we had babies, even the dogs didn't hear us. That's a woman's life. One has to bear pain. That's why I was so upset at the birth of another girl."

"Listen! It's the baby crying. Do you think she has a pain somewhere – in the stomach maybe?"

"Someone's evil eye must have touched her. I'll go to the Bez tomorrow and have him read a chant over the mustard seeds to put under her pillow ... Ei, get up, get up! It's very late. We have many things to do tomorrow – fetch water from thirteen different sources, collect the bark from the bael and the togor flower, gather dubari, rice grains, and so much more."

Before their footsteps died away, Togor quietly went and lay down on her bed. She felt her chest constrict. So much lacking in this house! Even the little ones were going hungry. And now these three days ... she felt overcome by shame. Now there would be more expenses, and all because of her.

She sank deeper and deeper in thought. All these household worries and difficulties completely destroyed her joy at the awakening. There were still a few grapes left – she had wanted to save them for later. Now, seeing them, she experienced a deep sense of gratitude to her mother.

The words of her mother and aunt continued to ring in her ears for a long time. What was that cursed label again – Patiheena! Husbandless! She suddenly remembered the mondoloni's words, "You'll be barren as soon as you flower."

An unknown fear sent a chill through her body. But it was a momentary sensation. And then a great wave of anger stiffened her spine. She felt angry with her mother, but then this anger, moving in her mind from person to person, focused on the astrologer. Why should he have asked for the goat? Suppose her mother gave away one of her goats? What would happen if these ridiculous rituals were ignored?

Deep into the night, Togor tossed restlessly in bed. Her ear caught the sound of her mother groaning in her sleep, the shrill cries of the night birds, the howls of foxes, the faint whimpering of the newborn, and her father's hacking cough. She was hot and the dust blown in by the wind made her mouth and skin gritty. She felt truly unclean. The smell of her own sweat, and her unwashed body, made her nauseous. It made her recall the smell of blood and sweat in the room where her sister-in-law had given birth. She could no longer bear the thought of remaining in the tiny room without being allowed to wash herself. She imagined herself walking through the garden of tamul-paan to the river, and slipping from the branches of an overhanging tree into the cool depths of the river.

Towards the middle of the night, a strong wind began to blow and the rains came pouring down. The first rains of the year! It was very important, this shower of rain. The steady pitter-patter drowned out the other sounds of the night. Togor felt comforted. The rhythmic beat of the rain calmed her and gradually she fell asleep. She began to dream ...

She was sitting naked near a tall plantain tree and a group of women were rubbing a paste of lentil and turmeric on her, before bathing her gently. They sang a sad and plaintive song whose words she couldn't decipher though the tune was familiar – like the lullabies of childhood. For some reason, she felt it was her mother who was singing the song. She turned her head around to look for her mother and thought she saw her standing beneath a tree. She cried, "Aai! Aai!" and ran towards her, but saw instead a figure in white, with an unfamiliar dark face. Not finding her mother anywhere, Togor ran down the forest path like a ball of cotton borne by the wind, looking here and there. At last she found her in a strange place near a rice mill, sitting with a group of women, winnowing the grain. Togor went and flopped down onto the ground beside her mother and saying, "Let me do it, Aai," she took the kula from her mother and started to toss the grain into the air. The chaff flew out in a cloud.

At this point she heard a voice from somewhere in the distance call out to her. "Togor! Togor!"

As the voice came closer and closer, the petals of sleep brushed off her. She opened her eyes and saw that it was morning and it was her mother who stood calling out her name.

Golapi, who had come to awaken her, had stopped herself when she found her daughter mumbling in her sleep. Her heart softened at the sight of the young face, flushed with sleep. She asked gently, "My love! What were you saying – Give it to me, Aai! Let me do it! Do what, child?"

Togor looked up at her mother, a little shy, a little embarrassed. "It was only a dream, Aai!" she said, "I think ..."

In what a short time my little daughter has grown up, thought Golapi, looking at Togor with love and joy as she heard her say, "Aai, don't leave me at the mondol's house again. Let me go with Moini Pehi, to their Society ..."

MY DEAR JAYU

DARWIN'S COUSIN

TRANSLATED BY TRIDIP SUHRUD
NOMINATED BY KANTI PATEL

First published in Gujarati as "Darwin no Pitrai" in *Vi*,
May-June 1998, Gujarat

To tell you the truth, I have walked each path and dirt-track of my village as also those of the surrounding fields, so going anywhere, at anytime, is usually no problem for me. But that night when I passed under the haunted amli, I almost wet my pants. The cold of night had descended, the skies were moonless, and wandering clouds dribbled showers every now and then. There was an icy chill in the air. I shivered. There was an exorcism on at Natha's house and I was headed there. I could hear the drums of the bhuvas thrum in the distance. Standing under the ghost-infested amli, I quaked with fear, leaden feet refusing to budge.

"Why did you stop?" a voice asked, making me jump. I turned around and saw Bhagatbapa standing right beside me, asking, "Going for the exorcism? I am going there too." He started walking briskly on. I was deeply relieved to see him – as if all the thirty three crore gods had come to reside within me. Natho is a friend. I used to visit his house often till his wife came to live with him. By then he had also acquired new friends I didn't approve of. His wife was no apsara, but she wasn't bad looking either. In deference to her, even the scum of the village had begun to call Natha, "Nathabhai."

I don't care for things such as exorcisms, but each to their own, I guess, after all who knows what fate has in store for one. It humbles even the mighty, let alone the likes of Natha's wife. People say that one night Natha saw a man coming out of his house and completely lost his head. The wife denied the charge. Natha gave her two hard slaps – You whore, you rand, are you saying I'm lying? The wife retorted, Yes, you are. Natha's temper flared. He picked up a stick and thrashed her on the back with it. The wife yowled like a cat, then grabbed one end of the stick and both of them grappled with it for a while. Suddenly she stopped fighting. Don't raise your hand, she said in a quiet voice, there is Sat in me! Her body trembled and shook, as if from an aftershock of violence and sex, her face flushed, her eyes widened. Convulsing uncontrollably, she shrieked, I, Khijada, I have come to destroy you – I'll uproot you, root and branch!

She was the goddess incarnate. Fierce, bright-eyed, body drenched in sweat, clothes in wanton disarray, her hair undone, wild, dishevelled. And she kept screaming. The women of the neighbourhood had gathered by then. They threw themselves at her feet and pleaded, "Khamma, Ma Khamma, be kind and generous, O Ma." After a while the convulsions subsided. An old woman gave her some water and she quietened down. Natha slunk away to crouch in a corner. His mind was a blank. Was his wife a woman or a god?

From that day on, Natha's wife grew completely dull and listless. She didn't cook or eat, didn't go out to fetch water, didn't sleep. She was as if turned to stone. The entire village started talking about her. People said that the spirit of the goddess had indeed entered her body.

News of the incident reached Savabhuva. Savo said, "Lies. Are goddesses to be found wandering on the streets? No spirit can enter the town without my permission! Don't you know who I am? I am Savaji Jamadar. All the sixty four jognis play in my yard. They need my permission even to move." The village believed him. Opium or something else made his eyes glow red. Everyone agreed that there was a need for exorcism.

And so the tussle began. Savabhuva thundered, If I don't strip naked whatever it is, in a fraction of a second, I am not Savaji.

I felt a little queasy when I heard of the exorcism. Should I, or should I not go? What if the truth emerges? Several thoughts crossed my mind. Finally I mustered up enough courage, but my legs grew wobbly each time I thought of it.

And now, "Arre, come, come, you are extremely slow," Bhagatbapa said as I inched reluctantly towards Natha's house. "The bhuva's drums are beating out there and you here shaking like one possessed?" he taunted.

"I know nothing about such matters," I stammered, "That's why I am frightened."

"How the hell does it matter to us? We are just spectators. If it becomes too frightening, just get up and leave. Are we the ones who have sinned?" he asked as we entered Natha's house.

The courtyard was littered with charpais. A few people sat around, bidis dangling from their lips. The veranda was packed. The exorcism was underway in the inner room. The only lamp in the house was inside the room. Outside it was pitch dark and I could sense any number of ghostly shadows hovering around. I peeped into the room. A fire burned, swirls of smoke and an overpowering fragrance danced around it. Natha's wife, her hair wild and unkempt, sat huddled in one corner, facing the fire. Savaji sat across from her, flanked by two padhiyars. All three men with their long, matted hair and flaring sindoor on their foreheads looked frightening in the light of the fire. In a corner, two ravaliyas were beating drums as if possessed, while two others twirled the zanj. One of them was chanting something that could hardly be heard. The padhiyars were making more noise than all the others.

I crept in and took my place next to Bhagatbapa, wondering how long they had been at it.

Savaji cleared his throat and signalled for the din to stop. And Natha's wife, whose eyes had been glued to the floor all this while, jerked her head up.

I was there, squarely in her field of vision.

Savaji took some grains in his hands and said, "Let's begin."

One of the ravals nodded his head vigorously. Savaji's face instantly brightened. And people more knowledgeable than me about what was going on, sat up. A whispering began. I looked at Bhagatbapa inquiringly. Bapa said, "His gods have assented, he will be on his haunches soon. Whatever it is, he won't rest till he catches it."

Jehmat Babar passed around saucers of tea that people drank, slurping noisily. Bidi packs were pulled out and proffered, smoke filled the veranda. And in her corner, Natha's wife all of a sudden removed her blouse, tossed back her hair and cleared her throat. Everything was ready.

"Invite the goddess Amba," Savaji said.

The ravalias started beating their drums, the zanj players plucked at their instruments and one of them started to sing:

Ma Amba, come and play at the chowk,
Ma, come start your play at the gabbar ...

The padhiyars continued to make strange noises. Savaji's finger shook, his eyes grew larger, more protuberant. Drums and zanj beat rhythmically, acquiring a life of their own, and the raval sang louder and louder in a shrill voice. Suddenly Savaji shouted loud enough to be heard in the next village, "Ma, come down, Ma, come down and play, O Mother!"

Savaji was on his knees now. I trembled. But Natha's wife sat unmoved.

The drums rolled louder, faster, the song was a high pitched screech, and Savaji siddled up close to Natha's wife pleading, "Come and play jogni! Your sisters are waiting. Come down from your abode, O Mother!"

Natha's wife sat like a statue.

Even though the smoke from the fire had cleared, the bodies of the bhuvas appeared aflame. The drums played on insistently, pleading, cajoling, but Natha's wife held her ground.

Savaji held up his hand. Everything came to a halt. He spat loudly, "Haa ... kathu ..." and out fell a gob of spit like a silver coin. People wiped the sweat off their bodies. Savaji took some grains and set them aside. The raval counted them. And then suddenly Savaji slapped Natha's wife, a tight sharp slap. But she continued to sit inert, as if made of stone.

"This is no goddess! It is a demon. A good spirit would have revealed itself by now. She is possessed by an evil spirit," Savaji proclaimed.

Bhagatbapa leaned forward on his haunches, "But she claims to be the goddess of the Khijada tree."

Savaji lit a bidi, "Will the evil one ever say it is evil?"

Bhagatbapa said, "Whatever it is, it has to be exorcised."

Savaji rose, cobra-like, "Why just it, even its father has to get out. If it doesn't reveal itself by the third slap, I am not Savaji."

Then, tucking a wad of opium into his mouth he said, "First, offer a coconut to the goddess and get some tea. We will take care of the other things, by and by."

Tea started doing the rounds. The lamps and agarbattis were rekindled. Natha smashed open the coconut and handed it around. People munched the coconut not bothering to even look at Natha's wife. She continued to sit still, very still.

I looked out. The sky was overcast, making the night even darker. It was almost midnight. I didn't have the guts to go out alone but some of the men were going out to relieve themselves so I went with them. One of them said, "When Savajibhai gets angry, most people wet their clothes." Another said, "All the gods reveal themselves to him. He can converse with any one of them."

I went back in. Now a chillam was being passed around. Savaji and his assistants drew hard on it, Bhagatbapa took a puff too, whispering, "One should do as the community does." Savaji had the last puff. He sucked so hard that the chillam flared red. His eyes were bloodshot. Everyone fell silent. One of the ravals put some guggul in the fire and the room was once again filled with smoke. The only light in the room emanated from the thin flames of the sputtering fire that threw more shadows on the people gathered in the room than light. Savaji straightened his back and the ravals readied their drums. Savaji said, "Invoke the Meladi Ma. Khamma, be kind and generous, O Mother!" With that, the drumming commenced and the zanj joined in. One of the ravals began to sing:

Khamma, visit my house, Ma Meladi!
O Khamma, the long haired one,
Khamma, the one eyed goddess,
Come Khamma, the one with two tongues,
O you who holds the sword
Khamma, come visit my house, Ma Meladi!"

The drums beat faster and faster. Someone joined in the chant while many others fervently cried out "Khamma, Khamma, Khamma." The padhiyars started trembling as more people took up the chant. I had never witnessed such a scene before.

Suddenly Savaji reared up and his fist came smashing down on the ground. He roared fit to rent the skies, rolling his head wildly, tossing his long hair around, so it grazed the woman's face. Natha's wife stared into Savaji's eyes as he jerked and juddered on his knees like an epileptic, raising his arms and moving rhythmically, mesmerically, like a goddess astride her bull. He began to laugh loudly. "Khamma, Khamma," shouted the crowd, prostrating themselves at his feet. Savaji looked like the Meladi herself when he gave Natha's wife a resounding slap, shaking her out of her trance. The padhiyars rained blows on her back as Savaji shouted, "Speak, speak! Who are you? Whatever you are, present yourself. Or I'll beat you to pulp. Speak out, who are you, speak!" Savaji cracked his palm against her face again and, finally, Natha's wife began to tremble.

All the three bhuvas hovered over her shouting and screaming, "Come out, come out into the open, you bitch. Whoever you are, face us." They were shaking so that everyone present in the room felt a tremble inside them as if the room itself was quaking.

Maybe the goddess would reveal herself any minute. Natha's wife was trembling, too, and Savaji picked up a chain and roared, "Are you coming out or shall I rip your hide? Come out, you rand shankhini!" He lashed her with the chain. The padhiyars grabbed the woman's hands. Savaji caught her by the hair and held her face to the smoking fire. Then started beating her with the chain screaming, "Are you coming out or not? I'll make you shit in your clothes. Speak out, who are you – A dakin? A chudel? A shankhini? A vantari? A witch, a vampire, a sorceress, who, who, speak!"

The fire spewed smoke, the drums and zanj beat a crescendo, the bhuvas screamed and Savaji beat the woman till she convulsed. Savaji threw some dried chillies into the fire. The people started to cough and ran out of the room. Savaji did not relent. He kept striking her with the chain, eyes aflame, shouting, "Who are you? Will you come out or not? Why don't you speak? A shankhini? A dakin? A shikotar? A vantari? Who are you?"

The woman, drenched in sweat, her eyes and nose streaming, on the verge of passing out, finally acknowledged defeat. As if hanging on to Savaji's last word she whispered hoarsely, "A vantari. I am a vantari."

Savaji released her hair, slapped her once more and sat back in exhausted triumph.

He held up a hand. Immediately, the gyrations began to slow down, the shaking stopped, the drums and the zanj ground to a halt. The people in the room grew still.

Savaji said, "Fan the room," and two people took their shoulder cloths and waved the smoky air out of the room.

Pointing to the fire, Savaji ordered, "Throw it out," and the embers were duly whisked away.

Babar brought some water. Savaji gave a glassful to the woman who drained it in a single gulp. People lit their bidis. Some started to go out. Savaji sat still. Bhagatbapa sat where he was, I beside him. Saucers filled with tea started making the rounds once again. Even Natha's wife drank some tea this time, as compliant as a docile girl.

You made her confess," Bhagatbapa said appreciatively slurping his tea as noisily as the others.

"Did she have a choice? The presence of sixty four jognis cannot be slighted!"

"Never heard of a vantari possessing people," Bhagatbapa said chattily, as if he and Savaji had all the time in the world. "Where did she find her?"

Savaji puffed his bidi meditatively. "Vantaris are known to roam around, if you don't hassle them, they let you be."

"How did this one get to her?"

"The vantari was visiting her when Natha beat the daylights out of her, and the rand decided to stay put."

Bhagatbapa was enthralled. "What are these vantaris like? Where do they belong – among the devs or the dakins?"

"Neither," Savaji said between puffs on his bidi.

Bhagatbapa was perplexed. "But I must understand from which world this evil one comes. The night is still young. I can be at peace only when these things are explained."

Bhagatbapa had great prestige in the village. No one could slight him.

Savaji threw away his bidi. He smiled. "If you really want to know, I'll tell you, but Brahma will have to be invoked. The story should be heard from him."

Turning to his raval he said, "Put out the fire, sprinkle clean water, light a lamp and four agarbattis ... and everyone, go wash your hands and feet."

Everyone did as they were told and then trooped back in to sit down, cleansed and pure. A raval reached for his drum. Savaji said, "No need. I'll recite a mantra and Brahma will be here."

Savaji closed his eyes, took a deep breath, and mumbled a mantra. When he opened his eyes, a beatific smile played on his lips. He wasn't the Savaji of a moment ago.

"Long long ago, there was an ocean of milk, the ksheerasagar. Sheshnag swam in it and Bhagvan lay there with Lakshmi massaging and pressing his legs. They talked endlessly, of this and that, smiling and laughing and luxuriating in themselves. You all know that, don't you?"

Some heads nodded.

"One day, Goddess Lakshmi said, Bhagvan, I don't like things as they are, do something new.

Bhagvan said, What should I do? Aren't you happy sitting around with me?

Lakshmi said, No, do something that will be fun.

So Bhagvan caressed his navel and out came the lotus that lay coiled within and Brahma sitting on it.

Bhagvan said, Brahma, create something to amuse the goddess.

Brahma opened one of his four mouths and out came a ball of his breath. Brahma disappeared and the ball began to roll, now showing itself, now vanishing. Lakshmi laughed at this game of hide and seek.

Some days went by. Lakshmi was bored again. She said to the Bhagvan, There is no fun in watching this empty ball rolling around. Do something!

So Bhagvan caressed his navel again and out came the lotus and Brahma on it.

What is this ball called? asked the Bhagvan.

Prithvi, said Brahma. Earth.

Bhagvan said, Do something more to this Prithvi.

Brahma opened his second mouth and breathed on to the ball. Out came wind, water and fire, each pursuing the other. The ball kept rolling. The wind pursued the fire all over Prithvi. The fire would hide in the water and the wind would raise the water to the skies. Lakshmi enjoyed the fun and frolic. But how many tricks could wind, fire and water invent? Lakshmi complained again one day.

Bhagvan expertly touched his navel once again and once again out came Brahma. Bhagvan said, Lakshmi needs further novelty.

Brahma opened his third mouth and out poured the rain. Trees began to grow on Prithvi, trees of all kinds, shapes and sizes, big trees and small trees, thick trees and thin trees, trees on the mountains and trees in the water. There were trees everywhere. Prithvi was covered with trees."

"Who can match Brahma!" exclaimed Bhagatbapa.

Savaji took a deep breath and continued:

"The trees flowered, bore fruit, the winds swayed them. They provided shade. There was bliss on Prithvi. Even Lakshmi was pleased. Till she grew restless again. Couldn't something more happen?

Bhagvan said, Let's ask Brahma. Again the navel and again Brahma. Bhagvan said, Give Prithvi the play of life.

Brahma said, There is life in the trees.

Bhagvan said, Not enough. They are rooted to one place. What fun is there in that?

Brahma said, I don't want to cross you but it is not good to give living things too much life.

Lakshmi said, Let's see. After all they can play around only on Prithvi, they won't be able to come to swarglok.

Brahma said, Your wish is my command. He opened his fourth mouth and exhaled on Prithvi. And out came buds and seeds and insects of all shapes and sizes. The whole earth was covered with them. They were everywhere, on land and in the waters, small and big and medium-sized, some with four legs, others with thousands, some with wings, others with tails. They all ate and drank and slept and copulated and made the females pregnant. Soon new life forms were seen, crawling, and squalling.

Lakshmi was thrilled. What fun it was! She never tired of watching them. One day Bhagvan said, These days your hands don't press my feet as well as before. Lakshmi chuckled and said, These insects, some of their antics are such that I forget myself watching them ..."

Savaji winked hugely at Bhagatbapa, who responded with a weak smile.

"Many years passed. The creatures enjoyed themselves on earth and in devalok, Lakshmi derived great pleasure watching them. But, Lakshmi began getting bored again. Once it had been fun to watch a buffalo being hunted or a sparrow trying to catch an insect. But, all this happened on its own, repetitively.

One day she was deep in thought. Bhagvan, unable to see her quiet asked, Is anything wrong? Why are you so preoccupied these days?

She replied, There are many things on my mind, but how do I tell you? You will get needlessly angry.

Bhagvan said, Have I ever been angry with you? Please tell me.

Lakshmi said, I want you to bring some more novelty on earth.

Bhagvan said, There are eighty four lakh creatures out there who lead individual lives, enjoy themselves differently from one another.

Lakshmi said, I agree, but all the creatures are speechless and predictable, can't we have more complex creatures?

Bhagvan touched his navel with a finger. Nothing happened! He caressed his navel again, but no sign of Brahma! He rubbed his navel vigorously. Brahma finally appeared, looking weary and tired. Bhagvan said, Can something new be done on earth. Brahma said, I can't do a thing now. I have only four mouths, I have blown wind from all four and created the earth and the creatures. Now my navel is cleaned out. Bhagvan said, But I have already given my word to the goddess, what of that? Brahma replied, Only I can make changes on the earth and now I am powerless. There is no strength left in me. But Bhagvan pleaded with him to come up with something.

Brahma scratched his head. He thought for a while and said, Let's ask Hanuman. He has lots of strength.

But does this thing require strength or brains, asked Bhagvan.

Brahma replied, First we require strength. For whatever has to be done now can be done only by using what exists. We need to inhale all the air from the earth, and, with that, all the creatures will also be inhaled. Only then can we turn them into something new.

Bhagwan agreed and Brahma flew off in search of Hanuman.

Hanuman was sleeping on a tree. Brahma said to him, Aei, you lazy creature, we have work for you.

Hanuman jumped down and stood attentively with folded hands as Brahma explained what the Bhagvan wanted.

How many such creatures do you want? asked Hanuman.

Brahma thought for a brief while, then gave Hanuman a mala, saying, One for each bead, and promptly fell asleep under the tree.

Hanuman started in right earnest and was shaping two legged creatures, your human beings!"

Everyone was wide-eyed. Savaji spoke as if he had been witness to the entire process of creation with Bhagatbapa beside him saying

Hanh, Hanh! right through, with great incredulity.

Savaji, quite forgetting Natha's wife, continued his story with great relish.

"As you know," he said, "Hanuman is not known to worry about the finer details. In a short while, all the beads were done. And Hanuman nudged Brahma awake, Prabhu wake up! Everything is ready in accordance with your wishes.

Brahma woke up and saw rows upon rows of human beings. Then Brahma suddenly stopped short. You have forgotten the main thing. It's not your line of work, so I can't blame you. But you've forgotten to make the sticks and the holes. How will they procreate without them? Once that's done, push them down on to Prithvi once again.

Saying this Brahma went off to sleep once more. And Hanuman set to work once more till finally, satisfied with his work, he came to Brahma, wiping his hands, saying, Prabhu, it's done. Here is your mala.

Brahma took the mala asking, Did you divide the sticks and the holes equally?

Hanuman said, Most certainly.

So you did leave out the single large bead on top?

Hanuman scratched his head. You didn't ask me to, he said.

Oh no, groaned Brahma, that was the odd bead. Now one bead is without a partner. And the bead that got left out will be neither male nor female. It will have to become a vantari and roam the earth."

Savaji brought the tale to an end. His finger stopped trembling. He gulped some water. Bhagatbapa shivered. Some others, who had forgotten about their bidis, took a hurried puff.

Savaji turned to his assistant. "Get some tea. Then we will deal with her. We also have to go to the smashan."

The tea arrived. Savaji downed it in one long gulp then leaned against the wall, as if it was up to the padhiyars to manage the rest of the affair.

The ravalia took his drum. He lit a fire in the centre of the room and put some guggul in it. Bhagatbapa inched closer to me. I asked him, "Bapa, what will they do now?"

"They will ask the vantari, who the bhadvo was. Once she speaks, and reveals the name of that miserable pimp, they will take the vantari out of the woman and leave her at the smashan," explained Bapa.

"Leave who at the smashan?" I asked.

"The vantari, of course."

I looked out of the window. It was still quite a while before dawn. The night was silent and awfully dark. I didn't have the guts to go out.

"Put some grains before her," Savaji was ordering, still chuffing at his bidi. "She will now throw the grains in the direction of her bhadva. Or we'll give her some more lashings with the chain." He turned to the raval, "Invoke Savand, their family deity."

The assistants of Savaji picked up the beat on their drums and the zanj. They untied their hair. One of them started to sing, "Oh Ma, I invoke you, Ma please respond, come Mother." He chanted this a few times and one of the bhuvas shrieked. Everyone present said, "Khamma ... Khamma ..."

One bhuva picked up the chain, and Natha's wife began to tremble. "Pick up the grains, or else we will skin you ..." The bhuva raised the chain to strike her and Natha's wife immediately scooped them up.

In that instant I lost my mind. I shot up, leapt from the veranda to the courtyard, and ran for the door. Just before I stepped out, I turned.

Natha's wife was flinging the grains at the door ...

ROSCHEN SASIKUMAR

SUMMER ON THE ISLAND

NOMINATED BY PANKAJ MISHRA

The summer vacation has begun. Everyone has gone home except Lissy and me. Lissy's brother has chicken pox and her mother does not want her home at this time. I, of course, have nowhere to go. My aunt certainly does not want me to go to her and I prefer to stay at the Home than to be the constant target of her nasty remarks. Moreover, Sister Maria will be here.

Usually the other girls pity me when they go home for vacation. But this time some were actually jealous that I could be with Sister Maria. I asked her why she didn't want to go to the Mother House like the other Sisters. She said, "It is much more fun to be with you here, Uma." But I have a feeling she is sad about something. Before she came here she was studying in Trivandrum, even now she is studying for something called PHD. Sometimes we see her writing all kinds of funny things, lines and lines of numbers and English letters mixed up on big sheets of paper – this is for her PHD. We ask her what she is writing and she says, "This is a kind of maths that you will learn in higher classes." She hadn't finished her studies when Mother Agnes brought her over here and she continues to work at it when she gets the time.

Our Home is on an island that is flanked by a river on one side and a lagoon on the other. The whole island is crisscrossed by canals. Coconut trees grow in every nook and corner. Our Home is a white washed bungalow with blue painted windows and a veranda all around. From our veranda we can watch the boats peacefully floating on the river. Sister Maria says it is the most beautiful place on earth. She has lived only in cities until now. She grew up in a big two-storeyed house. We visited her house when we went on an excursion to Trivandrum. Her parents still live there. We liked her bathroom the best – there is a chain that one can just pull and water comes rushing into the toilet bowl. We talked about it for days – she must have been very rich. We are all poor. Most of the girls have mothers, but no father. I am the only one with no father or mother. Each of us has a sponsor in Germany who pays money to the Home for all our expenses until we are eighteen.

I was born on this island. So I can show Sister Maria around. I run and skip ahead while Lissy and Sister Maria walk slowly behind. Sister Maria has problems walking over the single-log bridges across the canals. I run across them while she has to first imagine that she is Peter walking on water looking at Christ. We sit on the banks and watch the boats loading sand from the river. The water becomes orange as the evening deepens. Sometimes we stop by my aunt's house and talk to her. She lives in a thatched hut amidst the coconut trees. There are always big heaps of coconut fibre in front of her yard and she makes ropes along with the neighbouring women. She is very nice to me in front of Sister Maria. "Uma does not want any of us now that she has you," she says to Sister Maria smiling with all her red stained teeth. The last time I stayed with her she was always cursing her fate that she had to put up with "that mad man's child" in addition to all her other burdens. And she would spit out the red betel juice with a loud "thoo!"

My father had been a boatman. When I was about two years old, he went mad and killed my mother and then hanged himself. When I told Sister Maria about this, she held my hand tight and asked, "How do you know this? Who told you?" "Everybody," I said and she looked angry. I think she likes me very much. She hugs me often and lets me sit on her lap. In all these ten years, I can't remember any one else ever hugging me (though sometimes there is that vague hazy sensation of warmth from a time long ago, another life, soft arms with glass bangles pressing into me ... a sensation which is immediately blotted out by an unnamed dread).

Sister Maria seems to love all of us. The new girl, Daisamma, used to get up in the early hours of the morning and cry loudly until Sister Maria came and carried her into her room to comfort her. Daisamma got to like Sister Maria's pampering so much that she made it a daily practice. She even took to going to bed early so that she could get up early and cry! Only our merciless teasing broke the habit. The other sisters are not big huggers like Sister Maria. "Children need touching," says Sister Maria.

Sometimes I wish Sister Maria liked only me. I can't help feeling that she does like me specially. Anyway now I am glad I have her almost to myself for two months. But she does look a little preoccupied sometimes and sits in her room for hours writing long letters. When I pester her for stories she sometimes tells me to go away. But I like to sit there and look at her, sitting and writing, with her long plait thrown over one shoulder. She keeps playing with her silver cross when she is thinking.

Good Friday and a long boring church service. Before Sister Maria came, I could not have dared to say church was boring, even to myself. Unlike Bindu P G who is not afraid of anything or anyone. She always grumbled about the church, and once someone carried tales to Sister Maria. "Sister, you know this Bindu P G, she says that Church is boring!" And Sister Maria laughed! She said, "Really? To tell you the truth, I feel the same sometimes." We were stunned! If it had been Sister Joyce or Sister Molly, Bindu P G would have got a real long lecture on the dire consequences of irreverence – not that Bindu P G would have minded; she challenges even God and dares Him to smite her down. Sister Maria calls her Doubting Thomas and she calls me Vazhakali. I know that everyone thinks I am bad-tempered and quarrelsome – but when *she* calls me Vazhakali ... it does not seem as if she thinks I am a terrible person, only that I am a silly stupid girl. Since Sister Maria came I don't get into trouble as much as before. She usually laughs me out of my bad moods.

At dinner Sister Maria declares, "I happen to know that on Easter Day our hens are going to lay coloured eggs. Make sure that you pick them up first thing in the morning!"

Of course, we scoff at the idea – one of Sister Maria's wild tales. She is always telling us these tales – how she can do magic, how she turns herself into a bird at night and flies around, how she once went to the moon, how the dolls in the play room come alive at night and talk to her ... We always make it a point to scoff at her tales, then she makes up more and more stories and the wilder they get, the more fun it is. I know that some of the younger girls half believe her tales, but they follow the rest of us and try to make objections.

Once we were all below the mango tree looking up at the mangoes and hoping for a wind to blow one down and Sheelamma ran to Sister Maria and begged, "Sister Maria, please do some magic and bring a mango down." Sister Maria came and stood under the tree and dramatically raised her hands and turned round and round in circles chanting magic words, "Om hreem haim ... mango fall, mango fall, FALL ..." and, at that moment a wind blew and a mango fell down. What fun! But Sister Maria looked most surprised when we begged her again and absolutely refused to repeat the feat. "No, no, magic should not be repeated often," she said.

Anyway I don't believe that she can manipulate hens to lay coloured eggs. Not just coloured, but spotted too, she says!

Easter Sunday. We go to church early in the morning – Sister Maria, Lissy and me. The sermon is not as long as usual. We gather the yellow and red flowers under the tree on the church compound. For breakfast we have appam and stew. And then Sister Maria says, "Girls, did you look for coloured eggs in the hen house?"

"Of course not," I say, "we are not such fools."

"Come on, why don't you go and see?"

She persuades and persuades till finally, willy-nilly, we go to the hen house and look ... the eggs *are* coloured, one blue with yellow spots and the other red with green spots! We squeal and yell and run back shouting. Sister Maria looks smug. "Look, a little of the colour has come off on my hands," says Lissy.

"The egg must be warm since the hen has just laid it."

Lissy and I talk about what the girls would say when they hear our story. "We have to keep them safe, otherwise they will never believe us," we tell ourselves. We call Johnny over the fence to show him our miracle.

"Nonsense, it was not the hens – it must have been your Sister Maria," says Johnny's mother, "She must have painted those eggs herself."

We are furious. We storm back and ask Sister Maria if what Johnny's mother said is true.

"Well ..." she says. She rolls her eyes and smiles mischievously. This Sister Maria! She is always playing tricks on us! We pummel her with our fists. Later she shows us pictures of how in Germany people make coloured eggs for Easter. And the pictures of the Easter Bunnies and chocolate eggs make our mouths water. I wish one of our sponsors would send us chocolate eggs.

Mother Agnes has come from Kottayam. We all like the Mother. She is short and plump and has the serene face of a Madonna. She is the one who brought Sister Maria here. Mother knew her when she was in Trivandrum and they are very close, but now there seems to be something wrong. She sits on the steps and watches while Sister Maria plays Jhansi Rani with us.

The Rani of Jhansi orders that all kinds of crazy things be brought to her and the team that brings it to her first gets a reward. Of course now the teams are just Lissy and me. Sister Maria makes a big drama of being the Rani. She walks around majestically and does not give us a clue to what she is going to demand next. "The Rani of Jhansi wants a ... wants a ... WANTS A ..." We wait in suspense ready to run. "A BLUE AND YELLOW FEATHER!"

We squeal and start running. It takes a while to find this. When we return, Sister Maria and Mother are talking seriously.

"You are so good with them. They love you so much. How can you ..."

Mother stops abruptly when we arrive on the scene. They talk late into the night. I can hear arguments. "You are acting against God's will. You are meant for higher things ... You are hurting everybody ..."

Sister Maria's voice is raised in a way I have never heard.

"I said I will think and pray about it for a year. I will submit myself to God's will. I am doing it. Let me be.

"Mother, other people need not understand me, but you ..."

I bury my head in my pillow. A year? Is Sister Maria here only for a year? It's already six months since she came.

The girls are back. The Easter eggs story is a great success – we have to repeat it all the time. We could not keep the eggs because they became stale. But we keep the shells.

Sister Maria, has made new rules. Nobody should go to school without a pencil. If you have lost your pencil you have to go to Sister Maria, get a beating and then get a new pencil. And Sister Maria's beatings are hilarious! I suspect she introduced the beating part to satisfy Sister Joyce who feels that our tendency to lose things must be curbed. "But then, they should not go to school without pencils," Sister Maria said when she found out that many of us go without a pencil for days because we are afraid to ask for a new pencil. And now, "Oh God, I am late for school. Sister Maria, please give me a beating quickly and give me a new pencil" has become a usual yell in the mornings these days. If we crowd around her in her room and she wants us to clear out and leave her alone. She would shout "Everybody out!" and then start counting. We all have to be out before she says Ten. We push and scream as we run out. Bindu P G asks her what would happen if we stay where we are. Sister Maria says, "You could try and see." But even Bindu P G has not yet tried. By the time Sister Maria reaches nine, Bindu P G slowly walks out.

There are days when the dark cloud settles over me. I mope around with a sour face. "Uma has got the devil in her again," says Sister Molly. I snap at everyone and pinch Minikutty. Minikutty runs to Sister Maria crying. I wait mutinously.

"You are in for it," says Bindu P G, "You know what Sister Maria feels about bullying."

I don't care. I hate Sister Maria too. Sister Maria does not come out of her room. She puts Minikutty on her lap and continues her writing. I am disappointed. I want her to scold and punish me like Sister Joyce did last time. Then I can hate her more.

But Sister Maria ignores me. I wander around aimlessly sunk in my darkness when "Hoi, there!" she calls me from her window. "What a horrible face you are making!" she rolls her eyes and makes a face. "Come up here!"

I feel suddenly lighter, but I keep my long face and drag my feet to her room. "Bow!" I jump out of my skin when she pounces on me from behind the door. She lifts me up and swings me round and round till I am breathless. "That will teach you not to bully little girls," she says as I plead for her to stop. Soon I am sitting with my head on her lap. And telling her about my recurring nightmare.

But later when I'm in bed I remember, Only four months more.. after that?

Sophy has got a new doll from her sponsor in Germany. A big, beautiful one. Sister Maria has got a big glass shelf made for keeping all the toys. They used to be dumped in cardboard boxes before and we never got them for playing. Now we have play times when we can choose what we want from the shelf. We have better toys than even the rich kids in our school because our toys are from Germany. There are some sponsors who are always sending presents (like Sophy's) and some sponsors who just send the money to the Home and don't even write (like mine). So the ones who get presents should share, Sister Maria says. The real owner of the toy gets a little preference over the others.

Once a month we have to write letters to our sponsors. We get nice white sheets on which Sister Joyce draws lines with pencil. We usually write the same things – I am fine. Hope you are fine. I pray for you everyday ... Sometimes we draw a picture on it, usually a cross. Sister Maria says these are the most boring letters she has ever seen and that it is a pain to translate them. "Why don't you write real letters, tell your sponsor what you are doing, feeling ..." I don't think my sponsor reads my letters. I have his photograph. He has white hair – but Sister Maria says he is not old, Germans often have white or pale yellow hair. I wonder what he thinks of my photograph. I have a scowl on my face. Maybe that's why he doesn't like me. Sophy's sponsor is visiting her next year.

We all get nice new dresses. Not the same dull uniforms as it used to be – we chose the materials ourselves. Sister Maria took us to Quilon for that. Another real nice day. My dresses are pink and yellow and both have bows on them. Sister Joyce says Sister Maria is spoiling us. "You are taking them above their station in life," she tells Sister Maria. "It is nice to see them happy and their sponsors are paying us for that," Sister Maria replies.

Even though Sister Maria is the youngest of the Sisters, she is the warden of our Home and the one who can decide. Everything about her is different, her light complexion, her long straight brownish hair smelling of shampoo, her slow drawling walk, the way she talks with lots of English words coming in between the Malayalam words ... Sister Joyce is the oldest, she is short and dark and kind in her way, but she is always giving us sermons and telling us that we should always be grateful for the good fortune of coming to this Home. I don't like the thin-lipped Sister Molly, she is often bad tempered. We don't get to see much of Sister Beatrice and Sister Mamy, they are in charge of the kitchen. The other Sisters talk about Sister Maria a lot – they laugh about her "crazy" ways, but concede that she does not put on superior airs. But these days they are whispering something about her and stop when we go by, something about Sister Maria wanting to leave the sisterhood. Something about a Hindu boy in Trivandrum. "Unbelievable ... seems so dedicated ... how can she?" I see Sister Maria in a red saree with a big red pottu on her forehead. A man walking with her; a child in her arms ... her bangles pressing its skin. Her own child. Something rises up from the pit of my stomach.

I want to run away to some place where there are no people.

There is going to be an exhibition at Bangalore where everyone from all the Boarding Homes is going to participate. Sister Maria is making us do all kinds of things – she has brought a book of ideas from a library in Trivandrum. She goes around with her camera taking photos of us playing, working, eating ... she hides behind doors and windows and snaps us unawares. There is a picture of me sulking under the mango tree. We stick the photographs on a big white cardboard and Sister Maria writes funny captions under each picture. She writes in English because the people who come for the exhibition may not know Malayalam. She will take one girl from here with her. Probably Jessy or Sheeja. She will never take me because I am not good at anything. Jessie can sing and dance and she is clever. How nice it would be to go by train with Sister Maria to Bangalore.

It is boring for everyone without Sister Maria. The girls are always talking about her – "If Sister Maria were here, she would be ..." "Nothing seems much fun without Sister Maria." I don't join in these conversations. But for me, it is an effort even to open my eyes in the morning – the day seems so dreary.

"You are going around like a drooping plant, Uma," says Sister Joyce. "We are all here, don't you like us?"

She doesn't understand. Sister Maria loves me. I think of how she sometimes carries me on her back holding my arms around her neck. "You are a featherweight, Uma," she says, "You could be just four years old!"

"But look at her face, her face is old," says Sister Molly.

Sister Maria looks quickly at me to see if I have heard. She pinches my chin and smiles conspiratorially. I feel I belong to her.

I have the nightmare again. I am again looking up at the hanging feet. The Dread is there. Sister Maria takes my hand. "Come, let's go for a walk." I skip away holding her hand. We come to a single-log bridge. "Uma, hold my hand when I walk on the bridge," she says. But I laugh and run across. "Uma!" she cries out from behind me. I look back and see her falling into the canal. I run back and look down. She is not there. I scream and call out. Nobody comes. I scream until I cannot breathe anymore. I wake up gasping. And I cry myself to sleep.

Jessy and Sister Maria are back. Our Home got a prize for the most original exhibits. Jessy has not stopped talking about it. She thinks she is someone very special now. When I said so to Sister Maria she just said, "You are just being jealous – don't be." I do not tell Sister Maria what Jessie is whispering about the bearded young man who came to the station to see them off. About how he looked intently at Sister Maria through the window as the train was pulling out of the station and said, "Your Kurukshetra is beginning. Be strong." And how Sister Maria sat absolutely still for a long long time ...

Sister Maria is more and more preoccupied. She sits alone on the steps lost in thought. If I go near her she puts her arm around me, but does not talk much. I try to provoke her into one of her wild stories. "Is Sophy's doll visiting you at night? Has she come alive too?" She smiles and says, "Ha, wouldn't you like to know ..." and she slips back into her reverie. Then she suddenly starts up and says, "Call the others, let's play!" and for the next half hour we are running and laughing and yelling. But there is something different about Sister Maria. She is laughing a little too much. When we are tired and panting, we sit on the steps around her.

"Sister," Jessie says, "Will you be with us always?" Sister Maria does not say anything for quite some time. I want to get up and walk off. I don't want to hear her answer. But I sit riveted.

"But none of you will be here always, will you?" says Sister Maria finally. "Next year all you fifth standard girls will go to the senior Boarding Home and the year after that, the fourth standard girls ... Nobody is here forever."

We sit silent looking at the sun set. When the last rays of light have disappeared, she says, "Don't you remember the song that I taught you. There's a season for everything under the sun ..." And she starts humming it softly.

"There's a season for everything under the sun,
A time to do and a time to be done,
A time to laugh, a time to cry,
A time to meet, and a time to part,
A time to live,
And a time to die"

Some of the girls are humming along with her. I feel a painful lump inside my throat, I cannot sing.

Mother is here again. The air is thick with tension. They argue throughout the night.

"I have to follow what I believe is God's will for me."

"You should be ashamed of yourself making God the justification for your selfishness."

"There is nothing specially selfish about marriage and nothing specially unselfish about being a nun."

"To leave your religion ... how can you be so disloyal?"

"My religion is in my heart. It is not something external that I can leave."

"Your intellect is your downfall."

Mother looks tired and worn out when we assemble for morning worship. She opens the Bible and then closes it again. She beckons to Sister Maria to take the Bible. Sister Maria looks steadily at her for a moment and then opens the Book of Job:

"My thoughts today are resentful, for God's hand is heavy on me in my trouble.
If only I knew how to find him, how to enter his court,
I would state my case before him and set out my arguments in full;
Then I should learn what answer he would give

And find out what he has to say.
Would he exert his great power to browbeat me?
No; God himself would never bring a charge against me ...
My feet have kept to the path he has set me,
I have followed his way and not turned from it
I do not ignore the commands that come from his lips,
I have stored in my heart what he says,
He decides, and who can turn him from his purpose?
He does what his own heart desires,
What he determines, he carries out;
His mind is full of plans like this ...
God forbid that I should allow you to be right,
Till death, I will not abandon my claim to innocence.
I will maintain the rightness of my cause,
I will never give up;
As long as I live I will not change."

There is a stunned silence in the room. Then Sister Joyce motions to Jessie to start the singing. We are relieved when the prayers are over.

The Sisters are not whispering any more.

"She has decided to leave. My God, how can she ..."

"I thought all along that God would save her from the temptation."

"Too much education is bad. Mother should not have allowed her."

They don't care now if we hear. We have to know anyway. We huddle together in corners and watch, too scared to talk. Sister Maria's face is swollen with crying. She does not even look in our direction; maybe she does not want us to see she has been crying. Maybe she is afraid that she may change her mind if she looks at us. Maybe she has forgotten all about us. She has decided to leave us. Her face reminds me of something, some memory long buried, something that chills me to my bones ... there is despair and determination on her face. I keep away from her.

I get up in the middle of the night for a drink of water. Sister Maria is in the dining room looking out of the window with her face pressed to the bars. She turns around and sees me. I remain at the door. She holds out her hand. I go to her slowly. "I am sorry, Uma," she whispers, drawing me close, "I am really sorry." Her voice breaks. I lean my head on her arm. Still, you are leaving, I think. But I don't say anything.

Sister Maria left today. It is raining on the island. The summer is over.

MOHAMMAD KHADEER BABU

ZAMEEN

TRANSLATED BY PRANAVA MANJARI N
NOMINATED BY AMARENDRA DASARI

First published in Telugu as "Zameen" in *Andhra Jyothi*,
September 1998, Hyderabad

Listen, it's you I am talking to! I don't need rotis. There's no time," said Hussain, pulling a terrycot kurta over his head. Rehana, who had been hurriedly chopping onions and making rotis, looked up at her husband, bewildered. Irked by his stubbornness, she washed her hands in the basin, and got up from the stove.

"Who can tell this man anything? In any case, he is carrying the chobapuri basket with him ... will it hurt his lordship's bones to carry a few more rotis in it? Won't he feel hungry on the way?" As she could not say all this to her husband directly, she spoke looking at her son.

The son didn't look up at all. He sat brushing his teeth, facing the door. As for the daughter-in-law, busy washing the dishes in the backyard, she pretended not to have heard a word.

Neither of the two had the wherewithal to argue with Hussain. For that matter, even after all these years of being married to him, nor had Rehana.

Rehana pursed her lips and looked with frustration at her husband. He was looking into the mirror on the wooden cupboard to make sure his hair was in place, then he threw a glance in his wife's direction to indicate that he was leaving.

Rehana continued to stand near the kitchen door, watching him. It seemed as if her entire being was pleading with him to say yes to the rotis. At the same time she was afraid Hussain would kick up a ruckus if she insisted. Hussain would not have relented normally but this time he was embarking on an auspicious journey. Why hurt her feelings? The expression on Rehana's face brought a smile to his.

"Don't look so woebegone. Give me the rotis. I will take them," said Hussain with a smile that did not quite reach his eyes.

Brightening immediately, Rehana quickly packed the rotis and thrust them into the wire basket Hussain was carrying.

"Take care now, convey my regards to Brahmaiah and Seethammavadina. And try to get a good bargain for the land," she said, walking behind him till the door.

It was already time for the train. Hussain quickened his pace fearing that he would be late. His new lungi chaffed against his legs as his steps fell into a hurried trot.

The train had just pulled into the station when Hussain arrived. It would be one thirty in the afternoon by the time he reached Kaavali from Chiraala, and that too, provided the signals came down on time.

Hussain rushed to the counter to buy his ticket and then occupied his seat. It was only after he had settled down with the chobapuri basket in his lap that he relaxed, not worried now about when the train would start.

To think that he was going to meet his friend Brahmaiah after all this while! More than the prospect of buying land in Kaavali and building his own house, the thought that he would be meeting his childhood friend suffused him with joy. It had been four years since Hussain had last visited Kaavali for Brahmaiah's daughter's wedding. But Brahmaiah was so caught up in last minute preparations that Hussain didn't get a chance to really talk to him, then or later. Hussain had stayed on till after the wedding feast and returned home with a heavy heart.

And now, he was making another visit to Kaavali!

Brahmaiah and Hussain were born in Kaavali. They grew up together, and studied in the same zilla parishad school. Brahmaiah was from Maalapalem. Hussain hailed from Kasaabgalli. Perhaps, because of the proximity of the localities to each other, there was a running feud between them, with violent incidents occurring on a daily basis. That a Kasaabgalli girl had been teased by a Maalapalem youth became the cause for heads to roll one day, while on another there would be bloodshed because a Maalapalem boy had been harassed by a Kasaabgalli boy. The local hoodlums lived off the hostility between the two localities, some diehards even drinking the blood of donkeys, in the hope of enhancing their fighting abilities. Then, fights were instigated to digest it. But all this never came in the way of Brahmaiah and Hussain's friendship.

"Don't you make friends with that pariah," Hussain's mother scolded him every day. Blithely unmindful of her advice, Hussain and Brahmaiah spent their time swimming in the well near their school. They went to Ayapureddy's tank to catch fish. Every evening, Brahmaiah would pick up his books and go to Hussain's house. Brahmaiah had only a kerosene lamp in his house, while Hussain's house boasted an electric bulb. Although Hussain's mother grumbled, both studied under its light. And as they grew up, there was no end to the hours spent aimlessly hanging out, or to the countless toddy drinking sessions in the palm groves of Tallapalem.

Hussain does not remember what Brahmaiah's father did for a living. Brahmaiah, however, remembers even today, what Hussain's father did for his. He was a butcher!

Brahmaiah would watch in wide-eyed wonder when Hussain's father brought out a joint of a lamb dipped in water and chopped it deftly into smaller pieces. The look on Brahmaiah's face seemed to convey that he would give his life to be allowed to wield that knife. Whenever Hussain's father left the shop for Hussain to mind, Brahmaiah would indulge this desire and hack away on the empty cutting block.

One day, while Hussain's father was chopping meat, he collapsed on the cutting block and died. The neighbours said it was a heart attack; fellow butchers claimed it was drink.

Whether or not there was enough to eat, Hussain's house had always been cheerful, full of smiling, radiant faces. With his father gone, the house acquired a desolate look. Shock and grief reduced his mother to a bedridden state.

In those difficult times, Brahmaiah's mother, Raavamma, provided the warmth and tender care of a mother to Hussain. She fed him thrice daily, gave him money for snacks, and murmured many words of comfort and courage. In short, noble soul that she was, she cared for him more than she did for her own son.

As for Brahmaiah, he guarded Hussain like a shadow, shielding him from fear and misery.

A few days later, Hussain's father's brother arrived from Chiraala. He was a petty cloth merchant, who went from door to door, hauling along his bundle of dhotis and bedspreads. He could barely look after his own family. To shoulder the responsibility of his vadina and Hussain was clearly beyond him but, moved by his vadina's plight, he nevertheless resolved to take them to Chiraala.

When Hussain learnt about his chinnaayana's plans, he protested, sobbing inconsolably. He fell on his knees and pleaded to be left in Kasaabgalli with his Brahmaiah. His chinnaayana had to tie him with a rope, and force him into the bus. When the bus began to pull out, Hussain bade a tearful goodbye to Brahmaiah between huge, uncontrollable hiccups.

Hussain's studies came to an abrupt end in Chiraala. He did various odd jobs like welding, and electrical work – even carrying the bundle of dhotis and bedspreads, and following his chinnaayana around the town for a bit. For some time he worked as a butcher, and finally settled down to become a mechanic.

Wherever he was, whatever he did, Hussain never forgot Brahmaiah. He wrote to him regularly. Brahmaiah, too, made friends in school and college, but nobody could replace Hussain or lay claim to the special place that his friend held in his heart.

When Brahmaiah landed a job as a railway guard after completing his BA, he took Hussain with him to Hyderabad on a goods train. On that unforgettable moonlit night, when the two friends sat in the guard's cabin, drinking and reminiscing about their childhood days, even the train fell silent and listened.

Hussain married Rehana and continued to live in Chiraala. Brahmaiah married Seethamma, was transferred from place to place, and finally came back to Kaavali. He built a house in Satram, a suburb of Kaavali with the money he received when he took voluntary retirement, coupled with the money he had saved up over the years. His daughter was given in marriage into a prosperous family. Hussain vaguely remembered Brahmaiah telling him about his son in a letter. Ramana either had a job or was looking for one.

Ever since Brahmaiah had settled down in Kaavali, Hussain too yearned to get back there. The secret wish that had lain buried in his heart all these years, was about to be realized now. He had set out to make real his dream of settling down in Kaavali one day.

Hussain had saved up some money after his son started earning and now he added to this the entire dowry he had received at his son's wedding. If need be, he was prepared to take a loan of five or ten thousand rupees.

Hussain's son was not in favour of settling down in Kaavali. He liked Chiraala. Moreover, his in-laws lived there. "We will remain here. You go to Kaavali if you want. We could visit each other often," the son said.

As if waiting for these words, Hussain started writing to Brahmaiah, asking him to find a plot of land for him in Kaavali. He hoped to build a hut or a tin shed on a plot of land, and spend whatever remained of his life, in his birthplace. Brahmaiah matched Hussain's urgency with an expeditious and prompt response.

"I have found a place ... Come over," he wrote.

When he received this postcard from Brahmaiah, Hussain was as excited as a child. All those years of namaaz had borne fruit, he thought.

"Chiraala is not our town. We will go back to where we belong. We will go to my native town. Now I have no more worries. I too will build my home in the town where my father died," said Hussain, clasping Rehana's hands and swinging them in his excitement.

He posted a card to Brahmaiah, informing him that he was coming, and set out that very day.

Only if the train reaches on time, will I be able to finish my work satisfactorily, he thought as he sat in the train. But the train that had raced swiftly after crossing Ongole, made a half hour stop at Singarayakonda. It was one o'clock already. Hussain was feeling very hungry. Knowing it was useless waiting for the train to start, he devoured the rice rotis he had made such a fuss about in the morning, and washed down the hearty meal with lots of water.

The train chugged along once again. By the time it reached Kaavali, it was two o'clock in the afternoon. Brahmaiah was waiting in the blazing heat of the sun to receive him.

Brahmaiah spotted Hussain even as he was getting off the train. Calling out loudly to him, he ran to Hussain and enclosed him in a warm embrace. Hussain's heart overflowed with joy at the sight of his friend.

"I did not think you would come to the station," said Hussain, holding Brahmaiah tightly.

"How could I not when you were coming?" said Brahmaiah, laughing.

"Where shall we go first? To your house or to the site?"

"We will go home first. I will take you to the site in the evening," said Brahmaiah, kick-starting his scooter.

Brahmaiah's house was located on the outskirts of Satram, some distance west of Kaavali. It was a proper house, made of brick and concrete.

Seethamma walked up to the gate on hearing the scooter approach. "Come, come, Hussain anna, how are you?" she said, welcoming him with a smile. Hussain smiled back, "How are you?" he enquired, handing her the chobapuri basket. "These are chobapuris. Rehana grated coconut all of yesterday to make them. You know how fond Brahmaiah is of them."

Ramana, who was sitting in the veranda rose abruptly and walked out in a huff when he saw Hussain. Not a word was exchanged. Not even a smile.

All that Hussain could do was stare in surprise.

"Wasn't that our Ramana? What is the matter with him?" asked Hussain, recovering a little. Seethamma was about to say something when Brahmaiah intervened, "It's nothing new with that scoundrel. You come in," he said to Hussain.

Declining lunch, for he was not feeling hungry, Hussain got

talking to Brahmaiah. In no time, it was evening.

After tea, the two friends started for the site.

The site was on the other side of Satram from Brahmaiah's house. It was a small plot of six ankanas, surrounded by green tamarind trees. A little beyond were the chilla trees. "The rates are rather high in the town. You won't be able to afford it. Moreover, this way, you will be closer to me," said Brahmaiah, walking around the plot.

Hussain looked around unbelievingly. For years he had dreamed of this! His eyes grew misty.

"How much does it cost? Will I be able to afford it?" he asked anxiously.

"Don't you worry on that count. The owner is a good man. He will accept gratefully whatever you pay," said Brahmaiah.

"Then let us go and talk it over," said Hussain, not wanting to delay things further.

"Go where? I am the owner," Brahmaiah laughed, patting Hussain on the shoulder.

Hussain was nonplussed. At the same time, overwhelmed with gratitude for his friend, he hugged him. "You never told me you had a site as well," he said, laughing happily.

The moon was just a thin line in the sky. Looking at it, it was difficult to ascertain whether it was the onset of the new moon or the end of the full moon. Gusts of wind blew in from the fields. Somewhere in the distance, dogs barked intermittently. Seethamma was busy cooking pedda koora in the kitchen while the two friends sat nursing their drinks on the terrace. The conversation rolled on, but the ease and liveliness of the earlier hours was missing. Both seemed a little lost in their own thoughts. The conversation was interspersed with pregnant silences till Hussain brought up the issue that had been weighing on his mind.

"Where is your son? No sign of him at all," broached Hussain, gently.

Ramana's behaviour had hurt him greatly. Was this the same Ramana who had laughed happily as a child when Hussain carried him and played with him? The same Ramana who called him Hussain Mama and tightly clasped his legs? Hussain was tormented by these thoughts.

Brahmaiah had anticipated the question. His face fell at the mention of his son.

"You were witness this afternoon to his rudeness and arrogance. He is beyond my control. I have given up on him," he said sadly. "We have tried talking to him but to no avail. He refuses to marry. He does not want to work. Talks about serving the nation."

Hussain could not see Brahmaiah's face clearly in the twilight.

"Hussain, it frightens me to see him. Every morning, he puts a vermilion mark on his forehead and strides out of the house with a stick in his hand. We have tried to dissuade him from it all, but he will not hear of it. He reads all kinds of books, mouths all kinds of rubbish ..."

Hussain listened puzzled.

"We lived in a certain town when he was doing his degree. He was a carefree youth till he contested the elections in his college. They drilled all sorts of rubbish into him and brainwashed him. Slowly, he has degenerated to this. I sought voluntary retirement and we moved in here hoping he would change his ways. But he has started his activities here too. In the town where we lived earlier, I visited the places he frequented, observing everything that he and those like him did. I even tried to reason with them. Not just my son, I know so many sons of my friends and acquaintances who are involved! And most of them are children of potters, dhobis, cowherds and maadigas ..."

Hussain's heart sank.

"Re, and do you know who they are wielding their sticks against? Against the likes of you, your wife, Kasaabgalli. What injustice is this!" lamented Brahmaiah, his voice choked with emotion.

Quite involuntarily, Hussain huddled himself closer, his legs pressing into each other.

"Hussain, let alone Ramana, even others are being pushed to wield sticks! People who have always lived amongst us are being lured into this ... in the name of idols and processions ... in the name of revenge."

Even as Brahmaiah was saying this, a commotion was heard from the street below.

Brahmaiah rose to his feet in a trice and strode across to the parapet. Hussain followed him.

Outside the gate, Ramana was kicking up a fuss. Seethamma was saying something in an effort to placate him. "There is nothing of that sort, Ramana. You come inside first. We'll talk tomorrow," she pleaded. There was another man standing next to Ramana.

"Seethamma, what is all the commotion about?" thundered Brahmaiah.

"You want to know? Come down, I'll tell you. With whose permission did you put up that site for sale? How dare you show the site? To a Muslim at that! Aren't you ashamed?" said Ramana, thrusting his chest out aggressively.

On hearing this, Brahmaiah did not even wait to look at Hussain. He stomped down the stairs and reached the gate.

"What nonsense, get into the house first!"

Ramana did not budge.

Brahmaiah turned to the other man. "Panthula, you may be the Sarpanch, but don't try any of your dirty tricks in my house. Leave now," he thundered.

"What have I done, Brahmaiah? I came here because your lad asked me to. He has been making a scene in the bazaar since evening. Is it true that you are selling the land to a butcher?" said the Sarpanch.

"Of course, he is a butcher. My father is selling the land to a fellow who slaughters animals. These fellows butcher animals first, then they'll target us," said Ramana.

Brahmaiah felt as if a thorn had pierced his heart.

"What do you mean by that? This is the town where Hussain was born and where he grew up. Is it only we who have a right to this place? Doesn't this place belong to Hussain also? I am going to sell that land to him." Brahmaiah was shouting by now. "I dare anyone to stop me."

"What right are you talking about? A non-Hindu has no native town anywhere here. He can't claim any rights here. First tell that old man to get out," bellowed Ramana, belligerently.

Brahmaiah lost his control. He punched Ramana hard in the chest. "Bastard! Get out. Go into the town and destroy yourself. Ruin lives. But never show yourself to me," he screamed, shaking uncontrollably.

Hussain, who was watching from the terrace all this while came rushing down the stairs to Brahmaiah, and held his hands.

"Re, Brahmaiah, let this quarrel end here. I don't want any land. Even if you sell it to me, I am not buying it. If I wanted to come to this town, it was only because I wished to die peacefully, secure in the knowledge that I would be buried in my native soil. I never meant to cause trouble. I will never be able to live here ..." Huge tears poured from his tired eyes.

"Hussaina, that land is yours. If it is not yours, it cannot be anybody else's. I am not going to sell it to anyone else. It can go to ruin. But don't let all this upset you. Listen to me. Stay here. With me ... re ... wait. At least have your food ... re ... Hussaina," Brahmaiah cried out in anguish.

But Hussain was not listening. He was already past the gate and into the thickening night that draped the house in a black shroud.

ꠖ

CHANDRA PRAKASH DEVAL

BLACK BUCKS IN THE BUS

TRANSLATED BY RASHMI CHATURVEDI
NOMINATED BY VIJAYADAN DETHA

First published in Rajasthani as "Bus Mein Rojh" in *Binjaro*, 1997, Rajasthan

On and on, from birth to death, a living being travels. He chooses the path he wishes to take and then abides by it. At times he deliberates long and hard, at times he just stumbles on to his desired path. It does not matter whether the man seen ensconced today in his comfortable chambers scoffs at the cremation ground, because without a doubt, if not today, then tomorrow, he too will reach that well-known, eternal destination. It seems simple, but it is only deceptively so. With ease or without, in whatever way, what is called life has to be carried to its culmination. It is exactly like taking a bus. Twisting, writhing, in luxury, in discomfort, whatever, it is the dream of every passenger to squeeze himself onto a bus.

And so was mine that day. The bus bound for Jodhpur arrived at its expected time – late as always. And what did I see but a bus packed to bursting. Of course, can anything be called a bus if it isn't overflowing with people? Perhaps the wheels of the bus refuse to turn unless they are weighed down completely. I thought of staying back to participate in the efforts of the next bus, but that would have meant waiting for an hour and a half. And to start out late means to arrive late. It was hardly as if I was going to my in-laws' house where I'd be feted and garlanded on arrival. I was on duty and was hoping to stay with a friend after getting to Jodhpur, and I was not keen to arrive at someone's house at an ungodly hour. So I plucked up courage and tried to burrow into the bus through a window. You want to know what courage has to do with it? You see, one can get ahead only when one can get on and that day I was willing to travel standing on one foot. If I wanted to save having to spend on a hotel, I had to board this very bus. Alas, we all know, to desire is one thing and to realize the desire quite another. (Every one tries to kill his or her desires – and so did I, but that's another matter altogether.)

"What, is Akha Teej forcing its way into winter?" I asked the conductor as I tried to negotiate my way. "It's not the wedding season and I have heard neither of a fair or a play being held, nor of any guru or sant visiting during the Chaumasa. Why all this crowd then?"

"You think *this* is a crowd?" the conductor retorted, "You haven't been anywhere, have you – to a court, a hospital, a cinema. You won't find space there to even set a toe."

"You have forgotten to mention one other place – liquor shops," I said, grinning.

"Yes," he said, "But if you really want to see numbers, do a round of the jails and the rail stations."

It was on the tip of my tongue to ask, I wonder why these poor politicians squander so much money to pull a crowd. I pulled out some tobacco from the pocket of my trousers and tossed it into my mouth and concentrated on being steady, balancing all my weight on one leg – like Angad.

Beawar took a long time coming as if the place had uprooted itself and was running ahead of the speeding bus. But speed is wasted on muffosil-bus speed – we soon caught up with speeding Beawar. Here the bus almost emptied and I effortlessly captured a seat, precious as the throne of heaven, and then set in it like curd. Ignoring my body's pleas for tea, I pushed my bag under the seat, stretched out and pulled a book from my bag – *Letter of an Unknown Lady*, by a loved contemporary of our times, Stephan Zweig. I started to read the book and became so engrossed in it that I did not notice when the bus set off again. I felt as if I neither existed in the bus nor in the space in which it was moving.

God knows how far away I was, peeking into an alien land. Strange clothes, never seen flora, unfamiliar hills, roads and unintelligible speech, but the expressions of love and affection were no different. Out there too the men breathed like us, ate, drank and slept as we do except, I told myself, except that the women of my land, trapped under the delicate veil of the ghunghat, can neither dream like the women there nor can they exchange places with them when awake.

Whatever the reason, this other world seemed so fascinatingly different from mine that I had no qualms surrendering myself to its labyrinthine streets and alleys. Perhaps, left on her own, even the girl in the novel wouldn't have cared to visit so many streets, but in Zwieg's story she had to do the author's bidding and dutifully went wherever he chose to take her.

The real journey was out there, thousands of miles away from where this bus moved, and I, sweetly oblivious of myself, wandered the streets of an unknown city. Which one of the two journeys was real? This one in which I was so deeply immersed or the other which I was trying to shut out of my mind? I could stop to ponder this only if Zweig would let go of my arm. I was so completely caught up in his tale, that the fine line between the two realities was beginning to blur. Perhaps, I thought, I am there in that space and time which existed much before I was born. I opened my mind to a whole new realm of possibilities and then, reluctantly, shutting my book, I bowed out of it to land back into the moving bus.

Were all the other passengers also back from their various peregrinations? I tried to find out.

The passenger sitting in the front seat was frowning, no doubt in deep discussion with his lawyer on whether he would be able to directly inherit the land given to his grandfather after independence. He seemed desperate to know if he had any share in the freedom earned by his predecessor ... Another appeared to be far away in his village, sitting under the old neem tree that leaned against the fence of his field that dipped into the big village pond, his heart bounding like a deer, following the mirage of property and possession ... One passenger was in his office and another at home The student sitting ahead of me was on campus, plucking a rose and shyly offering it to his lady-love ... The passenger sitting at the window seat, perhaps an oil-merchant, was deep into the art and craft of adulteration ... Where was the man from the desert with a turban and hoary beard? He was lost in the good old days of his childhood. In his vision there was water all around ... The young girl in the front seat was preoccupied with the hairstyle of her favourite film hero ... Vakil Saheb, suffocating in the blackness of his lawyer's black attire, was with the government doctor and public prosecutor, passionately and convincingly arguing the case of a homicidal maniac indicted for four murders. In seat numbers nine and ten sat two young men who were completely absorbed in each other. They had no idea how far they had reached. Both had started the journey as bachelors but one was no longer unmarried, even though no one in the bus had noticed him taking his pheras ... The couple on seat numbers twelve and thirteen were ostensibly together but the distance between them was so vast that even if the bus had travelled on forever it would not have been able to bridge that chasm ...

The conductor too was far away, in his village in Jalore district, running after black bucks that had broken into his fields and were ruining his crops. He had somehow managed to procure enough seeds and fertilizer, but had not been able to find a farmer and had to, poor absentee landlord he, sow the seeds himself. Trapped in this bus what could he do to guard his crop from being plundered by black bucks? He imagined the black bucks fleeing down the road as he looked out of the windscreen and in urgent anxiety said "hsht-hsht" aloud, to shoo them off. And then, still in his own world, still livid at the black bucks, he approached a passenger sitting on the floor and blurted out, "Arre rojda, where do you want to get off?"

Shocked by the abrupt and uncivil manner in which he was addressed, the passenger raged: "What did you say? I dare you to repeat it!"

"Dear brother, where do you want to get down," said the conductor quickly, "At the corner of Nimaz or in the village?" And as quickly he hurried down the aisle to the driver's cabin, pretending to get the bus stopped, chuckling sheepishly to himself.

The affronted passenger muttered on. "The poor and meek are like black bucks to these upstarts. How times have changed! You pay through your nose to travel and then you have to put up with such talk."

The babuji sitting next to him piped up. "Only a black buck

thinks others to be black bucks. What is so new about it."

"Men who lick away the earnings of others *are* only black bucks," the old woman said, seizing the chance to put in her bit.

This exchange was reason enough for everyone on the bus to get involved in the discussion. For the next ten minutes the entire bus was abuzz with the saga of the black buck. What is its colour? How many legs does it have? Does it belong to the family of the cow? Is it a sin to kill a black buck because in Hindi the word "cow" is used in its name? What methods and means could be used to drive black bucks away from a field? Does it spoil more than it grazes? Can a scarecrow frighten it away and if yes, for how long? How many times does it breed? The female has only two udders – then how can it be called a cow? How many fields can it graze in a day? Black buck in the night ...

Silence set in after ten minutes, and the three or four passengers who had initiated the discussion withdrew into themselves, and instantly escaped the confines of the bus.

When there is little to be done, the monotony of the rumbling bus, the lurching and swaying, makes the passengers drowsy, and this drowsiness plucks them out of their environs and traps them, each in his own fantasy. Is this entire bus a vision or have all these dreams slithered into it through the open windows? And if so, what would happen if the dreams of the front seat passengers were to slip unawares into the sleep of the back seat passengers? So I wandered to other questions: Do dreams travel? If yes, in this travel within a travel? Which one will come to an end first? And how? Who knows?

Immersed in these thoughts I started to descend once again into Zweig's novel and at once found myself at the site where I had left off. The heroine, by way of writing a letter, was revealing her mind, layer by layer, like an onion. Will anything remain, after all the layers are peeled off?

When I lost track of this strain of thought I cannot say, but I suddenly found myself right in the middle of Farrukhabad. Through the lanes of the story I saw a bungalow right before my eyes. It was as splendid as the bungalow in Zweig's story. But where had I seen this before, I who had never been beyond Delhi. She was standing in the barsali, the front room, leaning against the pillar, her face bathed in tears, her eyes still brimming with them. But this woman was quite unlike the heroine of Zweig's story. The master of the house stood in front of her, haranguing and screaming, while the children bawled in the backyard. A face shimmered in her wet eyes. It was mine. Cut, complexion, contours – exactly like mine.

Am I lodged in the lines of this story or have these lines catapulted me into the unknown city of Farrukhabad? But this bus, isn't it going to Jodhpur and taking me with it? What kind of spell is this?

The saying that the horses of the mind go berserk the moment they are let loose is not true. In fact what one has in one's mind are black bucks not horses which are always uncontrolled, forever free to graze, run around, ransack ... Why does this vision of evil and destruction obsess my straying mind? Does this image come to delude me for a while or are such evil visions inherent in me?

The black bucks of the mind, with their raised manes, are struggling to break free of their tethers. Why is it that they come in the moment they find a weak spot in the fence? Why do they come bounding to ransack the property and the honour of others? Is it to fill their bellies with food or their hearts with pleasure? Why do they trample the lives of others just to fulfill their own urges?

This I know – if there are black bucks, you're bound to have standing crops ready for them to spoil, and if you have raised a crop, black bucks are bound to be close by – whichever happens first, will the fields and barns ever be free of black bucks?

Wedged on my seat, drenched in sweat, I felt like a black buck lashed by the scorching wind, the loo, my hunger fired and enflamed by the summer heat. All of a sudden it struck me that I *was* a black buck and as I looked around, I realized that, from the driver down to the last passenger, so was everyone else. The bus was full of black bucks. And that, brother, is the truth of this land. Each journey is just a mindless gambol of black bucks. And where are we headed? Towards destruction. After annihilating one field we will turn to the next and if the guard scares us off with his gun, we will simply move on, setting our sights on the next field to plunder. This incessant run is no journey. It is an aimless flight ...

When the bus reached Jodhpur I pushed and jostled my way out like all the rest, joining the herd of black bucks coming to ravage the city, in search of new pastures ... Let Zweig's sensitivity be left to him!

PRATIBHA RAY

KETAKI GROVE

TRANSLATED BY APARNA SATPATHY AND THE EDITORS
NOMINATED BY R P MISHRA

First published in Oriya as “Ketaki Ban” in *Jhankara*,
April 1998, Cuttack

The realization that I too had aged hit me for the first time when I met Subha. Though I was due to retire from my government job in a year, the fact that I had grown old had never before been brought home so emphatically to me.

Subha was much younger than I and such a baby-face that I'd never imagined she would look old one day. Meeting her after thirty two years, I was saddened to see that not only did she look old, she actually *was* old. As for me, I could no longer deny the truth of my own advancing years.

Of course, even if one were to acknowledge the passing of the years where is the time to dwell on it? Who allows you the luxury of revelling in it? Your wife, children, grandchildren, whom will you plead with to leave you alone because you've grown old? Who among them enjoys perennial youth that makes it all right for you to bow out of an active existence, pleading old age? Actually, the older you get the more mired you are in all kinds of worldly affairs and illusions. One is not a yogi. The Government declares you old at the age of fifty eight but you cling on, like a politician clings to his seat unto the last. Besides, as a member of the middle class, when are your dreams ever fulfilled, and when are you ever absolved of all responsibilities – your life partner is not your wife but your never-ending needs. Some people in my position believe that it's foolish to chase dreams of becoming a millionaire, but we do, don't we, nevertheless?

Of course, I knew long before I raised a family that I was not destined to be rich. My family was in dire poverty when I cleared my matriculation. To continue with my studies I had to tutor students in my mama's village. My father, my uncle and I have always held that had I not wasted my study time giving tuitions, I would definitely have secured a first division. At the time, however, I was content to pass the IA and then my BA.

Many boys from lower middle class families of my generation paid for their own education by giving tuition and, years later, engaged five private tutors each for their own offspring! I decided not to do this for my children even if I was financially in a position to do so, on a matter of principle. For if I did, my children, like Subha, would always depend for every small thing on their tutors.

Subha was so spoon-fed that not only was it necessary for me, her tutor, to do her maths and drawing, but I also had to ghost-write the "Autobiography of a Cow" for her. Mercifully, since she was a student of Class Nine, Subha didn't have to write the cursive regularly. Otherwise, I would have had to do even that! I had no great expectations of Subha. I knew that passing the matriculation exam was a hobby for the delicate, pampered daughters of the rich and ranked alongside drawing alpana with rice paste, embroidering "Sweet Dreams" on pillow covers (though bereft of any knowledge of the English language) and enshrining the good character certificate of God in the form of a *God is Good* picture and hanging it on the wall. All these achievements were then reeled off to impress prospective suitors and their nosy entourages.

I knew for sure that Subha would get married before she matriculated because she was already twenty, having flunked twice in each class. I was also the oldest in my class as I had started my education late and then wasted more time in tutorial assignments. However, I must confess, I didn't want Subha to be married off immediately. There was no noble motive for this, merely an ambitious boy's selfish wish – I was paid handsomely by Subha's father and fed an occasional delicious meal, so I prayed to God to delay Subha's marriage by three, four years, just long enough for me to complete my BA. But why would any eligible bachelor postpone his nuptials in deference to my wishes?

Subha suddenly discarded the load of matriculation anxiety and instead donned the crown of marriage. After one last sumptuous feast, on the occasion of Subha's marriage, I began looking for another job. I never saw her bridegroom, who was a big officer, because he arrived, as all bridegrooms do, in the middle of the night. The desire to see Subha's bridegroom was not nearly strong enough to keep me awake.

I didn't stop dreaming my big dreams because of Subha. Nothing stops for anyone. After struggling for many years, I not only managed to pass my BA but my MA as well. Then I got married and settled down. There was neither the opportunity nor the need to keep track of Subha. I was completely caught up in my own life, the love of my wife, the drudgery of household affairs, disappointments on the job front, petty injustices, transfers from one place to another, new friends, the struggle to make ends meet, survival in this competitive world. And now I stood on the brink of retirement.

Some years ago, Subha's son had scored a distinction and his name was printed in the newspaper. The newspaper mentioned that he was the son of Shri Manmohan Mohanty and Shrimati Sobharani Mohanty and the grandson of Chaudhary Jagmohan Ray. Of course, I immediately knew that Sobharani was Subha. There may not be much difference between these two names Subha and Sobha, but for me, the difference was significant. Why do people name their daughters after renowned beauties – Sobha, Sundari, Menaka, Urvashi – each followed by a Rani? For one thing, such names make them unnecessarily proud, especially if they are, in fact, endowed with some physical charm. But if the names are beautiful and they are not, then it gives them a sort of inferiority complex. Moreover, how many of them are lucky to be a rani? And even if they are, are they really happy? That was the reason why I had changed Sobha's name to Subha. But I was the only one who called her that. Anyway, if Subha had again become Sobha in her husband's home, what did I care? I had heard that her husband earned a lot, had power, fame, and lots of property. He was a lakhpati. He had given Subha her own car and driver.

I had to struggle to remember whether Subha was pretty, which only means that hers was not the extraordinary kind of beauty that gets indelibly impressed on one's mind, though, like every other girl of her age, Subha was endowed with a fresh innocence and a sweet, virginal charm that was pleasing to the eye. Some young rivers swell and overflow their banks, some are placid and steady. Subha was always grave and decorous even in the impulsive and unpredictable years of her youth and showed a wonderful sense of proportion in the amount she laughed and spoke. And she did not do this deliberately. She was naturally grave. It is also entirely possible she was this way because of the scolding she received from me for not doing her homework regularly, and for her inability to grasp a point even after repeated explanations. Another reason could be that she was distracted most of the time – which is something quite natural at her age. Whatever the reason, the fact was that Subha was a quiet person.

On the day before she was to be married she came up to me. "Sir, I am very sad," she said, hesitantly.

"Why feel sad? Every girl has to get married one day."

"Yes but ..."

"So, is it because you have to discontinue your studies?"

"No Sir, I am not at all sad about dropping out of school. I am not particularly fond of studies, you know that! It is good Baba allowed me to get married before the exam. Actually, I ... I am upset because there will be no more tuitions."

"Very strange! You need my tuition only because of your studies. You are not upset about having to discontinue your studies, but you are sad that the tuition would stop?" I burst out laughing.

"Sir, I am afraid that your graduation studies might stop. Everything happens as willed by God. If you are destined to pass, you will but ..." I gave her a quizzical look as Subha blushed. And I stepped out into the rains lashing the city, her last words still ringing in my ears, "Sir, you must come to my house."

It is my opinion that for girls "my house" is more important than "my husband." Women just love being in charge of a house. They may not like the husband chosen for them but get along with their lives, concentrating all their attention on "my home." They may not be free to choose their husbands but when it comes to setting up a home, they are in full control. It is possible to get on with one's life without loving the husband, but it is well nigh impossible to do so without loving one's home. Who knows if Subha's husband was to her liking or not? However, when she saw her new house, it must have met with her approval. And a home must have blossomed with Subha at the helm, anointing everything with her auspicious touch, a home that was bound to fall apart without her.

After thirty two years I chanced on Subha in a saree shop. Grey hair, flab, black and red paan-stained teeth with one gold-capped molar, heavy gold ornaments that dug into thick arms and neck, a round, plump face and dark patches under the eyes. I didn't recognize her but my eyes kept going back to her face. The abandon with which she was selecting sarees from a heap of very expensive ones indicated that she was a rich woman. It also indicated that she gave more importance to her possessions and status than to herself. Even the salesman paid her more attention than he did me. Probably a regular customer. I was trying to haggle down the price of a saree with a much more modest price tag, for my wife. The saree was beautiful. It caught the woman's eye. Then she looked from the saree to me. Suddenly, she got up and folded her hands, overwhelmed with joy.

"Sir, how come you are here, Sir?"

Taken aback I asked her who she was.

She replied, "Don't you recognize me? I am Subha." Her voice had cracked along with her face – she sounded as if her throat was choked with phlegm.

"No. Really, I could not. You have changed so much ..."

"Sir, why don't you just say that I have grown old? I have three grandchildren. We are celebrating the youngest one's birthday – that is the reason I'm shopping. He is happy with anything. As for my daughter-in-law, she ..." Subha gushed – like a river overflowing its banks.

I said, "I read of your son's success in the newspaper. It is fortunate that he has turned out to be such an outstanding student."

"Exactly like his father. You know how intelligent *I* am."

Subha's voice was full of pride for her husband and son. I noted the totality of her happiness. Only mindless girls like Subha are capable of such happiness – if their children study well and their husbands earn good money, there can be no sorrow.

Subha whispered, "Sir, were you able to pass your BA?"

I was momentarily taken aback. Nevertheless, the guileless question made it clear that even though Subha's appearance had changed, she had not. She remained as clueless as ever. It was obvious that she had no idea what I did or who I was. How does one answer such a question in a shop?

Ignoring the question, I said, "I was transferred to this place a year ago and retire in a year's time. I am glad to have met one of my students after all this time." I asked her to give me her address. "I'll drop in some day," I said.

Subha took her husband's visiting card out from her purse and I cut the conversation short by taking it and leaving the shop abruptly. If she had asked me any more idiotic questions – whether I ate good food, for instance – I would have completely lost my cool.

One day I decided to honour her request and look her up. At least, she should know that though she had escaped her education by marrying early, I had not only passed my BA, but my MA too and had managed to get a prestigious job. I could afford fish, meat, milk, fruits, and ghee. I did not have to depend on tuitions any more. Her husband may be well to do, but I was not poor either – though one must admit it is not easy to run a middle class household in a country like ours.

When I reached Subha's house at five in the evening, she was sitting near a bucket full of milk. Seeing me she said, "You must have to buy milk. You could have got pure, unadulterated milk from us if you lived a little closer. We milk cattle throughout the year. I have become a veritable vendor, what with figuring out what to do with all this milk." Nowadays, side businesses on the domestic front like selling sarees, training dogs and selling milk have become the latest status symbols of the rich.

Subha hurriedly made some paneer and served me a full plate of nuts and sweets with great enthusiasm. Thirty two years ago, I would wolf down everything that she served and more often than not, I did not have to eat supper afterwards. However, now when I saw so many delicacies in front of me, at that hour, I said, "So much? Am I a cow or a Kumbhakarna? Besides, I have food restrictions. No sweets and nuts. And I just want half of this piece of paneer."

Subha was aghast. She could not believe that I had acquired a rich man's blood.

"I am not lying. I ate a lot when I was young. Now my health does not permit any overindulgence. A middle class man usually spends everything on food. Food is his chief luxury because he cannot afford any other." I wanted Subha to know that I maintained a reasonable middle class home.

"My doctor has also imposed severe food restrictions on me," said Subha, as she started devouring the sweets and nuts she had put out for me. "But who cares? Human beings will die in any case, with or without food. Then why not die eating everything? I have never had any hobby other than eating."

Soon I became a regular visitor at Subha's house. Though there was no real reason to go there I felt I was neglecting my duty if I did not turn up every two or three days. My wife and children also met her once or twice and were treated very well. Subha too visited our place with her grandchildren. Her husband of course didn't have the time to come over, being a highly placed officer with many responsibilities – he even brought work home from the office, as if there was nothing more important than it. The life of officers like him is pathetic. It is as if they have nothing to live for, in spite of all the happiness in their personal and family lives. I had not misunderstood Subha's husband. I would have felt awkward if he had come to my house thinking that I was a middle-class man. I was not on friendly terms with him nor did I wish to be. The little I knew of him convinced me that he was quite the average husband, off-loading all the responsibilities of the household on his wife's shoulders, and residing in his own world.

People thought I was an old tutor hired for her three grandchildren. Everyone called me "Sir." Sometimes I felt not just Subha's husband, grandchildren and servants, even her cattle probably called me "Sir" in their language.

What kept taking me back to Subha's place? Definitely not Subha. And there was no question of it being her pompous and prestigious husband. Nor was it the tasty food as I had made it a point not to partake of anything at her place, except tea. They made the most exquisite green-leaf tea. They normally made dust-leaf tea for visitors but I was treated to the regular family tea. What flavour! Milk, sugar ... everything in the right proportion. Not once was the tea marred by an excess of milk or sugar, which is quite common in middle class homes like mine. Probably it was the cup of tea that drew me on my way back from office, like a suckling calf to its mother. Sometimes I used to ask for an extra cup. Subha's grandchildren had taken to calling me "Tea Sir."

Perhaps even the tea was not the main attraction. Perhaps it was her grandchildren. Because my own did not stay with me, my affection for hers grew day by day. My trips to her house were so regular that if I missed going there one day, Subha would question me about it on my next visit. "Why didn't you come yesterday? The kids missed you so much. They made my life miserable. I waited until eight o'clock for my evening tea. Was there a problem?"

Very strange! How can she push and force me like that? Have I been bought by a cup of tea? As if I was a tutor at her place, and was bound to go there every day. I went there of my own volition. Who was she to question me? Without answering her question, I would say, "Today I have planned to have two or three cups of tea, so hurry up and bring them on. Now where are the kids?" And my anger would be diffused by the delicate aroma of the green-leaf tea wafting out of my cup.

Slowly I discovered that the quiet girl had become a garrulous woman. The past was prominent in Subha's conversation, while the present barely warranted a mention. She pined for her village, its river, mango groves, orchards and the ketaki forest. She missed her circle of friends. The conversation would invariably start with food and quickly move on: How, although mangoes, guavas, plantains and berries were available in the city, some typical country fruits, like gooseberries, blackberries and the like were not to be seen. How among a variety of nurseries and gardens, country flowers such as the blue lotus and the ketaki were conspicuous by their absence. How the sky here was lost among the skyscrapers, and the moon forever unnoticed in the light of the electric lamps, the sweet chirping of the birds in the madding din of the city, the sweet smell of the earth in the smoke and dust. How human nature was blunted by selfishness, and how distanced people were even from close friends! The walls of buildings touched each other but the people didn't. There was neither dawn nor dusk, nor time for anything.

"Sir, it is our great good fortune that you were able to find the time to look us up, though you didn't have to," Subha said one day. "Your presence makes me feel as if our ketaki grove has not yet died; the blue lotuses still bloom in our village pond; the smoke of each hut continues to curl upwards and merge with that coming out of other huts. People still send dishes prepared for dinner to each other's houses, and everybody has time for everyone else. I have not been to the village for a long time. After all, who is there now? Every relative of ours is settled in some town or the other. Our village has grown old, only poverty, disease, and old, unwanted people inhabit it. Sir, do you visit the village sometimes?"

I looked askance at Subha. This lady had received much from the city, including her rolls of adipose and her advanced years. Yet how she pined for her ketaki grove.

I remembered how often I used to bring her the ketaki so her grandmother could make a catechu for her hair. I was adept at plucking the ketaki, at removing the dusky-green outer leaves with their long, needle-sharp edges, to reach the pale gold inner leaves and the flower inside, the colour of old, rich silk. What fragrance! Subha liked to weave the leaves into her plait. Once she had told me, "The ketaki smells better than the catechu made from it. Dadima unnecessarily destroys it to make the catechu."

What regrets could Subha have amidst such plenty and fulfilment? Surely the limited vision of a simple-minded woman like Subha will not notice anything lacking, will it? How was it possible then that a germ of discontent lay hidden all these years, within this obese woman's body and thought? But slowly, observing Subha daily, I was amazed that she was capable of fine thought. Though if an outsider observed her, he would have thought her a complete bumpkin.

I have stopped going to Subha's place. I have decided not to. It is better not to face her again. I sometimes remember the loud voices of her grandchildren – "Tea Sir has come!" – and the flavour of the tea. There is no fragrance in the tea at my place and no voices of grandchildren, either. Sometimes my feet turn on their own to Subha's house, but my judgement and conscience stop them from moving ahead.

The other day – a day of torrential rain – an unforgettable incident occurred as I sat relishing a cup of tea at Subha's, and I don't think it proper to go to her place now. Of course it happened so suddenly that even I was surprised. No one will know about it. Subha's husband, her well-established son, daughter, son-in-law, and daughter-in-law will never have a clue. Such a thing will never happen again. But then, what else is left to happen? The incident was conclusive. If I resume my tea-sessions now, sipping tea like a gentleman, or like the tutor of yesteryears, will it not be a farce? I won't ever have to meet Subha's husband – our earlier meetings were brief and superficial anyway – but I will have to face Subha. Maybe her eyesight is not as good as it once was but her vision certainly is. Will I be able to face her as I did before the incident? And what about Subha's feelings?

Oh God! Why did such an incident have to happen at this time, now when we are both so old? Will our lives change because of it? Had the incident not taken place, would our lives be incomplete? Perhaps, had the incident never happened, we would not have experienced the self-truth we both discovered about ourselves. But is it proper for such a situation to arise at this age? Could it not have been averted? Of course she started it but is it possible for a thick headed, easily satisfied, middle-aged woman like Subha, to create such an improbable situation without any encouragement? I know now, Subha's fat body conceals feelings as refined as the sweetest music.

The human mind is like a ketaki grove. It is very difficult to reach it, but does the silent fragrance of the ketaki flower remain undiscovered? Is there ever need for the ketaki to shout and advertise itself, "I have beautiful fragrance, come and smell me?"

After the incident, I realized that no girl is satisfied with a little bit, no girl is thick headed, and no girl ages. In one moment, Subha destroyed my strong male prejudice. Not only that, she also shook my unswerving opinion of myself. She has proved that neither of us has grown old. Old age is merely a shell – remove the shell, and within it brims rasa.

I do not blame Subha for the incident. My only regret is that what should have taken place thirty two years ago happened now. Who could benefit from the incident? The only outcome was that my visits to Subha's place came to an abrupt halt. Of course, Subha has not told me to stop coming, but I know that is the very least she expects of me. I know that even if I go back there, things will never be the same again. Perhaps the heart-wrenching rain was responsible for whatever happened that evening.

Nobody was at home. Her grandchildren had gone to their mama's place. The big house seemed as deserted and empty as a school building during the summer vacations. Just then it began to rain incessantly, as it had thirty two years ago.

Did the rain give a damn for the crops sure to be destroyed by the overflowing rivers? Did it stop for the houses that were being swept away by the floods? Once, on a similar day of rain, the twenty year old Subha had casually announced she was about to be married. She declared her sadness about her tuitions coming to an end. She invited me to visit her new home. She had looked no different than any other bride-to-be. The innocent young thing was full of sympathy for the poor, young tutor whose tuition would stop, who would no longer get his tea and snacks, and whose dream to pursue a higher education would remain unrealized.

And then, many years later, once again a day when it rained non-stop, Subha served me sizzling paneer pakodas, to counter the weather, she said which I categorically refused. I saw the pained alas-this-man-is-not-fated-even-to-eat-fresh-food look writ large on Subha's face and thought, My God, so much anguish? Wasn't she overdoing the hurt? Then I thought I saw Subha's eyes turn moist – maybe just drops of rain. Subha returned with a sugarless cup of tea for me. Her forehead and face were covered with beads of sweat.

And then a bolt of lightning struck. An oversized plantain tree that had been loaded down with a large bunch of plantains, collapsed. Oh Subha! Why did you do this? Have you taken me for a foolish, greedy and awkward man? Not everything is expressed verbally. Not everything is articulated in one lifetime. Don't you know that unsaid thoughts are deeper? The words one gropes for, struggling to convey a sentiment, can never match the eloquence and depth of feeling of the unsaid. Why don't you understand this, Subha? Who should know it better than you who has repressed so much tumult in her heart?

Oh why did you, in one second, Subha, make vulgar the secret words inscribed on the ketaki petals. Handing me the sugarless cup of tea, why did you abruptly say, "Sir, why didn't you speak your mind that night? Being a girl, how could I have made so bold myself?"

I came out of Subha's house that day, soaked to the skin in the torrential downpour. As her tutor, could I not have tossed back the same question at her now, so many years later – Why did you not stop me by saying, "Don't go out in this rain. You will get wet to the skin." Did you not know I was anyway completely drenched by then?

PREM GORKHI

WHO LIVES LIKE THIS?

TRANSLATED BY HINA NANDRAJOG AND THE EDITORS
NOMINATED BY RANA NAYAR

First published in Punjabi as "Bhala Iyon Wi Koi Jeonde" in *Nagmani*,
March 1998, New Delhi

Jarmanjit has filled up the clotheslines with the washing. She starts the washing machine the moment she gets up. A zesty girl, Jarmanjit. Ever since she has come to Hoshiarpur to complete her internship, life has become comfortable. She comes home every Saturday and we, bhua and bhatiji, have a wonderful time. My mother says the same thing, "With Jarman here one doesn't know how time flies."

Jarman has just finished her MBBS. While she was studying in Amritsar, she would visit us every month or so. I remember how my brother ran around trying to get her into a Delhi college. Not that getting her admitted in Amritsar was easy. Amritsar is about seventy to eighty kilometres away from us, but as my brother always said, "I have no worries now. She's in our own place."

When Jarman used to come home from medical college, she would bury herself in books, forgetting even her meals. And then she graduated. She sent up a quick prayer of thanks and started spending entire Sundays with me in the fields. First she made me teach her to drive the tractor, then to plough. Last Sunday when I went to drop the sugarcane off at the mill, she came along and drove the tractor all the way to the Dasooha mill.

One day she said, "Bhuaji, I'm going to stay here with you ... If Papa doesn't agree to this, let him not ... I like this village."

Her decision chilled my heart. But I knew for sure that she would be sent to America or England or be married off and then, she would forget everything. When I told Jarman this, "Bhuaji," she said, sharply, "Forget it, I'm not going anywhere now. I'm going to work here, in Punjab. I'll marry here, and stay near you. I've already hinted as much to Papa ..."

"Jarman, you'll have to think about inter-caste marriages not once, but a hundred times ... Look here, I'm not against inter-caste marriages. But still, you must ..."

"Preeti bhui, what are you trying to say ... what is there to see? I'm neither an illiterate, nor a fool. I know what I'm doing and what I should do ... I am *not* a child."

"Beta, I only meant that you should know everything about the boy, about his background ..."

"What is there to find out about the *boy* ... I told you that we've studied together for five years. We've been seeing each other for the past couple of years. One day both of us will be doctors. How does his background matter? Are people with very impressive backgrounds more able? I'm not going to fret over any boy's past. I'm going to live with the future. Do you understand?"

"Beta, we often compromise, we balance many things in life, to accomplish what we want to, but then silently, unexpectedly, our background creeps in, like a cobra with fangs spread out, and an entire life turns topsy-turvy."

"Oh Bhui, I don't believe in such stuff!"

I got up and patted her cheeks, dropped a kiss on her head. "Jarman, you're angry with me, I know. Beta, I am on your side. There's nothing to be angry about. Now come, let's go downstairs."

But she didn't get up. She just sat there, watching the clouds float against the red sun.

Jarman has told me that she's in love with this boy. His village is somewhere close to ours. Jarman has not told me the name of the village. Just that the boy is also doing his house job at the Hoshiarpur Civil Hospital, and that his name is Harjap. She says she cannot think of marrying anyone but Harjap.

Yesterday she returned from Hoshiarpur in the evening, bringing bags of fruit and clothes. When I asked her what it was all for, she said that she had invited Harjap. "He's coming here tomorrow."

At times I feel such happiness when I look at Jarman. It gives me immense pleasure to see our children cross the insuperable ravines, rivers, and valleys that we ourselves have been unable to. The day Jarmanjit marries the boy of her choice, will be a day of great fulfilment for me.

I know Jarman is not the timid girl I once used to be. I was not able to marry the person whom I had loved with all my heart. I just hadn't been able to take a stand. Bhajji had kept beseeching me to marry him, taunting me and goading me, and what did I do to him?

"Preeti," he would say, "Preeti, I can't live without you any longer. Either run away with me or let me stay in your house. I'm willing to live as your servant for the rest of my life. You're the daughter of a Sikh, aren't you, now show some lion-heartedness!"

I would look into Bhajji's eyes helplessly. And when Bhajji left, I would sit by myself and answer his questions. How can I run away with you, there are all these webs woven around me. No one to look after this vast property ... and there's Biji and Dadi, old and infirm. Who will take over this big haveli, these sprawling fields and orchards? And then my powerful maternal relatives, all very worthy people, yes, but will my fauji-mamas let us live our lives?

This is what always happens. When conversation with Jarmanjit veers towards her boyfriend, I find myself enmeshed deep inside the invisible net that Bhajji had spread. Now look at Jarman, how excited she is at Harjap's coming! How efficiently she finishes her chores! I too had waited impatiently for Bhajji whenever he was to visit us. I would hurriedly finish all my work and keep myself free. But in the end, what was I left with but grief over what happened?

I have always wept over the time when I went with Pragaso to her parents' place. Everyone fussed about Bhajji. His name was on everyone's lips. All the girls were hysterical about him. The day the village tournament was over, Simar and Paramjit came over and began to say, "A waist-high trophy and he won it all by himself, this Bhajji of Passi, even Kirpal was amazed. How handsome he is, Didi," they said in chorus. "When looking at him, I even forget I'm hungry! Just imagine, even Jamla Jatt hugged him on stage as he sang along ..."

When my eldest mama came visiting, he also sat with my chacha and others, and talked about Bhajji. "Our villages should be proud of this boy. How strong he is, this rascal. He hauls a sack that weighs two, two and a half maunds onto his shoulder as if it weighs a mere five seers. This is God's blessing, otherwise where do you see this kind of vigour in poor families ..."

All these tales about Bhajji only made me despise Kirpal who used to show off his muscles all the time as if he were the strongest man on earth. I had casually praised him a couple of times and he started chasing me. He would strut about near our orchards, all dressed to kill. I scoffed at him, said there were plenty like him around. And now he's lost to Bhajji thrice. People say that at the tournament held at Dafar, Kripal couldn't even move the sack!

It was as if Bhajji had cast some kind of spell over me and I had not even seen him! One day I mentioned this to Pragaso. She had come to thread the quilt, and she just whisked me away to her village to see Bhajji. And so I saw him – how handsome he was, his face as radiant as a rising sun, looking like a son of Mahajans – and I felt this melting within me.

Bhajji sat beside me and talked. I couldn't take my eyes off his face. He said he worked as a clerk at the Electricity Board at Tanda. But when the tournaments were underway, he hardly ever went to office. Whenever at home, he helped out, he said. His family bought, cut and sold trees in our area. And I heard myself telling Bhajji, "We fell trees, too. So why don't you come over to our place and see."

He was just beginning to say that he would send his brother, when Pragaso butted in saying, "Bhajji, now you come and visit me, your sister. You can bless your nephew, too. He's also an enthusiastic kabaddi player."

Three days later, Bhajji came over when I was driving the tractor out into the field. Some four, five admiring boys had brought him to our place. Bhajji stepped into our main hall and stopped to look around him.

"Ji, how many medals!" he said in awe. "Major saab won these?"

"Yes, my brother used to sprint; my father too was an athlete." I said.

I was standing close to Bhajji, unable to fathom the secret ecstasy that made my heart dance.

Bhajji sat on the edge of the sofa. I brought him a glass of cold water straight from the refrigerator and sat close to him as he gulped the water down. I asked him all sorts of questions that came to mind ... about his job, his selection to the Electricity Board, his diet ... Commonplace talk. Finally I asked, "How do you manage to lift all that weight?"

"With these hands, bas!" Bhajji laughed as he spread his hands out before me.

"Your hands are not that hard," I said as I caressed them. He stared at me for an arrested moment.

"It's not just the hands," he said. "One's entire body must possess strength. And if in addition one's morale is high, then the hands automatically become iron ..."

"Boost my morale, too."

"Your grit is already famous," he said shyly. "People say you're a gutsy woman and that's how you've managed your entire household. Your courage is well-known in all the neighbouring villages. Even in my office they say that the daughter of the Grewal clan is not a woman! She's a man. She ploughs and tills the fields, sells and exchanges grain in the mandi. I myself have seen you on the tractor trolley in the town ..."

Such praise made my heart overflow. I placed my hand on Bhajji's lips, "Enough, enough, don't flatter me so much," I said, reluctant to draw my hand away from his lips. At that instant, I saw my grandmother come down from the attic.

"Biji, look who's here ..." I called out.

Bhajji got up to pay his respects to Biji. I could see how this one gesture of his softened her. She embraced Bhajji. I went in to make sweetened milk for him as they sat there, talking. Soon, on the pretext of showing him the tree he had come to cut down for me, I brought Bhajji to the fields. I pointed out the distant tahli trees at the edge of the mango orchard. But even as he assessed them, I had eyes only for him. The proximity of Bhajji's body did something to me. Then suddenly, I lost control and grabbed his hand.

"Bhajji," I said, "I don't know what is happening to me. I need your support. I'm not able to express what is in my heart. You don't know what you have done to me. I am strong, really, but for the past month or so I find myself losing the struggle against myself."

I didn't even realize that I was clinging to Bhajji.

Bhajji caught hold of me and shook me, "What's happened to you?" he asked, aghast. "At least be heedful of that labourer who's crushing stones!" Then as suddenly, his diffidence returned and, "I'm a sportsman," he said. "Everyone knows, you know, I ..."

"Why are you so petrified? I'm not about to swallow you up." I marched off towards the well.

It was at the well that I managed to remove his fears. When finally he took leave, I gave him a tin of ghee that was lying with me saying, "I'd kept this, just for you. Do take it."

I walked out with him and stood watching till he crossed the big orchard, till he took the path that would lead to his village ... taking with him a strand of myself. The spool within me was being unravelled, slowly, leaving me threadbare.

One day I went to his office at Tanda to meet him. Another day I went to his house. Once I even dropped in at the adda at Dasooha. I was following Bhajji's footprints everywhere, fearful that he might slip out of my grasp.

Then came a day when Bhajji came to our well. He came a second time. He came home. Then he came once again; then a fifth time in my absence. He had lost his shyness. His personality gradually unfolded. I heard a totally different person whenever he talked solemnly, seriously. He was very fond of reading stories, and his conversation reflected this.

But soon, I started feeling that Biji didn't like Bhajji's coming and going though she didn't say anything openly. One day she began talking about Bhajji: "His grandfather was Jwala, and he had a brother, Mehnga. They were very poor. All day they would stoke the fire, and at dusk take two seers of gur. Often they only got the dross, scraped off the top of the boiling gur, to eat with four handfuls of rice thrown into it. Or for days on end, the entire family would survive on roasted potatoes."

"Biji, why on earth are you telling me all this?"

"Why not? Can't I speak about them? I ..."

I jumped up and stomped off to the well. Three days later, my younger mama came over. He told us that there was a good boy belonging to a place near Jalandhar, a captain in the army. Ah, so after two years, his concern for me had suddenly resurfaced. I promptly refused, saying I had wiped out all thoughts of marriage from my mind.

When I next met Bhajji, I told him not to come home ever again. I told him the truth. We arranged to meet in the dense arbour next to the orchard. We had become each other's weakness. Bhajji still won trophies in tournaments. He could now lift five more kilograms of weight than before.

One day I stole Bhajji from himself – I surrendered to his love. Many a times I had wanted to yield to Bhajji and had forced myself to contain my emotions. But in the dense arbour, on the golden sand, both of us forgot the world. We became one. We soared high into the skies. When we came back to reality, I saw my blood streaking the bleached sand, but I felt no regret. I lay in Bhajji's arms, in a stupor, and heard him relate a story.

"Preeti, do you know, about five years ago, in this meadow, your chacha, Zailla, strangled a girl to death?"

"Mmm," I said drowsily.

"First, he abducted this girl who was crushing stones, then ground her honour into dust, and when she said that she would return to the village and report, Zailla strangled her with her own dupatta. The police came, the court case went interminably on, but the witnesses went back on their word – your grandfather had bought everyone with his money. The witnesses as well as the cops."

I sat up. Bhajji was still on his back.

"Preeti, do you know who that girl was? She was my bhua's daughter ..."

And suddenly, I felt a storm rise in my breast, my eyes blaze. My thoughts went a-circling a million billion times but kept returning to a single point: Why has he told me this, about his cousin and my chacha? And that too now, at a time when I have showered on him all the wealth that I possessed. Had Bhajji deceived me? Was possessing Bhajji – something that I considered to be *my* triumph – actually his victory? Was Bhajji's merely a calculated interest in me? Had he sensed my weakness and led me on, to take revenge? He has not appreciated my love. He has nursed wickedness in his heart from the very first day. He has fooled me with all that talk of running away with me ... A spark burst aflame inside me and I, smarting with rage, jumped onto his chest, grabbed his neck with both my hands, and pressed with all my strength.

Bhajji was still laughing. "What are you doing, Preeti? What's happened to you, you bitch, I can't breathe ..."

Within seconds his eyeballs popped out and his body was limp. I stood up. I looked at him with demonic eyes for a long time. Bhajji's head had rolled to one side and his heels had dug deep depressions in the sand.

I turned and walked away. I reached the well, started the pump and sat under the full blast of the water. Then I burst loudly into tears, like a child. Even under the streaming cold water, I could feel the hot tears on my cheeks.

That entire night I could neither sit at home, nor could I go outside. I started feeling that my body would wither away in tiny flakes and my innermost thoughts would spill out. I couldn't sleep. At about ten o'clock, I went to the Sarpanch's house. I told him that I had gone to the meadow searching for the cattle, and had seen a corpse lying there. I asked him to inform the police. The Sarpanch first went towards the arbour with some men, and then headed straight to the thana.

Within minutes, the news of Bhajji's death had spread like wild fire and I, thinking fast, sent the labourer who had been crushing stones to distant Hoshiarpur, ostensibly to pay the installment on the tractor.

For about a month, many possibilities were discussed. Twice I visited Bhajji's mother. No clue had been found. The police gave up the search and fell into their customary silence. I didn't go to the fields for several days.

In the past several years, a lot has happened. My eyesight has gone bad. I can no longer work as before, so I employ labour to do the work at the well. I feel very weak. I have realized that Bhajji was totally innocent; killing him had betrayed my own insecurity, had been an expression of my cowardly vanity. I have committed a great sin, by killing Bhajji. For this I have suffered day and night for the past many years.

For a long time, Biji did not talk to me. The day she quarrelled with me was when she discovered a photograph of Bhajji and myself in the crevice of my clothes cupboard.

"Preeti, you are a very deceitful girl!" Her voice exploded in anger. I went numb at her words.

When she passed away, I cried uncontrollably. I could see Bhajji, and not Biji, dead.

This morning, "Preeti bhui, today you must wear a nice suit, sit with Harjap and talk to him. But please, not of timber or some such thing!" Jarman had said, putting her arms around my neck while I was sorting the clothes for washing.

"My dear, why should *I* dress nicely ... He's coming to meet you!" I said, laughing. I went about little odd jobs as Jarman washed the clothes in the machine and crowded the clotheslines with them.

Suddenly a bell pealed and I rose, startled. Someone had come on a motorcycle. I tried to look out and realized that my eyes were brimming with tears. I wiped my tears just as Jarman came out of the bathroom.

"Preeti bhui, keep sitting, I'll open it. It's only Harjap."

How happy Jarman is. Her feet don't seem to touch the ground!

When Jarman went to the gate, I too walked out. I looked at Harjap very carefully. He was a good-looking boy, a light beard on a fair complexioned face, a maroon turban, a checked shirt and black trousers.

"My Bhuaji," Jarman introduced me, and he bent to touch my feet. I caressed his shoulder affectionately.

Harjap and I sat on the sofa, facing each other. Jarman sat next to him for a moment, and almost instantly got up saying, "I'll make some juice. You both keep talking."

"Harjap, where are you planning to work after your house job?" I asked, for the sake of saying something.

"I had thought that both of us would stay either at Tanda or Dasooha. We want to serve our own people."

"Vaah ... What a noble thought ..." I smiled.

I could see Jarman outside the room. I wanted her to come and sit with him and for me to be out there by the well.

"Harjap beta, which is your village? Jarman says it is close by."

"Didn't she tell you? I belong to Passi, right here in your neighbourhood."

With great difficulty I said, "Passi?" staring at Harjap's face, fondly and longingly. My eyes kept delving into his. Surely, this was not Harjap, but Bhajji!

"Is your house close to the shops? Are you, by any chance, from Mistri Chand Singh's family?"

Harjap laughed, "It seems Jarman has not told you anything about me!" He stopped to look at Jarman who had just come in, carrying the glasses of juice, and then turned once more to me, saying, "Bhuaji, I'm Bhajji's nephew ... The same Bhajji who was murdered near your orchard."

I stared at Jarman and then at Harjap. Finally I put the glass of juice on the table and stood up, mumbling, "Please carry on. I ..."

I came out of the main room and went to the bathroom. I turned on the shower and stood under it, fully clothed, feeling a chill creep over me from head to toe. I felt as if the dust accumulated over the years was peeling off me. I saw the dignity and respect I had garnered over the years disappear, in that instant ...

MINAKSHI SEN

SNEHALATA

TRANSLATED BY KALYANI DUTTA
NOMINATED BY DEBES RAY

First published in Bangla as "Snehalata" in *Dainik Pratidin*,
Puja Special, 1998, Calcutta

The man arrived in the middle of the afternoon when Snehalata was asleep. He was a large, muscular man with a hard, cruel look. As he entered, he cast a long shadow over the huge water tank in the courtyard.

"Anybody home?" he called out, but there was no reply.

"Why would anyone build such a huge water tank?" thought the man irrelevantly, and then called out again, "Is there anyone home?"

Snehalata stirred. Though the marks of dissatisfaction and worry on her face deepened, this call too failed to rouse her.

The man walked towards the long open veranda and stood outside Snehalata's room, that is, the only room with its door open. A quick glance had shown him that all the other rooms were locked. He saw Snehalata through the open door.

Snehalata was lying in bed so the man was unable to guess her age. But he had no trouble gathering that she was quite old.

Since he bore ill tidings, he hesitated, wondering if it would be proper to deliver such news to a lady so old. The next moment he tried to shrug off the feeling. He had finished his work and was just about to leave for the day when Borobabu thrust this unpleasant task on him. He was new to the job. It was not possible for him to refuse anything that Borobabu asked him to do, even when it was couched as a request. He could not refuse, but he was irritated. All he wanted was to be done with it and go back home. Oof! It was terrible to sit and sweat in the thana all day. Time passed better when one was on outdoor duty, he thought and then called out loudly, "Can you hear me?"

Now the door of a side room opened with a bang. The man hadn't noticed this room earlier. When a man stepped out of the room, the policeman sighed in relief. It was easier to break the news to a man, and a middle-aged one at that. The person approached him, "What is it? Whom do you want?"

"Here, this is it ..." he was about to fish something out of his pocket, when he paused, and asked the middle-aged man, "Are you related to Kanakendu Roy?"

"Kanak? Yes, yah sala, the little shit!" The middle-aged man or

Pranabendu, turned around and began to laugh soundlessly, shaking in silent mirth.

Hell! This one's completely mad. Can't give it to him, thought the man and put the piece of paper back in his pocket. If he could just hand it over to somebody, his work would be done. But Borobabu had given him strict instructions: Tell them the family must get in touch with me immediately. There had to be someone he could entrust the message to. As the man pondered over this, Pranabendu walked out of the courtyard and down the narrow lane to the street.

"Great. Now I am really stuck!" Dashing the sweat off his brow he called out, "Here, listen, I have to talk to you," in the harsh voice of his duty hours.

Snehalata woke up. She asked, "Who is it?" calmly, as though she was used to waking up to such shouts. She sat up and the man saw Snehalata's fair skin, the colour of melted gold, smooth and glowing, in spite of the muscles being lax with age. Fine grey hair, streaked with black, gave her an aristocratic look but her thin face and wrinkles belied that nobility.

But Snehalata's appearance did not make much of an impression on the man. He felt no compassion – instead her well-born air made him feel a little hostile. Snehalata climbed out of bed, asking, Who is it? She arranged her saree and threw her anchal with its bunch of keys over her shoulder in the old-fashioned way. Her fumbling approach filled him with a strange sense of pity. He noticed that the lady was practically blind. Perhaps Snehalata could discern the presence of another. Besides having woken up all of a sudden, she was too groggy to walk straight. By the time she finally managed to totter up to him, her right hand feeling the air in front of her, he was thrusting the piece of paper back into his pocket.

"Is this the home of Kanakendu Roy?" he asked in a softer voice.

"Kanakendu? Yes, he is my son. But he doesn't live here."

"Never mind, someone else must be around," said the man in a pragmatic tone. "Someone does stay here with you, right?"

"Yes. My other son."

"Where is he now?"

At the man's question, Snehalata turned and called out, "Pranab? O Pranab ... Please look in the next room," she indicated the room next door with her head, and anxiously asked, "What do you want?"

Seeing Snehalata point towards the small room next door, he shook his head dejectedly, "O, that craz ... No, don't you have another son who is an important officer somewhere?"

"Officer? O, Rupendu? It's been a long time since he's lived here. He comes sometimes, drops in off and on."

Snehalata had felt a little alarmed at the man's enquiries, but now, relieved that he was looking for her officer son, she was more forthcoming.

As soon as he heard that Rupendu did not live there either, the expression of pity on the man's face vanished. An expression of mocking incredulity appeared instead. "How strange! Do you live here all by yourself in this huge house with that loony?" he asked, and then, gruffly, "How is Krishnendu Roy related to you?"

Snehalata visibly shook at this question and the lines of anxiety on her face deepened. The man had to admire this woman – she was more than seventy years old but she controlled her shivering and anxiety with an extraordinary act of will and in a near normal tone answered, "Krishno? Yes, he too is my son. But he doesn't live here either."

"I know that." His desperation to leave was making him rude. He said, "I have a message."

"Message? But Krishno doesn't come here often. How will I inform him of it?" she asked warily.

Snehalata's last words were a lie. Krishno hadn't come home in a year. It wasn't as if he visited infrequently – he didn't visit at all.

Though she had started off speaking calmly, her control soon gave way and she looked alarmed. Fixing suspicious, half-blind eyes on the man, she asked, "Why? What do you have to tell him? What is the message? Who are you? What is it?"

The man's expression softened again at Snehalata's anxiety. Fact was his face did not tell the truth about him. He was probably not cruel by nature, or he wouldn't have melted so quickly.

Impossible. Can't give such news to this old lady, thought the man. What should he do? Return to the thana, inform Borobabu that he had found no one to receive the message, then go home? He had already wasted enough time and he was off-duty. Surely Borobabu would relent and send someone else instead.

The thought that he may not have to deliver the message at all made the man feel relieved, almost cheerful. He had the ration to collect, the shopping to do, and the wife had said ... All the chores he had to do when he reached home came back to him. Muttering something like "Well, I'll be off," he quickly started walking towards the courtyard.

Just then, humming a popular Hindi song, "Tin tin tin, tin tin tin tina, ek dui tin, char panch chei ..." a short, fair boy, walked in. He wore a pink T-shirt and jeans, and his hair was carefully shampooed and styled.

"Didima! O Didima! How are you? Is there anyone at home besides you?"

Didima?

Though he had walked past the huge water tank, the man stopped. Didima meant that the boy was the lady's grandson. He was quite young and strong. There seemed to be no harm in telling him the contents of the message and his job would be over as soon as he handed the slip of paper to the boy. Remembering once again all the chores that awaited him, the man, forgetting the sensitivity and thoughtfulness he had shown earlier, thrust the paper into the boy's hands without further ado.

"Look, I've come from the thana. Pass on this message to your mamas or to Krishnendu Roy's wife if he has one. Ask them to meet Borobabu at the thana. He will explain everything."

The boy was standing near the window of the room next to

Snehalata's when he was intercepted by the man's urgent whisper. The boy was so startled that he screamed out, "Thana? What thana? Which thana?" Then, unfolding the paper he read the message out aloud. The message, sent on wireless from one thana to another, was written on a dirty piece of paper in faded ink. The boy found it difficult to decipher it and read haltingly but loudly, "Krishnendu Roy, known by local residents as brother of the famous singer Kanakendu Roy, was found dead ..." The boy repeated in a choked voice, "Dead?"

"Aei, why did you have to roar it out like a bull? Fine specimen you are! And here I have been all this time, for this lady's sake, what have you done! Your own grandmother ... this old lady!" The man was furious.

"Didima?" The boy was a little more in control now but hadn't lost his ashen and stunned look, "Didima can't understand English."

"Can't?"

The man breathed a little easier. Possible. A woman of over seventy might not know English. It was quite possible, he thought, reassured. Still, how could the boy so rashly announce the tragedy to the lady, rendering futile in one second all the time and effort he had spent! Calming down a little, the man thought that the lady had to learn about the tragedy sooner or later. Now that one of her own kin was here, if she did have an inkling of what had happened, it wouldn't bother him so much.

"Is she your grandmother? That is, you are her daughter's ..." he asked getting on with his job.

"No. No. Not of her own daughter. I am her grandson by way of a d-i-s-t-a-n-t relationship." The boy stretched the word "distant" in such a way as to imply that he wanted to completely detach himself from the present circumstances. He faced a difficult situation – now, even if he wanted to dodge responsibility he couldn't, some unpleasant task was bound to fall on him, and he was unwilling and afraid to take on any. The boy waited, distressed and frightened, ready to run at the first opportunity.

Though Nandan had tried to comfort both himself and the man by declaring that Didima didn't understand English, this was not strictly true. Nandan really was a distantly related grandson. He painted and made sculptures and had come down from Murshidabad to pursue his talent and try his luck. He had not known Snehalata for long so he couldn't have understood that real education does not come only from books or schools and that one's lifestyle and milieu can teach a person a great deal too. Anyway, as a doctor's wife, how could Snehalata not know the meaning of the word "dead"?

Besides she had picked up a number of English words by listening to the conversation of her highly educated sons, daughters-in-law and grandchildren. Her ordinary speech was so polished that no one could tell she was not educated.

Snehalata heard "dead," Kanakendu's name, and "brother" in relation to Krishnendu. She knew with certainty that the word had been spoken about Krishnendu. The word smashed into her heart with the impact of a heavy rock hurled at tremendous speed. She felt no pain but her body grew numb. She thought she was going to collapse. She pulled herself together with a great effort. The next moment the world seemed to be exhausted of air. She opened her mouth, like a fish out of water and gasping, turned around. Her left hand clutched at the air even more piteously than before, and she tottered up to the bed and sank down on it resting her back against its high, carved teak headboard.

She was seventy five years old, a mother of seven. She had had to suffer the untimely death of her husband and the descent into madness of a competent able-bodied son who had held a good job. People say there is no grief to equal the death of a child. Now that sorrow too had hit her at the age of seventy five.

How did she feel? She couldn't quite tell. The first person to come to her mind was the son who was farthest away from her – Nobendu. The child who cared most about the welfare of the family, who kept an eye on everything, who had had to move far away, unable to find a job in this country. Travelling from where he stayed was both time-consuming and expensive. He couldn't visit often with his family. She had thought that on his next visit she would ask him to search for Krishnendu.

Snehalata felt as if Nobo, her expatriate son, was standing next to her, holding her in his arms saying, "Ma. Please don't cry. I am here ..." She felt she could see Kanak, also dear to her heart, standing behind Nobendu, looking at her anxiously.

Then the dizziness passed. It was not Nobo, but Nandan who held her, "O, Didima, Didima."

As Nandan looked at her, Snehalata's lips moved imperceptibly, weakly. Her voice seemed to come from far away: "What should I do now?"

This was the first time that she spoke in her own East Bangla dialect. Because she wasn't addressing Nandan or the man, but herself. And then, as if she had found the answer, she raised her head and moved her fingers, the movement testifying to her long and sole guardianship of a large family. "Nandan, do you know where No'mami lives? Her father's house?"

"Ye–s. I did go once. I think I can find it," said Nandan hesitantly. He wanted desperately to escape the events that were about to unfold. Hoping his job would be done after informing No'mami, that is Krishnendu's wife, he asked, "Should I go there, Didima?"

"Yes. Don't divulge the details if you meet Mami or her mother. Ask Mami to come and meet me here immediately. If you find any of her nephews, let them know everything. Then come and tell me what happened ..." Snehalata was trying visibly to get a grip on herself. Her firm voice however faltered towards the end. The last few syllables were lost.

Even so the two present understood what she was trying to say.

"Achcha. I'll leave for Mami's house." Carrying the scrap of paper in his hands as if it was a rock weighing ten maunds, Nandan clambered off the veranda and walked wearily down to the street. The Nandan who had entered a little while ago, blithely singing "tin tina tin," looked devastated.

"Ei listen, please return soon. I can't leave this old lady alone with no one here."

The man was surprised at himself. Why am I not leaving? Why am I still sitting here? I have delivered the message, I have informed a relative that Borobabu would like to meet them, the dead man's wife is being informed, so what the hell am I doing here? He could find no logic for staying on. But he could not leave the old lady alone.

Meanwhile Pranab was back home and had come into Snehalata's room two three times. Once he asked his mother for money and once, for food. The man watched Snehalata as she sent him away with, "Buy a cake or something from Dulu's shop." He felt a sort of pity for the old woman. He realized once more how unsuited he was for a policeman's job. He was just too sentimental. His colleagues joshed him about it, his boss shouted, his workload increased. But how can one change one's nature?

There was a reason behind his discomfort at having to be the bearer of the news of the old lady's son's death. His mother had died when he was nine years old. So he did and did not have memories of his mother. He remembered the tenderness of his gracious mother, her limitless love, the infinite care she took in feeding him, lulling him to sleep. How soft and tender her hands, how sweet her voice.

What he didn't remember he filled in with his imagination. Imagination and reality blended in his memory and created a soft hazy mist of tenderness, care and love.

For him this was the image of all mothers. How could such a mother bear the grief of the death of a son? He could find no answer.

He had been brought up by his aunt. Mashi had constantly dinned into his head that his gentle and quiet mother, unable to bear the drunken, tyrannical nature of his father, had fallen sick and died.

He had been deprived of his father's company. His father who was a home guard, married a second time and didn't bother about his son, and when the father died of a burst liver, there being no children from his second marriage, his stepmother received all the money. He laid claim to the job, yet, hesitant about joining the police for a long time, he scouted around for another. But when he fell in love and married, he lobbied for and secured the job.

The mashi who brought him up was quite aggressive by nature. Yet he grew up with a tender side to his personality because he had, perhaps, been nurtured by the memory of his kind and gentle mother. Mashi used to say, "He has inherited his father's murderous looks, but in his nature he is the spitting image of his mother."

He still felt so much love for his dead mother that having to bear the news of a son's death to a mother made him feel like an executioner. He was troubled by the apprehension that, like his father, he was about to be the cause of a mother's death.

"What does that paper say?"

It was not Snehalata's voice. A sound had emerged from deep under water. The man started.

"Dead? Is he really dead?"

The man's throat went dry. The sound of a car coming to a halt near Snehlata's house saved him.

"I hear a car. Could that be your son?" the man asked Snehalata. He thought Kanakendu Roy had arrived and was excited at the prospect of meeting such a famous singer face to face. Borobabu had said that if he could get hold of the phone number, he would ring up Kanakendu to ask if the dead man was his brother. Borobabu was aware that Kanakendu didn't live in this house any more.

The grave, self-confident person who climbed up to the veranda, filling the narrow lane with the crunch of his expensive shoes, was not Kanakendu. The man could instantly tell – he was familiar with Kanakendu's pictures from the newspapers.

This man was much older than Kanakendu. His bald pate, his pink cheeks and fine rimmed gold spectacles gave the impression of a seasoned bureaucrat. He was dressed in a suit and tie. He held a small expensive briefcase in his hand.

Imperiously, as though there was no cause for him to look around and acknowledge his surroundings, the man walked straight up to Snehalata's door, looking right through the other man. He took out a long slim envelope from his briefcase and held it out to his mother: "Here Ma, keep this money. It was delayed. Are you all right?"

With this he placed the envelope with the money on a table next to the bed, put a glass over it, and turned to leave without waiting for his mother's reply.

"O, Rupu, something terrible has happened," Snehalata's voice was diffident, her words cautiously treading the air.

Rupu, that is Rupendu, Snehalata's eldest son, who was an executive in an important company, halted in his tracks and turned around.

"What? Are Nobo and the others all well?" It was as if all his concern was for Nobo and Nobo alone.

"No. Not Nobo. It's Krishno."

Snehalata seemed to have nothing left to say after this. She watched speechlessly as Rupendu's figure moved away from her door, squinting to catch a glimpse, through her nearly sightless eyes, of her son who was walking away the moment he heard Krishnendu's name.

The man was forced to obstruct him even though Rupendu Roy's powerful personality made him somewhat nervous. Rupendu Roy halted on being accosted by the man and asked coldly, "And you are?"

The man was immediately conscious of his own grubby, sweat-soaked shirt. After eight hours on duty and one whole hour of waiting here, his face must be haggard and dirty. Self-consciousness made him feel even more diffident. But the information had to be given. Now that the son himself had arrived, he would surely make the necessary arrangements. He would, no doubt, visit the thana too.

"Can we move away a bit?" asked the man quietly.

"No. Say what you have to, right here." Rupendu Roy's voice was harsh. So the man explained what had happened. In as low a voice as possible.

That afternoon Bhowanipore thana had received a message from a thana in South 24-Parganas. The tenant of a family, one Krishnendu Roy, had been discovered dead. Local residents reported that the man used to introduce himself as the brother of the famous singer Kanakendu Roy. People hadn't given much credence to his claim. Krishnendu Roy also had said that their family home was in Bhowanipore, where they all lived together. As soon as a relative was found, he would have to proceed immediately to identify Krishnendu's body.

In a flash, Rupendu Roy's strong presence, his worldly-wise tough exterior, vanished. For one moment he stood like a wooden statue, then his limbs sagged making his snugly fitting trousers and shirt hang limp. He fought to control his emotions. His voice seethed with contempt, "So? What am I supposed to do? I am not his legal guardian." Turning towards his mother, he called out, "Ma ..."

"O, Rupu! What is going to happen now? What shall I do?"

The tone of mourning in Snehalata's voice reassured the man. The voice of the bereaved mother had sounded very dry to him all this while.

"Inform Deepa. Let Krishno's wife do what she thinks is best. I came on an urgent inspection duty. The car is waiting. I've to return to the office. I'm off," said Rupendu Roy in a detached, dispassionate voice.

"Leaving? Won't you stay? What will I do? Won't you come again?"

"Not today. Your grandson has fever. I'll try tomorrow morning." Rupendu walked out of the courtyard and vanished into the lane. His shoes no longer had the stamp of authority.

"O Rupu! Suppose Deepa doesn't want to come. What am I to do then?" Even as she asked, Snehalata realized that Rupu had left. She fell silent.

The man was completely horrified by Rupendu Roy's exit. A terrible rage overcame him. Arre! Arre! The man is leaving. Her own son leaves while I stay stuck here. What a situation!

He had never been able to bring himself to thrash pickpockets and thieves but now he had an urge to punch the man, drag him by his collar and throw him down on the veranda in the typical manner of the police. He ran out on to the street. But it was too late. Rupendu Roy's Ambassador was turning into the main road.

What an ass I am. Why am I still here? Her own son went away leaving his mother alone. He cursed himself. He was so overcome with anger and amazement that he sat down on the veranda, perspiring profusely.

Even more benumbed than before, Snehalata sat thinking of Krishno's marriage. Her eldest, Rupendu, had repeatedly advised against getting Krishno married. Not Rupendu alone, Nobo and Kanak too had warned her against it. She had refused to listen. Rupendu had found him a job but Krishnendu was not regular, he got drunk and passed out at all times of the day. Yet after six months of being employed, Krishno had wept at Snehalata's feet, "Ma get me married now. I'll be completely cured."

Rupendu had cautioned again, "Ma, don't get taken in by all this play-acting and spoil someone's life." She had refused to listen. She was convinced that all his problems would be solved once he got married and had a wife at home. So many boys went astray in their youth. With marriage, family, children, he would not be able to afford the drinking.

But Krishno didn't improve at all. His wife, his two beautiful children – nothing could change his ways. Sometimes he went to work, sometimes he didn't. At the end of the month he didn't bring a paisa home. His brothers looked after his family, his wife took up a job ... The brothers didn't mind helping the family financially but finally the prestige of his famous brothers was affected. Krishno would be found lying drunk in all sorts of places. When passersby offered to take him home, he would give Kanak's and Rupu's names. He was arrested several times and would mention his brothers' names to secure his release. The brothers were intensely annoyed and now could not bear to hear his name.

Rupu had been angry ever since Krishnendu got married. He refused to accept Krishno's wife. His annoyance included his mother as well. But what else could Snehalata have done? She could still feel the wetness of Krishno's tears on her feet.

Krishno was sensitive. "You could say, I am the useless one amongst your lot," Krishno used to say in his self-deprecatory way. "That is the reason you don't love me."

All his three brothers were well-educated. Kanak had not been academically brilliant but had made a name with his music. If Pranab had not become mentally sick he would have been an even more important officer of the central government than Rupu. Academically, Nobo was the best, and a writer of repute.

Krishno was convinced that she didn't love him and she could not rid his mind of this thought. Can a mother not love her son? He wouldn't believe her. Perhaps it was this hurt that led him to drink when he entered college. He couldn't even complete his graduation.

"That's not it, Ma. He fell into bad company. None of you realized that. If he could have been checked at that time ... But what could you have done after all? In a family without a father, Ma, one or two are bound to go astray," said Nobo, trying to comfort her.

Though he was younger, Nobo had spared no effort to try and rehabilitate Krishno. If he had stayed on in India maybe Krishno would not have gone so completely out of hand.

Krishnendu babu ... Was he married?"

The man had risen from the veranda and had been watching Snehalata for some time. Now he spoke. He asked the question though he knew that Nandan had gone to fetch her daughter-in-law. Snehalata's dry eyes and silence upset him. He was trying to assess her mental condition by making her talk. Besides he had to know whether Krishnendu's wife would bother to come or remain as indifferent as Rupendu Roy.

"Yes, there is a wife. There are children too. Who else would be left to cry for him otherwise?"

"Don't they stay with him?"

"No. Not any more."

A deep sigh escaped Snehalata at long last. She had tried hard to change her daughter-in-law's mind. "Stay together. Try to change him by talking to him. Persuade him."

"He is not going to change, Ma. I have put up with so much. Not any more. Besides, I have to bring up the children."

She had left for her father's house. Now, she had forever lost the right to wear the noa on her wrist, the sindoor in the parting of her hair.

Wretched girl! Snehalata tried to feel angry. But instead her heart twisted in sorrow and sympathy. The man wondered how to keep the conversation going in the face of Snehalata's monosyllabic replies. The old lady knew it all now. So why didn't she burst into loud tears? He couldn't understand why she just sat there, numb.

Snehalata, the mother, was engrossed in remembering the special qualities of her dead son. None of her other sons were as jolly or as warm as Krishno. The whole house had been filled with laughter before his problem with alcohol. He had got on so well with Nobo's wife, with Kanak's wife and many others.

Krishno had always been ready to help. Whether it was someone in the locality who needed to be hospitalized or someone who needed to go to the cremation ground in the middle of the night, Krishno would put his heart and soul into helping whoever was in trouble. She had seen so many people bless Krishno. Could no one's blessing save him?

He was already addicted to alcohol when some devil started him on drugs. This was the most destructive thing of all. His home would have been free of trouble if he had not started on them. He began disappearing from home. Doctors, hospitals, nothing was of any use. A sudden wail burst out of her.

"O, Krishno, will I never see you again?"

The cry was so sudden that the man, startled, stepped into the room. As soon as she saw the man, Snehalata bit her lip and swallowed her tears. She couldn't understand why the man had been waiting all this while. This accursed, ill-omened person had brought the news and delivered it, so why didn't he just leave?

The sight of her room broke his heart. Kanakendu Roy, a famous singer, had a huge flat at Lansdowne and great wealth. And this was the state of his mother's room! There was a stove and a coal oven in a corner. No doubt the cooking was done in the room itself. Huge cobwebs hung from the ceiling. A grimy mosquito net hung from dusty bed frames. The red floor had turned black. An old, battered trunk sticky with dirt made the room look worse than a godown.

He imagined how happy he would have made his mother and with what comfort and wealth he would have striven to surround her, had she been alive, and he as rich as Kanakendu. Yet the mother of such a well-known son lived in this condition! The behaviour of the other officer son, he had seen with his own eyes.

The anger inside him resurfaced. He asked in an angry voice, "Does Kanakendu Roy visit this house?"

Irritated, Snehalata replied, "Yes. Of course he does. Why won't he come to see his mother? He comes whenever he is free."

"And your other son? The officer? Even news of this kind couldn't make him wait an extra two minutes?"

"He is like that. Doesn't think." Snehalata tried to make excuses for her son.

Her fear and suspicion of the man increased. Who was he to ask so many questions? Should she be angry and ask him to leave? She found that instead of anger, fear was what she felt. Now that the house was empty she felt fearful all the time. The house had scared her like this for a long time after her husband's death. She felt all at sea with seven children of different ages. Then things settled down again. Rupu got an important job. He married. The grandchildren appeared. Nobo went into politics. His friends filled the house all day. Kanak was beginning to make a name for himself. Many people, parties, clubs tried to please Snehalata so that they could get Kanak to come to their functions. "Ma, please speak on our behalf. He won't refuse you. He is a devoted son."

Yes, Kanak did love his mother. He earned a lot of money. Whenever she asked for money he filled her palms with it. Then he too got married and had a daughter. He had become so famous that he kept going away to America.

How could this dilapidated old house hold such an important man? He moved to a flat in another locality. Rupu had already moved out. Not able to get a job in the country, Nobo had migrated. Ever since then the house had begun haunting her again. Then there were Krishno's excesses, his drug addiction. His wife left. Krishno left last of all. Now only Pranab and she remained in this huge house.

The house seemed to want to swallow her ... it made faces at her, taunting her. These days she felt very afraid of staying alone there. The emptier the house became, the wilder Pranab got. She felt afraid of him even though she was his mother – Pono could strangle her to death.

No, her children were not inhuman. They all wanted her to stay with them. They would have all kept her in comfort. Rupu too would not refuse. Kanak and Nobo would keep her in luxury. But no one offered to look after Pranab. Nobo would have looked after him if he had been here. But the others would not even let Pranab enter their homes. How could she let her mad son roam the streets, while there was life left in her body? What will become of Pranab when she dies? She asked Nobo to find out if there was a place where he could be institutionalized.

"No place will keep him. The government taxes able-bodied people. It takes no responsibility for the disabled, old, helpless and mad. That responsibility falls on the family."

"He has no wife."

"He doesn't. Nor a father. When you die, we, the brothers might look after him. If we don't, no one can legally compel us to. When you can no longer look after him, he will go onto the streets, scrounge for food. If he is lucky, he will be placed in an asylum either under his own name or an assumed one."

These were the kinds of things Nobo used to say. Snehalata could not quite follow all that Nobo said. She understood that she had no alternative but to live alone with Pranab. As the days passed, no medicine or treatment had any effect on him any longer. He had begun by being violent with his sisters-in-law, then towards his brothers. Of late he had started trying to hit his mother and take away her money by force. Who knows if he was frightened too, like his mother. Was it fear that was driving him deeper and deeper into insanity? These days Snehalata was in the grip of an acute fear. Everything scared her. She was afraid of everyone. As if there was nothing left to receive from life. There was only this living in fear.

That terror had manifested itself in the shape of a piece of paper in the man's hands, wrapping itself all over her body. She wanted to scream out loud at the cold slippery touch of fear, from the rib-crushing pain ... But suddenly a fire rushed from her stomach to her throat and choked her voice. As though not only her heart but her belly too was aflame. Suddenly she was hungry, very hungry.

"What has happened? Why drag us into affairs concerning Krishnoda?"

The man's mind had wandered. He started out of his reverie and saw a well-built young man, about twenty five years old, standing in front of Snehalata's room, speaking gruffly to her, "Everything is over between him and Didi."

"How is it over? It is in his name that she still wears shankha and loha on her wrists and applies sindoor in her parting," mumbled Snehalata in a faint voice.

"That is Didi's personal affair and no reason for you to force her to go to the thana," the boy retorted aggressively. His chest muscles swelled beneath his T-shirt. He seemed prepared to lay down his life to shield his sister from all troubles.

"What will happen then? About Krishno?" Snehalata cried out in a pathetic bewildered tone no doubt wanting to ask about Krishno's funeral but unable to bring herself to it.

"What more can happen? It's all over now. Everything is finished," the boy said boorishly.

The man felt a strong urge to get up and slap the boy until he realized that the boy did not offend him half as much as Rupendu Roy.

"Kiltush, my son, don't get angry. I'm helpless. I can't see. Please make a trunk call to Nobo. I'll pay for it."

With trembling hands Snehalata tried to undo the knot in her saree. Nobo's address and phone number was tied up in her pallu. Only she knew why she kept Nobo's address and phone number tied up in her saree like that. Perhaps that address and number – like Nobo's love and concern for his mother – had become akin to his presence, and she held it close, always next to her body, wherever she went. When she went for a bath, she undid the knot and placed the piece of paper in a safe place. She never forgot to tie it into her saree again when her bath was over. It was this very paper she was trying to take out now. But her fingers trembled so much that she could not undo the knot.

"Where does your son live?"

"Far away. Takes three days to reach here," Kiltush answered him before she could.

"He'll fly. The moment he learns about Krishno, he'll take a plane. He loved Krishno." Tears at last overwhelmed Snehalata's words.

"Even then, not before tomorrow ... late afternoon or evening," said Kiltush, forgetting his previous hostility, and entering into Snehalata's predicament.

But the man grew impatient once more. "This is strange. Why don't you inform Kanakendu Roy? He lives nearby."

"Oh yes. Inform Kanak," Snehalata said suddenly remembering Kanakendu. "His address and phone number are inside the trunk. Please take a look, Kiltush."

Snehalata lowered her legs to the floor to point out the box, but her body trembled violently. Watching this, Kiltush softened his stance.

"Arre, I know Kanakda's address and phone number. I'll ring him up."

It was clear from Kiltush's tone that while he was ready to reject any connection with his brother-in-law Krishno, he was rather proud of the familial link with Kanak.

The man beckoned to Kiltush. He had realized that it was futile to either fear or be angry with this boy. He used his policeman voice, "This is an unnatural death. Has your sister divorced Krishnababu?"

"No, not yet," the boy answered nervously.

"In that case, no matter how many brothers go, the police will not release the body without the presence of his legally wedded wife. She will have to identify the body."

"Unh! Is that so?" Kiltush was visibly upset.

The man lied. "Of course. I have come from the thana and have been waiting for your sister for a long time."

"Oh really? I thought you had left after delivering the news. That is ... I don't know. Nandan didn't say that you were the one who brought the news," Kiltush was confused, his arrogance vanished. Then a strangely soft and sad expression shadowed his face and he asked quietly, "Is it really the body of Krishnendu Roy? Is it our Krishnoda's body? Are you sure?"

"How can we be sure till it is identified. That is why ..."

But Kiltush spoke on not really listening to the man's words, "You know, Krishnoda was a fine man. He was a nice man. But his addiction ... No wonder they say that addiction kills. That one failing spoiled his whole life, ruined Didi, and my nephew and niece. Could it be that it isn't Krishnoda's body? What do you say?"

"Good if it turns out that way," said the man looking at Snehalata and feeling really happy for her at the thought of such a possibility. But suddenly the expression on Kiltush's face changed and he became as grim and hostile as before.

"No, no. Whatever has happened is for the best. Things had to be decided one way or the other. How long can you ..." Then looking at the man, he said, "All right. Since you have waited so long, please wait a little longer. I'll pick Didi up from her office and take her to the thana. I'll also ring up Kanakda. Don't worry Mashima," the last words were addressed to Snehalata. "Since Didi has always done her duty, let her do this last one too. That will be the end of all her worries."

And the agile and youthful figure of Kiltush vanished from the courtyard in a trice.

After Kiltush left, Snehalata began feeling nervous again. Will Krishno's wife come here? Who knows what she will say? It will be so difficult to face her. Once again she was aware of a scorching hunger that rose from her belly and made her head swim.

Snehalata's wealthy husband, a doctor, used to keep a sharp and caring eye on her diet. He used to say, "Feed the children and me too. But there is no need to neglect yourself, we do not lack in anything."

That care lasted for fifteen years. For a few years after that there was some scarcity. But once the sons started earning, she had no more problems. The sons put all their earnings into her hands. The store, the household, was under her control. Daughters-in-law arrived and left. She remained the hub of the household. She never had to suffer for lack of food.

When she became a widow at the age of thirty five, she gave up eating fish and mutton. But she still had to cook these for the children. To herself she admitted that sometimes she had felt a strong urge to eat some meat. Now, in her old age, she was obliged to eat fish and eggs again.

She used to send Pranab to do the shopping and he bought only fish. He refused to buy any vegetables. Some days he didn't even go shopping. Then the only way out was to buy potatoes and eggs from the grocer near the house. How long can one live on boiled potatoes and dal? Besides, it was convenient to cook only one curry and some rice. She couldn't see, and so was afraid to light the fire nor could she squat on the floor to cook because her knees ached. Eating food cooked by servants disgusted her. So these days she managed to cook only one dish. When there were guests at home, she reverted to vegetarian food, but Nobo's wife had sharp eyes. Once she said, "Ma, your sons are all progressive. They address meetings on the subject of women's liberation. You should eat fish and mutton freely. No one is going to say anything."

"At this stage of my life? Fish and mutton? Won't that be a sin?" It was her own doubt she needed an answer to.

"Why should it be a sin? You have cooked it all your life. If that was not a sin, will it be one if you eat it now? If it is, then let it be mine," Nobo's wife had said, placing a large piece of fish on her mother-in-law's plate. Since then, she had eaten fish and eggs along with everyone else. Only mutton she didn't start all over again.

But even arranging for that curry and rice had become a problem these days. All the sons contributed towards her expenses. Sometimes, Rupu, away on tour, would give the money only when he got back ... some months, Kanak's secretary would forget to send the money. And at times Nobo's moneyorder would arrive late. There was no way she could keep a large sum of money with herself. Because she couldn't see well enough to open the iron trunk she didn't lock it. Pronob swiped all the money from the open trunk and spent it on bidis, gave it away, just as he pleased. In spite of being given five rupees every day he even helped himself to the monthly sum meant for running the household. Snehalata was afraid to request her sons to increase their contributions for fear that annoyed, they might stop contributing altogether. She knew that they wouldn't do that, but was afraid. What would she live on if they stopped giving money? As she grew older, her appetite increased. Today, at this time of great sorrow, an excruciating hunger consumed her.

Today she had given Pono thirty rupees. That cursed fool had brought two foli fish and swiped the rest of the money. She couldn't eat fish full of bones and had managed only a few mouthfuls. Now she was very hungry.

She knew that the house would fill up with people in a little while. Kanak was very annoyed with Krishno. He may not come. But his wife was a good girl. She's bound to come rushing with her daughter. She will also inform the daughters. They will come when they get the news. Rupu's wife might come if she feels like it. There were other relatives as well. Only Nobo and his wife will arrive last of all. Who will do the cooking till then? How will these people be fed? Would it be proper to cook and eat before Krishno's funeral is over? She was the mother and there was no one she could ask.

But this terrible hunger was going to kill her, she thought. Then she remembered that after lunch, she had put four eggs to boil on the dying flame of the stove. They must be done by now. She decided to make some egg curry. There was a lot of rice left over from the afternoon. She was going to eat curry and rice right now. After satisfying her hunger, she would cover the rest of the curry and keep it for Pronob. He could eat whenever he wanted.

She thought of Pronob to justify her urge to cook. He would drive her mad as soon as it was evening, if he didn't get anything to eat. He would throw such a tantrum that everyone, including Kanak's wife, would leave the house. It was such a torment that she never had any peace, though she had given birth to him. Each of her sons had made her suffer in a different way. Now the burning in her belly became one with the pain in her heart. The belly, which having borne seven children, now clung to her, ugly, wrinkled and sagging.

She rose from the bed and stood with the pain still burning inside her. She looked at the man. "There is a moda outside the room, please sit there," she commanded him imperiously.

When the man went out, she shut the door. She pulled the stove close to her and lighting a match, dropped it on the stove's wick.

Even now people praised her culinary skills and called her the Draupadi of cooking. She didn't use onion or garlic in her egg curry. She used ginger, cumin seed, chilli paste and garam masala. The part-time maid had ground the spices in the morning. She boiled the potatoes. After shelling the eggs she heated the oil, browned the eggs in it and then put them aside on a plate. She poured a little oil into the kadhai and dropped the spices into it with her left hand, stirring the paste with her right, adding a few drops of water every now and then to keep it from sticking to the sides. When the oil separated from the spice paste she poured some water into the kadhai and when it came to a boil she put in the eggs, the potatoes and some sugar and salt. She cut open the eggs a little so that the flavour of the curry seeped into the eggs. The thick red curry bubbled. Tiny drops of curry rose and scattered. The air was filled with the smell of egg curry.

Snehalata derived immense satisfaction from the aroma. The lines of discontent and anxiety were smoothed off her aristocratic face. But a few folds of sorrow still remained. Tears began to well up in the dry surface of her nearly sightless eyes.

Sitting outside the man was growing worried. When a mother shuts her door upon receiving the news of her son's death, it is cause for anxiety. Besides the lady had been acting rather unnaturally. After that one scream she hadn't wept at all. She hadn't even lamented the death. He thought the old lady was very resilient.

The man wondered whether her strength and calmness was born out of a desperate grief that was dispassionately pushing her to take an extreme step. The moment he had this thought he began to sweat. Was he just going to stand by and watch the lady die after waiting around so long? He imagined the lady's body, its neck grotesquely twisted, hanging from the roof. Terrified he ran to the door. Suddenly the smell of kerosene and fire assailed his nostrils. Now he was certain the lady was going to set fire to herself. Maybe she already had.

Really, how could an old lady like her climb up high enough to hang herself he thought, giving the door a hard push. Then he saw that a side window was open.

What an ass I am! Why don't I peer inside through the window?

He ran to the window. By then the smell of the egg curry announced that it was done. The man found something being cooked in a kadhai licked with flames. Snehalata was turning the eggs over with a ladle and, with infinite precision, prising them open, a little at a time. Her face was absorbed in the cooking but tears coursed down her cheeks.

"Oh Krishno! I don't even know where and how you died. Will I never see you again my precious!"

First the man felt thunder had crashed inside the room, though there had been no flash of lightning before. Something came crashing down loudly. Whatever it was, at the same time it was followed by the touch of a cool wet breeze. Then, slowly slowly, pitter patter, a shower rained down, incessant, ceaseless.

For a long while, the man stood and tried to figure out the significance of the scene, the meaning of the sound. Then, a sad, wistful smile appeared on his hard and cruel face. He turned around to go home. There was no need for him here.

ক

VIBHA RANI

THE WITNESS

TRANSLATED BY VIDYANAND JHA AND THE EDITORS
NOMINATED BY UDAYA NARAYANA SINGH

First published in Maithili as "Rahtu Sakshi Chhat Ghat" in *Sandhan*,
October 1998, Patna

Rau Baap, Rau Baap! There has been a dacoity in Bhola and Ramchannar's house, Ha Daib!, even one's enemies should not see such a day!

Barely ten days ago, the whole family had turned out at the Chhat Ghat for the riverbank puja, a celebration the family attended every year – Bhola and Ramchannar, their wives, Gauri and Gayatri. And the lovely Munia, how she had shone like a moon among the brothers' star-like children, draped as she was in a red Banarasi saree and loaded with jewellery – tika, nose-stud, a seetahar necklace, cummerbund and anklets, her lustrous hair in an elaborate red cloth braid. Munia, just barely in her teens, had looked like a winsome child-bride, soft and smooth like the new leaves on a mango tree, and even as one looked, she had seemed unusually grown-up. And today the entire village is scurrying to their place, filling the frontyard and the inner courtyard. And what are Bhola and Ramchannar up to? Fainting, that's what, one after the other. For the brief moments when they regain consciousness they flay their chests with both their hands and with a cry of "Ha Daib!" fall into a dead faint again, now one, now the other. Bhola's wife is pulling out her hair and beating her breasts and abusing her God – "Rau Mudai, Rau Mudai! You could not bear to see even a single day of our happiness, Mudaia ... If I don't brand you with a burning wood, I am not my father's daughter." Ramchannar's wife sits in the other room, surrounded by women, dangerously quiet till she totters up once in every sudden while, looks around wildly, screams, "Baap re baap! Let me go, l-et me go, let ..." then just as suddenly her shoulders droop, and she lapses back into a stupor – Oh, such misfortune!

As children, Bhola and Ramchannar helped their father sell balloons, tops and whistles pegged on to a bamboo stick. They roamed the city, their usual haunt being the rickshaw stand outside the railway station. There were four trains which crossed the station every day – the up trains came in at seven in the morning and six in the evening, and the down ones at nine in the morning, and eleven in the night. Bauji never waited for the eleven o'clock train because, one, it was quite late in the night, two, people were in a hurry to grab a rickshaw or tanga as soon as they got off the train, and three, all the children were asleep. When it was festival time, be it Jhoolan, Janmashtami or other festivals, Bauji would land up at the melas without fail. They did brisk business there, Bhola and Ramchannar had to work harder too, inflating more balloons and making more toys. And come the kite-flying season, father and sons were into making kites, grinding glass to make the manjha, applying this bristling paste on to the kite string – better to cut other kites with!

Mai had a goat. Both brothers grazed it by turns, wishing desperately they were in school instead, studying. The teacher of the school, Ramnath Babu, used to let them in sometimes but how much can one study, without a slate, a pencil or books? Bauji wanted them to study but could not afford to educate them. He sat them at home and taught them how to count up to a hundred, to multiply up to twenty times twenty, to calculate fractions and multiply sawaiya and adhaiya – just some basic math, really. This little knowledge held them in good stead. Then Mai's goat gave birth to three kids, clean and small chagaris, and Mai made a pact with God: Settle my sons, O Bhagavati, and I will offer one chagari to you. At the festival of Chhat that year, she made another maanata to Chhat Maiya, I'll offer bamboo baskets to you Chhat Maiya, but please settle my sons. So ten days before the festival, Bhola and Ramchannar went out early in the morning and placed a red ekranga cloth in a bamboo basket and then religiously offered to Chhat Maiya, the alms collected.

Humans beings do their calculations while bidhna does its own. If the two match it's god's will, if not ... Luckily Fate smiled on Bhola and Ramchannar. In time, Bhola started helping out in Ramasra Babu's grocery store. Ramchannar worked in Baldev Babu's Mithila Cloth Store. Baldev Babu was a Marwari and had quite a range of fabrics of different colours. His clientele ranged from the very poor to the wife and daughter of the town's chairman saheb. Ramchannar displayed the rich fabrics to them, dreaming all the time of owning his own cloth shop.

Mai's household however continued to run on the money Bauji brought in. The brothers gave half their salaries to Bauji and Mai immediately appropriated them from him. With this she got made two nose-studs for her future daughters-in-law. And a pair of tikas from the money earned from the sale of the chagaris – Mai had sold two on her own, the brothers insisted on selling the third as well, saying, "Mai, by the time we are well-settled in life, it will be too old. Then nobody will give you the proper price for it. Let another chagari come. Then you can fulfil your maanata to the Bhagavati."

Both brothers dreamed of starting a business with the portion of their salaries that they saved each month. Bhola wanted a grocery shop. But Ramchannar had his heart set on a cloth store. Bhola was just three years older than Ramchannar, but a great deal wiser.

He said with a laugh, "Ram Bhai, with the kind of money we have, we won't get more than ten thaans of cloth and it is only a big and well-stocked shop that attracts customers. People look at twenty five thaans before they buy half a gaj. A cloth store is for people with a large capital. If you sit with ten thaans like a pauper, nobody will even come to your shop. Also, cloth is not bought everyday. Unlike groceries, a daily necessity. Somebody needs salt, somebody else turmeric. The business will not collapse even with less capital. Let's open a grocery store. We'll not spend the profit. And with the increased capital we'll expand our shop. Once this shop is expanded, we may even be able to open a cloth store. But, not just yet."

Munia sits silently in the room. She cannot understand the terror that fills the house. Why is everyone crying? On one side, Barka Bauji and Chhotka Bauji are having fainting fits and on the other both the mais ... Everybody says that there's been a dacoity, but no thief or dacoit has entered the house. Everything is as before. Then what dacoity are they talking about, and who's the dacoit?

Time befriended Bhola and Ramchannar. The grocery shop

prospered. Mai ordered two sets of silver hansuli necklaces and cummerbunds for her future daughters-in-law. Bhagawati's maanata had been fulfilled, so too the one to Chhat Maiya. Now all she waited for was daughters-in-law. Mai wished both brothers would wed on the same day, even if the ceremony had to be performed in a mandir. And then a bride came for Bhola. The bride's father said, "If you think it appropriate, my chhotki beti, Gayatri, is also of marriageable age. If along with Gauri for Bhola Babu, you accept Gayatri for Ramchannar Babu, then, my responsibilities will be over and I'll be able to go bathe in the Ganga."

Such marriages were not common in their family, but both Bauji and Mai agreed to it. If both brothers were married to sisters, they would be fond of each other and there would be no rifts over property and inheritance later. Anyway, some dowry was necessary for them to make their capital grow.

Munia comes out of her room and goes into Barki Mai's. The womenfolk stare solemnly at her, each experiencing a wetness in the eyes and a shooting pain in the heart. A sigh escapes every lip. Munia goes and sits near Barki Mai and holds her hand. Barki Mai looks up and seeing Munia, hugs her tight and starts howling again. Munia also begins to cry. But while Barki Mai cries from the pain of knowing it all, Munia cries, in imitation, without understanding why.

Gauri and Gayatri were wed to Bhola and Ramchannar respectively. They shimmered resplendent in all the ornaments Mai had got made for them. And soon Gauri and Gayatri worked inside the house as hard as Bhola and Ramchannar worked in the shop. The house became nicer and more inviting. Mai oversaw the work of both the daughters-in-law at home and Bauji sat at the shop. But, most of all, Mai and Bauji spent time in puja path and dan dakshina. Mai continued observing Chhat. Bhola and Ramchannar still went and collected alms, only now it was no more than a token ritual. They bathed in the evening of the penultimate day of the puja and collect alms from five houses each just as, on the day of the parana, they collected prasad from five ghats.

Munia is still in Barki Mai's embrace. The women seated around are openly shedding tears. One woman starts to break the lac bangles on Munia's hands. The red and yellow bangles crack with a soft chat-chat sound. The lahathi, which she first wore five months ago, breaks free of her arms and falls to the ground in pieces.

What an arduous wait it had been. For fourteen long years no doctor was spared, from Madhubani-Darbhanga to Patna, Mai did not overlook any healer, vaid, ojha, guni, or peer-maajar, and for their part, Gauri and Gayatri kept all the fasts recommended by all and sundry. The doctors said, There's no problem medically. The sants said, Have patience. But Mai was impatient. Bhola and Ramchannar also were. What was the use of toiling so hard at this business they had built up with their sweat and blood if they had no children to pass it on to?

Time passed. Mai, completely drained of all energy, handed over the Chhat fast to Gauri. Bhola stood waistdeep in water, doing penance each day. And every year, the same plea to Chhat Maiya. Bhola and Gauri wept and wept, Gayatri and Ramchannar were pleaded silently. Till at last Chhat Maiya came to their rescue.

Gauri and Gayatri both became pregnant at the same time and gave birth to a son each. Then, one after the other, both had sons again, with remarkable similarities. The third time round, along with the sons and their wives, Mai also said, "Chhat Maiya should give us a daughter this time. Without one, how do we do kanyadaan, how do we amass the punya of bathing in the Ganga?" Bhola and Ramchannar begged Gauri and Gayatri, "We want a girl this time, we want a girl." And the two sisters giggled in unison, hiding their faces in their ghunghats, "Is this in our hands?"

Gauri gave birth to a son. But Gayatri, she fulfilled everyone's long cherished desire with the adorable Munia. Everyone forgot Gauri's newborn, Gauri too.

"She's my daughter."

"No, she's mine."

Both the brothers wrangled as Gayatri smiled benignly, and

Gauri, too smiled. In the end Gauri said, "Don't strangle the child in your fights. Is there anything in this house which is exclusively mine or anyone's, then how can Munia belong only to any one of us? She belongs to us all."

Munia turned and Munia crawled, Munia grew, day by delightful day. Every year, people saw her on Chhath Ghat, Munia at her mother's waist, Munia running, the tinkle of pajebs around her small ankles, Munia twirling in a red dacron frock, her hair in two long chotis, standing up.

Then one day, Bauji collapsed as he sat at the shop: Mai too left for baikunth while offering water to Tulsiji. Alas, they both died without seeing Munia married.

The seed of this desire was taking root inside Bhola and Ramchannar, Gauri and Gayatri. They were impatient for Munia to grow up. If it were in their hands, Munia would have crossed each year in a second. Every year, throughout the month of Katik, Gauri and Gayatri made Munia light the lamp to Tulsi.

Oh, say the people gathered around, What sin did poor Munia commit, that far from protecting her through all her seven lives Tulsi Mai has wrecked even this one, snuffing out her marriage at such a tender age?

Years passed like seconds indeed and people started seeing Munia wearing a tika and nose-stud. She was still in a frock and pajamis but oh, she looked such a doll! People only had to see her, glowing and radiant, and they would break into smiles.

The whole town gathered for the bariyat. The arrangements were top class. Snacks and dinner were arranged for all the guests. There were eleven types of mithais and puris and bunia in unlimited quantities. One could eat as much as one liked. The son-in-law was handsome too. About sixteen or seventeen with just a hint of a moustache. A widowed mother and another brother in the family. And rich. Even if the brothers did not study or work, and just frittered away their inheritance, it would last them seven generations.

Bhola and Ramchannar had made their intentions very clear. "We will fill your whole house with things. The bride is young right now. We will not send her to you immediately. The bidagari will be only after five years."

The mother-in-law was adamant and said, "How can this be? Will the bariyati go back empty-handed? You have to follow the dharma."

"All right. Please send her back after the chauthari," Ramchannar and Bhola, Gayatri and Gauri requested. "This way you won't lose face. We told you, we got our young daughter married only because we wanted to see her future secure. But we are responsible for her still."

And so, with her aanchal full of rice and paddy, in a saree trimmed with yellow gota and an oversized blouse, Munia reached her husband's home, like a beautiful gift, warm, delicate and soft like an unbaked diya. The groom was taken aback. He was around sixteen or seventeen, and understood the special relationship between a bride and a groom, and the importance of the first night. But he could not muster enough courage to touch this fragile unbaked diya. He felt as if she would crumble if he touched her. So he drank in her face, talked a bit, and fell to sleep.

On the day of the chauthari, the fourth day of the marriage on which it should have been consummated, the brothers reached Munia's new home with the puchhari. The bidagari was done the next day. Little Munia flew like a bird from its cage, prancing around in a red and yellow saree, nakhi, lahathi filling her arms, two chotis and peepa sindoor in her parting. Whoever looked at Munia, radiant in the morning light, could not take their eyes off her.

And now, the whole Chhat Ghat was numb with grief. Gauri was offering the arghya – with a soop in her hands and tears in her eyes. Bhola stood in the waters of the pond with his head downcast. People came by, on some pretext or the other, stole a glance at Munia and went back. When they saw Munia, a deep sigh escaped their lips: Ha Daib! People were so used to seeing her in her tika, nose-stud and dacron frock. And just last year she had charmed them all in her red Banarasi saree, her body adorned with ornaments, the parting in her hair filled with sindoor. Newly-wed Munia had not known the meaning of marriage but the unforgettable picture she made, as a sweet and charming baalvadhu, was in everyone's mind. It was quite natural to sigh seeing Munia now.

Munia was in a stark-white saree, with arms devoid of bangles, and the parting in her hair without sindoor. No bangles, no large bindi on the forehead, no smile on her lips. It seemed as if she had aged thirty years.

When her mother-in-law had been widowed at a very young age, she had had her strapping sons, Ramkumar and Ramprakash, by her side. She had yearned for a daughter-in-law as deeply as Bhola and Ramchannar wanted to marry off their little daughter. There was no pressing need on either side, both sides were tied with just the thread of longing.

How the groom and his brother had opposed the wedding. "Neither are we adults nor is she. What is the point when she would be in her father's house for five years after marriage?" But the mother reasoned, "I know, but just the marriage will take place for now. Your father is no more. If I were to die suddenly who will arrange the marriage of two orphans? If you are already married, then even if I die, Ramprakash will not be called an orphan. The hand of his Bhai and Bhaujai will be on his head." But the person meant to extend his hand had disappeared himself. The doctors said his heart failed. Such an ailment at such a young age?

Who has ever understood the games of bidhna?

Bhola and Ramchannar approached Munia's mother-in-law. "How will she live a life of widowhood from such a young age? Though it's not done amongst us, we are willing to take on society for the sake of our daughter. But before that we want your permission ..."

"Permission, I give you agreement. You want me to agree, no? I agree. Who understands the travails of widowhood better than I? I had my two sons to help me live. I passed my time watching them grow. She, poor child, has not even seen her husband's face. I know, traditions and norms are made by us. If we break them, they are made afresh, in a more logical, more rational manner. You want to get her remarried. If you ask me, I too want the same. But now that she is the daughter-in-law of this house, how can I let her go to some other? She'll have to live with me."

"But, how is this possible?" Ramchannar had no idea what she was saying.

"Why? Why is it not possible? Only Ramkumar has gone away from us. Ramprakash is standing right here. May he live long. May my remaining years go to him. I am only concerned about my daughter-in-law. I need her."

Bhola and Ramchannar were speechless. They had thought that the sasu would not have much sympathy for them, her heart filled with bitterness after the death of her young son. They and their Munia would get nothing but the choicest of abuses and curses, that, though it was no fault of theirs, they would be branded dishonest and Munia declared an evil, inauspicious being, a dayan, a churail, a saikhauki. But here, instead of seething hate, was the gentle balm of chandan, fragrant, soothing and cool. Their wounded souls were anointed with affection, trust and adhikar.

This time round too, the Chhat Ghat bore witness. All the women there made a special detour to see Munia, who stood again, entrancingly innocent in her finery, a red Banarasi saree, sindoor in her maang, tika, nose-stud and lac bangles. She was at a becoming age, her beauty was like the sun dancing on the water. It was a year after Ramkumar's death. The anniversary had been observed. Bhola and Ramchannar had reached Ramkumar's place with all the sarees and ornaments which Munia had received in the marriage. A year ago Ramkumar's mother told them, "Wait a year. After that I will get Ramprakash married to your daughter. But there would not be any bariati this time. The wedding will be a subdued affair in some mandir." And true to her word, Ramprakash and Munia entered a new life together, with the blessings of Lord Shiva and Parvati Ma in the famous Garibsthan temple of Muzaffarpur. And people said, If there were more people like her on this earth, no bride would ever be tormented by her in-laws again.

No, the Chhat Ghat's story does not end here. The next year the people saw a Munia who could barely walk. Her face was pale. Each woman's eyes lit up with expectation as she placed the lamps on the arghya.

And then, the following year, Munia came again, not in her Banarasi saree with the bridal tika on her forehead and nathia in her nose, but with a bag of baby clothes! Ramchannar walked in with a six month old infant and handed him to Munia. Eyes glazed. Memories came of the dacron frock, the red Banarasi saree, then the white saree, and then the red Banarasi again. Whether time is a witness or not I can't say but the Chhat Ghat was. The women lit the lamp and sang:

Aihen ge sugani chhati mai
Hoinhen unhin sahai

The baby looked in fascination at the swaying flame – clapping his chubby hands and gurgling. And so evening came once more, time for people to offer arghya. A small smile played on the corners of Gauri and Gayatri's lips. Munia's baby clapped baby hands.

YOGENDRA AHUJA

THE WRONG

TRANSLATED BY NANDITA AGGARWAL AND NEER KANWAL MANI
NOMINATED BY ASAD ZAIDI

First published in Hindi as "Galat" in *Pahal*,
June 1997, Jabalpur

If you ever need to go to one of those shops where signboards advertise This & That Properties, or So & So Associates, remember that it is a complete hoax, a sham, a pack of lies. When the guy on the revolving chair, surrounded by registers, files, pictures and maps of houses and colonies on the wall, says that the plot, house or flat in question is the only one left, just for you, it's bound to be a lie. The price or rent he quotes will be a lie. When he says that some Mr Mathur is going to settle abroad and wants to dispose of his house at a throwaway price, that's a lie as well. Indeed, it's completely possible that it's not Mr Mathur's house at all. When he tells you that a plot or house can't be had any cheaper and that you'd better decide fast as three other clients are waiting, hoping to clinch the deal, he'll be lying to your face. When he clasps his wife close and murmurs endearments into her ear, he is lying (actually he can't stand her), and when, sometimes, in a benevolent and expansive mood, he tells his children to go ahead and ask for anything they want, he's lying again. What he really wants is them to go far away from him. When he says he's going to Delhi on business he's going to Muzaffarnagar or, at most, Meerut. When he claims to have a toothache it could be a cold, ulcers in the mouth, stomach cramps, a tickle. Anything. Or nothing. In all his life, of the thousands of things he has said, perhaps one will be true and even that unintentionally. All are lies, fabrication, nonsense – manufactured and meaningless. He tells all kinds of lies – the sort that are premeditated and deliberate and those he mumbles out of ignorance, not to mention all those ill-informed ones he premises on his own faulty learning. If you ever see him cry, don't stretch your hand out in sympathy as he's probably cracking up with laughter on the inside. If he's lying sick and his rattling last breath signals an imminent demise, you will be well advised not to rush in with a doctor, for at the precise moment that he's about to breathe his last and his harassed and tearful wife is ready to relinquish all control, his eyes will flicker alive, he'll pucker his lips and in a quavering, trembly voice (great theatre this, an emotionally wrought moment) gasp for a drop of water. In a few minutes he'll be sitting up, bright-eyed, whistling for his dog.

Keshav spoke acidly of all property dealers in those days. It was '80, '81 and the price of real estate had skyrocketed and property dealing shops had mushroomed everywhere. His elder brother had joined the burgeoning race of realtors, giving up his clerical job and shifting out of the family home with his wife and kids. Within a year he had a red Maruti and a house full of gadgets. Sarveshwar would listen to Keshav, calmly and then remark that there was no reason to stress the blatantly obvious.

Of them all, Sarveshwar was a totally different kind of man – if you can call a twenty year old, a man. He spoke little and was silent to the point of being dangerous. On special occasions, when he spoke elatedly, in a dreamy voice, words floated up from his blood and mingled with it again. Rarely, but when he did, even the bloodshot eyes on his pallid face would communicate. Of course he was difficult to understand – a hieroglyph in some ancient language – and was given to lying motionless on a mat in a corner, oblivious to the talk in the room, until Shirish Sharma, aspiring writer, would gesture and say, "Sh-h ... don't disturb him, he's communicating with the dead."

Sarveshwar was a thin, emaciated boy whose bones had a paucity of phosphorous and his mind a surfeit of thoughts, ideas and dreams, his life blood pulsating with an all consuming energy. He would pillow his head on his hands while within him beat a gypsy drum, like an incessant and inchoate song of human constance or a poem with very simple, everyday words that nevertheless shone with blinding light, and yet would leave you breathless if you were to read it.

A heater for boiling endless cups of tea stood in one corner of the room and a dilapidated cot in the other. They would gather in that room, ostensibly to study, and, behind its closed doors talk about everything under the sun – girls who moved like the murmur of leaves, select poems from world literature that kindled hope and fired desire, politics and culture, philosophical constructs like base and superstructure ... Heated discussions that either ended in mournful silence as they all shuffled outside into the descending darkness – or in a heady rush of blood, as if stepping into the gaudy lights of a marriage procession, in the glare of which, you find yourself, willy-nilly, breaking into the high notes of a snappy song, perhaps even grabbing a drink.

Sarveshwar's house was closest to the college and his cell-like room with its low damp roof and dirty walls was their favourite haunt. It was customary for everyone to peep in whenever they were going past. Adesh Awasthi, now an insurance agent, Gurvinder Singh, a cashier in the State Bank of Patiala, Alok Srivastava, doctor and owner of a large nursing home, Shirish Sharma, erstwhile Marxist and post-modern writer who had married only recently, much later than the rest of them, and Keshav, he who ... Then there were Shukla, Ghosh and all the rest who had been students in those days, all of them would hang around from evening till late at night, some of them occasionally sleeping over.

That was fifteen years ago. Memories of that time are now old, like unused junk in the dark recesses of the mind, wiped with moist hands in one's dreams, groped at and put back as they were – an old picture, a frame, a chessboard with a few missing pieces, a cane chair on its last legs, a wall clock frozen in time and a skeleton of a lantern waiting for its chimney. But there is also a violin that plays as beautifully as always, only much softer, to hear which you have to suspend your breath.

It was a derelict, hundred year old, double-storeyed house made of kuchcha bricks, with thirty three rooms, now let out to ten or twelve tenants. The first floor had a row of damp, unevenly tiled, attic-like rooms which were crammed with junk and always, a deep silence. Besides Sarveshwar's family, office clerks, a taxi driver, a teacher, a homeopath and a man who ran a teastall and whose room was always locked – no one ever saw him come in or leave – resided on the ground floor. Oh, and there was also a barber shop, the one room serving as home and workplace, which opened on to the back street and was plastered with posters of matinee idols and from which a radio blared incessantly. In another solitary dark room lived a smuggler – a middle-aged man with a tense face and narrow eyes, who would slink by silent as a cat and look up, startled, when called. He disappeared for days on end, engaged in the illegal traffic of timber with the full complicity of the police and the forest office. He remembered a lot of verse – by Mahadevi Varma, Dinkar and Ayodhya Singh Upadhayaya "Hariaudh" – that he'd studied at school. Sometimes he would hustle everyone to his room for a cup of tea. He said his family lived in Muzaffarpur, where, he claimed, his brothers had seized control of his sprawling assets. He was poised to wrest it all back, any moment now, and then it would be home, a lifetime of luxury and indolence forever – "You guys come too, it'll be great," he'd say and then try to cadge a few bucks.

Keshav said that there was something distinctly profane about a smuggler spouting poetry, that it seemed, somehow, to be a portent of doom and that one of these days he was going to accost him in the street and demand that he leave the world of poetry quietly, like a decent man. And he would have done so too had not the whole college been agog with rumours about a professor of literature who beat his wife with shoes.

Anyway, the house must have once belonged to the aristocracy and changing hands over the years had finally come to the lot of a retired subedar of the army who had rented it out, keeping a three-room set for himself. Two rooms housed his family and the third, a printing press in whose dingy, smoky confines sat a compositor picking out letters of iron in the partial darkness. Morning and evening, each tenant lit an angithi and the smoke coupled with the emissions from the printing press would drive the homeopath screaming out of his office, where having vented some spleen, he would rush back in and slam the door to keep the smell from ruining his tinctures.

In the night the house looked like a ship ablaze with light – every window was a glittering porthole and sounds emitted from everywhere – the trumpeting of the radio, it's rising and falling cadences, the clickety-clack of the printing press, people yelling, kids bawling outside ... The rest of the street was steeped in quiet, only the curtains on the windows of the houses flapping and flaring in the passing breeze.

The door to Sarveshwar's room was always closed and inside, young, formidable minds spoke in endless whispers, touching upon all that writhed in the dark viscera of time and beyond ... of a golden sunrise, books recently read, Marxism, the girls in the city, especially the one so beautiful – the only word to describe her was "cruel" – about whom the writer would say just this: Each city and town of India always has one girl like her, but only the one ...

And about the Omnipotent. (Yes, God too, and why not?) Every twenty two year old, save the very witless, wants to discuss the existence, and otherwise, of God. For they're at the age when the secrets of the body and the meaning of the classics are beginning to reveal themselves, like the sun that grows clearer and more distinct as morning progresses. It is completely untrue, like most things going around, that the existence of God concerns only the defeated and tired. Just listen in quietly to the talk of a twenty year old. By twenty five, at the most, he has an informed opinion on God. Either the antiquated view of He who stops your thoughts from straying – the traditional earmuffs handed out by parents – or the most fiery ideas and powerful thoughts regarding the haplessness of human existence which smelter in one's blood for a long while before one sits up, suddenly, at three in the morning, and for a heart-stopping second, crosses over to the other side, to perfect understanding, when in the darkest hush of night, the heart trembles like a leaf and then from somewhere appears that friendly consoling hand, offering solace. It is the moment of enlightenment, the moment to say goodbye to everything ... to up and leave with a compass, an Atlas and a few books in a shoulder bag. Yet, all that it means, or should mean, is that God, shedding his mysterious and spiritual aura, acquires a human shape. He who comes in the darkness, suddenly, is also God. For it must be remembered, that the philosopher who, with lantern in hand, declared God dead at high noon, was the same man who compiled the textbooks of the fascists, that the first and final endeavour of the fascists has always been that God endorses what they are doing, raises His hand in their support, and that, rebuffed, God comes still, in dreams this time, with the face of a beggar, leaning on a walking-stick, dark as the night. You want to say something to him but you fumble, nothing is said. He leaves, and you feel very, very inadequate.

These are not the author's views on God but an extract from the Sarveshwar Purana, which Sarveshwar would expound on a summer afternoon, when the sun swung dangerously close to the Earth's horizon, singeing its surface. Surrounded by books bought from a second-hand market or the library he would talk, and listening to him, Shirish Sharma would say – I believe, in fact, that Sarveshwar is "deeply religious" and that even when he's murmuring Marxism to himself he has metaphysics on his mind. Shirish predicted that Sarveshwar's life would be spent in the whisper and murmur of beautiful words, that he might even eke out a meagre living from them, but nothing more. And God forbid, if he ever became a writer, a poet or a professor. For when his readers and students, aflame with the great creative force inspired by his words and phrases, were ready to jump into that great battle of life going on every moment in this country, he would be riding the train out to Vaishnodevi.

Shirish Sharma never gave Sarveshwar a chance to counter these charges. However, one day Keshav pinned Shirish against the wall and in a fierce whisper made it clear that, one, he found his comments petty and silly because the conclusions he drew from Sarveshwar's conversations were false, and, two, in any case, it is better to deal with God in the very beginning because avoiding him means coming back to him in the end. Shirish just stared at him blankly, too nonplussed to speak.

And now something more about Shirish Sharma. He had entered this group only recently, he hailed from a village somewhere beyond the mountains, after his intermediate he came to the city to pursue higher education and was a paying guest in a beautiful bungalow owned by an Engineer Sahab who had retired from the PWD. This engineer's father, now long dead, had come to the city from the same village as Shirish, in search of a living. When Shirish spoke of his village, it was as if many auspicious and inauspicious grahas were in alignment with it, his memories of it were bittersweet ... The gently swaying trees that rustled in the mountain breeze like untethered horses; the quiet river that flowed in front of his house reflecting a myriad rosy hues that chased each other like hunting dogs and formed part of some extraordinary vast expanse of creation; an old bridge on the river which was like the battlement of an old Roman fort in ruins, looking down from which was like looking deep into Time, Meaning, and the Innumerable Expressions of Life ...

But though he spoke of it often, he never took anyone to visit his hometown. He never took anyone to his room either, claiming it was shabby and that there was no arrangement for tea, though everyone knew his meals were inclusive in the rent and that, when the JE's daughter (whose name, everyone knew too, was Dolly) got him his tea, he let his fingers linger on hers. And she too ... This girl had run away to Bombay with a filmi-hero type dude from her street to become an actress in Hindi films. The JE had followed in hot pursuit and scoured every studio and beach till he found her sipping tea with the neighbourhood lout in front of a film studio. He dragged her home though the boyfriend had stayed on.

Shirish Sharma had the sharpest mind among them, read the most, and had a keenly analytical brain but sometimes, desperate to prove himself, his arguments would become absurd and far-fetched. For instance, once when someone remarked that after the Russian Revolution, there had not been a single work that equalled Gogol's "Overcoat," Sarveshwar replied that after the revolution, millions found the right to express themselves and it was natural that their first outpourings be unremarkable, and anyway what about Sholokov, Gorky, Mayakovsky, Pasternak. Shirish had opined that the kitsch actually reflected the success of the Russian revolution because great works can only be produced in a depraved society. Then Keshav screamed at him to shut up and Shirish turned white.

And so the arguments continued. And all the while Sarveshwar read out his poems in a quiet, steady voice to a silent audience of rapt faces and dreamy eyes. Often they were passionate love poems addressed to imaginary girls with soulful eyes and warm hearts. Poems that sounded like mantras chanted at the shmashan to coax secrets from the dead. The most evocative word in these poems was "beloved" and whenever it came up there was a soft sigh of appreciation ("dualism" was standard fare in all their conversations).

Whenever there was a surfeit of poetry, Ghosh would remind them of the real business of life: What world are you living in, boys, what about earning a living when all this is over?

Ghosh's father had a small hardware shop and Ghosh himself was a student of commerce who spent every evening in the library reading the *Financial Express* and the business and economy pages of *The Times of India*, his brow furrowing in concentration as he tried to divine which way the country's economy was headed. He would often come to the room in the night and enter silently, his dark giant shadow swallowing the wall. He would stand in the corner and joke, What do you guys have to do with Brecht and Plekhanov anyway? And being met with a stony silence, no one deigning to answer, he would gather his hunched shoulders and dark shadows and step back into the night.

The door of the room was falling apart and creaked on its hinges even though it was always kept shut. It had many holes and crevices and at the very moment when one was about to grasp a particularly complex poem, the face of poverty would peep in, uninvited, like an ugly witch, and would stare into their face so that their smiles grew plasticky and fixed.

Sarveshwar's handicapped father lounged in the sun on a plank cot from where he would shower abuses on his older son and daughter-in-law throughout the day. His brother's one year old moved around the courtyard soiling the place at will. The brother was unemployed and did odd jobs around the locality like putting up shamianas and decorations at weddings to earn a couple of hundred bucks. The father had retired from the electricity department. People said that he'd lost his leg from an electric shock and been sacked from service. There was a sister of about twelve or fourteen who suffered convulsions and blackouts for which the local doctor's pills were proving useless. She'd come to after being splashed with water to stare at the faces gathered around her with uncomprehending, exhausted eyes. The brother's wife, pregnant again, moved around the courtyard in her petticoat, looking increasingly grotesque.

Fifteen years ago time had seemed to stand still, but of course it hadn't, it moved, like the film on a projector showing a freeze frame. But somewhere, deep inside, desires stirred and gathered spin and momentum with increasing frenzy. Everyone except Sarveshwar waited impatiently. Surely something would happen soon. They wanted to rush headlong into a vortex of excited talk, dramatic happenings and amazing events. It was only for the Benevolent Almighty to come and blow the whistle ...

Shirish Sharma wanted his first anthology published.

Ghosh was to join his father's shop after completing his BCom.

Alok Srivastava having cleared his medical entrance had gone to study medicine in another city.

Adesh Awasthi was playing the stakes.

And as for Keshav ... well, there had been an accident. In his inexperience, Keshav's elder brother had taken his red Maruti into the mountains where the roads were iced and as smooth as glass. The car had fallen into a deep gorge and from those heights looked like a speck of blood. They had to wait for the sun and warmth of the next day to recover the body. After the customary period of mourning, Keshav's bhabhi handed over the property business to him, incomplete deals and all, requesting him to help out in these bad times – if not him, who?

Sarveshwar vanished one day, suddenly, without a trace – like a bubble of water. He had got an ordinary teacher's job in some far-east border village and left silently, without telling a soul, without meeting a friend. He never came back – not even to meet his family. He sent them some money for the first two or three years, then lost the job for some reason, but didn't return. News of him came in snippets, and one had to fill in the gaps on one's own. After many years we heard that he had married, then later that he had fallen on tough times that allowed little by way of ease but not yet despairing and strained because wherever he went he was among like-minded people, both he and his wife and their friends and co-workers were involved in political and ideological work, street theatre, meetings and gatherings among students and daily wage labourers and also in a sporadically brought out newspaper. There was no time at all – he was completely cut off from the city – sometimes his articles would appear in some magazine, one would read some bit of news about him. The years passed between cracks of light and shade, silent, stuffy afternoons and nights black as sin.

Then the hundred year old house collapsed in the widely-covered, devastating earthquake that rocked the area wreaking widespread havoc. The house was reduced to a mound of rubble. Sarveshwar couldn't come even then and had sent a comrade who stayed with his family for a few days. Many tenants had been hurt in the house collapse. The homeopath was killed by a large chunk of falling masonry, and died surrounded by his tiny white glucose globules and the smell of alcohol. The smuggler was also injured and after some first aid left straight for Muzaffarnagar. Sarveshwar's father was wounded as he could not hurry out on his crutches and had to stay in hospital for a fortnight before being moved to another house in the locality. There wasn't a scratch on the landlord and his family and in the bargain, after years of stubborn occupancy, the land was vacated in a jiffy. Now he was free to build anything on that land – a marketing complex, an eight-storey building.

Sarveshwar had written to Adesh Awasthi after eight years, the letter – an angry emotional outburst in which he had talked about how the long absence from home had made him yearn to be back and how he could no longer contain himself. He was coming home for a few days. His sister was getting married. The actual time lapse between his leaving and coming back was a very long period, but looked at in a different way it was only a short while.

It had been raining since morning. Awasthi woke from a fitful sleep and in the loneliness of his room a thousand fearful words and thoughts tore through the layers of his mind – they dogged him in sleep by night and extended their drooling tongues and friendly paws in the wee hours. He was an insurance agent and he dealt with words the way a tailor deals with a pair of scissors, a barber with that strip of leather on which he sharpens his razor. Awasthi would stalk the residential areas, shops and offices of his city, telling all who cared to listen grim stories of the omnipresence of death, how it lurked behind them all the time, everywhere, ready to pounce, and God help their children ... His story became more and more realistic in the retelling and he himself would listen to the story each time till his own nerves were stretched to a fine point and fear stuck to his innards like green slime. He was his own best customer and would take out a policy every couple of months with most of his salary going as premium.

Awasthi rose slowly and went about his morning ablutions. He was waiting for the rain to let up and debating whether to attend office when, umbrella in hand, the building contractor who was constructing his house came to get the bathroom tiles approved. Just then the little girl next door threw a wet letter near the gate saying that the postman had delivered it wrongly to their place. He ran out in the rain to get the letter and spent a while trying to identify the handwriting on the envelope. Finally, he just tore open the letter and told the contractor to come back later.

"Some bad news?" asked the contractor, lingering on.

"Nothing of the sort, you carry on now," he replied.

His wife, fair and long-haired, with Barbie-doll looks, the daughter of a rich man from a large city, sat sullenly on a cane-stool looking out at the pouring rain. Awasthi called Alok Srivastava who, at that moment, was on the other side of town grappling with a large, fleshy woman in his clinic. The fat lady was bad-tempered and irritable and complained that even after six months of treatment, she had not been cured of the tingling sensation in her limbs and why did her ample chest feel so empty?

She was verbose and obnoxious in her familiarity.

"Yes?" the doctor said into the phone."

"It's me, Awasthi."

"Awasthi who?" the doctor asked again in a harassed voice.

"Leave Awasthi, first answer me," the fat lady demanded belligerently.

"It's me, Adesh Awasthi. Don't you recognize my voice?"

"It's the rain. I can't hear you properly."

"Sarveshwar is coming, maybe tomorrow or the day after. His sister is getting married."

"Sarveshwar who?" This from Awasthi's wife, listening in.

"Do I have to tell you this too? Sarveshwar ..."

"Sarveshwar who?" the wife asked again. She wanted to snatch the phone away from him, but warding her off with one hand, Awasthi continued somehow, managing a hurried conversation. The fat lady tried to interject again but the doctor angrily cut her off. The wife screamed, "Who is this Sarveshwar?" Awasthi couldn't stop himself and pushed her back irritably, "Do be quiet, yaar, will you let me talk?" Between the tirade of the two quarrelsome and shrieking women, he somehow managed to convey the news that Sarveshwar was coming in a day or two. When he replaced the receiver his wife pounced on him like a cat and plonked herself on the nearby diwan. "Who is this Sarveshwar? When is he coming, I should know everything."

The truth was that quite a few of Awasthi's friends were disreputable drunks and writers whom she had put up with silently for about a year after marriage. After that she'd started insisting on a transfer and slamming the door in the face of any visitors. And that wasn't all – she had got a few boys in the street to pelt stones at any of these characters if they were seen hovering around, for a price of course. Now nobody came. She said, "I have got rid of your useless good for nothing friends with great difficulty. If the same characters are seen again, I will have to run away."

She was also peeved because he was getting their house constructed in the same city not someplace else where there wouldn't be any tensions with writers and artistic types.

At the other end the fat lady sat entrenched on her seat at the doctor's clinic like a lump of clay. The doctor asked her to take her medicine then pressed the bell and told the attendant that he was going out for half an hour. Tell the patients to wait. He went to his house, which was just adjacent to the clinic, and lay down on the bed, as straight as if in a coffin. He felt a sudden need to look in the mirror, to check the circles under his eyes and to ponder the times he lived in, to dwell on how much of life was lost and how much of it remained.

Awasthi's wife was in a foul mood. She lay sulking on the bed as he dialled Gurvinder Singh at the State Bank of Patiala, who at that precise moment was surrounded by so much currency that had it been stacked one on top of the other, the tower would have gone through the ceiling. On the phone he said, "Sarveshwar? After so many years? When's he coming?"

"Either tomorrow or the day after. The letter was late."

"Oh? I wonder what it is going to be like meeting him after so many years. He didn't mention the date?"

"His sister's wedding is on the sixth, the day after tomorrow."

"Then he will certainly be there."

"A day or two after, all of us old friends must meet somewhere. A long get-together, the whole night, okay? I just wanted to inform you."

"Have you told the others?"

"I'm trying to get them on the phone. You can inform Shirish, he is not on the phone. He lives quite near your place."

Outside the meshed window, a few pairs of eyes watched Gurvinder Singh expectantly. He shut the window and wrote out an application for a half a day leave. The manager, anxious and unblinking, came out of his cabin and asked him what the matter was.

"Why the half-day leave?"

"I am not well. I'm feeling a little dizzy. Put someone here who can count all the money."

The people at the teller counter had started to grow restless. The manager cast a despairing glance at the crowd and told him to serve the customers at the window and that he would arrange someone in the meantime. The replacement came after sometime and, nimble fingered, started counting out the notes.

Gurvinder walked out silently. The sky was alive, the wind had dispersed the clouds and the thin warm rays of the sun peeped out. The rain had stopped completely now. He hailed an auto, squashed himself in between the other passengers and, shuddering along in the vehicle, reached home sometime later. His house was right in the middle of the city, a three-room apartment where he lived with his family – parents, wife and two children.

His wife saw him, "How come you're in so early?"

"Not feeling so well. Took half the day off."

"Why? What happened"? She grew alarmed.

"Nothing, nothing to worry about. I will go inside and lie down for a while. Tell the children not to make a racket. Ghosh might drop in after lunch – wake me up then."

He went inside and lay down in shavasan, relaxed. He slept on for an hour, two hours, dreaming. In his dream too he was lying in the same position and unable to asleep. That sleepless dream was invading his sleep like a dagger entering its sheath, smooth and fast. When he sat up after a long time, he realized that he hadn't slept at all, not a wink, not for a moment.

At that very moment the phone bell shrilled in Ghosh's house and someone calling from the city two hours away informed him that his pregnant sister had fallen down the stairs when she had gone out to hang the clothes. She had been taken to the hospital where she could be saved only after a lengthy operation. But she'd lost the baby. She was still unconscious and Ghosh was told to reach there immediately.

Ghosh remained staring at the phone, a suppressed scream trying to force its way out of his throat. Then he staggered to his father's room only to stop short and watch him as he slept. Like the dead. His mother had died two months ago. She had always been sad and anxious when they weren't well off and when they finally were, always in an apron of yellow and brown melancholy. She had removed that lifelong apron only when she'd died and her dead body had been serene, alabaster white. After she was gone, an oppressive silence filled the house and father and son would stare at each other with empty eyes, like sleepwalkers or blind men.

Suddenly Ghosh remembered something and, changing out of his clothes, moved to the porch where his shiny yellow car was parked. He drove out as quietly as possible and in a few moments reached the main road. The potholes were filled with rain water and the road was completely submerged in places. It took him a long time to reach Gurvinder's place.

"Where is Sardarji?" he asked as he entered.

"He is lying down inside. Please sit while I call him," Gurvinder's wife replied.

Gurvinder Singh came to the bedroom door. He looked tired and wan, and his eyes were full of leftover sleep.

"I'm in a hurry right now. Have you got the forms to open an account?"

"No, I forgot them."

Ghosh flopped down on to the sofa in despair, "What do you mean you forgot? Didn't we decide that today ... I came post-haste for this purpose only, even though I've just got some bad news. My sister has met with an accident, she is lying unconscious in hospital. I have to go there with Baba. I haven't even told him yet."

"Why? What's this? Your sister is lying unconscious and you haven't informed anyone at home. Yet you're bothered about your bank account?"

"I got the news over the phone. I thought first let me get Baba's signatures, then I'll tell him, but you haven't got the forms."

"Why? Why didn't you tell him?" Gurvinder asked angrily.

"Yaar, after Ma died he is not interested in anything. He is becoming spiritual now. He talks of going to live in an ashram in

Haridwar or Rishikesh. If he decided to just pack up and leave when he hears the news, leaving everything ... Okay let's sign the partnership deal at least. I've got the papers with me. You ask Bhabhi to be the wit ..."

Sardarni was making tea in the kitchen but her ears were on the conversation outside. And she heard Gurvinder interrupt Ghosh. "No-no, no signatures today. You should leave at once. Not today."

"But why?"

"Just this. Not today, we will see to this some other time."

"But why not today?"

"Your sister is battling for her life. At this time, all this ... no, you should leave immediately."

Actually, it was like this: Gurvinder Singh's father owned a small plot about ten or twelve kilometres from the city. The area was now being developed as an industrial estate. Ghosh had asked Gurvinder to sell him the plot at the going rate maybe at a premium of ten or twenty thousand rupees.

But Gurvinder Singh was smart – or, rather, his wife was. She was from a traditional business family and ever since they were married, had pestered Gurvinder to leave his job and set up a business of his own somewhere. Every night, after sex, they would talk in hushed tones about money and business till they fell asleep, to dream the same dream together, the recurring motif of which was a stack of steeply piled currency notes. So he had told Ghosh, "Arre, think of my plot as your own and just give me a twenty five per cent partnership in the Mineral Water Factory you're going to set up there." Ghosh had not agreed, saying, "Yaar, you take more money fifty thousand, one lakh but ..."

But the Sardarni had whispered on in Punjabi, with the persistence of a voice in the head: Be firm, don't give in! And in the end Ghosh had had to yield. Gurvinder was a government servant and Ghosh had tax problems, so the factory had to have Gurvinder's wife and Ghosh's father as partners.

However, the night before Gurvinder's wife had done some complicated calculations on their pocket calculator and after scribbling furiously in their child's notebook, had emerged visibly upset, pale and drenched in sweat to declare that to agree to a partnership of less than forty per cent was a suicidal proposition.

"I am just leaving. This will take five minutes. You call Bhabhi."

"No, not today. I've already told you. We will talk about it some other time."

"What more do we have to talk about?"

"If you return by tomorrow or the day after, we will sit at leisure, thrash it out and sign on the deed. Not today."

Ghosh stared at him with eyes full of despair. He was sweating now and breathing fast. Then he stood up and slowly walked out.

After he was gone, Gurvinder sat for some time lost in thought. Then he glanced at the clock and started dressing to go out. His wife came out of the bedroom and looked at him questioningly. He said he would be back in a little while. He took out his scooter and soon enough was at Shirish's place in the neighbouring colony.

The bungalow was shrouded in darkness. The front portion converted into a shop, was closed at the moment, the signboard – Dolly Beauty Parlour – lit by one dim light. Shirish Sharma, the post-modern writer lived in a rented room in the rear.

Standing outside, Gurvinder called out to Shirish. But getting no response he opened the gate. He heard voices raised in argument and then the muffled sounds of someone sobbing. Somewhere to his right, a voice asked: "What do you want?"

Trying to peer through the dark he saw Shirish's landlord, the JE, sitting on a chair wrapped in a dark shawl, as if waiting for someone. He stood up and walked across to Gurvinder. In the beam of light coming from afar he looked very old and his shoulders drooped in despair.

"Shirish," Gurvinder said.

"I think he's not in," the old man replied in an anxious voice.

"Where's he gone?"

"I don't know."

There was an uncomfortable silence

"I will wait for some time ... maybe he'll be back soon."

Shirish's room was plunged in darkness. A dim light glowed behind the drawn curtains. He called out Shirish's name but the silence persisted. Shirish never bothered to lock up if he was close by and Gurvinder pushed open the door. Inside he saw a rumpled bed strewn with books and magazines. The room was full of human smell – as if someone had left only a moment ago. There was another door on the far end of the room that opened into the landlord's portion of the house. Gurvinder sat on the bed and waited for a long while. Finally, he wrote out a note informing Shirish of Sarveshwar's visit and put it under a paperweight.

The landlord was still there near the gate. He asked, "Did you find him?"

"No he is not in."

The old man was satisfied. "If there's anything ..."

"I've left a message on his table," Gurvinder said.

A few minutes after Gurvinder had left, the inner door swung open cautiously and a dishevelled Shirish gripped under his arms by two men in leather jackets, stumbled out. Shirish's face was drasined of blood, dark like a broken shard of the night. Darkness seemed to be closing in on him. He felt faint and sank down on the cot, tired and trembling, and asked the two who stood menacingly close to him, "What do you want?"

The two thugs had entered silently only a short while ago when he'd been busy reading. Startled, a small scream had escaped his lips. One was a youngish chap, the other sported a goatee. They surrounded him and started shouting threats. When the bell rang he requested them to let the visitor leave, pleading that there be no scene in the visitor's presence. So all three had hidden behind the inner door, waiting for him to leave with bated breath.

"Do we need to tell you again?" one of them shouted after Gurvinder had gone. "Look, you're an educated writer. We've heard that your stories have been published. We respect writers and so are being very respectful to you. We aren't asking you to vacate the room immediately, or even tomorrow."

The other one said, "Find some other house at your leisure, take a week, ten days, if you like, take a month. If you stay here it will bring you a bad name and that won't be good for Dolly. Do you know what people are saying?"

Wrapped in his shawl, the JE sat in the darkness outside, his eyes fixed on the gate and his ears on what was being said inside.

"... And if you're really in love with her then marry her. What's the problem with that? Then you can stay on, rent-free forever. Whatever you earn from your job will be supplemented with what the Beauty Parlour brings in. Bhai Saheb ... if I were you ..." the guy with the goatee sniggered, the bastard.

Shirish remained seated on his bed, his head hanging low.

The intruders left quietly.

Shirish's heart was beating fast and he breathed deeply to steady his nerves. He was in shock. His head burst with random thoughts and ideas which were like shrapnel buried in a swamp, stuck any which way, and he felt compelled to take out each piece and inspect it closely, searching for some probable cause.

The temple bells started from afar, far enough to be soft and gentle on his ears. He tried to guess how much money the JE had got when he was superannuated and how old Dolly would be.

Suddenly, he saw the message under the paperweight. As soon as he read it, he was swamped by a host of memories. He read the message again. Sarveshwar was arriving either tomorrow or the day after. Then he remembered: he had scheduled a literary meet in the town hall to be presided over by a great post-modern theorist and expert the day after tomorrow. The meet was happening only because of his efforts and the arrangements – collecting funds, posters, pamphlets, invitation cards, had taken up an entire week. Now all that remained was the arrival of the great man in a UP roadways bus to a grand welcome replete with garlands and brass band.

He jumped up and dressed hastily, rushed to the PCO on the other side of the road and scribbled a number on a scrap of paper for the booth attendant. Red numerals sprang up on the monitor but a pre-recorded message regretfully informed him that all the lines on that route were busy. Shirish wanted to tell the post-modern theorist that something important had cropped up and that he would be out of station on the D-Day. When the call finally went through, the bell rang on without an answer – the post-modern theorist wasn't home. God alone knew where he was – Delhi is such a big town where everything is massive, oversized, a giant alive – sprawling expressways, high rises, cars, buses, dust, smoke, so much noise, so much literature, and dear God, so much literary discussion, so much culture, so many people.

The bell rang on in one empty room of that unimaginably vast metropolis like a portent of doom, a warning. Shirish replaced the receiver and returned to his room with defeated steps. He lay down on his cot and after resting awhile, pulled a stool to reach some books on the top shelf of his cupboard. Taking down three, he dusted them by simply striking them against the edge of the bed. Then he settled down at the table to read them, first silently to himself and then loudly, as if jogging sluggish memories, like a child preparing for exams who turns the pages fast, scared of time-out. One of the books was a thick, slow-moving novel about agricultural life in the pre-industrial revolution days in England; the second was an anthology of Mayakovsky's poetry which also contained the poem where the poet screams out at the burning sun of the summer heat, Hey, you loafer, come down some; and the third, he was surprised to see, was an old medical text. Perhaps Alok Srivastava had left it there on one of his visits. It had a couple of chapters on obstetrics and gynaecology along with diagrams of the reproductive organs, seeing which, he invariably imagined a half-clad woman, shoulders pinned down by a midwife, screaming in the throes of labour ...

His eyes suddenly went to the mirror. In the dim light he looked sweaty and sallow and seemed to be the only, the most lonely, being in the world. His shaking fingers combed the tangled mass of his beard of a few days. He suddenly felt very old. He noticed for the first time that the roof of his room had begun to sag, the plaster on the walls was peeling off, the dry bare walls beneath had begun to crack and crumble around him ... a veritable ruin slung low with cobwebs. And, amidst these ruins, sitting on a chair, wiping his tears on his sleeve, Shirish longed to be far away ... beyond the bare hills, in his village with its gently swaying trees and cool mountain breezes, beside the peaceful river, not as a five foot seven inch, forty two year old but as a child with a runny nose shouting his story again, this time with a new beginning.

Adesh Awasthi was rigging up the mosquito net on his bed when he remembered that Keshav had not been contacted. He picked up the phone diary and flipped through the pages till he found Keshav's number. Keshav's office or shop or whatever (he was still a property dealer) faced Jawahar Nagar's main crossroads. It was a room in a semi-constructed house with a table, a chair, a phone and a cot for quick snoozes. The power failure some minutes ago had caught him fumbling with the office lock and then the phone began to ring most insistently. Opening the lock, he answered the phone in the darkness. It was Awasthi, that familiar voice of many years ago.

"Remember me? Awasthi here."

"Yaar, my memory is not that weak though you're calling after a long time. Where are you?"

"In this city, where else?" Awasthi said. "Listen, Sarveshwar is coming in a day or two for his sister's wedding. Let's all meet somewhere after that. Sarveshwar says that he would like to meet all of us. I have informed most of the gang today."

Keshav was silent. Not hearing any response, Awasthi asked, "Keshav are you listening?"

And then Keshav said, "Sarveshwar who?"

Incredulous, Awasthi tried again: "You've forgotten Sarveshwar? Sarveshwar our old friend, who ..."

"He's been dead for many years, hasn't he?"

"What are you saying?"

"He has been dead these ten years, I believe. Is he still alive?"

It was Awasthi's turn to be silent.

"If he's alive he has no intention of coming here, and if he's dead then he won't be able to. Maybe on the way somewhere ..."

First the phone wires brought a panting, omnious sound to his ears, and then their own vibrations. The hum of the wires seemed to carry omnious tidings from afar, very far.

Locking his office in the dark, Keshav started for his house where an empty drawing room awaited him. His wife and children had gone to another city for a wedding. He walked reluctantly as if someone was pushing him from behind. He wanted to go straight to bed, to be soothed to sleep by a lullaby or a shower of cool kisses. Then again, he may have wanted to lie senseless and unconscious to escape being plagued by his memories, but knew that his sleep that night would be filled with ominous rumblings. I mean, how can one be sure of what these property dealers really want?

He wanted to spend time till then most carefully. He started walking to the side of the railway station where his friends, Pokhariyal, a contractor, Tiwari and another property dealer were waiting for him. Tewari had clinched a hotel deal that day and had earned a commission of fifty, sixty thousand. He had phoned Keshav, promising him a good time.

When they saw him, Pokhariyal and Tewari waved Keshav over to their table. People sat talking in low murmurs at different tables, and the blue light gave everyone a translucent ghost-like appearance. The manager at the counter kept accounts in the pool of light from the table lamp. They had a long drinking session and as his senses started clouding over, Keshav shut his eyes and rested his head on the back of the chair. He wanted to float but felt instead as if he was falling down a gorge. A few moments passed and then he felt himself shaken awake. He opened his eyes. Pokhariyal and Tewari were asking if he was all right.

He wanted to say something about capitalism and the salt of the earth, about Paris communes, about the great Lenin and Gorky and the first Indian Struggle for Independence of 1857 and about

Czechoslovakia where the fascists had strangled little children whose golden locks, nappies and soothers were now on display in a museum – and a lot more about what had once occurred in history and now churned in his mind. He had an honestly-earned masters degree in history but didn't say anything because it would have sounded like lies, or at least would seem tainted with falsehood. So he just pleaded tiredness in a small weak voice. Taking a short cut to his home through a dark deserted street he reached home and, closing his eyes lay down on his bed. A few moments before he fell asleep he heard the sound of wailing beyond the window. He opened the window and stared into the darkness. There was no one there. Closing the window he lay down again. The wailing continued.

The streets where Adesh Awasthi was looking for Sarveshwar's house, among all the noise and confusion, were twisted and tangled like a mass of steel wires or like human veins and arteries carrying blood. He had been through each street and road many times. The streets were choking with vendors' carts full of vegetables, mithai and teashops; the roads were slushy with the onset of the rains; flies and cattle nosing through rotting garbage and houses sealed like coffins. There was no house with a loudspeaker blaring or any signs of the revelry that normally marks a house where a marriage is to take place. He walked those endless streets filled with crowds and noise for a very long time. The noonday sun sank low and dusk began to fall.

He found Sarveshwar's house with great difficulty crammed as it was behind a timber store. It was very old with black dirty walls where the door downstairs was heavily padlocked and a spiral staircase rose up from one corner of the veranda. The whole place was shrouded in a wet, clinging smoke. He climbed the shaky staircase and knocked. No one answered. After a long wait, when he was about to turn back, the bolt moved inside. A child, whom he didn't recognize, opened the door and stood watching him silently.

"Is this Sarveshwar's house?"

The child did not answer, his expressionless eyes were fixed on Keshav's face. Sarveshwar's father hobbled out of an inner room on his crutches. He went to a corner and pressed a switch. The room filled with a dim, weak light. "Whom do you wish to meet?"

"Sarveshwar," Adesh Awasthi replied, wiping his sweaty face with the back of his hand. The room was devoid of furniture except for a cot in a corner and a crumpled mat on the floor. The child dragged in a folding chair from inside. Adesh sat on the chair and Sarveshwar's father on the cot in front, carefully laying his crutches aside.

"I am Sarveshwar's friend," he said, "His sister's getting married, no? He wrote to me. Has he arrived yet?" The house beyond was utterly silent. An inexorable, intolerable silence. "I came to find out whether Sarveshwar has come or not." Sarveshwar's father moved his head. He sat silently for a long time.

"I'll go now and come back tomorrow to find out," Awasthi finally said, standing up. But Sarveshwar's father sat on, unmoving. Adesh had the curious impression that he hadn't heard a word he had said. He came out quietly.

Sarveshwar sat in a crowded second class compartment. The train, filled with bulky trunks, beddings, rustics in smelly clothes and city folk in trousers, was crawling along somewhere between Bast and Gonda taking long halts at all the stations. It staggered under the weight of people everywhere, in the aisles, on the floor, yet was steeped in a strange unnatural quiet. Drowsy people swayed with the moving train and there was no sound save its rickety clickety-clack. A clamped, cramped silence. He carried a shoulder bag with a diary, two or three books, an empty tiffin box and some clothes. His face was all angles, bones jutting out; his gaze straight but spent. He looked tired.

As the train lurches forward the mind goes back.

The train ground to a halt at a small station. Someone coughed in the compartment and the sound sank into the stillness outside like a stone in water. Sarveshwar's eyes grew heavy with sleep.

They had lost their characteristic sparkle. Perhaps at precisely that moment, all of a sudden, or perhaps a few moments this way or that, who knows when, he had started losing courage. He took out a book from his bag and began to read, concentrating on each word, each sentence. The effort was too much, the words blurred and he felt a massive weight on his chest. He stood up somehow and cleaved through the crowd, groping his way to the toilet. He stood with his head bowed over the wash basin. Something yellow with last night's dinner and clots of blood.

He staggered back to his berth and fitting himself into its narrow confines, lay down, his haunted eyes boring into the roof. The train started with a jerk and his eyelids closed on their own.

Half an hour later the train stopped again, this time in a jungle. By now his pupils were dilated and he was gripped by a shivering fever. Seeing him shaking like a leaf the other passengers bent over him. The men pressing close, the women some distance away. A scream, the sudden wailing of a child beyond, and then a babble of confused, concerned voices.

"This fellow's sick. Is there someone with him?" But the question was met with silence. The train crawled into a tiny station and before it could come to a halt a thickset man had jumped out on to the platform to fetch some water. He came running back and pushing his way through the crowd tried to hold the bowl of water to Sarveshwar's lips. There was no response.

Sarveshwar had lost consciousness.

Meanwhile, a man in his fifties, tall, with intelligent eyes and a snow-white beard stepped out of the last compartment enraged beyond control. The blood flowing in this man's veins, like that of ordinary mortals, was begot from his parents but a little bit, perhaps just one test-tube, was from mankind's most glorious and great ancestors, the distillate of generations of mankind. For one's life-blood is not dumped into the sea with one's bones nor does it vaporize like ether from the fumes of an electric crematorium. Each individual is simply a pulsing conglomeration of many dead mens' bodies – their hopes, dreams, fluctuating blood pressure, snivels and tears – and what makes the difference, as in the case of this man, is *which* dead and *what* kind. And I don't mean greatness as in that of prophets or geniuses. I am talking of people of a different strain. People who reach past all obstacles to battle disease and death anywhere on this earth; a little like Dr Kotnis or Dr Louis Pasteur or like Marie and Pierre Curie.

Like the worthies mentioned above, this man was also a doctor though not a scientist. Besides which he was extremely short tempered, with a gut-wrenching angst that fellow doctors had warned him to control through meditation or shavasan, or be doomed to burst a brain vessel that would knock him off his feet some day, slamming him to the ground with a force that would send his glasses flying in the opposite direction.

A short while ago he had picked up a fight with a shopkeeper because the man had blocked the aisle with his packages making it impossible for others to cross. Now he had alighted to confront the guard because his compartment was without water and the distressed children on board were screaming, unable to use the toilet. When the guard was not found in his compartment he started to look around for the station master. Then he noticed the crowd near Sarveshwar's compartment and entering it, sized up the situation in a moment. Shouting and flailing his arms at the crowd he reached Sarveshwar and lifting his wrist in one hand, checked his pulse, pinching his skin to check for dehydration.

"Is there anyone with him? He is extremely ill, looks like heat stroke, maybe dehydration ..."

Not a murmur.

He said, "Call the station master, where's the railway doctor?"

He grabbed hold of a youth in sun glasses and ordered him to run and fetch the station master and then, in a stern voice asked some others to step aside. He moved Sarveshwar closer to the window and removed his shoes. The youth returned with the station master who was dressed importantly in white.

"This man has to be taken off the train. He can't travel any further," the man said.

"Sir, this is a small station. He'll get proper treatment in Lucknow or Barabanki."

"No," he said imperiously, "The railway hospital ..."

"There's no hospital here, sir. It's a small station."

The man grabbed his white uniform: "Mr Station Master," his voice was steely, "don't people fall sick here? What do they do?"

"Look there is a small primary health care centre here. The doctor comes once a week. Not today ..."

"I'm a doctor. There must be some medicines there. Get him down fast. Any stretcher, anything. Call one or two men. What are you waiting for?" His voice was hoarse with anger.

The train wasn't moving despite the guard's sharp whistles. People craned their necks to see what was happening.

"Look, that health care centre will be closed now."

"The key ... have the key found immediately If it isn't found break the lock ... If this man doesn't ..." The man was livid. His liquid brown eyes glinted ominously. Had the station master stood around any longer he would surely have been slapped. The doctor hurried to his compartment and threw out his baggage. Two passengers lifted Sarveshwar on to a stretcher and placed his bag near his head. The engine shrilled again. The train slowly pulled out.

The noon day sun poured down like a scourge. The station master strode out followed by the doctor with the stretcher and a porter carrying the luggage. The doctor halted mid-stride to catch his breath and it seemed to him that the faces gathered around him were impassive, unblinking, expressionless mummies. Suddenly his heart picked up the drumbeat of death. It was his sixth sense with him. The station master took out the key from his pocket and opened the door. The porters lay Sarveshwar down on the examination table in a dirty dank room stinking of ether. The doctor lifted his wrist – it was as cold as ice. He held a cotton thread to his nose. Frantic, he started pressing his chest, massaging it in haste borne of desperation. Slowly he gave up and, defeated, punched his fist into the sarcophagus-like table. He walked out, thrusting through the crowd. Trying to hide his face from the people around. Trying to find a place where he could accost his God. Alone.

That morning, Shirish Sharma remembered that he had forgotten to arrange the drinks for his wedding. Making some time from the ceremonies, he phoned Gurvinder, appointing him man in charge of the "programme."

Gurvinder promptly called a client, an ex-army man, and went to the canteen to fetch four bottles. He reached with the bottles much before time but his mood was spoilt the moment he saw the baraat getting ready at the colony's temple. This was the baraat which was to weave its way back to Shirish's house? He stood outside in a huff, braving the ear-shattering music. When he spotted Adesh, he signalled to him to complain about the "arrangements." He has chosen a temple as the baraat ghar. So much for our boozing session, he fumed.

Don't worry, yaar. I will make some arrangements, Adesh said soothingly. They went back to Shirish's house, and located the JE who was all dressed up in a safari suit and pink safa and, calling him Uncleji, they took him aside. The room behind Shirish's was occupied by his folks from the village and they had locked it, taking the key with them. However what use was the Beauty Parlour at a time like this? The JE slipped him the key saying, Please, there should be no noise as there are ladies present.

Rolling up the shutter a bit, the old small crowd sneaked in and ensconced itself on a bench in a room overwhelmingly fragrant with cosmetics and feminine toileteries. The loudspeaker was right above the shop and everyone had to shout to be heard above the noise of the Hindi film songs.

Keshav arrived late and a dozen glasses were raised to hail his arrival. They were all squashed in and everyone moved up a bit to accommodate him. When Gurvinder poured him a glass he declined saying that he had "left off drinking" but everyone knew he just wanted to be persuaded.

Adesh Awasthi shouted across to Keshav that he had been wanting to meet him for many months but hadn't managed to even though it was about something important. Ghosh changed places with him and Awasthi wedged himself in next to Keshav. In the din of the blaring loud-speakers Awasthi asked, How did you know that Sarveshwar was ... Do you have some power of looking into the future?

Keshav couldn't hear him. And Adesh shouted in his ear again, Do you have some special prescient knack? How did you know that Sarveshwar ... during the journey ...

Keshav understood him with difficulty and then shouted in his ear that he had said it just like that, the way a man says thousands of things without thinking. Now Adesh couldn't hear him and, irritated, shouted at a passing boy to pipe down. Then he asked his question again. And Keshav replied in a tired voice that he had just said it. It didn't mean that he was clairvoyant or that he had some special power to foresee the future. Adesh wanted to say something but suddenly the power failed and everything fell dark and silent. And in that terrible speechless dark Keshav added dryly, Besides, you don't need the gifts of a soothsayer or the brains of an Einstein to work it out...

It was time to take leave of dreams and ideas. Time for all thinkers and dreamers to file out one by one leaving behind a brightly-coloured eternal present, a constant sunshine, a constant crowd in the markets, the sun nailed firmly in the centre of the heavens, all clocks frozen in time.

But then someone went and switched on the generator and the lights and music flooded back and the huge mirrors on the wall cast spectre-like images of them, all huddled together. And then, someone present there, not knowing Keshav, asked Ghosh who he was. Ghosh introduced him as Keshav, a college friend. Then the person asked, What does the gentleman do? and Ghosh said, Well, he is a well-known property dealer. So the next time you have a plot house bungalow cemetery hospital cinema hall tower mausoleum anything to buy or sell ...

ക

GOPINI KARUNAKAR

THE MOON IN THE EARTHEN POT

TRANSLATED BY PRANAVA MANJARI N
NOMINATED BY AMARENDRA DASARI

First published in Telugu as "Dutta Lo Chandamama" in *Andhra Jyoti*, April 1998, Hyderabad

Once again Guddavva has taken out the moon from the earthen pot that hangs from our thatch roof, and thrown it back, up in the sky. Now the moonlight streams down, flooding the world.

Palakonda is resplendent in the golden moonlight.
The stones are awash in the wet moonlight.
The ripples in the pond are awash in the silver moonlight
The green grass glistens in the shimmer of moonlight
The tamarind tree is aglow in the tender moonlight
And on the wings of the white crane – a milky white moonlight!
The entire village rocks to sleep in the cradle of moonlight that hangs from the sky. But …

The moon has to be stolen tonight, one way or the other. My father's mother, my guddavva, will wake up early tomorrow and put the moon back in the earthern pot again. But I'll remove the moon from there and hide it away somewhere. Let me see what she does then! She has been fooling me every day about giving me the moon!

It all started one summer evening when it rained heavily. That night, stars appeared on our sunkeswari tree. I held the branches of the tree and shook them. The stars showered down. Collecting them in the folds of my shirt, I ran to show them to Guddavva.

"Avva, Avva, see what I have brought you!"

Peerugodu peeked into my dress. "So many stars!" he exclaimed, pressing his hands into his cheeks.

"Let me look, let me!" said Vasantha, jumping up and down, pulling at my hands. The stars slipped from the folds of my shirt and fell on Vasantha's head and clothes. With stars on her dress and stars in her hair, Vasantha shone like an apsara from heaven.

"Avva, see how many stars there are on my dress!" sang Vasantha, her laughter scattering like flowers.

"These are not stars, child. These are fireflies," said Guddavva.

"Fireflies! What are fireflies?" I asked.

"Come, I'll tell you a story," said Guddavva.

We sat down in front of her. I tossed some of the fireflies into the air. They floated along and settled on Guddavva's saree drying outside, winking their tiny lights. And my guddavva began:

"All night, the moon chaffs against the sky, scattering moondust. This dust is nothing but the fireflies. Once upon a time, the golden sparrows flew all the way to the kingdom of the gods to pray for light: Devuda, Devuda! Men light lamps at night, cobras have gems on their foreheads to light their way, and as for the owls, their eyes are their lamps. Our nests are filled with darkness. How are we to light our nests? We have our babies to think of, what is to become of us? they wailed.

"Moved to pity, god said, When the moon rubs against the sky and scatters dust, bring the dust to light up your nests. That's why, from then on, the golden sparrows build their nests with soft mud to catch the fireflies. And as for the fireflies, they have always been happy to light up the nests of the golden sparrows."

Even as I listened to the story, a thought struck me – if a little moondust could shower so much light, just imagine how much light the moon would bring. How very nice it would be to pluck the moon and put it in the nests of the golden sparrows!

So the next night, when I was lying in Guddavva's lap, I pointed to the moon in the sky, and said, "Avva, I want the moon. Will you get it for me?"

"The moon? Let's see, I'll get it for you tomorrow."

"No, I want it *now*," I said, pulling a face and I pulled at the pallu of her saree and beat her on her breasts. I liked doing this just as once I had liked to pull away her saree pallu saying, "I want milk, give me milk!"

"What a brat you are, just like your grandfather," Avva said, slapping me affectionately. "Won't the world plunge into darkness if I gave you the moon now? So wait and I'll give it to you in the morning."

The next morning, I ran to her asking for the moon.

"I've kept the moon safely in that pot. If I take it out now, the moon will just melt away in your hands, so wait till it is night," she said.

So I went again at night.

Guddavva untied the rope and slowly brought the pot down from the roof. She dipped her hands in and brought out the moon in her cupped palms. But just as she was giving it to me, her hands suddenly opened skywards and, "Oho, the moon has flown away!" she exclaimed, pointing to the sky.

I was very very angry, and my inside hurt. Grabbing Guddavva's hair, I started beating her, screaming, "You blind avva, why, why did you throw the moon back into the sky!"

Guddavva laughed through toothless gums. "I'll give you the moon tomorrow night."

The next night, she did the same thing again. And every night since then she has been cheating me somehow. A few days ago, she hid the moon from me and I couldn't find it for days and days. Only today did she put the moon back in the sky again.

That's why I *must* somehow steal the moon tonight. I have even brought the nest of the golden sparrows and tied it to a branch of our sunkeswari tree. I shall put the moon in the nest and then Peerugodu and Vasantha and I can go back to play, I thought giggling to myself as I walked towards the eucalyptus tree.

We all like Guddavva so much. And Guddavva, she loves us! She tells us stories. She gives us all lots and lots of special things to eat. She plays so many different games with us. And as for Vasantha and her friends, Avva plays other games – they are always drawing muggulu with rice flour on the ground, making flower garlands or plaiting one another's hair.

You got to keep an eye on Guddavva when she is telling a story for, in the middle of it she may suddenly prod the clouds with her stick and bring rain. Or she'll make the sun blaze red hot, or the great big seas to rise in fury. Sometimes she can even magic the trees to burst into flowers! She says, A magician spans the seven seas with a single step!

One day, Guddavva told us, "Listen, I have tied the seven seas with a single strand of my hair and dropped them in our well!"

I looked at her in disbelief.

"I swear on the green leaf," she said solemnly. "If you want more proof, taste the water from the well. See?" she asked, pouring some water into my mouth.

"Aak ... thoo ..." I spat out, adding, "Chee, the water is sooo salty."

Guddavva ran her hand over my head and dropped a kiss saying, "My eldest grandson is so naive!"

I believed everything she said, but not so my younger brother and sister. They were so suspicious!

The rakshasas in Guddavva's tales always stalked in meanly, menacingly, and then, one sight of the stick in her hand and they would quickly turn tail and flee! Do you know that the gods take her to their kingdom, offer her a seat equal to their own, and listen to her stories? Even the birds and animals sit as if made of stone when she tells stories, and sometimes they even nod their heads. Oh you should see Guddavva when she holds her stick. She's a total sorceress! She moves this magic wand of hers and suddenly it is now a bow, now a dagger or mace or flute, anything she wants! I wonder where she learnt all this from.

That's why it's sad that my guddavva of the wonderful tales has had a sad life.

My grandfather (whom I call Gorrela Thaatha) had a brother, Paramati Chengayya, who had two wives. My guddavva was his elder wife. Guddavva is the daughter of my grandfather's elder sister. That made Guddavva my mother's maternal aunt. Guddavva's parents' home was in Aarepalli-rangampeta, a town near Tirupathi. After marrying her, Chengayya Thaatha moved in with his wife's family and took up farming. It seems when my guddavva was very young, something happened to her left eye. They called a local doctor but she, telling them that she was treating the eye, pierced it with a paddy stick. And so Guddavva became blind in her left eye. After this, every one clean forgot the name "Ijilacchmi," and took to calling her "Guddidaava."

It seems Thaatha was terribly nasty to Guddavva. He had a bad, bad temper. Also it seems he liked lots of other women. One evening, when he came back home, he saw my guddavva sleeping soundly. Thaatha became mad with rage. He stomped out of the house, untied the bullocks from the yoke and secured them up in the shed. Then he stormed into the house and overturned the cot on which Guddavva was sleeping. Guddavva woke up with a start and was trying to regain her balance when Thaatha unfurled the strap he used to whip cattle and whipped her with it.

"Ayyo, ayyo!" my guddavva cried out. But Thaatha didn't stop. "You guddilanja! Aren't you ashamed of yourself, sleeping in the evening, wantonly baring yourself?" He kicked her and lashed her again and again. For Guddavva, such beatings were a daily thing.

Right in the midst of this terrible life, Guddavva had a son. And immediately after this, Thaatha married again and promptly forgot all about Guddavva and their son. Guddavva reached Tirupathi with her child and there, on the Tirupathi hill, she tried to do all kinds of jobs – she carried firewood, she carried hay, she even carried bricks on construction sites with her baby tied to her back. But after her son grew up, he went straight back to his father, married and settled down in Rangampeta. Guddavva continued to live on the hill, working sometimes as a servant in the merchants' colonies, sometimes selling hot water to pilgrims who came to Tirupathi.

It was then that my father brought her to our home. He had a hut built for Guddavva under the eucalyptus tree. My mother too takes great care of her but Guddavva doesn't rest for a moment. If she's not frying peanuts and making groundnut sweets with jaggery, she is selling them outside our school. After school hours, she sits beside the bus stand near the Muslim bazaar. After the day has retired into the nest of darkness, Guddavva returns home, the day's earnings tucked in a little pouch at her waist. She still earns for herself, says Amma.

This is my guddavva's story.

And so ... The moonbeam was flooding Palakonda. The moonlight dew fell on the leaves of the eucalyptus tree and then dropped gently on our heads. We, Peerugodu, Bujji and I, sat there, getting wet in the dewdrops, in the shower of moonlight.

Sakku Chinnamma came with her anapa ginjalu which had been soaked in water, and sat with us, skinning the pulses, as her mouth worked busily on betel. Every now and then she glanced at Enkatramanna from the corner of her eye and a laughter would bubble up in her. Next came Guddavva, bringing with her some groundnut sweets. She gave each of us one. Vasantha who came in behind Guddavva, was already eating her groundnut ball.

Guddavva set down her basket of groundnuts. She heaped them on the floor and began to shell the groundnuts one by one. Enkatramanna stopped playing and sat down, too. Guddavva took out betel nuts and a leaf from the little pouch tucked in at her waist. "Have some chunna?" she asked Sakku Chinnamma, who crooked her finger and scooped out some lime, smearing it on Guddavva's betel leaf.

"Attha," said Sakku Chinnamma looking at Guddavva fold the betel leaf expertly, and tuck it into her left cheek. "You are so fond of children. You are always making something for them to eat. You tell them stories. You play with them, you make them laugh. You are happy when they are happy. When they are sad, the day hangs heavily on you. Why do you love children so?"

"You crazy one," murmurred Guddavva through betel-stained teeth. "Is it possible to not like the moon? There is only one moon in the sky. See how many moons I have around me."

A tender moonlight shone from her eyes.

We started pestering her for a story.

"The Coconut Bride," I begged.

"The Fox and the Pig," Peerugodu clamoured.

"The Bottle Gourd's Brain and the Goat," Lacchukamma pleaded.

"I shall tell you a new story today," said Guddavva. And Vasantha promptly clambered on to her lap.

Guddavva said: Long long ago, there was a widow called Aakasamma. She had two sons. The elder one was called Suranna and the younger one Chandranna. Aakasamma had to work very hard to bring up her fatherless sons. She sent them to school, she taught them many arts.

One day, the sons came up to their mother and said, "Amma! If we have your consent, we would like to see the world."

"You two are like my two eyes. If you go away, what is to become of me?" sobbed Aakasamma. (Sakku Chinnamma's eyes filled up at this. She blew her nose and wiped her eyes with her pallu.)

"It's only fair that we put our education to some use. Let us go. We promise to return in a year's time. Please give us your blessings."

"If you are so determined to go, how can I refuse you?" asked Aakasamma. "But take care, my children. May success be yours." And then she added, "Remember to come back and marry your uncle's daughters, Pagatamma and Reyamma."

So the brothers set off on their travels – Suranna set off eastwards, while Chandranna travelled west.

After touring several kingdoms in the east, Suranna reached Indrapastha, which was ruled by Raja Vanapastha. Now, Raja Vanapastha had seven beautiful daughters. The princesses had declared that they would marry the man who would bring the seven flowers in seven colours from Indraloka.

The Raja had an announcement made in every street corner: Listen, listen! Raja Vanapastha will give his daughters in marriage to the hero who brings the magical flowers of Indraloka. He will also crown him Raja and give his new son-in-law half his kingdom.

Of the many princes who journeyed to the kingdom of the gods, several died after being bitten by the poisonous snakes that guarded the seven heavenly flowers. Others returned empty-handed, but glad that they were at least alive.

Many days went by. The royal drums announced the challenge everyday.

As days went by, the king began to panic. No prince had returned victorious. But the princesses still wanted only a man who could bring the seven flowers in seven colours from Indraloka.

Now it happened that Suranna heard the announcement. Straight he proceeded to the kingdom of the gods. He shot a string of arrows and built a stairway to the kingdom of the gods!

(Touching Bujji on the thigh, Ravigodu said excitedly, "Bujjakka, tomorrow I am also going to build a ladder of arrows to heaven." Irritated, Bujji shouted, "Shut up, you monkey! Can't you let me listen to the story in peace?" But you know Ravigodu. Unmindful of Bujji's protest, Ravigodu was on his heels, shooting arrows into the sky with his empty hands.)

Suranna entered devalokam. He pierced the eyes of the seven poisonous snakes with his arrows. He plucked the seven flowers and descended the stairs hurriedly.

Indrapastha was agog with the news of the young man who had come back triumphant. People flocked in the thousands to witness the rare spectacle. Suranna placed the flowers before the king on a gold platter. The people applauded. The flowers shone like stars, and their fragrance filled the air. The seven princesses wore the flowers in their hair. The king gave his daughters in marriage to Suranna, and also crowned him king of half his kingdom.

(Enkatramanna jumped to his feet, took off his upper cloth, waved it in the air and whistled in delight.)

Guddavva continued:

Now, while all this was happening in the east, Chandranna, who had travelled extensively in the west was passing through a dense forest on his horse. In that forest, lived a rishi with his beautiful daughter. A brahmarakshasa had been pestering the rishi to give his daughter in marriage to him. One day, when the rishi was not in his ashram, the brahmarakshasa kidnapped his daughter and carried her away beyond the seven seas and hid her in the branches of a banyan tree!

Chandranna, who was passing by, stopped for a drink of water. Dismounting from his horse, he walked up to the rishi's ashram and saw the rishi looking deeply distressed.

Is something wrong? asked Chandranna.

The rishi told him what had happened. If you rescue my daughter from the brahmarakshasa's clutches, I will give her in marriage to you, said the rishi.

Chandranna mounted his horse, and riding beyond the seven mountains and the seven seas, reached the banyan tree. (Vasantha, who was sitting in Guddavva's lap, clutched Guddavva in fear.)

On seeing Chandranna, the Brahmarakshasa jumped on him with a roar. ("I'm getting scared!" said Ravigodu and, running into the house, listened to the rest of the story from behind the door.) Chandranna leapt at the brahmarakshasa. The brahmarakshasa caught Chandranna and flung him away. Chandranna somehow got up to his feet, and, dusting his clothes, jumped at the Brahmarakshasa again. This time, the brahmarakshasa uprooted a tamarind tree and threw it at Chandranna. (Afraid that the tamarind tree would fall on me, I ducked from its path.) Chandranna swiftly stepped away. Then he uprooted a banyan tree and flung it towards the brahmarakshasa. The brahmarakshasa threw a huge boulder at Chandranna this time. Chandranna replied with a whole mountain! A fierce battle was fought, lasting seven days. At the end, Chandranna wrung the brahmarakshasa's neck who screamed a most horrible scream before falling lifelessly to the ground.

The rishi gave his daughter in marriage to Chandranna. (Ravigodu returned to sit with us from behind the door.)

The sons and their wives went to Aakasamma. and she said, "My sons, I want you to get married to your mama's daughters also." So, Chandranna married Reyamma. Even today, he lives with Reyamma for fifteen days in a month. The other fifteen days are spent with the rishi's daughter. This is why half of the month is dark, and the other half, bright.

As for Suranna, he married Pagatamma. Suranna's seven wives started disliking Pagatamma, especially because Aakasamma had bestowed the status of the eldest daughter-in-law upon Pagatamma. This was reason enough for the seven sisters to hate their mother-in-law too.

The days however passed peacefully.

Then, one day, Aakasamma fell seriously ill. The vaidyudu told her sons to churn the sea and bring back the extracted buttermilk for Aakasamma to drink. The brothers set off with a silver churning stick and a pot each. They churned the sea and collected buttermilk in a pot each.

Chandranna went straight to his mother with the buttermilk. Suranna, however, went to his seven wives first. Unknown to Suranna, they mixed chilli powder in the buttermilk. Aakasamma drank the buttermilk that Chandranna had brought her and her stomach was filled with calm. My son! You soothed my stomach with cool buttermilk. May you live happily with your wives. Not only that, you will brighten the world with moonlight and everybody will love you for it, Aakasamma blessed.

Aakasamma then drank the buttermilk Suranna got her. Her stomach was aflame. Burning with anger, Aakasamma cursed Suranna without thinking. How dare you burn my stomach! You will always be blazing hot. And everybody will curse you for the scorching hot sun that you will be. At this, Suranna's wives came running, and fell at their mother-in-law's feet. We are to blame, they cried. Your son is innocent. We mixed chilli powder in the buttermilk. So it was you, said Aakasamma. Because you caused hurt, you seven sisters will come together only on the days it rains and that is when you'll live with Suranna also.

("Have you noticed the rainbow after rain? The seven colours in the rainbow are the seven sisters. And they come together briefly only after rain," explained Guddavva, while, "That's why they say a mother's curse runs its course," said Sakku Chinnamma, with a huge sigh.)

But Aakasamma was deeply grieved that she had cursed her innocent son. She cried bitterly, saying, I am not a mother! I deserve to die for what I have done! And she ran to the top of a cliff and prepared to jump. Just then, Lord Siva and Parvathi, who were passing through the skies in their chariot, spotted Aakasamma.

Stop the Chariot, my Lord! A woman is trying to jump off that cliff there, cried Parvathiamma.

Aakasamma was just about to jump off the cliff when Parvathidevi caught hold of her pallu and stopped her.

On seeing Lord Siva and Parvathi, Aakasamma gave vent to her anguish and, between sobs, narrated what had happened.

Neither you nor your son is at fault. It is all god's game. They say everything happens for our own good. Your elder son will give light to all. Your younger son will shower moonlight. If we are the invisible gods then your sons are the visible gods! consoled Parvathi before she and Siva climbed back into their chariot and went back to their abode among the gods.

And a happy Aakasamma returned home.

Here ends our story. It is now time for *us* to go home," ended Guddavva.

We got up one by one. The crane that had perched on the tamarind tree, stood up and flapped its wings. The milky moonlight showered down.

"I must hurry, Attha. I still have to weed Anumanthumama's garden." Sakku Chinnamma picked up her vessel of anapa ginjalu and hurried away. Ravigodu followed his mother.

Vasantha was fast asleep in Guddavva's lap. Peerugodu picked her up and rested her head on his shoulder. Then, turning in my direction, he said, "Come on, let us go."

"I am going to sleep here. With Guddavva," I said.

Peerugodu went away, carrying Vasantha. Guddavva collected the shelled groundnuts into a basket. Then she swept the place, and spread out a quilt for me. She also gave me a pillow made of paddy husk.

I slept on the quilt. Guddavva turned out the lamp and lay beside me. She gave me her tattered blanket to cover myself. As for herself, she used the pallu of her saree to keep warm.

Moonlight flooded my face. The moon, like a butterball in a pot of buttermilk, would plunge down one moment, and reappear the next.

"Beware, I am going to steal you today!" I said, looking at the moon in the sky.

The next morning I woke with a start when the cock crowed. Guddavva was already gone off to fetch water from the well. She is always up before the cock crows.

I looked up. The moon was not in the sky. Guddavva must have put it back in the earthen pot suspended from the roof.

I stole up to the roof with soft steps. The pot was beyond my reach. So I climbed onto a sack of groundnuts. Looking back furtively in the direction of the door, to make sure Guddavva was not around, I reached for the pot.

I climbed down carefully and put the pot on the ground. Then kneeling before the pot I removed the lid. All at once, a brilliant light flashed across my face, blinding me! Inside the pot was the radiance of one crore lamps. It was the moon!

When I tried to lift the dazzling moon from the pot, it kept slipping from my hands like a fish. I sieved it with my fingers and slowly removed the moon from the pot. There! I had it in my palms! It felt like a ball of ice in my hands. I kissed it and my lips went numb. A shiver went up my spine.

Just then, I heard the sound of Guddavva's steps.

I jumped to my feet in a trice, and hurriedly stuffed the moon under my pillow. Then, pretending I knew nothing, I pulled the blanket over me and feigned sleep.

CONTRIBUTORS' NOTES

ASOMIYA

Pankaj Thakur has a post-graduate degree in Economics from Guwahati University and is Area Manager, Marketing with TELCO at Guwahati. He writes in Asomiya and is known mainly for his satires. He has been the Associate Editor of *Ajir Asom*, a popular monthly in Assam and has also edited works on developmental studies. A collection of his short stories, *Apuni Kiba Kaboneki*, has been translated into Hindi and he has recently edited a volume of short stories for Sahitya Akademi. He has also translated Ibsen, Strindberg, Sartre and Wole Soyinka into Asomiya from their works in English translation.

- The literary scene in Assam is fairly bright. Good literature sells and not a single publishing house has closed down in the past few decades. The Assam Sahitya Sabha is a very active body, involving itself in major projects and taking policy decisions, having far-reaching effects. Also, writers in Assam don't write because they have nothing better to do, which is why one can see a lot of good writing. They are, therefore, a cared-for lot and enjoy considerable respect.

  Amongst the stories published in 1998, **Pokhila** is an example of excellent technical craft and magical language. It is highly readable.

Imran Hussain is a post-graduate in Political Science, from Guwahati University. He is presently working as a lecturer at Sipajhar College, Darrang, Assam. He has contributed short stories, poems and articles to leading literary journals and his stories have been translated into English by Sahitya Akademi and into Gujarati by *Gujarati Samachar*. He was the Vice-President of the All Assam New Artists and Writers Association during 1991-92. He has won the titles of Best Literary Man, 1991 and Best Artist of the Year, 1991, bestowed by Guwahati University.

This section is organized language-wise. It contains the biographical details of the Nominating Editor; the state of the short story in that language and the Editor's reasons for nominating the chosen story/stories. This is followed by the biographical details of the Writer and her/his notes on the story; then the notes on and by the Translator. In languages where there are two stories, the reasons for the nomination of both stories come with the Nominating Editor's note, while the Writer's and the Translator's notes for each story have been placed together for ease of reference, and are alphabetically arranged according to the Writer's first name.

He is currently the editor of *Ajir Kabita* brought out by Guwahati University.

- The ritual, toloniya biya, a ceremony performed among Assamese Hindus when a girl attains puberty, was quite strange to me, being a male, brought up in an Assamese Muslim family. I wanted to know more about it and go deeper into its socio-psychological aspects. I felt I could see certain things associated with the custom, which one born into the culture may not notice.

Nandana Dutta has post-graduated from Guwahati University where she is now teaching English literature. She has just begun translations. "Sunset at Noon," her English translation of Phul Goswami's story, was published in the Katha title, *Imaging the Other*.

- The swear words and the colourful colloquialism had really no adequate English equivalents and a literal translation would have taken away the pithiness of the original. The story, written by a male writer, is about the awakening of a young girl, and I kept encountering what I thought was a rather definite "male" gaze.

BANGLA

Debes Ray is an eminent fiction writer, with twenty six books to his credit – of which about thirteen are novels – and nearly a hundred short stories. He received the Sahitya Akademi Award in 1990.

- The short story has developed into a very powerful genre in Bangla literature over the last one hundred years even as it has faced social crises and political upheavals. This genre has always excited authors to innovate and experiment, and there are few writers in Bengal who have not written at least one very good short story.

  Arthaheen Katha Balar Nirbharata is a remarkable story displaying mastery over language. Very subtle, it involves a complex narrative strategy and builds up claustrophobia with unerring motivation. Episodes like the journalist's search for attractive headlines, or presenting a bereaved neighbour with a telephone that trills like a bird on ringing, create a bizarre and weird atmosphere. A cruel comment on our times.

  I chose **Snehalata** for the interesting juxtaposition of the policeman and the old woman. The story turns allegorical towards the end and the pathos has been dealt in a stubborn style, never yielding to sentiments. The author's mature view of life simply overwhelmed me.

Afsar Ahmed post-graduated in Bangla from Calcutta University. He began his literary career as a short story writer but later switched to novel writing. He is now working with the Paschim Bongo Bangla Akademi on a collection of socio-economic articles. His published novels include *Gar-Garasti* (1982), *Basabas* (1988) and *Alowkik Divrat* (1999). *Afsar Ahmeder Galpa* (1989) and *Shreshta Galpa* (1999) are among his published short stories. He also has one children's book, *Bagnaner Bhoot* (1996) to his credit. Some significant awards received by him are the Somen Chandra Memorial Award for Short Story, Nikhil Bharat Banga Sahitya Sammelan Puraskar (1997) and the Sapan Puraskar (1993).

- I wanted to convey through my story that basic human rights cannot be violated in a democratic country.

Chandana Dutta has a doctoral degree in English Literature from Jawaharlal Nehru University. She has taught for some time at Sherubtse College, Bhutan, and at Jesus and Mary College, New Delhi. She heads the editorial department at Katha as Assistant Director, Katha Vilasam. Reading, music and travelling are some of her main interests and this is her first attempt at translation.

- The story is about a journalist who finds himself increasingly enveloped by meaninglessness, both in his experiences and expressions. The constant element of surprise arises from the fact that everyone around him is able to find meaning and beauty even as he despairs. Translating the force with which the Bangla words convey the meaninglessness that the protagonist feels, and the poeticness with which the others around him experience the beauty of words and expressions, into English, where the vocabulary is so different, has been very challenging. To convey exactly what the writer wishes to, and yet keep the translated version readable, was like walking a tightrope.

Minakshi Sen finished her schooling from Calcutta in 1970 during the turbulent time when many youths were responding to the call of the naxalites. She was not an exception and was arrested on false charges by the police in 1973, tortured and detained for a long time without trial. After her release in 1977, despite the traumatic experience, she went on to complete her post-graduation in Physiology with a gold medal from Calcutta University. She began serious writing in the late seventies and a large part of her prison memories was serialized in *Spandan*, a literary magazine edited by her husband. Much later, a book on her days spent in prison, titled *Jailer Bhetor Jail* was published in 1993 winning considerable critical acclaim. She is a Member Secretary, Tripura State Commission for Women.

- The main theme of my story deals with the inner strength of a mother who is a widow, and her struggle in a totally adverse situation. Her characterization may not fit into the traditional Indian idea of a mother but she is very much a mother in her own right.

Kalyani Dutta, educated in Delhi and Leeds, UK, has been teaching English Literature at Indraprastha College in Delhi for more than three decades. She reviews in and translates from Bangla into English and also writes articles on culture and environment. "Stove," her English translation of Premendra Mitra's story, appeared in the Katha title, *Imaging the Other.* She is currently researching on the life and works of the early twentieth century educationist and social reformer, Rokiya Sakhawat Hossain.

- There was the impossibility of conveying the East Bengal dialect in translation and the usual problems of long sentences which when translated, become awkward in English. There was also the difficulty of translating abusive and exclamatory phrases. The punctuation too is somewhat eccentric in the original.

ENGLISH

Pankaj Mishra is a writer based in New Delhi and Shimla. He is the author of *Butter Chicken in Ludhiana,* published by Penguin India. His new book, *The Romantics*, has just been brought out by India Ink.

- As regards the state of English short story in India, the tendency to make large generalizations on the basis of a very small fare should be resisted. There isn't enough evidence of high literary quality out there and I would hesitate to speculate why this is so or whether we can expect a sudden flowering of talent.

  Summer on the Island conveys a peculiar experience of childhood, and the simplicity of its prose and the directness of its tone help uncover all the hidden sources of feeling and emotion within that experience. It shows a writer in command of her material.

Roschen Sasikumar has a PhD in Theoretical Physics and she works at Thiruvananthapuram as Head, Computational Materials Science Unit, under the Council of Scientific and Industrial Research. She has been awarded the Alexander Von Humboldt Fellowship for excellence in research and has written 30 scientific articles in international journals and presented papers at many international conferences. She runs a centre for underprivileged children at Thiruvananthapuram.

- About eighty percent of the story is autobiographical, of my experiences when I took a year off in the middle of my PhD to work as the warden of Bethel Ashram Boarding Home, Munroe Island. We took care of 30 children with aid from German sponsors. For one of them, Uma, I think I was a little more than a "fun" adult in their drab lives. After I left, I sometimes wondered – I still do – whether I did her more harm than good by giving her a lot of affection for a short while. And that's what led to the story.

GUJARATI

Kanti Patel is a short story writer and critic. He is Head of the Department of Gujarati at Bhavan's College, Mumbai.

- Short story has always been the most loved genre in Gujarat and many good writers have helped develop it. The modernist period between the sixties and the eighties witnessed a revolution in Gujarati literature with Suresh Joshi primarily contributing to it. His writings and criticism had a tremendous impact. Contemporary Gujarati short story is more tradition-bound and straight forward. The focus has shifted to the village and the small town and one can read stories in different dialects.

  Narrated in Kathiawadi dialect, **Darvinno Pitrai** describes tantric rituals in a gripping style. The psychological dimension in the witchcraft is fascinating. The story of human evolution has been depicted in a characteristic manner which is why the story gets the title it has.

My Dear Jayu is the pen name of Jayanti Gohel. He teaches Gujarati at Samaldas College, Gujarat. He is the President of Bhavnagar Sahitya Sabha and Samaldas Parivar Trust. His published works include *Maranteep* and *Kamlpooja* which are novellas, two collections of short stories, *Thoda Otha* and *Jeev*, and a collection of critical articles, *Sa Pashyati*.

- The nativist concept of 1990 led me to conduct certain story-telling experiments. I felt that the story can be elevated if social life and mind are presented in their own style and structure. I, therefore, adopted Otha, a form of story telling like fable and legend for many of my works. This story gives a glimpse of the beliefs underlying our emotions, experiences and our concepts of evolution, astronomy and environment.

Tridip Suhrud teaches in the Science and Liberal Arts Programme at the National Institute of Design, Ahmedabad. His specialization is social history and literature of Gujarat. At present he is working on nineteenth century Gujarati autobiographies. He has translated Ashis Nandy's *Intimate Enemy* into Gujarati, and has edited and translated a selection of Nandy's essays, *Pratishabda*. His translation of Suresh Joshi's Gujarati novel, *Chinnapatra* was published as *Crumpled Letter* by Macmillan in 1998.

- The story retells the origin myth, with irreverent humour. The story is written in boli, and the writer depends upon the reader's familiarity with the oral tradition. To capture its echoes in an essentially written language like English was not easy.

HINDI

Asad Zaidi is a poet and critic with two collections of poems to his credit – *Behnen aur Anya Kavitaen* (1980) *and Kavita Ka Jeevan* (1988). He has received the Sanskriti Award for his contribution to Hindi literature. About half a dozen anthologies of poetry, fiction and criticism have been edited by him and he has translated the works of a number of European and Latin American poets and some classical Chinese poetry into Hindi and Urdu. He also writes extensively on media, culture and art. He is closely associated with the South Asian Network for Alternative Media (SANAM), a voluntary organization working in the field of culture and media and edits *Delhi Magazine*, a periodical on South Asian culture, art and literature.

- What salvages **Galat** from becoming a tale of loss, guilt and momentary collective remorse, is its considerable poetic vision, emotionally controlled choreography and power of evocation. The writer emerges as a responsible artist who does not let his sense of irony degenerate into cynicism and aesthetic nihilism. He has managed to subtly weave the socio-political undercurrents of the time and their manifestation in a city like Dehradun, which lends its personality to the story as it does in the works of, say, Allan Sealy and Ruskin Bond.

Yogendra Ahuja is a post-graduate in Economics from Bareilly College, Bareilly. He works as an officer in a nationalized bank. His published works include short stories in various Hindi magazines. He is an avid reader of poetry, and is interested in science, history, anthropology, computers and cinema.

- The story was perhaps written in a sombre mood lamenting the cultural crisis of our times, the triumph of consumerism and the endless, thoughtless jollification that the "great Indian middle class" indulges in. I wanted to spill the beans, to ruin this senseless celebration by adding an ominous wail to it in the form of this story. It is another matter that no one listens to a writer, and the party goes on.

Nandita Aggarwal is a consultant editor with Katha. A post-graduate in psychology from Punjab University, she has been a freelance editor for publishing houses with around ten years experience. She has worked with Penguin India for some time. She likes doodling and cartooning and has illustrated a Puffin book, *Grin and Bear it, Abhy.*

- The story is complex and detailed with the writer taking off at a tangent whenever he wishes to. In the original, these long and winding sentences slide along beautifully one after the another, underpinned with wry humour. The challenge was to not miss out on any of the details and yet maintain the writer's lightness of touch and gentle self-derision.

Neer Kanwal Mani teaches English Literature at Government PG College, Faridabad. Her areas of interest are modern literary theory and literary criticism, modern writing in Hindi and other Indian languages. She loves painting and translating.

- The story is contemporary and very realistic with a theme I could identify with. I enjoyed translating it.

KANNADA

Ramachandra Sharma, as writer, editor and translator, is considered to be one of the pioneers of modern Kannada literature. He has a doctoral degree from London University, has taught at schools in India, Ethiopia and England and has worked as a psychologist in England, Zambia and for UNESCO. He has to his credit, several collections of poems, short stories, plays, and literary essays. He is also the author of a collection of poems in English, titled *Gestures*. Many of his poems and short stories have been translated into English and other Indian languages. The Katha Classics title, *Masti* was edited by him and he received the Katha Award for Translation in 1992. He was the recipient of the Government of India Award for his play, *Seragina Kenda* in 1954 and the Government of Karnataka Award for the play, *Neralu* in 1965. Among other awards, he was honoured with the Karnataka Sahitya Akademi Award in 1985 and the Sahitya Akademi Award in 1998.

- Following the success of the navya tradition of narration, some of the leading writers of that school began to feel that the society around had been left out. As a result, there was a sort of Second Coming of the society into the genre of short story and Muslim, women and dalit writers helped in expanding its range. Most of the powerful stories today have a rural setting. There is great felicity and skill in the narrative techniques, which is a legacy of the navya and the navodaya movements.

  Doni beautifully depicts the elemental attraction between a boy and a girl against the elemental forces of the wind and the sea. There is a vivid description of the life of fisherfolk with the sea as an effective backdrop.

Na D'Souza is a retired officer from the Karnataka Public Works Department. He has thirty six novels, twenty five children's books, five collections of short stories and eight plays to his credit. Many of his writings have been translated into Hindi, Urdu, Telugu, Malayalam and Konkani. He has won the Karnataka Sahitya Akademi Best Children's Book Award in 1988 for *Belakinodane Banthu Nenapu*. He also received the Karnataka Sahitya Akademi Award in 1993. The film based on his novel, *Kadina Benki*, won several national and state awards in 1990. He is a member of the Karnataka Konkani Sahitya Akademi.

- This wonderful mass of water called sea has a special character. It has never bothered about gender, caste, and creed and has inspired me many a time to write. In my story, for the boy, the sea is unknown, for the girl, her destiny is undecided. But together, they sail towards the sea in a new doni ...

Bageshree is a journalist with the *Deccan Herald*. She translates from Kannada into English and this is an area of special interest to her.

- A deceptively simple story, it confronts the issues of caste, class, gender and modernity. The different varieties of boats and fish in the story are very specific to the language of fisherfolk. They don't have English equivalents and are also not used in the standard Kannada speech. The fact that the story is about a Tulu-speaking community, conveyed in the original through occasional use of Tulu words, is entirely lost in the translation.

MAITHILI

Udaya Narayana Singh is a Professor of Linguistics at the University of Hyderabad. A gold medalist from Delhi University and a Jubilee Awardee of Calcutta University, he is a playwright and poet in Maithili. He has also written books on syntax, translation, stylistics and socio-linguistics. He has been a visiting professor at the Indian Institute of Advance Study, Shimla. As a Fellow of the Linguistic Society of America in 1978, he has taught linguistics, English, anthropology and comparative literature in leading universities across the country.

- Maithili short story emerged prominently only after 1947, and along with poetry and essays, is one of the strongest genres. Prior to that, there were only four writers with anthologies to their credit. Stories, however, appeared in literary magazines right from Kali Kumar Das's "Bhishan Anyay" (1913). Among writers like 'Suman,' 'Kiran' Yoganand Jha, Umanath Jha and Upendra Nath Jha 'Vyas,' the ones who made their mark then and continued to do so in the post-independence period were Harimohan Jha and 'Yatri'. Maithili writers have always represented different trends. Some like Manmohan and Sudhanshu Sekhar Choudhury tilting towards emotional, some like Manipadma, Mayanand or 'Kiran' showing a preference for the realistic and others like Lalit and Dhirendra leaning towards socially relevant themes. There was yet another group continuing with the tradition of humour set up by Harimohan Jha. The best known writers of today, like Somdev, Prabhas Kumar Choudhury, Dhoomketu and Rajmohan Jha, have shown preferences for psychoanalytical, political, symbolic and realistic topics. Amongst the youngest generation, Sukant Som, Shivsankar Srinivas, Vibha Rani and others have shown a lot of variety and freshness in their treatment of characters, style and choice of themes.

  The sheer simplicity of the plot and superb use of the female register of speech to write the story tilted the scale in favour of **Rahtu Sakshi Chhat Ghat**. Here, the context is highlighted, which is, the Chhat Ghat, a silent witness to the joy, sorrow, trials and tribulations of a community. And as time heals their wounds, as men and women bring in revolutionary changes in their attitudes and practices, the Chhat Ghat too lights up with earthen lamps floating on the water.

Vibha Rani holds an MA degree in Hindi. She presents programmes on All India Radio and Vividh Bharathi, Mumbai. She has previously been a radio announcer, drama artist, compere and folk singer on All India Radio, Darbhanga and Calcutta. She regularly contributes short stories, poems, features, and reviews in Maithili and Hindi dailies and magazines.

- I come from Mithila, a small town in the northern part of Bihar where women in my opinion, are like sealed envelopes, not allowed to express themselves and live their lives the way they want to. Their destiny is in the hands of their family members. A real incident inspired this story.

Vidyanand Jha teaches organizational behaviour at Indian Institute of Management, Calcutta. He has a doctorate in management from the Institute of Rural Management, Anand where he has also worked for more than three years. His poems have been published in Maithili magazines and have also been translated into Hindi, Bangla, English and Telugu. He translates from Maithili into Hindi and English and from English into Maithili. He had also been a political activist with an underground communist party from 1981 to 1986. He likes listening to nirgun bhajans, Indian classical and jazz and loves watching movies and going on long walks.

- It is a tough story to translate as it is replete with a whole lot of words associated with rituals and ornaments, some of them long out of fashion. This required that the reader be given some exposure to the ceremonies associated with chhat and marriage. But bringing all these details into the story would have made it an anthropological treatise. Footnotes too, after a point, hinder the smooth flow of the narrative.

MALAYALAM

K Satchidanandan is an eminent Malayalam poet, critic and translator, who has so far written eighteen collections of poetry, seventeen works of literary theory, social theory and criticism, two plays and sixteen collections of translations of world poetry. His work has been translated into all the major languages of India and many languages abroad. He has three published works in English – *How to Go to the Tao Temple* and *Summer Rain* which are poetry collections and *Indian Literature: Positions and Prepositions*, a book of essays. He has also edited several anthologies of stories and poems in Malayalam and English. Previously, a professor of English and the editor of the journal, *Indian Literature*, he is now the Secretary of the Sahitya Akademi. The honours he has received include the Kerala Sahitya Akademi Award (thrice, for poetry, essay and drama), the Bharatiya Bhasha Parishad Award, the Oman Cultural Centre Award, and Senior Fellowship from the Department of Culture, Government of India. He has represented Indian poetry in several literary festivals abroad.

- The Malayalam short story is now passing through what critics call an uttar-adhunik or post-modern phase. While modernists like Kamala Das, O V Vijayan, M Mukundan, Sethu, Punathil Kunhabdulla and Paul Zacharia are still active, the scene is dominated by a generation that emerged in the seventies and the eighties. Their writing rejects the essentially solipsistic ideology of modernism based on the urban experience of solitude, alienation, existentialism and irrationality and focuses instead on a straight forward idiom. This generation includes a number of excellent writers like Sarah Joseph and Gracy who take an aggressive feminist stance, dealing directly with patriarchal ideology and its diverse manifestations in our daily lives. Chandramati uses invective and satire to laugh at the hypocrisy of man-woman relationships. Ashita and Priya in some sense continue in the tradition of Kamala Das and have kept tenderness alive in their tales while being acutely conscious of the status of woman in Kerala's society. Pathos and affection, more than sarcasm and hatred govern the contents of their lyrical narratives.

  Panchali is a typical instance of revisioning patriarchal myths and the assertion of female sexuality as an act of resistance. The writer tells the story in her own style, in short sentences, mixing the past and the present to create her own space-time theatre for the unfolding of a violent "anti-erotic" drama.

Gracy comes from a family of farmers and she started writing while studying for her BA degree and her first story was published in 1972. She later worked as a Malayalam lecturer. Her first short story collection, *Padiyirangippoya Parvathi* was published in 1991. *Narakavathil* and

Bhranthan Pookkal came out in 1993 and 1996. The latter fetched her the Thoppil Ravi Award in 1997. A volume of nineteen stories by her has also been published in Tamil as *Pothu Panikkalam*. In 1995, Gracy won the Lalithambika Antharjanam Award. Other than literature, she loves dance and music.

- I have never tried to impose my own idea on any of my stories. I usually let out the story in its own way.

Rukmini Sekar is Director, Performing Arts, at INTACH (Indian National Trust for Art and Cultural Heritage) and has been actively working with SPIC MACAY (Society for Promotion of Indian Classical Music and Culture Amongst Youth). She started YOUNG INTACH, a cell aimed at involving the youth in the preservation of heritage and also the SPIC MACAY magazine, *The Eye*, and was its editor till June 1998.

MANIPURI

Robin S Ngangom is a bilingual poet and translator. He studied literature at St Edmund's College, Shillong, and earned his masters degree from the North East Hill University, Shillong, where he teaches now. He has written two books on poetry, *Words and the Silence* and *Time's Crossroads*.

- Beginning with romantic stories about unexceptional lives, the Manipuri story, **Ahing Ama** has faithfully portrayed changing realities over the years. There are writers who use the allegorical or satirical mode or who depict seemingly trivial incidents and characters belying existential situations. Writers today seem to be preoccupied with ethnic violence, corruption, extortion, terrorism, drug addiction. As a result, experimentation has slowed down a little.

  I chose the story for its human interest aspect, psychological fidelity and universal significance.

  While translating this story, one problem was the absence of pronouns and articles in the Manipuri original. For example, the personal pronoun "I" is not used but only implied in Manipuri.

Keisham Priyokumar is a civil engineer by profession and he has three volumes of collected short stories in Manipuri to his credit. He has been the editor of two journals, *Wakhal* and *Sahitya*, and a literary bulletin, *Sahityagi Pao*. He is the only Manipuri writer to win the maximum number of awards for a single book, *Nongdi Tarakkhidare* in 1997 – the Dr Khoirom

Tomchou Memorial Gold Medal, the Teleuns Abir Memorial Award, and the Dineswori Sahitya Award. In 1998, he received the Sahitya Akademi Award and the Manipuri State Kala Akademi Award. He is associated with various literary organizations in Manipur.

- During the past few years, the Nagas and the Kukis have been engaged in perennial conflict. So many lives have been lost and villages gutted, in this relentless strife. It seems unbelievable that people who had been living peacefully for many centuries have suddenly started moving apart. The impact of this strife is the source of my story.

MARATHI

Usha Tambe is a lecturer with an MPhil degree in English from Bombay University. She writes book reviews regularly for *Maharashtra Times*. She is a member of the Executive Committee of Mumbai Sahitya Sabha. Her translations of Shashi Deshpande's stories have appeared in Marathi magazines and she has compered programmes for Doordarshan and All India Radio.

- The short story continues its hold over the readers and writers of Maharashtra and new writers are constantly emerging while at least some of the old masters still continue to write. This genre seems to be more aware of the changing socio-cultural situations. On one hand, it appears bolder in expression, on the other, it is entering new areas like science fiction, which is gaining popularity. Dalit writers have also carved a niche for themselves. In many stories of this year, the plight of parents whose children have settled abroad, holds centre-stage though the conventional themes of mother-in-law versus daughter-in-law have not totally disappeared. Philosophical questions are also being raised through the medium of the story.

  The strength of **Athrawa Unt** is not so much in the chain of events as in the complexity of emotions. The gradual deterioration of a relationship, the frustration felt by Sujata, the slow revival of her self-respect, her courage, are all poignantly portrayed. The world of theatre, its inner manipulations, insecurities and doomed relationships are all skilfully revealed by the writer. Life itself becomes a play, with the spotlight always on these actors.

  Jaala is about the young generation that has migrated abroad, bearing the constant burden of guilt of having left their parents behind. The nuances of emotions, the delicate emotional and practical threads binding the characters are so subtly but powerfully suggested that reading it becomes a moving experience.

Meghana Pethe has been associated with Marathi Amateur Theatre since 1982. She has won the prestigious Natya Darpan Award for Best Amateur Actress. She has written two one-act plays and her articles and columns have appeared in various Marathi dailies like *Aaj Dinank*, *Apla Mahanagar* and *Sanj Dinank*. Among the short stories she has written, seven were published as *Hans Akela*, in 1997 for which she received the Anandibai Shirke Award from Maharashtra Sahitya Parishad. She has also won the Priyadarshini Award in 1997 for contribution to Marathi literature, Shri Bal Sitaram Mardhekar Award, 1998 for being a new and promising writer in Marathi literature and the Shantaram Award in 1997.

- What happens when a woman decides to realize her potential? The decision has inevitable repercussions on her personal life and her priorities crumble and rearrange, leaving scars and strains on the relationship called marriage. She is confronted with new questions, which will have to be answered by her all alone – bravely. I have tried to capture all these turns in a marital relationship.

Sumedha Parande graduated in Chemistry from Bombay University, and in Education from Nagpur University. She also holds a diploma in travel and tourism. She taught in schools in Mumbai and Delhi for over ten years before deciding to take break and devote herself to other interests. Translation is a recent interest.

- It is not always easy to translate the idiom of one language into another without some loss of effect. The same holds true of cultural undertones in the original. However, apart from that, I faced no specific problems.

Sarita Padki has been writing since the age of eight or nine! She has handled various literary forms including translation and literature for children. Among the many awards and recognitions she has received are four state awards for literature.

- I wanted to write about how different are the memories of the mother. I am always apprehensive that our children living abroad will not be with us when we are unwell. But what I wanted to say is that though children move away from their old parents, it should not be assumed that they have no affection for them. The separation is almost always, equally painful for both.

Mukta Rajadhyaksha has an MA in French from Bombay University and a diploma in social communications media. She started her career in advertising, moving on to freelance writing, scripting and so on. She has produced and directed documentaries and television serials (notably, "Humraahi," a fifty two-episode serial for Doordarshan in 1992-93.) She writes theatre reviews and features for the Mumbai edition of the *Times of India*. She has translated a significant work, *Gandhi Viruddha Gandhi*, from Marathi into English as *Mahatma vs. Gandhi*.

- The story is an apt comment on migrant Indians who cannot shake off ties with their motherland. It also deals with relationships and misunderstandings between people supposedly close to each other. The narrative, as usual, is more emotive in the original language than in translation. However, there were no huge problems.

ORIYA

Rajendra Prasad Mishra is a post-graduate in Hindi and has a doctoral degree in Comparative Literature from Jawaharlal Nehru University, New Delhi. He has worked as Hindi Officer in the Bank of Baroda for three years, as Associate Professor of Hindi Translation at Jawaharlal Nehru University for a year and is at present working at National Thermal Power Corporation, New Delhi as Manager, Raj Bhasha. Translation is his only hobby and he has translated more than forty three books into Hindi out of which sixteen have been brought out by Bharatiya Jnanpith, New Delhi. The Central Hindi Directorate Award in 1986 and 1993, the Sauhard Puraskar Lucknow (1994), the Dwivagish Puraskar from Bharatiya Anuvad Parishad (1995), the Somdutta Samman (1994) and the Sahitya Akademi Award for Translation (1998) are among the major awards received by him.

- Orissa has a long literary history, one of the oldest in the country. Even modern Oriya prose fiction is more than hundred years old. With several brilliant writers, contemporary Oriya short fiction, has a rich past, an enriched present and a bright future.

  I chose **Ketaki Ban** for its artistic excellence. The language, style, narrative and a firm grip on the storyline hold the reader's attention leaving a strong impact on life itself.

Pratibha Ray referring to the glorification of her works on injustices against women says, "I don't relish being called a feminist, I am a humanist." Her novel *Yajnaseni*, received the Moorti Devi Award by the

Bharatiya Jnanpith in 1991. The Orissa Sahitya Akademi Award was conferred on her novel, *Shilapadma*, in 1985, and the film based on her novel, *Aparichita*, won the Best Film Story Award from the Culture Department, Government of Orissa in 1980. She has also received the Katha Award for Creative Fiction in 1994. Several of her short stories and novels have been adapted for radio plays, television serials and films. Pratibha Ray has a PhD in Educational Psychology and has been teaching in different colleges around Orissa for about twenty five years. She attributes the boldness, the revolt and the humanism in her writings to the influence of Vaishnavism.

- What comes across through my story is that love is natural, unselfish, has self-esteem and is not a sin. There is a lover inside every human being, needing no language or verbal expression.

Aparna Satpathy has graduated in Psychology from Utkal University. She lives in Delhi. This is her first attempt at translation.

- The story probes into the depths of human relationships built around what is said and what forever remains unsaid. Some colloquial expressions were difficult to translate and the writer uses some very typical Oriya phrases defying one's best attempts at translation. There are thematic, ideational repetitions, which seem awkward in translation, but are almost necessary for the original.

PUNJABI

Rana Nayar is a Reader in the Department of English, Punjab University, Chandigarh. Recepient of the Charles Wallace India Trust Fellowship to work on short stories of UK based Punjabi writers, his main areas of interest are drama, pedagogy and translation, and he has translated extensively from Punjabi into English.

- Punjabi short story is primarily a twentieth century phenomenon. In a long march over hundred years or so, it has acquired a distinct character of its own, evolving into a highly self-conscious art. To a large extent, this self-consciousness is reflected in the stories short-listed for this volume. Drawing upon the oriental, indigenous forms of story telling, Punjabi short story has experimented with every known form or mode of expression that one can speak of, in relation of any other genre or language available anywhere in the world. If there are stories in fabulist modes, there are others in romantic or realistic modes as well. There are stories in the traditional forms of folk narrative and those that are out and out modern in spirit and tone. Such experiments with new forms and newer contents have not only given a certain vitality and vibrancy to this form but also enabled it to discover uncharted boundaries. It is this openness, this restlessness that puts Punjabi short story on par with the best available anywhere in the world. A continous, uninterrupted tradition starting with S S Charan Singh Shaheed, Hira Singh Dard, and Joshua Fazal Din, has furthered and developed through Nanak Singh, Gurbaksh Singh, Kartar Singh Duggal, Sant Singh Sekhon and is now being ably nurtured by Prem Prakash, Gurbachan Singh Bhullar, Ram Swaroop Ankhi, Prem Gorkhi and several others. Unfortunately, Punjabi short story has not found the kind of exposure it richly deserves as not much is being done to promote its translation into other Indian languages including English.

I chose **Bhala Iyon Wi Koi Jeonde** for economy of detail and expression, control over language and characters, and for its authentic portrayal of the culture milieu, gender and caste politics.

Prem Gorkhi was detained by the police soon after his matriculation because of naxalite activities. Three years of police excesses, and trials in courts nearly uprooted him. After his release, he started studying privately and got a job in a Punjabi daily. From 1971 to 1978, he dabbled in journalism at Jalandhar and later moved to Chandigarh. After his first story was published in the popular Punjabi magazine, *Nagmani*, he made a decision to write only for and about the deprived and disadvantaged sections of society as he felt that the literary world almost ignored them. His first collection of short stories, *Mitte Range Lok* evoked a good response and was followed by a second collection, *Jeen Maran* in 1982. He has also written two novelettes, *Tittar Khambhi Juh, Budhi Raat Te Suraj* and an autobiography, *Ek Gairhazir Aadmi.* Gorkhi was the recipient of the first Giani Hira Singh Dard Award in 1981, the Dr Ravinder Ravi Award in 1992 and the Dr Ambedkar Award by Bharati Dalit Sahitya Akademi in 1995. He has also been awarded by the Punjab Lok Sabhayachark Manch in 1993, the Punjab S C and BC Employees Union in 1998 and has bagged the Nagmani Award thrice.

- I want to spread the idea of universalism that all are equal and that caste barriers are created by man. But I do see rapid changes emerging in our society, as the modern generation has a progressive outlook. As regards the impact of my writings on my readers, only time will tell.

Hina Nandrajog is a lecturer at Vivekananda College, Delhi University. She completed her Masters in English from Punjabi University, Patiala and did her MPhil from Delhi University. She was inspired to take up translation after going through Katha's publications at an exhibition. It seemed to be a fruitful and enjoyable way to keep in touch with the Punjabi language.

- It was difficult to convey the easy, conversational style, peppered with typically Punjabi culture. I would especially like to mention the term, "vaddiyan paggan wale" – used to indicate well-off and influential people – which literally means "those with large turbans." The narrative also rambles on from one tense to another rather liberally.

RAJASTHANI

Vijayadan Detha is a pioneer of modern writing in Rajasthani. He began writing in Hindi and Rajasthani while still a student and has edited numerous journals, magazines and anthologies in both languages. His works include *Batan Ri Phulwari*, a collection of stories in thirteen volumes, *Roonkh, Duvidha and Alekhoon Hitler*. He has also written stories for children. He is the recipient of several awards and honours that include the first Sahitya Akademi Award for Rajasthani Literature (1947), the Rajasthani Sree (1977), the Great Son of Rajasthan (1985) and the Bharatiya Bhasha Parishad Award (1990). Presently, he is working on literary projects for Rupayan, an organization he has founded, dedicated to the culture and literature of Rajasthan.

- Writing in Rajasthani has traditionally been dominated by poetry while story telling has often been verbal. However, modern story writing began in the late forties. Writers like me have tried to give a new dimension to the short story by adapting tales from our rich folklore and giving them contemporary connotations. For instance, Annaram "Sudama" comes down heavily on the evils in our society, making an effective use of symbolism in his many stories. Narsingh Rajpurohit has brought alive the rural scene and successfully depicted human emotions and relationships in his writings.

  I do not see the necessity for citing my reasons for choosing **Bus Mein Rojh** as the story speaks for itself.

Chandra Prakash Deval teaches in the Department of Biochemistry at Jawaharlal Nehru Medical College, Ajmer. He has a PhD in Biochemistry from Udaipur and Jodhpur Universities. Among his published works are nine volumes of poetry, which include, *Paagi*, an anthology of Rajasthani poetry (1977) and, *Avasaan*, an anthology of Hindi poetry (1998). *Upanishadawali*, is his Rajasthani translation of the seven Upanishads and *Saja*, the Rajasthani translation of Dostovesky's *Crime and Punishment*. He has received the Sahitya Akademi Award (1979), the Bharatiya Bhasha Parishad Award (1993), the Sahitya Akademi Translation Award (1995), the Rajasthani Sahitya Akademi Award, (1980) and Meera Puraskar, the highest Hindi award conferred by the Sahitya Akademi. He was executive member of the Rajasthani Bhasha Sahitya and Sanskriti Akademi, Bikaner for ten years. He is a member of the Advisory Board (Rajasthani) of the Sahitya Akademi and has given editorial inputs to its literary digest, *Uttara*.

- To intrude into someone else's personal life in thought or imagination is also a kind of violence. To intervene stealthily in the common place yet established institution of marriage is an act of cowardice. They are a sort of indirect exploitation, even if there is sublime love in the background.

Rashmi Chaturvedi, has been teaching English since 1974 and is presently the Principal of Kanoria Mahila Mahavidyalaya, Jaipur. She has actively participated in the activities of women's organizations and teachers' unions. Apart from acting in plays she has also directed several Hindi plays at the college level. She has translated one story for Sahitya Akademi.

- The story is rich in local, colloquial idiom and simple spontaneous utterances , which cannot be expressed as eloquently in any other language.

TAMIL

Jayamohan's mother tongue is Malayalam but he writes in Tamil as well as Malayalam. He has written more than sixty stories. The Akilon Memorial Award for his novel, *Rubber* (1991) brought him recognition. His other published works include *Vishnupuram* (1997), two short story collections, *Desaigal Naduvil* in 1992 and *Manai* in 1996. He was the recipient of the Katha Award in 1992. Other awards won by him include Sanskrita Sammana Elakia Viruthu in 1993, the Janakiraman Memorial Prize for a novella, and the 1994 Sanskriti Award for Literature. At present he works in the Telephone Exchange, Dharmapuri in Kanyakumari district.

- Tamil short stories in the forties were fast-paced. This was because authors like Pudumaipittan, K P, Mauni, and R Gopalan wrote some very good stories based on real and contemporary life. Stories then came to be written in a new way where brief depictions, subtle voices and descriptions of human nature were missing. Now, after the eighties, a new style of writing is being attempted where the plot of the story or its depiction is not important. The story unfolds through the words of the protagonist, with no uni-linear narration. Through the images flitting through the story, one goes through the literary experience of reading. Short stories today have made a place for themselves through this characteristic style of narration.

  As compared to stories that are generally uni-linear in their narration, the story, **Ottrai Siraku** seems to travel in several directions, faster through the mechanics of human psychology than through incidents of virtual reality. Explaining the possibilities beyond life through the significance of the events in one's life, is the highlight of the story.

Sutradhari, is the pen name for M Gopalakrishnan. A post-graduate in commerce and Hindi literature, he is an official in The New India Assurance Company Limited. He is also the editor of *Soll Puthithu*, a Tamil quarterly. He has a poetry collection, *Kuralgalin Vettai* to his credit. His maiden short story "Iruppu," published in *Puthiya Parvai* was awarded by Ilakkiya Chinthanai. He was one of the editors of *Kuthirai Veeran Payanam*, a literary magazine from Tirupur. He is the treasurer of the state level office of the Federation of Film Societies of India, Tirupur and actively participates in poetry sessions and conferences.

- What I wanted to portray in my story is human pain. I have tried to recapitulate the agony of a man who longs for a child. To achieve this I have taken recourse to emotions and images.

N Ramakrishnan has an MA in Mass Communication from Jamia Millia Islamia University and a degree in Journalism from Delhi University. He is a filmmaker by profession and translation is a hobby to be indulged in, whenever he is not producing documentaries and short films under his banner, Ideosyncs Media Combine. Ramakrishnan treads the line between English – his first language by his own admission – and Tamil, his mother tongue. He also writes articles and features for several mainstream English dailies.

- Any story replete with symbolic and allegorical references carries its own challenges to translation. The only phrase which posed some difficulty was "olirum pachaiyum," which crops up towards the end of the story, where the protagonist's attempts to immerse himself in his work are described. Literally translated, it means the lights and the green. It took a few moments for me to realize that the object being described was a computer, which the protagonist was working at – something supported by the fact that he had to tear himself away from the "four cornered screen" in front of him.

TELUGU

Amarendra Dasari is a writer and literary enthusiast stationed at Delhi and working for Bharat Heavy Electronics Limited. He has two published travelogues to his credit and is working on a short story collection.

- Telugu short story dates back to the year 1910. It has witnessed four to five generations of short story writers. Despite being dominated by the poem and the novel during the seventies and the eighties, short story has emerged as the foremost literary form in the nineties. The new generation of writers has been touching upon a range of issues starting from class conflict, to present-day realities. The Andhra revolutionary movement is also a popular theme.

  Dutta Lo Chandamama effortlessly depicts life with all its miseries. Despite a serious context, the story unfolds in a jovial way and engulfs the reader instantaneously. It contains all the elements of the oral literary tradition.

  Zameen is a story which deals with the finer aspects of religious harmony and religious intolerance. A sensitive issue handled with great care and craftsmanship, it is a powerful statement on the present day society.

Gopini Karunakar, a poet and fictionist is assistant director to N Shankar, a noted director in the Telugu film industry. Many of his poems have found place in well-read Telugu journals and dailies. He particularly admires the oral style of storytelling – a legacy of his blind grandmother – recreating it in his writings. His profession naturally leads him to present his stories in a visual form. He has assisted Bharati Raja in directing the Tamil film, "Karuthamma."

- I didn't particularly have a pre-conceived idea for my story. Girish Kasarvalli's film, Krowrya, inspired the character of the blind grandmother in my story. Basically, I wanted to relive the memories of my childhood nights full of dreams and visions.

Mohammad Khadeer Babu is the sub-editor of *Andhra Jyoti*, the prestigious Telugu magazine. His publications include *Darga Mitta Kathalu*, an autobiography of a Muslim boy.

- I felt that the present generation needs to be made aware of the value of friendship between the two religious communities and not get carried away by any fanatic ideology.

Pranava Manjari, translator, reviewer and editor, has a doctoral degree in English from Bangalore University and teaches in a Delhi College. She won the Katha Award for Translation in 1997 for her Kannada translation. She writes reviews for the Sahitya Akademi journal, *Indian Literature* and has translated both the Telugu stories in this volume.

- The swear words in the story was the problem area. I devised an alternate method as a literal translation would have made no sense in English.

URDU

Sadique is a distinguished poet, critic and artist, and a professor in the Department of Urdu, Delhi University. He has published a significant work, *The Progressive Ideology and the Urdu Story*. Alongside Urdu, he has been writing in Hindi.

- Urdu is an incomparable language, not belonging to any particular region of India even though it is spoken, understood, written and used all over the country. The Urdu short story has had an exceptionally rich past and its present is no less glorious. Today's writers have once again discovered the protagonist who had disappeared in the sixties, who does not merely appear in the context of a specific atmosphere or background but rather becomes the text itself. In this, there is certainly some politics with its own meaning but there are no prescribed norms to understand a person with, which can be labelled as existential, psychological or marxist. That is the very reason why the story today lends itself to a number of dimensions experienced by the person living in the present times. At the surface level, one can see how the contemporary Urdu short story presents the picture of good craftsmanship, which is taut and tight. At another level, it has within its folds, a whole silent world filled with doubts as well as questions. With every reader, the nature and the relation of its meaning changes.

Jeelani Bano knows the art of storytelling and she has skilfully portrayed the psyche of a man and a woman in **Ashtray Mein Sulagta Hua Cigarette**.

Jeelani Bano started writing stories in 1955 and has so far published sixteen works, which include two novels, a story collection and two collections of novellas. She strongly associates herself with developmental and anti-communalism movements and her second novel, *Baarish-e-Sang* dealt with bonded labour. She has been the chairperson of an NGO working for women's empowerment and has written and produced television programmes on similar themes. Her stories have been translated into several Indian languages, besides Russian, German, Norwegian and English. She has been conferred the International Award 1998 by Majlis-e-Frogh-e-Urdu, a literary organization based at UAE, the Soviet Land Nehru Award and the Ghalib Award among others. She is a member of the Urdu advisory board of the Sahitya Akademi, National Book Trust, India and National Council for the Promotion of Urdu Language.

Aateka Khan is studying for her post-graduate degree in English literature from Delhi University. This is her first attempt at translation and it has been done jointly by her and the editors of this volume.

A SELECT LIST OF REGIONAL MAGAZINES

The Award Winning Journals of 1999

Prantik (Asomiya) Ed: Bhabendra Nath Saikia
Navagiri Road, Chanmari, Guwahati 781003

Dainik Pratidin (Bangla) Ed: Swapan Sadhan Basu
20 Prafulla Sarkar Street, Calcutta 700029

Baromas (Bangla) Ed: Ashok Sen
63/C Mahanirvan Road, Calcutta 700029

Vi (Gujarati) Ed: Rajendra Jadeja
Ballabh Vidya Nagar, Gujarat 388120

Pahal (Hindi) Ed: Gyan Ranjan
101 Ram Nagar, Adhartal, Jabalpur 482004

Karmaveera (Kannada) Ed: K Shama Rao
Samyukta Karnataka Press, 2 Field Marshal Road, Bangalore 560025

Sandhan (Maithili) Ed: Ashok
C-407 Officers Flat, Belly Road, Patna 800001

Mathrubhumi (Malayalam) Ed: A Sahadevan
1 KP Kesava Menon Road, Kozhikode, Kerala

Sahitya (Manipuri) Ed: L Damodar Singh
Manipuri Sahitya Parishad, Paona Bazar Road, Imphal 795001

Miloon Saryajani (Marathi) Ed: Vidya Bal
33/225 Erandwan Prabhat Road, Lane 4, Pune 411004

Huns (Marathi) Ed: Anand Antarkar
4 Bhardwaj Apts, Near Krishna Hospital, Paud Road, Kothrud, Pune 411029

Jhankara (Oriya) Ed: Bhartruhari Mahtab
Prajatantra Prachar Samiti, Bihari Bag, Cuttack 752002

Nagmani (Punjabi) Ed: Amrita Pritam
K 25 Hauz Khas, New Delhi 110016

Binjaro (Rajasthani) Ed: Nagraj Sharma
Pilani, Rajasthan

Kalachchuvadu (Tamil) Eds: Kannan & Manushya Puthiran
151 K P Road, Nagercoil 629001

Andhra Jyoti (Telugu) Ed: K Jagadish Prasad
Road no 8, Banjara Hills, Hyderabad 500034

Tanazur (Urdu) Eds: Balraj Verma & Qamar Jamali
C117 A G Colony, Yousufguda Post, Hyderabad 500045

Other Journals

ASOMIYA

Ajir Asom, Omega Publishers, G S Rd, Ulubari, Guwahati 7
Anvesha, Konwarpur, Sibsagar 785667
Asam Bani, Tribune Bldg, G N Bordoloi Rd, Guwahati 3
Budhbar, Shahid Sukleshwar Konwar Path, Guwahati 21
Prakash, Publication Board of Assam, Bamunimaidan, Guwahati 24
Prantik, Navagiri Rd, Chandmari, PO Silpukhuri, Guwahati 3
Pratidhwani, Bani Mandir, Panbazaar, Guwahati 1
Sadin, Sadin Karyalaya, Maniram Dewan Path, Chandmari, Guwahati 3
Sreemoyee, Agradut Bhawan, Dispur, Guwahati 6
Sutradhar, Manjeera House, Motilal Nehru Path, Panbazaar, Guwahati 1

BANGLA

Aajkaal, 96 Raja Ram Mohan Roy Sarani, Calcutta 9
Amrita Lok, Binalay, Dak Bungalow Rd, PO Midnapore 721101
Ananda Bazar Patrika, 6 Prafulla Sarkar St, Calcutta 1
Anustup, P 55 B, C I T Rd, Calcutta 10
Bartaman, 76 A Acharya Bose Rd, Calcutta 15
Bartika, 18 A Ballygunge Station Rd, Calcutta 19
Basumati, 166 Bepin Behari Ganguli St, Calcutta 12
Chaturanga, 54 Ganesh Chandra Avenue, Calcutta 13
Galpapatra, C E 137 Salt Lake, Calcutta 64
Ganashakti, 31 Alimuddin St, Calcutta 16
Hawa, 49 Brahmapur, Bansdroni, Calcutta 70
Kuthar, Canara Bank, 25 Princep St, Calcutta 72
Madhuparni, Sitbali Complex, Balurghat, South Binajpur 733101
Manorama, 281 Muthiganj, Allahabad 3
Nandan, 31 Alimuddin St, Calcutta 16
Parichaya, 30/6 Chautala Rd, Calcutta 17
Pratidin, 14 Radhanath Choudhuri Rd, Calcutta 15
Pratikshana, 7 Jawaharlal Nehru Rd, Calcutta 13
Proma, 5 West Range, Calcutta 17
Raktakarabee, 10/2 Ramnath Majumdar St, Calcutta 9
Yogasutra, TG 2/29 Teghoria, Calcutta 59
Yuba Manas, 32/1 B B D Bag (South), Calcutta 1

GUJARATI

Abhiyan, Shakti House, Ashok Rd, Kandiwali East, Mumbai 1
Buddhiprakash, Gujarat Vidya Sabha, Ashram Rd, Ahmedabad 9

Dasmo Dayako, Sardar Patel University, Vallabh Vidyanagar 388120
Etad, 233 Rajlaxmi, Old Padra Rd, Vadodara 15
Kankavati, 24 River Bank Society, Adajan Water Tank, Surat 9
Khevana, 9 Mukund, Manorama Complex, Himatlal Park, Ahmedabad 15
Navchetan, Narayanagar, Sarkhej Rd, Ahmedabad
Navneet Samarpana, Bharatiya Vidya Bhavan, K M Rd, Mumbai 7
Parab, Govardhan Bhavan, Ashram Rd, Ahmedabad 9
Shabdashrushti, Gujarat Sahitya Akademi, Sector II, Gandhinagar
Sanskriti, Sandesh Bldg, Gheekanta, Ahmedabad 9
Uddesh, 2 Achalayatan Society, Navarangpura, Ahmedabad 9
Vi, 6 Vishwamitra, Bakrol Rd, Vallabh Vidyanagar 388 120

HINDI

Dastavej, Vishwanath Tiwari, Dethia Hatha, Gorakhpur
Hans 2/36 Ansari Rd, Darya Ganj, New Delhi 2
India Today, F 14/15 Connaught Place, New Delhi 1
Indraprastha Bharati, Samudaya Bhavan, Padam Ngr, Delhi
Kathya Roop, 224 Tularam Bagh, Allahabad 6
Pahal, Ramnagar, Aadhaar Taal, Jabalpur
Pal-Pratipal, 372 Sector 17, Panchkula, Haryana
Pratipaksh, 6/105 Kaushalya Park, Hauz Khas, New Delhi 16
Sakshatkar, Sanskriti Bhavan, Vaan Ganga Chauraha, Bhopal
Samaas, 2/38 Ansari Rd, Daryaganj, Delhi 2
Samkaleen Bharatiya Sahitya, Sahitya Akademi, Rabindra Bhavan, New Delhi 1
Vartaman Sahitya, 109 Ricchpalpuri, PB 13, Ghaziabad 1

KANNADA

Lankesh Patrike, 9 E A T St, PB 416, Basavanagudi, Bangalore 4
Mayura, 16 M G Rd, PB 331, Bangalore 1
Prajavani, 66 M G Rd, Bangalore 1
Rujuvathu, Kavi Kavya Trust, Heggodu, Sagar 577 417
Samvada, Samvada Prakashana, Malladihalli 577 531
Shubra, Shubra Srinivas, No 824, 7th Main, ISRO Layout, Bangalore 78
Tushara, Press Corner, Manipal 19
Udayavani, Manipal Printers and Publishers, Manipal 19

KONKANI

Chitrangi, Apurbai Prakashan, Volvoi Ponda, Goa
Kullagar, PO Box 109, Margao Goa 1
Rashtramat, Margao, Goa1
Sunaparant, BPS Club, Margao, Goa 1

MAITHILI

Vaidehi, Samiti Talbagh, Darbhanga
Mithila Chetna, 1/C Kakeshwar Lane, Post Bali Howrah 1
Janaki, Similtil, Damodarpur Road, Dhanbad
Pravasi, Mithila Sanskritik Sangam, Kendranchal, Allahabad
Sandhan, 40 Officers' Flats, Bailey Road, Patna 2
Pallak, Shri Mahal Pul Chowk, Lalitpur, Nepal

MALAYALAM

Desabhimani Weekly, PB 1130, Kozhikode 32
India Today, (Malayalam), 98A Radhakrishnan Salai, Chennai 4
Katha, Kaumudi Bldg, Pettah, Thiruvananthapuram 24
Kala Kaumudi, Pettah, Thiruvananthapuram 24
Kerala Kaumudi, PB 77, Thiruvananthapuram 24
Kumkumam, Lakshminanda, Kollam
Madhyam, Silver Hills, Kozhikode 12
Malayala Manorama, PB 26, Kottayam
Manorajyam, Manorajyam Press, T B Junction, Kottayam
Mathrubhumi Weekly, Cherooty Rd, Kozhikode 1

MANIPURI

Ritu, The Cultural Forum, Manipur, B T Road, Imphal
Sāhitya, Manipur Sahitya Parishad, Paona Bazar, Imphal
Wākhāl, Nahārōl Sāhitya Premee Samiti, Imphal

MARATHI

Abhiruchi, 69 Pandurang Wadi, Goregaon East, Mumbai 36
Anushtubh, Anandashram, Near D'Souza Maidan, Manmad 423 104
Asmitadarsha, 37 Laxmi Co Chawani, Aurangabad
Dhanurdhari, Ramakrishna Printing Press, 31 Tribhuvan Rd, Mumbai 4
Dipavali, 316 Prasad Chambers, Girgaon, Mumbai 4
Grihalaxmi, 21 Dr D D Sathe Rd, Girgaon Mumbai 4
Jatra, 2117 Sadashiv Peth, Vijayanagar Cly, Pune 30
Kathasagar, Akashdeep, Milan Subway Marg, Santa Cruz East, Mumbai 55
Kavitarati, Vijay Police Vashat, Wadibhikar Rasta, Dhule
Lokaprabha, Express Tower, Ist Floor, Nariman Point, Mumbai
Lokarajya, New Admn Bldg, 17th Floor, Opp Secretariat, Mumbai 2
Loksatta, Express Towers, Nariman Point, Mumbai

ORIYA

Anisha Sahitya Patra, Chandikhol Chhak, PO Sunguda 754 024

Jhankara, Prajatantra Prachar Samiti, Beheri Bag, Cuttack 2
Jiban Ranga, Stoney Rd, Cuttack 2
Nabalipi, Vidyapuri, Balu Bazar, Cuttack 2
Pratibeshi, 236 Acharya J C Bose Rd, Nizam Palace (17th flr), Calcutta 20
Sahakar, Balkrishna Marg, Cuttack 1
Samay, Badambadi, Ananta Aloka, Sankarpur, Cuttack 12

PUNJABI

Kahani Punjab, Kuccha Punjab, College Rd, Barnala, Punjab 148 101
Nagmani, K 25, Hauz Khas, New Delhi 16
Preet Lari, Preet Nagar, Punjab
Samdarshi, Punjabi Academy, New Delhi
Samkali Sahithya, Punjab Sahit Sabha, 10 Rouse Avenue, New Delhi

RAJASTHANI

Binjaro, Pilani, Rajasthan
Jagati Jot, Sahitya Evam Sanskriti Akademi, Bikaner
Manale, Jalori Gate, Jodhpur
Mansi, Ambu Sharma, Calcutta
Rajasthali, Rajasthani Bhasha Parishad, Shri Dungarpur, Bikaner

TAMIL

Arumbu, 22 A Tailors Rd, Chennai 10
Dinamani Kadir, Anna Salai, Chennai 2
India Today, (Tamil), 98A Dr Radhakrishnan Salai, Chennai 4
Kalki, 84/1-6 Race Course Rd, Guindy, Chennai 2
Kal Kudhirai, 6/162 Indira Ngr, Kovilpatti 2
Kanaiazhi, 245 T T K Salai, Chennai 18
Kanavu, MIG 189 Phase II, TNHB, Thiruppatur 635602
Kappiar, Kaliyakkavilai, K K Dist, Tamil Nadu 629153
Kavithaasaran, 31 T K S Ngr, Chennai 19
Pudia Paarvai, Tamil Arasi Maligai, 84 T T K Rd, Chennai
Puthiya Nambikai, 13 Vanniyar II St, Chennai 93
Sathangai, 53/2 Pandian St, Kavimani Ngr, Nagercoil 629002
Semmalar, 6/16 Bypass Rd, Madurai 18
Unnatham, Alathur PO, Kavindapady 638455

TELUGU

Aahwanam, Gandhi Ngr, Vijayawada 3
Andhra Jyoti, Lubbipet Sunday Section, Vijayawada 10
Andhra Patrika, 1-2-528 Lower Tank Bund Rd, Domalguda, Hyderabad 29

Andhra Prabha, Express Centre, Domalguda, Hyderabad 29
Chatura, *Eenadu* Publications, Somajiguda, Hyderabad 4
India Today (Telugu), 98-A Dr Radhakrishnan Salai, Mylapore, Chennai 4
Jyothi, 1-8-519/11 Chikadapally, PB 1824, Hyderabad 20
Mayuri, 5-8-55/A Nampally, Station Rd, Hyderabad 1
Maabhoomi, 36 S D Road Hyderabad
Rachana, PB 33, Visakhapatanam 1
Srijana, 203 Laxmi Apts, Malakpet, Hyderabad 36
Swati, Prakashan Rd, Governorpet, Vijayawada
Vipula, *Eenadu* Compound, Somajiguda, Hyderabad 4

URDU

Aajkal, Publication Division, Patiala House, New Delhi 1
Asri Adab, D 7 Model Town, Delhi 9
Gulban, 9 Shah Alam Society, 12 Chandola Lok, Davilipada, Ahmedabad 28
Kitab Numa, Maktaba Jamia, New Delhi 25
Naya Daur, PB 146, Lucknow
Shabkhoon, 313 Rani Mandi, Allahabad
Shair, Maktaba Qasruladab, PB 4526, Mumbai 8
Soughat, 84 III Main, Defence Colony, Indiranagar, Bangalore 38
Zehn-e-Jadeed, PB 7042, New Delhi

NB: This is by no means an exhaustive list of all the contemporary journals, periodicals, newspapers (the magazine sections), little magazines and anthologies which give space to the short story. But, for the most part, these names represent the range of publications consulted by the Nominating Editors in their respective languages. However, since the compilation of a more detailed list of publications is one of Katha Vilasam's objectives, the editor would welcome any additional information on the subject, particularly with respect to languages not covered in this list.

INDEX OF NOMINATING EDITORS, AWARD WINNING WRITERS, TRANSLATORS AND JOURNALS OF KPS VOLUMES 1 TO 8

NOMINATING EDITORS

Sudha	5
Udayavani	4, 7
KONKANI	
Chitrangi	4
Jaag	8
MAITHILI	
Katha Disha	8
MALAYALAM	
India Today	2, 4, 5, 6, 7
Kala Kaumudi	1, 3, 4
Malayala Manorama	3, 6
Mathrubhumi	1, 2, 3, 7
MARATHI	
Anushthub	1
Dipavali	6
Gulmohar	1
Loksatta	1, 6
Mauj	2, 3, 4
Sadhana	5
Saptahik Sakal	4
Shree Vatsa	2
ORIYA	
Jhankara	4, 5, 6, 7
Journal Emporium	4
Sharashjya	2
PUNJABI	
Arsee	6, 7
RAJASTHANI	
Jagati Jot	7
Rajasthan Patrika	8
TAMIL	
Dalit	8
Dinamani Kadir	7
India Today	1
Kavitasaran	6
Manaosai	2
Navina Virutcham	8
Sathangai	6
Subhamangala	2, 3, 4
Unnatham	5
TELUGU	
Andhra Bhoomi	8
Andhra Jyoti	1
Andhra Prabha	1, 2, 3, 5
Andhra Prabha Sachitra Vara Patrika	5
India Today	4
URDU	
Aajkal	1, 3, 6
Daar Se Bichhre	5
Dastak	8
Shabkhoon	7
Soughat	2, 7
Zehn-e-Jadeed	1, 4

ABOUT KATHA

Katha is a registered nonprofit organization working in the area of creative communication for development. Katha's main objective is to enhance the pleasures of reading amongst children and adults.

Kalpavriksham, Katha's Centre for Sustainable Learning, is active in the field of education. It develops and publishes quality material in the literacy to literature spectrum, and works with an eye to excellence in education – from nonformal education of working children to formal education, from primary through higher education. Katha also works with teachers to help them make their teaching more creative. It publishes learning packages for first-generation schoolgoers and adult neo-literates. Specially designed for use in nonformal education, every quarter Katha brings out *Tamasha!*, a fun and activity magazine on development issues for children, in Hindi and English. The *Katha Vachak* series is an attempt to take fiction to neo-literates, especially women.

Katha-Khazana, part of Kalpavriksham, was started in Govindpuri, one of Delhi's largest slum clusters, in 1990. Kathashala and the Katha School of Entrepreneurship have over 1000 students – mostly working children. To enhance their futures, an income-generation programme for the women of this community – Shakti-Khazana – and the Khazana Women's Cooperative were also started in 1990.

The Katha National Institute of Translation strives to help forge linkages between writers, students and teachers. Launched in 1997 as Kanchi, KNIT has been conducting workshops in schools and colleges all over the country to enhance the pool of translators, editors and teachers of translated fiction. KNIT operates through five Academic Centres in various universities in the country – Bangalore University, IRIS, Jaipur, North East Hill University, Shillong, SNDT Women's University, Mumbai, in addition to its Delhi Centre.

Katha Vilasam, the Story Research and Resource Centre, seeks to foster and applaud quality fiction from the regional languages and take it to a wider readership through translations. The Katha Awards were instituted in 1990. Through projects like the Translation Contests, it attempts to build a bank of sensitive translators. KathaNet, an invaluable network of Friends of Katha, is the mainstay of all Katha Vilasam efforts. Katha Vilasam publications also include exciting books from Kathakaar, the Centre for Children's Literature which brings out the Yuvakatha and Balkatha series, for young adults and children respectively.

LOOKING FOR KATHA BOOKS?
FIND US IN THE BOOKSHOP CLOSEST TO YOU!

AGRA
Modern Book Depot
4, Taj Rd, Sadar Bazar
Agra

BANGALORE
Books for Change
28, Castle Street
Ashok Ngr
Bangalore – 566025
Ph: 080 – 5098240
Vinayaka Book Distr
No 13, K Kamaraja Rd
Bangalore 560042

BARODA
Baroda Book Centre
20 Step-N-Shop Plaza
Offtel Tower Premises
Alka Puri Rd
Baroda – 390005

BHUBANESHWAR
Modern Book Depot
Unit III, Station Square
Bhubaneshwar

BIKANER
Sugan Nivas
Chandan Sagar
Bikaner, Ph: 521200

CALCUTTA
Book Line
7, Tottee Lane
Calcutta – 700016
Ph: 244-0903
Indiana Distributors
2/1, Shyama Charan
De Street
Calcutta – 700073
Seagull Books
26, Circus Avenue Ist Flr,
Calcutta – 700017
Ph: 2407942
Timely Book Centre
30, Chittaranjan Avenue
IInd Flr,
Calcutta – 700012

CHANDIGARH
The English Book Shop
SC0 31, Sector 17 E
Chandigarh
Capital Book Depot
SCO 3, Sector 17 E
Chandigarh – 160017
Ph: 702260

CHENNAI
Fountainhead
Laxmi Towers
27, Dr Radhakrishna Rd
Chennai – 600004
Ph: 8280867
Odyssey Dev Agency
6, First Main Rd
Gandhi Ngr, Adyar
Chennai – 600020
Ph: 4420393
Higginbothams Ltd
814, Anna Salai
Chennai – 600002
Ph: 8520640
Landmark Plaza
3, Nungambakkam
High Rd
Chennai – 600034
Ph: 8279637
The Book Plaza
G-16, Spence Plaza
769, Anna Salai
Chennai – 600002
The Book Point India Ltd
160, Anna Salai
Chennai – 600002
Ph: 8523019
Tulika Publishers
7, Prithvi Avenue
Ist Flr, Abhiramapuram
Chennai – 600018
Ph: 44-44981639

COCHIN
The Book Mart
33/272 Pullepady Rd
Ernakulam
Cochin – 682018

GOA
The Other India Press
Above Mapusa Clinic
Mapusa Goa – 403507
Ph: 0832-263306

GUWAHATI
United Publishers
Pan Bazar, Main Rd
Guwahati – 781001
Ph: 517059

HYDERABAD
Akshara
8-2-273 Pavani Estate
Rd, No 2 Banjara Hills,
Hyderabad
Ph: 213906

JAIPUR
Books and News Mart
M I Rd, Jaipur – 302001
Ph: 337261
Books Corner
M I Rd, Jaipur – 302001
Ph: 366323

Rajat Book Corner
8, Narain Rd
Near Trimurti Circle
Jaipur 302004

KANPUR

Kitabwala
PO Box No. 468
Kanpur – 208001

LUCKNOW

Bharat Book Centre
17, Ashok Mrg
Lucknow – 226001
Ph: 280381

Dastavez Prakashan
Masjid Lane
Hazratganj, Lucknow
Ph: 391610

Shri Ram Advani BookSellers
Mayfair Bldg
Hazratganj
GPO Box No. 154
Lucknow 226001
Ph: 223511

UBDC
A-1 Arif Chambers
Kapoorthala, Aliganj
Lucknow – 228020

Universal Book Sellers
Hazratganj
Opp. Allahabad Bank
Lucknow

MUMBAI

Crossword
Mahalaxmi Chambers
22, B Desai Rd
Mumbai – 400026
Ph: 4938311

English Edition
404, Ravi Bldg
189/191 D N Rd Fort
Mumbai – 400001
Ph: 5243531

Lotus Book House
516, BSV Rd
Bandra (West)
Mumbai – 400050
Ph: 6400199

Strand Book Stall
Dhannur Sir P M Rd,
Fort, Mumbai 400001
Ph: 2661719

NEW DELHI

Alpine Book Shop
H-1536, Chittranjan Park
N D – 19, Ph: 6478338

Arora Book Stall
DAV School Bldg
Yusuf Sarai
N D – 16 Ph: 6518703

Bahri & Sons
Khan Mkt, N D – 3
Ph: 4618637

Cambridge Book Depot
3, Regal Bldg
Parliament Street
N D – 1 Ph: 3278368

Capital Book Stall
Gopinath Bazar
Delhi Cantt
N D – 10 Ph: 5691364

Crossword
EBONY Bldg
II nd Flr, D-4 NDSE–II
N D – 49 Ph: 6257645

Dass Book Depot
2/2, Mall Rd, Tilak Ngr
N D – 18 Ph: 5190077

D K Pub & Distr (P) Ltd
1, Ansari Rd, Daryaganj
N D – 2 Ph: 3278368

D K Agencies (P) Ltd
4788 90/23 Ansari Rd
N D – 2 Ph: 3201567

E D Galgotia & Sons
17 B Connaught Place
N D – 1 Ph: 3322876

Famous Book Depot
25, Janpath Bhawan
New Janpath Mkt
N D – 1 Ph: 3311810

Fact & Fiction
39, Basant Lok
Vasant Vihar
N D – 57 Ph: 6146843

Faquir Chand & Sons
18, Khan Mkt
N D – 3 Ph: 4618810

Geeta Book Centre
JNU, Near Ganga Hostel
New Campus
N D – 67 Ph: 6178081

Gulati Stationery
14, Prithviraj Mkt
Khan Mkt, N D – 3
Ph: 4635827

Hem Book Centre
JNU, Near SSS Bldg
New Campus,
N D – 67 Ph: 6162312

India Today Book Club
Living Media India
(P) Ltd
B – 318, Okhla Phase I
N D – 20 Ph: 6812225

Jawahar Book Centre
JNU
Near SSS Bldg
New Campus, N D – 67

Jawahar Books & Stationers
179, Sarojini Ngr
N D – 23 Ph: 4100510

Jolly Book Depot
47, New Mkt, Tilak Ngr,
N D – 18 Ph: 5191853

Krishna Book Shop
Hotel Claridge
12, Aurangzeb Rd
N D – 11

Malan Book Shop
Lodhi Hotel, N D – 3
Ph: 4362422

Manohar Pub & Dist
4753/23, Ansari Rd
Daryaganj,
N D – 2 Ph: 3262796
Midland Book Shop
Aurobindo Place Mkt
N D – 16 Ph: 6867121
New Book Depot
18-B, Connaught Place
N D – 1 Ph: 3220020
New L & R Distributors
5-B, Surya Kiran Bldg
19, K G Marg
N D – 1 Ph: 3336444
Om Book Service
1690, Ist Flr, Nai Sarak
Delhi – 6 Ph: 3279823
Om Book Shop
E-77 South Ext Part-I
N D – 49
Paramount Book Store
88 M M, Janpath
N D – 1
People Tree
8, Regal Bldg
Parliament Street
N D – 1 Ph: 3734877
Prakash Book Depot
M-86, Connaught Place
N D – 1 Ph: 3326897
Rama Book Depot
61, Central Mkt
Lajpat Ngr
N D – 24 Ph: 6834324
Ritika Book House
The Oberoi Hotel
Dr Zakir Hussain Mrg
N D – 3
Sehgal's Book Shop
F- 38, South Ext Part-I
N D – 49 Ph: 4647783
Teksons Book Shop
G-5 South Ext Part-I
N D – 49 Ph: 4617030
The Book Shop
14-A, Khan Mkt
N D – 3 Ph: 4625066
The Book Mark
A-2 South Ext Part-I
N D – 49 Ph: 4644071
The Book Review
239, Vasant Enclave
N D – 57 Ph: 6140383
The Book Worm
B-29, Connaught Place
N D – 1 Ph: 3322260
UBS Pub & Distr Ltd
5, Ansari Rd,
N D – 2 Ph: 3273601
University Book House
15, U B Bunglow Rd,
Jawahar Ngr,
Delhi – 7 Ph: 2919154
Variety Book Depot
AVG Bhawan
M-3 Connaught Circus
N D – 1 Ph: 3382567

PATNA
Anupam Pub and Dist
Opposite Patna College
Patna – 800004
Books en Amee
Boring House
Patna – 800001
Ph: 232888
PONDICHERRY
Books Plaza
Rue Mahe De
Labourdonanas
Next of Chamber de
Commerce
Pondicherry – 605001

THIRUVANANTHAPURAM
Modern Book Depot
M G Road
GPO Junction
Thiruvananthapuram
Kerala – 695001
Prabhu Books
Old Sreekanteswaram Rd
Thiruvananthapuram
Kerala – 695001

VIJAYAWADA
Ashok Book Centre
Opp Maris Stella
College
Vijayawada – 520008

VISAKHAPATNAM
Ashok Book Centre
13-1-KST Anthony's
Church Compound
Jagadamba Junction
Visakhapatnam
Ph: 565995

Booklovers ... Katha thanks you for giving pride of place in your shops to Indian fiction in translations!

Be a Friend of Katha!

If you feel strongly about Indian literature, you belong with us! KathaNet, an invaluable network of our friends, is the mainstay of all our translation-related activities. We are happy to invite you to join this ever-widening circle of translation activists. Katha, with limited financial resources, is propped up by the unqualified enthusiasm and the indispensable support of nearly 5000 dedicated women and men.

We are constantly on the lookout for people who can spare the time to find stories for us, and to translate them. Katha has been able to access mainly the literature of the major Indian languages. Our efforts to locate resource people who could make the lesser-known literatures available to us have not yielded satisfactory results. We are specially eager to find Friends who could introduce us to Bhojpuri, Dogri, Kashmiri, Nepali and Sindhi fiction.

Do write to us with details about yourself, your language skills, the ways in which you can help us, and any material that you already have and feel might be publishable under a Katha programme. All this would be a labour of love, of course! But we do offer a discount of 20% on all our publications to Friends of Katha.

Write to us at –
Katha
A-3 Sarvodaya Enclave
Sri Aurobindo Marg
New Delhi 110 017
Fax: 651 4373
E-mail: katha@vsnl.com
Internet address: http//www.katha.org
Or call us at: 686 8193, 652 1752

THE KATHA AWARDS

The KATHA AWARDS were instituted in 1990.

Katha requests an eminent writer, scholar or critic in each of the regional languages to choose what she/he feels are the three best stories published in that language, in the previous year.

Our Nominating Editors sift through numerous journals and magazines that promote short fiction. Many of them consult their friends or other Friends of Katha in the literary world to help them make their nominations. The nominated stories are translated and from these are chosen the Prize Stories.

Each author receives the KATHA AWARD FOR CREATIVE FICTION which includes a citation, Rs 2000, and publication (in translation) in that year's *Katha Prize Stories* volume.

The editor of the regional language journal that first published the award winning story receives the KATHA JOURNAL AWARD.

Katha celebrates the living tradition of storytelling with the KATHA AWARD FOR ORAL LITERATURE.

The translators are handpicked from the list of nearly 3000 names we have at Katha. Each of them gets the KATHA AWARD FOR TRANSLATION which includes a citation, Rs 2000, and the chance to translate a prize story.

The A K RAMANUJAN AWARD goes to a translator who can, with felicity, translate between two or more Indian languages, as Ramanujan himself was able to. A K Ramanujan was a Friend of Katha and this award was instituted in 1993.

Every year or so – as and when we can afford it! – Katha holds a literary workshop. The award winning writers, translators and editors are invited to it.